Violent Echoes

A Brooks & Banks Novel

PJ Mouchet

Paul Mouchet Publishing

Contents

Dedication   VII

Preface   VIII

1. The Villain   1

2. Jackson and Ruby   8

3. Willow and Ranger   14

4. Jackson   23

5. Willow   30

6. Jackson   35

7. Willow   41

8. Jackson   47

9. Willow   53

10. Jackson   58

11. Willow   68

12. Jackson   74

13. Willow   81

14. Jackson   87

15. Willow   94

16. Jackson   97

17. Willow   103

18. Jackson   112

19. Willow   117

20. Jackson   123

21. Willow   131

22. Jackson   136

23. Willow   141

24. Jackson   148

25. Willow   155

26. Jackson   165

27. Willow   170

28. Jackson   175

29. Willow   181

30. Jackson   189

31. Willow   195

32. Jackson   201

33. Willow   207

34. Jackson   213

35. Willow   221

36.	Jackson	228
37.	Willow	236
38.	Jackson	244
39.	Willow	249
40.	Jackson	255
41.	Willow	261
42.	Jackson	267
43.	Willow	273
44.	Jackson	281
45.	Willow	288
46.	Jackson	295
47.	Willow	301
48.	Jackson	310
49.	Willow	317
50.	Jackson	323
51.	Willow	330
52.	Jackson	336
53.	Willow	342
54.	Jackson	346
55.	Willow	352
56.	Jackson	358

57.	Willow	364
58.	Jackson	369
59.	Willow	373
60.	Jackson	376
61.	Willow	382
62.	Jackson	386
63.	Willow	390
64.	Jackson	394
Afterword		399
Also By		400

To my wife, who believes in me, even when I struggle to believe in myself. Without her support and infinite patience, I would have never realized my dream of becoming an author.
And, to my big sister Louise, thank you for helping me bring my stories to life.

Preface

In the winter of 2024, I took my first trip to northern Alabama. My wife, Candice, our Golden Retriever, Gizmo, and I stayed at a charming Airbnb on Wilson Lake. Our hosts, Christine and Al, lived next door and welcomed us like family from the moment we arrived.

The city of Florence is more than just the setting for this story—it's a character in its own right. The places and restaurants mentioned are real, drawn from our experiences during that unforgettable stay.

That said, this is a work of fiction. Any resemblance to real persons, living or dead, is purely coincidental, even if certain characters or events may be inspired by real life. While I've done my best to capture the spirit of these locations, I've taken creative liberties where the story demanded—like imagining a restaurant as dog-friendly or tweaking small details to fit the plot.

I hope this blend of authenticity and imagination brings Florence to life, deepening the mystery and drawing you into its streets. And if you ever visit, I hope you'll discover the same charm and character that inspired this novel.

Paul

Chapter One

The Villain

Florence, Alabama—April 23, 8:47am

I draw a deep breath as I walk the streets of Florence, Alabama. The morning air is intoxicating, carrying the scent of fresh coffee from nearby cafes and the lingering dampness from last night's rain. I run through the plan in my head once more, each step clear and precise. As I visualize the outcome, a rush of endorphins courses through my veins, heightening my senses. I've killed many times before, but the idea of executing two people in broad daylight, in front of dozens of witnesses, thrills me in a way I hadn't expected. But my window of opportunity is small, and I can't let elation derail me.

As I round the corner onto North Court Street, I scan for Levi Benson, a homeless man who panhandles for spare change. He had a promising career in the District Attorney's office until he broke off his engagement with Rachel Persie, the mayor's prima donna bitch of a daughter. Rachel went crying to daddy, and within a week, Levi lost his job and became radioactive. Nobody asked why he ended the relationship. Nobody cared. All that mattered was that the princess of Florence had been slighted.

Thankfully, there's no sign of Levi. It wouldn't have been good for people to see both me and him at the same time. It would have broken my carefully planned illusion. All it took was for me to throw a cup of coffee at him earlier this morning. Even as a homeless man, the ex-DA is fastidiously neat, and incredibly predictable. He must be off to the laundromat, doing his best to get the coffee stain out before it sets.

My hair and beard are more unruly than Levi's, but it won't matter. When the shit hits the fan, the onlookers won't notice. They'll see what I want them to see—just another homeless man with a gun.

I wrap my fingers around the Beretta in the pocket of my hoodie. Its weight is reassuring. The texture of the grip, the coolness of the metal, the slight resistance of the trigger under my finger—all of it combines to create a visceral connection between me and my weapon.

My destination is a block up the street. Yumm is an upscale Thai restaurant that caters to a younger crowd. Rachel and Tanner should both be there by now. I know because I arranged their meeting. They're childhood friends, and they haven't seen each other in many months. I emailed Tanner, spoofing it to look like it came from Rachel. I left a cryptic message saying that she had information that she could only share in person. The idiot is too righteous not to show up. I also spoofed an email to Rachel from Tanner saying that he wanted to see her and to meet him at the restaurant. That's all it would take to get her to come. Tanner had been a star quarterback for the local North Alabama University. Go Lions! It's been nearly eight years since Tanner graduated, but he's still a celebrity with football fans and the college crowd, and she'd never pass up an opportunity to be seen with him.

As I approach the restaurant, a fat, pimple-faced young man has his phone out. He's got it pressed against the window while he peers inside. His reason for being there is irrelevant. He'll just be yet another witness able to describe how a homeless man murdered two people eating their breakfast. I move in next to him, taking in every detail of the restaurant and its patrons. The smell of bacon and fried potatoes waft out, mingling with the morning air. The chatter of diners and the clink of cutlery create a backdrop of normalcy that will soon be shattered. From my vantage point, I can see Tanner and Rachel talking over their morning coffee. Tanner has chosen a table that would keep his back against the wall. It ensures he has a clear view of the entrance and every person in the room. Even though he is only an analyst, his FBI training would ensure he maintained a tactical advantage. Rachel's back is to the front door. She'll never see me coming until it's too late.

A grim calmness settles over me as I push open the all-glass door and step inside. The temperature change is immediate, the frigid air conditioning a stark contrast to the warmth outside. The smell of food intensifies, making my stomach growl despite the circumstances. The waitress, a tiny bit of a thing with horrid platinum hair, looks me up and down and sneers. The name embroidered on her smock reads *Evelina*.

"You're not welcome here." She points to the door I just stepped through, offering me her absolute best bitch-face. "Leave or I'll call the police."

"Relax, Evelina. I'll only be a moment." I motion to where Rachel and Tanner are sitting. They're deep in conversation, oblivious to my encounter with the waitress. "I've got a message to deliver."

Evelina follows my stare to where Rachel is sitting. She cocks an eyebrow and huffs. It seems she doesn't like Rachel any more than I do. Not totally unexpected. She's a waitress, and the mayor's daughter has likely treated her like shit from the moment the self-important bitch walked into the establishment. "Be quick about it, okay? I'm not supposed to let vagrants inside." She drops her voice low. "If you can embarrass her, I'll bring you a fresh breakfast in the alley."

"Thanks, but I'll do more than embarrass her." I give the young woman a wink and turn to address my quarry.

Evelina's reaction is a pleasant surprise. It's a reminder of Rachel's never-ending toxicity. For a moment, I consider sparing the waitress, warning her to leave. But I dismiss the thought. Sentiment has no place in my plan. Everyone in this restaurant is a potential witness, and witnesses are exactly what I'm counting on.

In five long strides, I'm standing beside their table. I move past Rachel and position myself shoulder to shoulder with Tanner.

"Excuse me, sir," Tanner says. His voice is calm and controlled. "Is there something I can help you with?"

"Leave, creep," Rachel says. She snaps her fingers at the waitress to call her over.

I purse my lips and shake my head to let Evelina know I'll only be a minute. When I see the waitress smile at me, I turn my attention back to Rachel and look her square in the eye. All she sees is a filthy, homeless man with raggedy hair and beard. The woman looks at me like I've got leprosy.

"Leave," Rachel says. "Now!"

I ignore her protests and bend closer to Tanner, whispering unintelligible gibberish into his ear.

"What?" Tanner leans in, trying to hear me over the dozens of nearby voices. "I didn't understand what you said."

I hover over him until our bodies are so close that nobody can see me aiming the handgun from within my jacket pocket. The proximity is uncomfortable. The heat of his body and the smell of his cologne invade my senses. But discomfort is a small price to pay for the perfect shot. "I'm sorry." I feel bad. He doesn't deserve what's about to happen to him. He's a decent man, doing his job like a good little FBI soldier. I press the barrel against his chest and pull the trigger. Between the suppressor and my jacket, the gunshot is no more than a light pop. The bullet's mushrooming head would have ripped through his chest, guaranteeing extensive internal damage without exiting out his back. I hold Tanner close, giving his brain time to process the fact that his body is already dead. A small gasp escapes his lips as he takes his final breath. When I pull back, the unfortunate man slumps over onto the table.

The moment of Tanner's death is oddly intimate. I feel the life leave his body, the sudden weight as he goes limp. There's a strange beauty to it, a finality that's both terrifying and exhilarating. I push the thought aside, focusing on the task at hand. I turn to my next target and smile. "Your turn."

Rachel's face crumples. She's trying to process what's happening. Fear is flooding her consciousness. Her bloodstream is overflowing with ketamine, adrenaline, and cortisol. They'll cloud her judgment and help her see me as her ex.

Freezing up will be her first response. Screaming will be her second. I've got a few seconds to act before she does. My heart is pounding against my ribs. Satisfaction is moments away. I can taste it. It's sending shivers up my spine, but I need to remain calm. I have things to say, and people to control. One small error on my part and I'll be arrested before the dinner bell rings. I pull out my gun and hold it high in the air. "Remain calm." I keep my voice sure and steady, ensuring they know I am in complete control. "Nobody moves, nobody speaks, and everybody lives."

College kids pack the restaurant. The majority are self-absorbed idiots. They should be smarter—but they're not. Half of them whip out their cell phones, snapping pictures or recording videos of me. What they're not doing is panicking, which is positively perfect, absolutely expected, and completely to plan.

"When I'm finished talking with Ms. Persie here," I say, making eye contact with every cell phone in the restaurant. "You can all leave. I have no interest in harming any of you, but while I'm talking to the mayor's daughter, I expect complete silence. If any of you makes a noise, I will shoot you in the face."

A smart-mouthed little bitch from the next table over engages, fluttering her overly long eyelashes at me. "And how will we know you're done?" She doesn't realize Tanner's dead. I doubt she would care. The twit is using my audacious behavior to boost her social media presence. She's willing to risk her life to be seen and heard, to let the entire world know that she was here. I'd like to shoot her too, but that would deviate from my plan—and I don't deviate from a plan unless the situation forces me to. Like right now, I'm here in Florence, Alabama, deviating from my plan.

Her interruption grates against my nerves. "You'll know," I say, meeting her gaze with practiced calm. "You'll all know." I turn to the other patrons, and they all nod their understanding. All except for a table near the back. Four oversized meatheads are sizing me up, thinking they can rush me. I make a mock shooting action at each of them and their resolve wavers. In a fist fight, they might stand a chance if they all attacked me at once. But against me with a gun, three of them would be dead before they got off their asses. They all settle back into their chairs and hang their heads. I take a quick scan of the room. Nobody is trying to call the police. I'm almost done here anyway, so it doesn't matter if they do. In less than a minute, I guarantee there will be dozens of phone calls. The thought thrills me.

I turn back to face Rachel. She has regained control of herself, at least enough to put on her mask of hate-filled superiority. But I can see the truth of it. Her pulse is so quick she's on the verge of passing out. Sweat is dripping from her temples, her hands are trembling, and her overly-made-up eyes are much too wide. "You really are a cunt, Rachel. I've known a lot of people in my life, a lot of criminals even. They don't hold a candle to you."

The air between us is charged with tension, thick with fear-sweat and the cloying scent of her expensive perfume. Her mask of bravado slips, and I savor the exact moment she realizes her status and connections mean nothing.

"Levi?" she says, narrowing her eyes and raising her chin in defiance. Her voice is wobbly. "You've lost weight. It seems the streets are not treating you kindly." She's got a sharp tongue, and she is always so happy to use it. It gives her courage. "That's what you get for fucking with my life."

Her attempt at defiance is pathetic, a last-ditch effort to maintain her illusion of control.

"And this is what you get for fucking with mine," I say, letting my pent-up rage pour out. "You treat people like dirt. You act all superior, but you're a fraud. Your whiff of glory came from daddy's wealth. Without it, you'd be groveling in the gutters with the rest of the wannabe authors of this world." I savor how each word makes her flinch. "And you'll never hurt anyone ever again."

I fire three shots at the woman in rapid succession. The first hits her mouth, splitting through her upper lip, shattering her veneered teeth. The second goes through her left eye. The third goes through her right, exploding out the back of her head. The first three bullets I fired today were hollow points. The fourth was a full metal jacket, causing maximum visual effect.

Rachel crumples, her body sliding from the chair with a wet thud. The social media junkie sitting at the next table never stops filming. Her face blanches at the horror of it all, but she refuses to miss her moment of glory. I reach into my other jacket pocket and pull out a grenade. "It's time to scream and run!" I yell just before I pull the pin and toss it behind the bar that stretches the length of the room. "You've got seven seconds before it explodes. Everybody out!"

The chaos that erupts is beautiful in its own way. The screams, the frantic scrambling, the primal fear on every face—it's a symphony of panic. I can feel the rush of bodies as people push past me, their fear palpable. It's intoxicating, this moment of pure, unfiltered human reaction.

As I sprint out the rear exit and down the alley, a grim satisfaction settles in my chest. This was more than murder—it was a necessary correction. I've worked too hard to let a few loose ends unravel everything.

Chapter Two

Jackson and Ruby

50 Minutes Earlier

Special Agent Jackson Brooks found Levi and his border collie begging outside Trowbridge's diner, a fresh coffee stain darkening the shoulder of Levi's white shirt. Jackson's K9, Ruby, whined beside him, echoing his frustration at seeing the former Deputy DA reduced to this. "Good morning, Levi," Jackson said. "That job offer at my kennels still stands. If not for yourself, do it for Boone."

Levi stroked his dog's fur, sending his tail thumping against the sidewalk. "I'm not looking for charity."

"It's not charity when I genuinely need the help." Jackson checked his watch—he was already cutting it close for his morning appointment.

"You might need the help, but you can't afford to pay a full-time worker. I know how much you Feds make. To be frank, I can't imagine how you can afford to run the shelter at all."

Jackson bristled at the insinuation. "You let me worry about the money. Okay?" The agent glared at the well-to-do couple who strolled past and averted their eyes, like Levi was something less than human. They only saw a dirty homeless man. They didn't see the human being who'd received a raw deal and lost everything because of it. Like many of the people who grew up in Lauderdale

County, Levi was taught to be proud and self-sufficient. Welfare was something almost nobody accepted, which made no sense to Jackson. It was a safety net. Something that helped you get through a rough patch. He had tried explaining that to Levi, but the man was stubborn to a fault. "Can we talk about this later? I've got a meeting in a few minutes, and I need to get to it."

"Don't let me stop you. I got nowhere to be and all the time in the world."

"You can't beg out here. Chief Wheeler said the next time the PD picks you up for vagrancy, they're going to charge you."

"What choice do I have?" Levi wrapped his arm around Boone. "From what I heard, you and the chief are thick as thieves. Surely, you can get him to keep looking the other way."

"We're not that close." Levi's comment about Jackson's relationship with the chief took him by surprise. How could a homeless man have any inkling about his connection with Wheeler? "And if they do pick you up, they'll take Boone and likely put him in a kill shelter." The thought of the sweet dog being put down wrenched Jackson's heart. He'd never let it happen, but he needed Levi to get the message. "I'll tell you what. Go back to your place behind Big Bad Breakfast, and I'll bring Boone some food after I'm done here. He might even share some of it with you. Boone will do anything for you, you know."

"Although..." Levi pulled at his t-shirt, looking at the unsightly stain. "I do need to get this washed." He picked himself up off the ground and held out his hand for Ruby to give him a sniff. "Okay. I'll do it for my dog. Can you bring Ruby too? Boone really enjoys her company."

"He'd have plenty of company if you took my job offer." The comment earned Jackson a flat stare from Levi. "Okay, I'll let it go. For now. I'm not sure how long I'll be, but wait for me, okay? I promise I'll be there."

"I'm going to get my clothes cleaned, and then I'll wait for you at my home. If you beat me there, can you leave the food behind? Boone needs a meal, and the passersby have been less than generous. Then again, it's Monday, and everyone is always a bit grumpy on Mondays."

Levi walked to the street corner with his dog at his heels. Jackson watched as they crossed the street together and continued on to where the local laundromat was. He considered Levi's makeshift home tucked in behind the restaurant. The alley was quiet and, except for garbage day, hardly anybody ever went there. Jackson would keep his promise and bring them some food. It would also give him another chance to convince Levi to take the job. Truth was, the kennel needed full-time help, and Levi was extremely good with animals. More than anything, the man needed to catch a break. He'd been in a downward spiral for five months—ever since he broke off his engagement with the mayor's daughter. With nothing more to do at the moment, Jackson pushed open the door to Trowbridge's, triggering its electronic chimes. He would survive his meeting, bring Levi and Boone some food, and get on with his day.

"Mornin', Violet," Jackson said as he stepped through the door. The diner looked like something straight out of the fifties, with black-and-white tile floors and gleaming chrome and Formica surfaces. A white counter stretched the length of the narrow room. Every table was taken, all awaiting Jackson's special guest—a perfect setting for his meeting.

Everyone in the restaurant greeted Jackson and Ruby as they made their way to the back of the room and the only unoccupied table. Jackson inhaled the kitchen's heavenly aroma, causing his stomach to growl. He took a seat with his back to the wall, allowing him to see the entrance. He wanted to observe Special Agent Willow Banks and her K9, Ranger, from the moment they walked through the door. While he waited, Jackson pulled out a notepad and started writing out the makings of a contract, one that he would give to Levi. Once he saw that he was being offered real work, for real compensation, he might accept. If he didn't, he'd have the paper to review later—when the temperatures dropped at night and the streets became less than safe for a homeless man and his dog.

Jackson drained his second cup of coffee, looked at his watch again, and groaned. He was scheduled to meet with Special Agent Banks at eight a.m., and it was nearly twenty to nine. "She could have at least called to say she's running late," he mumbled to himself. Ruby whined in response. Unlike Jackson, she'd already had her breakfast, but the smells of bacon and eggs were likely driving her to the brink as well. "I know, Ruby. We're late for work and the captain's going to ream us out. Again."

"You can tell the old curmudgeon to stick it up his arse," Violet said, the fifth-generation owner of Trowbridge's—Florence's only dog-friendly diner

"I can't talk to Captain Sawyer like that." Jackson rubbed his neck, tension building at the base of his skull. "He's my boss, regardless of how he treats me."

"The old fart's just sour because the chief brought in outside help." Violet rolled her eyes. "You'd think he could show a little appreciation."

Jackson shrugged, absently stroking Ruby's head. "Being close to Mom is worth dealing with Sawyer."

"You're too nice." Violet held her hands wide, palms up. "It's why you haven't found a woman yet. I've told you time and again, we like strong, take-charge men—wild stallions that ain't been broke yet. It gives us something to work on." She smiled and gave Jackson a playful nudge. "You show up all tall, handsome, and perfect... it doesn't leave anything for a woman to fix."

Heat crept up Jackson's ears, turning them scarlet. He hated receiving compliments. He simply didn't know how to respond to them.

"Oh, dear." Violet chuckled and pursed her lips. "I've gone and made you blush. We can't have you all red-faced when your date shows up. What's she going to think if you're all sweaty and stammering?" The woman tutted and looked to the door. "Where is she, anyway? She's over thirty-five minutes late. People got lives to get back to."

"Oh, we're not going anywhere." An elderly woman seated at the next table clutched her Chihuahua against her chest. She nodded slowly while stroking the little dog's head. "We're here to help, but we all want to see Jackson's new girlfriend."

"She's not my girlfriend, Mrs. Foster," Jackson barked. His already bright ears turned scarlet. "I'm sorry, Grace. I was rude. It's just..."

The old woman's smile broadened. "Come on Jax, there's no need to apologize. I've watched you grow up, and you know that I can take as good as I give. We're all aware that your *date* is coming for work, but there's no reason you can't mix some pleasure along with it." The old woman waggled her brows, making Jackson even more uncomfortable. "Just tell me when you don't need me anymore. I've got bridge club that I need to get to for ten. If I'm late, I'll get partnered with old man McPherson. I swear to Jesus, I can't understand a thing the man says. And he's the worst bridge player."

Jackson patted the woman's hand. "I'll always need you, Grace, but you can leave anytime. I'm thinking Agent Banks has changed her mind about coming." The chime of the restaurant's doorbell announced a visitor, cutting off Jackson's conversation. A tall, slender blonde woman was holding the door open with her back while she was wrestling with a Belgian Malinois, yanking on his leash and trying to convince the dog to follow her into the restaurant. The black and tan dog was resisting with everything he had while barking at his owner to not take him inside.

I'm going to be very late.

Chapter Three

Willow and Ranger

"Ranger, come," Special Agent Willow Banks commanded, pushing as much dominating energy as she could muster into her words. That's what people said. Speak with authority and the dog will listen. Apparently, Ranger didn't subscribe to the same school of thought. Willow's mind jumped back to her partner, Special Agent Kate Wilmington, who used to be Ranger's handler. The dog would literally do anything for her, and as it turned out, Kate would do anything for him—even take a bullet to save her K9's life. It had been Willow's fault. All of it. Had she not acted brashly... Had she followed Kate's advice... The wound was too fresh. She couldn't think about it. Not now. She'd already shed a river of tears, and now was not the time to start again.

"Come on, dog. We're both tired and we need to get this over with. It's your last chance." The words caught in Willow's throat. It really was the Belgian Malinois' last chance. If this so-called dog whisperer she was meeting couldn't fix him, the K9 agent was going to be euthanized. He was unstable and too aggressive to be re-homed. The FBI refused to accept the liability. Willow's supervisor wanted the dog destroyed immediately after he bit a fellow agent and put him in the hospital. If it wasn't for Ranger's guardian angel, Assistant Special Agent in Charge, Alice Baldwin, he would have breathed his last breath that day.

Several high-pitched barks from inside the restaurant changed Ranger's mind about not wanting to enter. He immediately switched from flight to prey mode. He dashed past Willow, nearly knocking the tall woman off her feet when the leash suddenly went taut. Using every ounce of strength, the agent gripped onto the heavy leather lead and yanked. Her efforts were less than useful. The seventy-pound dog was dragging her into the packed restaurant, and there was very little she could do to stop him. Just as Willow thought she was going to be hauled off her feet, Ranger stopped pulling and snarled. She knew that sound. Her K9 was about to rip out someone's throat.

"Ranger, heel!" Willow yanked on the leash and repeated the command. As she scanned the area, her breath caught. She tightened her grip on the leash, quickly wrapping it around her wrist. Directly in front of Ranger stood a small, wide-eyed girl holding out a strip of bacon. A woman in her late twenties rushed over and scooped the child into her arms.

"What are you thinking, bringing that monster in here?"

What was she thinking, indeed? Ever since his handler died, Ranger wasn't himself. He was terrified of entering any new building, and she had just forced him into a situation that would set him off. And why, of all places, would the trainer suggest they meet here?

A tall, thin man dressed in a heavy leather coat and gloves quickly moved to block Ranger's path to the woman and child. Despite the situation, he appeared calm. Did he not realize the danger he was in?

"Ranger, come!" Willow commanded, desperately trying to drag the dog outside. "Ranger!" She yanked at the leash again, pulling the dog off balance enough to gain some ground. Electronic chimes announced the front door opening again.

Can this day get any more horrific?

The thought had barely registered in her head when an enormous golden-red dog came bounding forward from the back of the diner. He let out two deep-chested barks, drawing Ranger's attention. The dog's head was high and his tail straight up, swishing slowly from side to side. Willow didn't know much about dogs, but she knew a Golden Retriever when she saw one.

Ranger lunged. The sudden lurch yanked Willow off her feet. Her forehead bounced off the floor, sending a wave of pain shooting through her skull. Bright lights exploded into her vision. She lay on her chest disoriented, trying to regain her senses. Snarls, barks, and yelps echoed in her head. Each noise felt like a spike being driven into her brain. A powerful hand grasped her upper arm.

Am I being attacked?

Willow rolled over, gripping the handle of her Glock 19.

"Special Agent Banks, I presume?" a deep male voice asked. "I'm Special Agent Jackson Brooks. Welcome to Alabama."

Willow stared at the hand for a moment. She raised her eyes long enough to take in the man standing in front of her before noticing the room filled with people gaping at her. "Are you insane? Why in God's name would you bring me here? What is wrong with you? Where's Ranger?"

"Your dog is in excellent hands," Jackson said, motioning with his head for Willow to look behind her.

Slowly she turned, finding Ranger sitting perfectly calm beside the tall thin man in the leather coat. The Golden Retriever was on his other side, giving her dog a good sniff.

"Good morning," he said with a crooked smile. "I'm Jason. I'm here to help Jax with Ranger's evaluation."

The cold linoleum floor did nothing to cool Willow's burning cheeks as she watched her supposedly unstable K9 sitting calmly beside a complete stranger.

"Okay people," Jackson said, addressing everyone in the small restaurant. "Show's over. Go back to your breakfasts."

Willow hopped to her feet, and the world spun. She grabbed onto the back of a stool for balance. "Show's over?" she repeated, her voice's pitch rising much higher than she'd have liked. "Does my dog nearly attacking a small child amuse you?" She pressed her face forward. Despite Willow being five-eleven, the man was at least four inches taller. "You put me and Ranger into this position... on purpose?" She was about to explode. She wanted to punch the prick in the face and continue until the light went out in his eyes. What kind of maniac would put her and a fearful, extremely dangerous dog in such a highly charged environment?

"He needed to see you and your dog in a real-life situation, sweetie," a slender woman in her forties said. She was wearing a thin cotton dress with a simple white apron. "We've got a place set up for you with plenty of room at the back." The woman motioned towards the rear of the diner.

"Follow me," Jackson said, his voice calm and reassuring. "Ranger's fine. Ruby and Jason have got him. They'll join us shortly."

Willow struggled to take it all in. She recognized Ruby's name from her earlier research on Agent Brooks, but she had no idea who the man was. "Who's Jason? Ranger never lets strangers or other dogs come near us."

"Dr. Jason Simmons is a behavioral vet. Ruby is my K9. Follow me and ignore Ranger. Keep your eyes forward, shoulders back." The lanky agent demonstrated the posture, keeping his head high and his shoulders straight as he strode to the back of the restaurant.

"What the hell is going on here?" Willow asked. The sharpness in her tone made Jackson visibly cringe. "Why would you bring me into a situation like this? You could have warned me. I could have been better prepared."

"And that's why I didn't say anything," Jackson said, pulling out a chair for the woman. "I needed to witness you and Ranger as you are together. If you had known, everything would have been different, and I'd have no useful information on either of you."

Willow sputtered at the comment. She understood the rationale. She had used it many times during impromptu interrogations in the field. There was much more to be learned about people when they were being themselves. Still, she didn't appreciate the tactic being used against her. The entire ordeal had been humiliating, much like how everything else had been going for her since she'd arrived in Alabama two hours earlier.

"And look at Ranger now," Jackson said. Ruby was standing next to the nervous shepherd. "Look at his head and his tail. His eyes are bright, and his ears are relaxed, and Ranger's tail isn't tucked nearly so tight under his belly. He knows he's got a pack leader, and he doesn't need to worry about anything but her."

Willow's eyes darkened at the comment. "I'm doing the best I can. I don't need some smart-ass trainer to tell me I'm a terrible owner."

"You're not terrible at all." Jackson waved his hands in front of himself in a defensive gesture. "I think you're amazing. Ranger lost his handler during a traumatic event, and he's struggling to cope with his new reality. Hair missiles are a difficult breed at the best of times—"

"What the fuck is a *hair missile*?" Willow took a step closer. "Why are you insulting my dog?" Ranger immediately started barking, earning himself a nip from Ruby.

Jackson swallowed hard while he continued his defensive pose. "I meant no disrespect. It's a nickname I picked up from a TV show I used to watch. The special operators had a Belgian Malinois who looked a lot like yours. That was her nickname, something she earned because she was extremely fast, and she never missed her target." He stammered out the last words and swallowed hard.

Willow smiled to herself. She had somehow gained the upper hand in the conversation. It seemed that he didn't like close-quarter confrontations. It might have also been that he struggled with angry women. From what she'd read about the man, he was an exemplary tracker and dog trainer. He and his dog, Ruby, belonged to an elite search and rescue team, but the pair also handled manhunts. In these tight confines, it seemed Jackson was out of his element, and he simply didn't know what to say or do to diffuse the situation. But the word was, the man was a burnout and had taken on a lollypop K9 assignment back in his hometown. A twinge of regret and sympathy knotted in her stomach. The sweat gathering on Jackson's brow made Willow feel bad for the agent, a man who was here to help her the best way he knew how.

"Sorry," Willow said, pressing her palm to her forehead. She winced as she felt what was likely the start of a lump—a direct result of her head bouncing off the linoleum floor. "It's been a trying twenty-four hours. I drove through the night with Ranger barking non-stop in the back seat of my truck. I had hoped he would either bark himself hoarse, or he'd exhaust himself to the point he'd just lay down and fall asleep. I should have been in town last night, but I had to keep making stops. Letting Ranger out for a drink and a walk was the only way to get him to stop barking. I didn't get to my hotel until six a.m., and the prick at the front desk wouldn't give me my room because my dog was too disruptive."

"I'm sorry you went through all that," Jackson said. "Have a seat and I'll get you some coffee and a bowl of water for Ranger."

"You just sit yourself down," the woman in the summer dress and apron said. She was carrying a pot of coffee, a mug, and a dog bowl full of fresh water. "You might be the world's best dog trainer, but I'm the world's best waitress, and I know how to care for my guests."

"Listen to Violet, Jax," an elderly woman said. She was clutching onto her Chihuahua like it was a life preserver. The little dog was likely the source of the high-pitched barks that Ranger had reacted to when they'd arrived. "You and the pretty lady need to get acquainted. Your new relationship has already had a rocky start." The meddlesome woman turned her attention to Willow. "He's single you know."

"Oh, God save me," Jackson muttered. "Grace, please don't. You've done your duty helping me today. Don't you want to get to your bridge club?"

"Mercy, no," Grace said, leaning in to get closer. "I want to meet the pretty lady. I'm a bit disappointed that you haven't introduced me yet. Your momma raised you better than that. If your pa was still around, he'd tan your hide."

Willow's eyebrows lifted as she turned to face SA Brooks. His body language screamed that he wanted to crawl under a rock and die. Rather than tell the old busybody to mind her own business and shut the hell up, he took her crap. The man was a doormat. He needed to grow a pair, or the world was eventually going to eat him alive.

"Pleased to meet you, Grace." Willow inclined her head to the overly friendly woman. "I'm Special Agent Willow Banks, and I'm afraid I've done everything wrong since the moment I came through the door. Please allow me to remedy my indiscretions."

"Don't patronize me, missy. And your errors started long before you got here." Grace wagged her bony finger at Willow. "You left my Jax sitting here for near forty minutes waiting for you. A proper lady would have called to let a gentleman know she was running late."

"I would have," Willow said, fishing her phone out of her pocket. The screen was cracked and punctured, and the device was bent at an unnatural angle. "I was trying to call when Agent Ranger decided he didn't like my phone. Unfortunately, it contained all my information, including Agent Brooks's phone number, as well as the name and address of this restaurant. I've been walking up and down Court Street looking for where I was supposed to be for over an hour."

"No need to apologize," Jackson interrupted. "Stuff happens. And you've found your way, and all is as it should be. You can go now, Grace. This is FBI business and not for your ears."

The old woman blew a raspberry. "Nonsense. It's a free country and this is a public restaurant, and listening in on other people's conversations is my favorite pastime. Are you going to take that away from me, Jax? Are you going to deny me my God-given rights? What would your mother say?"

"I don't mind if she hears what you have to say to me," Willow offered. She turned to the nosey woman and pasted a saccharine-sweet smile on her face. "I mean, it's only fair. In the last two minutes I've learned a lot about you. Things like, you're recently a widow. You like to appear important to people around you, but deep inside, you're terribly insecure. It's why you're clutching your little dog the way you are. I think it's a terrible shame that you need a shield while you're sitting among friends."

Grace blinked and sputtered. Her gaze shifted to Jackson as she waited for him to come to her rescue.

"Don't look for another shield," Willow said. "In the short time that we've met, I've also learned that you are a willful, independent woman, and you have strong moral standards. I'm sure if you stick around for an hour or so, I can learn a lot more about you. I think I'd like that very much."

With a huff, Grace stood from her chair, loosened her grip on her dog, and stuck her nose firmly in the air. "You're not as clever as you think you are, missy." She raised her brow at Jackson. "Don't let this one get away, Jax. She smart, she's pretty, and she'll drag you out of that shell of yours. Your mother would like nothing more than to see you with a fine woman before she passes, and she's not going to keep her cancer at bay forever, you know." The old woman spun on her heel, clopped through the dining room, and exited without ever looking back.

Oh shit. That's why he's working in this small city with the police K9 unit. That wasn't in his files. I thought he had burned out.

"Nice job with Grace," Jackson said. His expression said he was desperate to fill the momentary lull in the conversation. "How did you know she was recently widowed?"

"Mostly," Willow said with a sheepish smile, "it was all guess-work. She was wearing a wedding ring, which told me she was married. Her husband wasn't with her, which may or may not have been normal for her, but I think that's why she was using her little dog like a shield. She's not accustomed to being alone in public. And, lastly, she had a small heart-shaped amulet. My church back home gave my grandmother one just like it when my grampa passed away. Grams's amulet tarnished within a month, and Grace's still looked shiny and brand new."

Willow liked the appreciative expression that spread across the man's face. She had no need or desire to impress him, but after her horrific entrance, it gave her a more solid footing for their conversation. She had dug herself into a hole, but her small display of skill had helped her climb out of it. A little, at least.

A loud BANG outside sent Ranger scrambling, his claws struggling for purchase on the slick tiled floor. Willow recognized the sound. It was a flashbang grenade, the type used by military and law enforcement. She drew her gun and raced through the mass of patrons, rushing to get a look at what was happening outside.

Chapter Four

Jackson

Jackson groaned, his attention split between the frantic Malinois and Agent Banks's hasty departure. Ranger crouched behind a table, barking incessantly. Even with Jason and Ruby present, leaving the dog behind was risky. If approached, Ranger might attack out of fear, his bite-training making him a serious threat.

Every patron crowded towards the front of the restaurant, eager for a glimpse of the commotion outside. Many had already stepped onto the sidewalk.

"I've got him," Jason assured. "Go."

"Thanks, Jason." Jackson commanded his retriever with practiced authority. "Ruby, hold!" He pointed at Ranger. "Don't let him out." The Golden Retriever positioned herself between Ranger and the exit.

"Sorry, Violet," Jackson said, gesturing to the dogs. "Jason and Ruby will keep him contained, but can you make sure nobody goes back there?"

"Go, sweetie." Violet waved him off. "Go save the world. I'll take care of my guests."

With a nod, Jackson pushed through the throng blocking the exit. The bright morning sun assaulted his eyes, the late April heat already climbing despite the early hour. To his left, a university-aged crowd had gathered outside Yumm.

A young woman hurried up, her face pale with shock. Jackson identified himself, "I'm FBI Special Agent Brooks. What happened?"

"He shot the couple," she stammered, glancing back fearfully. "A homeless man… he walked in, shot them, and then set off a bomb. Everyone ran, me included." She clung to Jackson's arm like a lifeline.

"Ma'am, were you in the restaurant? Did you see him? What did he look like?" The questions went unanswered, the woman too shaken to respond. Despite wanting to question her further, the active scene demanded his immediate attention. Agent Banks was nowhere in sight. "Ma'am, wait inside Trowbridge's," he instructed, pointing to the diner. "There are two officers inside. They'll protect you."

It wasn't entirely truthful—Ruby and Ranger were K9s, not officers—but it served his purpose. Hoping she'd follow his directions, Jackson dashed towards Yumm, shouldering through the crowd of university students, all with phones aloft.

"Nobody leaves," he ordered, flashing his badge. "I'm going to want to talk to all of you." Without waiting for acknowledgment, he pushed into the restaurant.

The scene inside made him recoil. A young woman stood amid the carnage, taking selfies with two victims visible behind her. She tugged open her blouse, revealing blood spatter on her chest and neck. Beyond this macabre spectacle, the room appeared empty.

"Give me that," Jackson demanded, reaching for the cell phone. The woman yelped, trying to pull away, but Jackson was quicker.

"Give it back," she protested, swinging at him. "I have every right to take pictures."

"You're impeding a criminal investigation and you're tampering with a crime scene." Jackson held the phone out of reach, fending her off. "You're standing in blood."

"Gross! Damn, I missed that. Give me my phone so I can get some pics." She began moving, leaving bloody footprints in her wake.

"Stop moving around," Jackson commanded, grabbing her elbow. She lashed out, striking his face and shoulders, screaming incoherently. He pocketed her phone and swiftly cuffed her, bringing her to the floor. With a knee on her back, he removed her shoes.

"You're going to lose your job over this, asshole. I'm pre-law and I'm going to sue you for every worthless penny you have." When Jackson didn't relent, she began screaming for help, claiming rape.

"Ma'am," he said, voice steady. "You're under arrest for assaulting a federal agent and hindering a criminal investigation. Anything you say can and will be used against you in a court of law. I'm removing you from the murder scene for your own protection. I strongly suggest you keep quiet and don't make this any worse for yourself."

"Those aren't my Moranda rights," she yelled, still struggling. "I'm going to sue you, asshole."

"It's pronounced Miranda rights, Ma'am." Jackson pulled out his notebook. "What's your name?"

"Fuck you," she sneered. "I want my lawyer."

"You can call your lawyer when we get to the station. For now, what is your name?"

She rolled her eyes dramatically. "My name's Fuck You, and I'm not saying another word until I've spoken with my lawyer."

Exhaling slowly, Jackson led her to the exit, acutely aware of the half-dozen people recording the encounter. This was precisely why he preferred search and rescue—less scrutiny, more straightforward problem-solving. Still, these phone-wielding observers could prove useful.

"I'm going to want your cell phones," Jackson announced, stepping outside. The young woman had quieted, much to his relief. "You are all potential witnesses to the crime and you're all going to stay put until I finish processing the scene." Several spectators began protesting, citing their rights. They were wrong, of course, but did he want to deal with the mountain of paperwork that enforcing compliance would generate?

"Listen," he said, securing the woman to a metal bench. "Two people were just murdered. If you saw anything, or if you've got video, you may be able to help catch a killer. If you want to post your exploits on social media, why not post something about how you performed a public service?" It was a good speech, he thought, but it highlighted a disturbing reality. "And, if any of you took pictures of the deceased, for the love of God, do not post them to the web. Can you imagine finding out about a family member being murdered like that? I know you're not so interested in earning a few likes or hearts that you're willing to destroy someone's memories of a loved one."

As phones lowered, Jackson felt a glimmer of hope. It vanished when a device was thrust into his face. "It's my constitutional right to film and post whatever I want, whenever I want," a young man said. His smug expression screamed privilege, the kind that came with old money in Florence.

"You're absolutely right," Jackson conceded. "But it is within my right to secure the scene, and right now, you're in my space and you're potentially destroying evidence. So, you will either back away from this restaurant, or I will arrest you for hampering a federal investigation."

"I've got him on video, Agent Brooks. I've got everyone on video."

Jackson turned to find a short, pimple-faced young man behind him.

"Johnnie Walker, Sir," the man said. "Like the whiskey. My parents thought it was funny. I'm a journalist major at UNA. I've got everyone. I was right outside when it happened. I got it all. I've been filming ever since. I got everyone coming out of the restaurant. I'll give you my phone and the video. Just give it back, okay? I want to help, but I can't lose this. There's a Pulitzer in it for me. I'm sure of it."

"Thanks, Johnnie. Keep recording. Look for anyone suspicious. I'm going back inside." Jackson's instincts told him this kid would stick around. His footage could prove invaluable. "Did you see a blonde woman dressed in white and blue, and carrying a handgun?"

"I did. I got her too." Johnnie pointed down the street. "She came from that direction. She ran into the restaurant, yelled at Charlie to get out, and that was the last I saw of her. I'm assuming she ran out the back, or she's still inside."

"Charlie? Is that the name of the young woman I cuffed to the bench?"

Johnnie grimaced and nodded. "Her name is Charlie Shanahan. You're going to make her the meme sensation of the week. Maybe even the month. She's a liberal arts major, but she spends more time recording herself on social media than she does attending class."

"You seem to know a lot about this young woman," Jackson observed, glancing back. "You're not stalking her, are you?"

"Stalking her?" Johnnie bit his lip, averting his gaze. "No. Not at all. But she is pretty famous with the college crowd, and I thought that maybe I could... you know... help her get to know me if I did some fluff pieces on her." He scuffed his shoe on the ground. "Not that it's helped."

Jackson jotted down the woman's name. "Okay then... thanks for the information." Breaking off the conversation, he returned to the restaurant and called the station. "Hey, Marcy," he said to the desk sergeant. "We've got a double homicide at Yumm, the Thai restaurant on North Court Street. Get the ME, Franklin, and Castor down here, along with as many officers as you can manage. There's a large crowd out front, and I need help getting their information. Inform the officers that there is another federal agent on scene searching for the shooter. She's Caucasian, with long, wavy blonde hair, five foot eleven, and an athletic build. She's dressed in navy blue pants and a white button-down shirt, and she's carrying her service gun, a Glock 19."

"I'll send Dawson and Reeves, instead," Marcy replied. "There's a squad car already enroute. I'll send more, and I'll let them know that your girl isn't the shooter."

Jackson considered the suggested officers. They were trained in scene processing, but he preferred Franklin and Castor. Despite evidence of their corruption, they were excellent detectives with an impressive close rate.

"Where's Franklin and Castor? I need detectives on the scene."

A pause. "Franklin's been called away on a personal matter, and Castor's at the mayor's press conference. Oh, and Captain Sawyer's pissed that you're late. He's making a big show of how irresponsible you are." Marcy chuckled softly. "He's going to look like an idiot when he finds out why you're not here."

"Thanks, Marcy. You're the best."

"You know it, sugar."

Ending the call, Jackson pocketed his phone. He wasn't equipped to handle a crime scene properly. Observation from a distance was his best option now. When he'd left the Violent Crimes Against Children task force, he'd thought he was done with scenes like this. The brutal murders and exploitation had been too much. Unbidden, his memory of the terrified boy in the closet, gun pointed at Jackson's face, surfaced. He pushed it aside. The victims needed his full focus now.

Pulling out his phone, Jackson began documenting the scene, capturing Charlie's bloody footprints and noting a single boot print—someone else had stepped in the blood, leaving a perfect impression before smearing subsequent prints. It seemed only

Charlie and this unknown person had been careless enough to contaminate the scene.

With a deep breath, Jackson turned to the woman on the floor. Her face was unrecognizable, a bloody ruin that made his stomach churn. The male victim, slumped over the table, showed no visible wounds, but his clothing was soaked in blood. Based on the lack of blood on the table and the state of his shirt, pants, and chair, Jackson surmised he'd been shot in the torso. Without moving the body—which he wouldn't do until the ME arrived—there was no way to confirm. No exit wound was visible on his back.

"Freeze!" a high-pitched voice commanded. "Show me your hands."

"At least you didn't shoot me, Fisher," Jackson said, turning to face the police officer. "I appreciate that."

Chapter Five

Willow

Upon confirming both victims were deceased, Willow flashed her badge at the few remaining patrons and kitchen staff, instructing them to exit and remain nearby for questioning. Her instincts suggested the killer had likely escaped through the rear door while others fled out the front.

"Damn it," Willow muttered, scanning the area as she stepped outside. She might have erred. The back alley stretched empty in both directions, a narrow road winding between buildings. The only notable feature was a homeless encampment a block away.

Approaching the makeshift shelter—a blue plastic tarp riddled with patches, held together by binder twine and fishing line—Willow called out, "Hello? Anyone home?"

A gravelly female voice responded from within, "Whatcha want?"

"I'm Special Agent Willow Banks, FBI. I have some questions for you."

"No!"

Perplexed by the curt response, Willow pressed on. "Ma'am, please come out. There've been two murders. I need your assistance."

"I ain't helping with dead bodies," came the reply. "I'm safe here. Go away."

"Ma'am?" Willow gently pulled back a tattered flap and peered inside. Sunlight filtered through the tarp's holes, illuminating an unexpectedly tidy living space. Everything was neatly arranged, save for the disheveled woman wearing a pulled-up hoodie and an N95 mask. "I apologize for intruding, but your help is crucial. Did you see anyone pass by in the last five to fifteen minutes?"

"You're trespassing," the woman snapped, futilely attempting to smooth her scraggly black hair. "I got rights. You feds think you own everything. I know you can't be here. Get out!"

Undeterred, Willow asked, "Are you hungry? I'll give you twenty dollars to step outside and talk."

"Make it forty, and I'll stay put."

"How about this?" Willow proposed, retrieving a money clip from her pocket. She peeled off a twenty and offered it. "Take this twenty. Answer my questions, and I'll give you twenty more."

"I don't know nothin'. Might as well leave."

"All I need is for you to tell me if you saw anyone come through here recently. That's an easy twenty bucks."

The woman leaned forward. "Maybe I did. Show me the other twenty."

Willow smiled inwardly. "Here," she said, handing over the second bill. "I trust you'll share what you know. No need to withhold payment."

"Not too bright, are you, agent?" The woman snatched the money and retreated. "Now I got your cash, and you got nothin'."

"Fair enough," Willow shrugged. "I've met many in your situation. Most are good people facing hard times. If you can't help, I understand."

Willow paused, letting her words settle. She knew displaced individuals rarely trusted strangers, especially law enforcement. But silence often prompted people to fill the void.

After a moment, the woman spoke. "One man passed by fifteen minutes ago. Had a dog. Tied it up and went into that building."

She gestured vaguely toward the restaurant. "Came out after the loud bang. Grabbed his dog and took off. I hid when I saw him. Didn't see where he went after."

"Can you describe him? Did you get a good look?"

"Good enough, I guess." The woman leaned closer, her striking blue eyes contrasting with her grimy skin. "White guy, pretty tall. Nearly six foot. Long black hair like mine, shaggy black beard. His dog was one of them yappy collie-type dogs, the herding kind."

"What about his clothes? How long ago exactly?"

"Dark colored. Black or brown." The woman's brow furrowed. "Maybe five minutes ago. Ran by full tilt. Didn't even try to hide his face. Like he didn't care if I saw him. That's why I hid. Figured if he didn't care, he might kill me." She patted herself. "Still breathing, so guess that wasn't his plan."

The story puzzled Willow. It didn't align with the calculated assassination she'd witnessed. The killer had targeted only two victims, injured no one else, and created a diversion to cover his escape. Revealing his face seemed an unnecessary risk.

Thanking the woman, Willow headed in the indicated direction. At the cross street, she found herself amid a crowd, with no way to guess the killer's whereabouts. Sirens wailed nearby, signaling the local PD's approach. She needed to return quickly before someone contaminated her crime scene.

Willow backtracked a block and turned right onto North Court Street. Across the way stood Trowbridge's, where she'd met Agent Brooks. She wondered about Ranger, regretting abandoning him but knowing she couldn't manage the unstable animal while pursuing a murderer. Not today. Concern for the dog's behavior gnawed at her.

He's in good hands.

Hoping it was true, Willow hurried toward the crime scene. As she neared Yumm, the crowded sidewalk forced her to slow. University-aged kids milled about, discussing how the man had shot someone named Rachel Persie in the face. Some sounded almost glad, as if she'd deserved it. While Willow had encountered her share of reprobates, the casual disregard for human life disturbed her. She recognized it as reactionary talk, but it troubled her that this woman—someone's daughter, sister, or mother—was being dehumanized. Respect for life seemed to be waning.

"Excuse me," Willow addressed two uniformed officers taping off the area, flashing her badge. "Why is that woman handcuffed to the bench?"

The taller officer, his nameplate reading "Martin," chuckled as he lifted the crime scene tape for her. "You'll have to ask Agent Brooks. She was like that when we arrived." He gestured toward the door. "He's inside, but I wouldn't go in. He's not in a great mood."

Willow glanced at the officer's feet, noting a missing shoe. "Let me guess. You stepped in blood? Contaminated the scene? That's why he's upset?"

"I was trying to help," he scowled, glancing back at the entrance. "I used to be a paramedic."

A paramedic turned cop—not something Willow encountered often. People found their way into law enforcement for various reasons. Perhaps EMT work hadn't suited him. "How long have you been on the force?"

The officer winced. "Just over six weeks. Depending on how Agent Brooks writes this up, today might be my last."

"Well," Willow offered a half smile, "if it's your last day, make it count. Tell me what you've observed since arriving."

"Lots of people in the restaurant," Officer Martin straightened. "Mostly from UNA." He nodded up the street toward the North Alabama University campus. "They all gave similar accounts. Many have video, though I heard some complaining the footage came out blurry." Willow nodded, encouraging him to continue.

"According to witnesses, the victims are Rachel Persie and Tanner Montgomery. They identified the shooter as Levi Benson."

"They know the murderer?" Willow almost laughed. This might be her easiest case yet.

"Well, no," Martin clarified. "But Ms. Persie said his name was Levi, and she used to be engaged to Levi Benson." He moved closer and lowered his voice. "Apparently Ms. Persie destroyed his life after he broke off with her. In less than a minute, he went from being a big deal in the DA's office to a homeless man panhandling on the street."

"Levi was a prosecutor?"

"Not just any prosecutor," Martin said. "He was the Deputy District Attorney."

"Jesus. What kind of pull did this woman have to get him fired?"

"She's Mayor Persie's daughter."

"Damn." This wasn't as straightforward as Willow had hoped. "And the other victim, Tanner Montgomery?"

"Local hero," the officer beamed, clearly a fan. "Star quarterback for the Lions. Holds records in passing yards and touchdowns. Took the team to nationals three times, winning twice. Would've been three if the refs weren't homers. Couldn't let their precious Fighting Irish lose to us three years running."

"I see," Willow nodded. "A big deal, then."

"More than that," Martin continued. "He's one of the only feds who doesn't catch flak around here. Him and Jackson Brooks. They're both hometown boys."

"Tanner's federal? Which agency?"

"FBI."

"Christ," Willow's eyebrows shot up. "The victim was an FBI agent?"

Chapter Six

Jackson

Jackson's grip tightened on the young woman's cell phone. If not for the evidence it contained, he'd have smashed it against the wall. A profound emptiness consumed him as he gazed at his childhood friend slumped over the table. They would never again share lunch or debate the dark underbelly of humanity they both knew too well. Tanner's endless technobabble and conspiracy theories about bureau corruption had been silenced forever.

Their heated debates echoed in Jackson's memory. Where Tanner saw widespread immorality, Jackson clung to his belief in human goodness. After nearly three years of hunting child predators, he had to believe these monsters were anomalies. The alternative was unthinkable, twisting his stomach into knots.

The selfie-girl's continued recording of the brutal murder left Jackson reeling. Without the video, he might never have identified Rachel Persie's ruined face. The killer clearly hated her. Ironically, the lengthy list of people with motive to harm Rachel included Jackson himself. Her character assassination of Levi had been unforgivable.

Yet the video provided a crucial lead: a clear image of the killer's face. The resemblance to Levi was striking, but the eyes were wrong. Colored contacts, perhaps? But the suspect appeared far too disheveled. Even at his lowest, Levi maintained a certain standard. In Jackson's experience, people's core nature rarely changed so drastically.

"Nobody enters," Officer Fisher said firmly, standing just inside the glass doors of the restaurant. The sharp command broke through Jackson's thoughts, and he glanced toward the doorway. Outside, through the smudged pane, Willow paced, her expression tight with frustration as she stared in at them. "Let her in," Jackson said, powering down the cell phone. "She's FBI and was first on scene." Willow had already presented her credentials, but the officer remained obstinate until Jackson's order.

"News crews are already outside," Willow reported. "I don't understand how they got here so fast." She studied Jackson's face. "Are you okay? You look ill."

"No, I'm not okay," Jackson admitted, struggling to maintain composure. "I knew both victims. Tanner was an FBI agent." He paused, collecting himself. "I've alerted the Birmingham office. They're sending agents to assist. For now, it's our case."

Willow's expression shifted, concern mixing with something deeper that Jackson couldn't quite place.

"I'm getting Ruby," he continued. "All signs point to the killer exiting through the back. I want her to track the suspect."

"Wait." Willow's brow knitted together as a pained expression crossed her face. "I can't manage Ranger and the crime scene simultaneously. He'll lose it if I bring him in here."

As if on cue, frantic barking erupted outside. People scattered as flashing white teeth strained against a leash.

"Are you insane?" Officer Fisher shoved the door open, bellowing at the dog's handler who was standing outside the door and doing his best to restrain the Malinois. "Get out of here. Leave. Now!"

Jackson muttered and bolted for the door, tucking the cell phone into his back pocket. "Ranger, hush!" he commanded, approaching the agitated dog. Jackson shouldered past Fisher, following his verbal command with a hand signal. Ranger instantly quieted and sat, eyes locked on Jackson, awaiting further instruction.

Meanwhile, Ruby waited calmly off-leash beside Jason. The veterinary behaviorist turned to Jackson with a shrug. "Sorry. Ranger is... single-mindedly persistent. Short of sedation, he was coming here with or without my permission. Calling him strong willed would be an understatement."

Jackson sighed. "I can't let him in, and I need Ruby." He glanced back at Willow's stern face and the bloody scene beyond. "Can you get Ranger safely back to the kennels? He's an unnecessary distraction right now."

"Sure thing, if I can convince him to come with me," Jason said, smiling down at the shepherd. "I'd like more time with him anyway. He'll push me to my limits, I expect."

"Thanks, my friend," Jackson said. "I owe you one."

"You owe me more than one, Jax," Jason raised his eyebrows pointedly. "And I expect to collect sooner rather than later."

"Absolutely," Jackson winced internally at the word choice. "Your next fundraiser. I'll be there." He tried to ignore Jason's skeptical look, knowing the man often ran bachelor auctions for his free vet clinic. "Come on, Ruby. We've got work to do." The Golden Retriever bounded into the restaurant, heading directly to the dead bodies. "Thanks again, Jason. I'll try not to be too late. Call if Ranger gives you any serious trouble."

"Heel," Jason commanded, tugging Ranger's leash. The Malinois' attentive gaze gave Jackson hope that the dog wasn't beyond help. His issues likely stemmed from Willow, who'd require the bulk of the training. Jackson shifted his attention to where his own dog was working the scene.

"Ruby's awfully close to the blood," Willow observed. "Should you call her off?"

"She's fine," Jackson assured her. "She knows what not to do. She needs proximity to isolate relevant scents." In truth, watching Ruby work never failed to impress him. While most SAR K9s were well trained, Ruby displayed an almost preternatural instinct. During their time with the VCAC task force, she'd shown an empathy for people without becoming overwhelmed by the horrors they encountered.

Images of that terrified young boy in a closet flashed unbidden through Jackson's mind. The gun in the child's hand, a desperate last resort. Jackson had watched the boy's finger tense on the trigger, a moment in time that still haunted his sleepless nights. The bloody crime scene now before him did nothing to dispel the disturbing memory.

Ruby barked, leaping over blood-soaked tiles. She pressed her nose to the floor, snuffling her way towards the restaurant's rear. When no one followed, she barked again and vanished from view.

"Ruby, come," Jackson called. The dog reappeared, confusion evident in her expression. This deviation from their usual investigative pattern clearly puzzled her. "We can't leave yet," he explained, as if she understood every word. "We need to wait for the ME."

Jackson knew better, of course, but he'd learned that his actual words mattered less than his tone and emotion. Ruby used those cues to determine her next action.

"Go," Willow urged. "I'll secure the scene. I've already checked the back alley. Apart from the homeless woman, I saw nothing of interest. Maybe you and Ruby can spot what I missed."

"Homeless woman?" Jackson frowned. He knew most of the area's transients. The few women who frequented Court Street returned to shelters at night for safety, as did most of the men. Only Levi maintained a full-time encampment, generally left alone by local law enforcement who felt he'd been through enough. Those who might hassle him had to contend with Boone—small, but lightning-fast and fiercely protective.

"Yeah," Willow confirmed. "She's behind the restaurant at the alley's end. The tarps forming her shelter were barely intact, but the space was immaculate. I wish my own home was that clean."

"That's Levi's home." Jackson's throat constricted as he realized another friend might be in danger. Friend might be too strong a term, but he cared about Levi's welfare. "What did this woman look like?"

"Scraggly black hair, blue eyes, thin. She never came out of the tent, and she was wearing a black hoodie and an N95 mask."

"Fisher, guard the scene." Jackson didn't want to leave, but he had no choice in the matter. "Agent Banks and I are going to check out the encampment. Nobody but the ME enters. I don't care if you have to shoot them. Understood?"

"Sure, Agent." Fisher hesitated. "But... what if other cops want access?"

Jackson glanced towards the entrance. "Not just the ME. Franklin and Castor should arrive shortly, with Dawson and Reeves. Let them in too. Nobody else."

"Remember," Willow added, "this is now a federal crime scene, but until more feds arrive, we need all available help."

Jackson nodded appreciatively. "You're coming with me. Show me what you saw." He sprinted towards the back of the restaurant. "Ruby, seek." The dog barked and bolted ahead, already at the back door by the time the two FBI agents caught up.

Using a handkerchief, Jackson carefully depressed the heavy metal door's crash bar, mindful of preserving potential fingerprints. Years of experience had taught him the importance of maintaining crime scene integrity, even when urgency pressed. As the door unlatched, he gently pushed it open with his elbow.

Ruby darted out first. "After you." Jackson held the door for Willow. While it might have appeared chivalrous, his primary in-

tent was to prevent the visiting agent from contaminating potential evidence. Before they had fully exited, Ruby's excited barks
were already fading down the alley.

Chapter Seven

Willow

"This is where I saw her," Willow said, peering inside the tent structure. "It's only been, what, ten minutes since I was here." Ruby's frantic barks drew her attention. "Has she got her scent?"

"Possibly," Jackson said. "I'm waiting to see what you might have found inside Levi's home."

Well, shit. I'm off my game.

"It never dawned on me to search the encampment. I don't know these streets at all. I assumed it was the woman's home. She never gave me any indication that she was somehow connected..." Jackson's silent disappointment stung more than she expected, even if she deserved it.

"Ruby, seek," Jackson commanded. The Golden Retriever sniffed the air and bolted down the alley.

Jackson dashed after his dog, forcing Willow to run full tilt to keep up. Her shoes, chosen after years with her partner and Ranger for their suitability for sudden sprints, proved inadequate today. Jackson and Ruby quickly outpaced her, disappearing around a corner two blocks ahead.

Willow's footfalls echoed in her head as she ran, the bustle of cars and pedestrians fading from her awareness. At the corner, she scanned the street posts for cameras. None were visible, but she knew they might be hidden.

"The trail went cold right here," Jackson said as Willow approached, wiping sweat from her brow.

"She got into a car?" Willow searched again for surveillance cameras. "Any chance she was caught on surveillance video?"

"I'll get some unis to canvas the area, but I expect we'll find nothing. Whoever she was, she chose her escape route carefully. All the buildings here face the main street until you get to the next intersection." Jackson absently rubbed Ruby's head. "We need to get back to the scene."

"We need to get the homeless encampment processed," Willow countered. "It's in an alley and it might already be compromised by passersby."

"Unlikely. That street sees almost no foot traffic, and about the only time a vehicle uses it is on garbage day." Jackson caught Willow's flat stare. "But you're right. It needs to be processed. I'll leave Ruby to guard it until we can get the crime scene investigators here."

"You've got your own CSI?" Willow asked skeptically. "The city population can't be more than fifty thousand. The local police force couldn't possibly be that big."

"No, but there are a couple of officers in the PD who are trained to handle a crime scene. They're not the best answer, but they know enough not to compromise any evidence while they gather what they can." Jackson pulled out his cell phone and dialed. "Hey Marcy. Can you redirect either Dawson or Reeves over to Levi's place for processing? There was a woman using it, and I suspect she's connected to the shootings." His eyebrows shot up as he listened. "Okay, Marcy. Look. Do what you can. I'm on my way back to the restaurant now. I'm going to put Ruby on guard duty, but I can't leave her there all day." A smile tugged at his mouth. "Thanks Marcy. You're the best."

He pocketed his phone and strode past with Ruby at his heel. "Let's get going."

En route to the restaurant, they paused at the shelter. Jackson verified it was undisturbed and ordered Ruby to "Guard." Willow marveled at the dog's instant compliance, knowing Ranger would never obey so readily.

"Who's Marcy?" Willow asked, noting the familiarity in their exchange.

"Desk sergeant at the Florence PD," Jackson replied quickly. "Captain Sawyer's already called in the Alabama State Bureau of Investigation. He wasn't too keen on waiting for the FBI." He huffed in frustration. "Swear to God, the man's doing it just to tick me off. At least he agreed to let Dawson and Reeves process the scene and Levi's home until the FBI arrives."

"Why would a police captain try to piss you off?" Willow pressed. "Why bring in the SBI?"

Jackson hesitated, his eyes shifting for a moment before he shrugged it off. "Sawyer's been a thorn in my side since day one. He threw a fit when Wheeler put me in charge of the K9 unit. Didn't think I should have any say in how the department was run."

"Wait... what?" Willow's eyes widened in surprise. "You're a cop now? You left the bureau?"

Jackson's jaw clenched, his gaze hardening as he turned away. "No. I'm still with the bureau but Chief Wheeler needed me seen as part of the PD. Officially." His words were sharp but withdrawn, as if he regretted revealing that much. He moved ahead, distancing himself.

Willow stared after him, something clicking in her mind. "Hold up... you're not just here for the K9 unit, are you?" Her voice lowered, the realization settling in. "Wheeler brought you in for something more." She paused, watching him carefully. "Something involving Captain Sawyer?"

Jackson stiffened but kept walking.

"Holy shit." Willow jogged to catch up, her voice barely a whisper. "That's why he's giving you hell. My boss warned me there were some bad actors in the PD, but I didn't think it was this deep."

Jackson's step faltered, but he didn't stop. His hands flexed at his sides, as if fighting the urge to respond.

"I knew it," Willow muttered, lowering her hands in a gesture of peace. "I get it, okay? You don't have to say anything. But it makes sense. I just wish you'd trust me."

Jackson exhaled, finally slowing down. His voice was quieter now, laced with exhaustion. "I'm not investigating anyone. I'm just trying to do my job."

His words were evasive, but his expression gave him away.

Willow took a breath, deciding to ease the tension. "You mentioned before that you knew the victims. How did you know them?"

Jackson's shoulders sagged as if the weight of the situation had caught up with him. His eyes glazed over with a sadness that Willow hadn't seen before. "Oh shit." Her voice softened. "You didn't just know them. You were close to them."

He cleared his throat, nodding. "Tanner and I grew up together. We went to college together. We even went through Quantico together." His voice dropped to a hoarse whisper. "We were more like brothers than friends. I'd have done anything for him."

Willow's heart clenched. Though she hadn't grown up with her partner, Kate had been closer to her than anyone. Unwilling to deal with it, she changed the subject. "What about the mayor's daughter? Rachel, was it?"

Jackson closed his eyes, lost in thought. "I only knew Rachel by association. We were at the same parties, or school functions, but I didn't *know* her. Not that I wanted to. I never liked her, but after what she did to Levi..."

Willow sensed there might be more to that relationship. It might not be relevant to the case, but this unassuming dog trainer had more layers than an onion. Unraveling his story would be interesting. Though initially reluctant to come to Florence, Willow was glad she had. It was giving her plenty of distractions from her own troubles.

A heavy-set police officer in his mid-thirties approached. "Hey, Dawson," Jackson greeted, his voice thick with emotion. "Are you on your way to process Levi's home?"

The man nodded, struggling to maintain eye contact. He wrung the brim of his Florence PD ball cap. "I'm sorry for your loss. Tanner was a good man. Reeves is back at the murder scene..." His plump face reddened, and he cleared his throat. Beads of sweat dotted his forehead. "Mayor Persie's there too, throwing his weight around. The first thing his detail did when they arrived was confiscate everyone's cell phone."

Jackson's eyes narrowed, his hands balling into tight fists. He straightened his back, like he was desperate to hold in his emotions.

"He's trying to obstruct the investigation?" Willow asked incredulously. "What the hell?" Her outburst earned a glare from the officer.

"And who are you?" he demanded, leaning into her face despite having to crane his neck.

"Special Agent Willow Banks," Jackson intervened, stepping between them. Willow bristled at his interference. "And she's right. Unless he's willing to give us the phones, the honorable mayor is intentionally impeding a federal investigation."

"The mayor doesn't want footage of his daughter's death hitting the tabloids," Dawson explained. "His public affairs team is trying to suppress any photos or video that might have been posted of Levi murdering his daughter." He looked down. "Persie was holding a press conference up the street when the bomb went off. Someone had already shared an image of Levi holding a gun to Rachel's face to her Instagram feed."

Bile rose in Willow's throat. Losing a daughter was difficult enough, but learning about her execution on social media? Unimaginable.

"Did he get inside the restaurant?" Jackson asked, clearly dreading the answer. Dawson's face crumpled.

"We need to get back," Willow urged, her eyes pleading. "The woman's father shouldn't be there. That sight cannot be the last image he has of his daughter."

"She was covered up," Dawson assured them. "The officer on the scene draped a tablecloth over her."

"Fisher tampered with evidence?" Jackson muttered. "Thanks, Dawson. Ruby's guarding Levi's home. I'll call her off when I'm ready for her." He gestured for Willow to follow and set off at a brisk pace.

Willow jogged to keep up. Police tape cordoned off the area, squad cars serving as barricades. Reporters swarmed, thrusting microphones at bystanders while camera operators filmed everything in sight.

"You need to set up a bigger perimeter," Jackson ordered Officer Martin, who stood idly behind the tape. "Do something right today, will you, and get the reporters as far back as you can."

Willow noted that Martin's career prospects seemed dim. Though new, he lacked the initiative to function without constant supervision. Where was his training officer?

"Tread lightly with the mayor," Jackson murmured to Willow. "He's got many influential friends, and he won't hesitate to use them against you if you come on too strong."

"It's not my first rodeo," she retorted, eyebrows raised. She pulled back and took a beat. She didn't need his help to do her job, but she needed to keep in mind that, like her, he was dealing with a painful loss. Willow softened her stance. "I'll go easy. The man is a grieving father who is accustomed to being in charge." Jackson gave her a dubious look. "Trust me, Jackson. I can handle this."

Chapter Eight

Jackson

Electronic chimes announced Jackson's entry into the restaurant. The space teemed with unauthorized personnel. Officer Fisher intercepted him at the entrance.

"What part of *nobody gets in here* didn't you understand?" Jackson demanded of the flushed officer.

Officer Reeves intervened, gesturing toward the mayor and chief hovering near Rachel Persie's body. "Jesus, Jax. I'm sorry. We tried to stop them, but what could we do when ordered to stand down?"

Jackson's heart ached at the sight of the grieving father, triggering a painful sense of kinship with the man. They had both lost someone irreplaceable, leaving behind a profound emptiness. Tanner's parents still needed to be notified. Jackson couldn't bear the thought of them learning the news from a stranger.

Instinct urged Jackson to flee, but he suppressed it. For Tanner's sake, he had to compartmentalize his pain, just as he'd done after the incident with the boy in the closet. Visiting Tanner's parents would have to wait.

"Where's Mr. Benson?" An irate voice cut through Jackson's haze. "Why haven't you arrested him?"

The blurry figures resolved into Chief Wheeler and Mayor Harlan Persie. Jackson blinked, trying to clear his mind. Officer Reeves retreated, avoiding the confrontation.

"The mayor asked why the homeless man isn't in custody." Chief Wheeler was in full dress uniform. "At least a dozen witnesses saw him murder the mayor's daughter."

"The eyewitness accounts are inaccurate," Jackson replied. "I have definitive proof that Levi Benson was not involved in the shooting."

The mayor sputtered, and Wheeler immediately stepped up his commands. "You're here on *official duty* until I say otherwise, Special Agent Jackson. While you're in my city, you will do as you're instructed, or I'll let SAC Greene know that our arrangement has come to its end." He raised his eyebrows in a wordless challenge. When Jackson didn't answer, he pressed harder. "Am I making myself perfectly clear, Special Agent, or do I need to spell it out for you?"

Willow interjected, "Excuse me, Chief. I'm Special Agent Willow Banks, FBI. You need to vacate this crime scene immediately." She addressed the mayor directly, "I'm deeply sorry for your loss, Mr. Mayor, but you can't remain here. We'll do everything possible to find your daughter's killer, but your presence compromises our investigation. Please step outside with your entourage."

"I'll do no such thing," the mayor snarled. "This is my city. I'll go where I please."

Chief Wheeler added, "You'd do well to learn your place, ma'am. This is *my* crime scene. I decide who has access. Your presence here is at my discretion. I didn't invite you in on this investigation and I can easily have you removed."

"No, sir. It isn't *your* crime scene," Willow said. Her voice was strong and laced with venom.

Jackson knew he should intervene before Willow went too far, but right now, he didn't care about the consequences.

Willow stepped closer. The chief was a big man, but Willow could nearly meet him eye to eye. "Tanner Montgomery was an FBI agent." She practically spat the words in the man's face. "That makes this a federal matter. As a courtesy, I will include the local PD where possible, but make no mistake, Chief, you are, most definitely, not in charge here."

Wheeler crossed his arms, clearly unwilling to yield. It didn't matter that Willow was completely right in everything she'd just said. He had no intention of backing down.

"Chief," Jackson pleaded, glancing at Rachel's shrouded form. "I'm begging you. Get the mayor and these people out of here. A compromised crime scene could jeopardize the entire case. I want justice for this as much as the mayor does. Tanner was like a brother to me..."

"He's right, Dawson." The mayor straightened, his public persona replacing raw grief. "Find Levi and arrest him. I want to be present for his interrogation."

Jackson watched as the mayor's group departed, including Chief Wheeler and several officers in dress uniforms. The chief's parting glare promised a future confrontation.

"Any word from the ME?" Jackson asked Reeves, who had returned. Jackson resisted the urge to reprimand him further. The damage was done.

Reeves checked his watch. "Should be here any minute. He had a university lecture this morning." As if on cue, the door chimed, admitting Medical Examiner Dr. Jim Johnstone and his assistant.

"Hey, Doc," Jackson greeted the lean, middle-aged man. They'd met before, but never at a crime scene. Johnstone had a reputation for professionalism, competence, and arrogance in equal measure. "The scene hasn't been processed yet, so if—"

"Don't worry, Special Agent," the ME interrupted. "I'll document everything as I proceed."

"The mayor and his people have already compromised the scene," Willow interjected, extending her hand. "I'm SA Willow Banks. I'm leading this investigation."

Anger flared in Jackson's chest. He wouldn't relinquish authority to an out-of-state agent he barely knew—one who couldn't even control her own dog. The idea of being sidelined grated on him. He clenched his jaw, inhaling sharply.

"Well then, Special Agent Willow Banks..." Dr. Johnstone paused, donning protective gear. His assistant, already suited up, readied the camera. "If you approve, I'd like to begin. I promise not to further contaminate your scene."

"Sure, Doc," Jackson said, glaring at Willow. "We'll talk while you work."

Agent Banks returned an icy stare. "I'm taking charge," she hissed, leading Jackson by the arm toward the back of the restaurant. "You're too close to the victims to be objective."

Jackson yanked free, speaking through gritted teeth, "I'm the only one here who knows this city and its quirks. Locals don't trust federal agents. They tolerate me because I grew up here. You're an outsider. You'll get nowhere. Unless you want this killer to escape, I suggest you—" He bit off the rest, waiting for her response.

Willow's piercing gaze met his. Each camera flash illuminated golden flecks in her blue eyes—a striking effect Jackson had never seen before.

"Fine," Willow conceded. "I'm in charge, but you handle local interactions. I admit you know the people and politics better. I won't waste time chasing dead ends."

Jackson maintained his stare, silent.

"Where's your friend Levi? We need to bring him in."

"Levi's not my friend, and he didn't do this."

"A dozen witnesses say otherwise."

Jackson lowered his voice. "I'm telling you, he's innocent. But we do need to find him. If local PD gets to him first, they might shoot on sight." It was just one more hurdle keeping him from reaching Tanner's parents.

"They wouldn't try to arrest him?" Willow glanced at the officers by the door. "That's twisted."

"The mayor despises Levi. I fear Captain Sawyer will do anything to curry favor, including killing an innocent man. He wants to be chief, and he'll do anything to get the job. The man is corrupt, and he's got a good number of officers involved in his schemes."

Willow raised an eyebrow. "So, I was right. There is more to your assignment than K9 training."

Jackson stifled a groan. This agent was perceptive. Maybe working with her wouldn't be so bad. He was too close to the case, emotionally compromised. She had no personal stake blinding her. But could he accept her leadership, even if she let him handle local interactions?

"We'll discuss that later," he deflected, glancing toward Dr. Johnstone who was busy examining Rachel. "Okay?"

Willow strode toward the ME. "I'm not sure what else you'll learn from her. Cause of death seems obvious."

Dr. Johnstone stood, removing his mask. "Astute, Agent. Three bullet wounds to the head, one exit wound. What does that tell your expertly trained eyes?"

"Several possibilities," Willow replied sharply. "All requiring autopsy confirmation. Why aren't you examining Agent Montgomery? We can't see his injuries. We assume he was shot, but there's no visible evidence."

The assistant's camera flashed repeatedly.

The ME sighed. "Two rhetorical questions, Agent. I don't expect answers, but they should resolve your query." He paused as Willow gestured for him to continue. "Have I offered suggestions on how to do your job? And are your eyes so untrained that you can't see my assistant photographing Tanner?"

"Tanner was shot," Jackson interjected, hoping to defuse the tension. Antagonizing Dr. Johnstone would only delay results. Both the doctor and Willow turned to him, clearly wondering how he knew. "I saw the student's video of the murders. The killer leaned close to Tanner and shot him in the chest. Couldn't see the gun, but the muzzle flash was clear."

"Where's this video?" Willow demanded.

"Dr. Johnstone?" Jackson ignored her question. "How long until you're finished? I'm not rushing you. The SBI is sending a CSI team, and I have other matters to attend to. "

"Like finding Levi?" The ME removed his gloves. "Word is, he's the one who killed your friend."

"It wasn't him," Jackson insisted, glancing at the frustrated Willow. "I saw the video. The killer looked right at the camera. It wasn't Levi. The man was disguised as him, but it wasn't him. His face was filthy, hair and beard unkempt. Levi may be homeless, but he's meticulous about cleanliness." Indeed, Levi visited the laundromat weekly. After food and shelter, hygiene was his top priority. Jackson's urge to leave intensified. He knew where to find Levi—his last words had been about getting cleaned up.

"Well, Agent, everyone thinks it's him—so you'd best get moving. I'll stay until the CSI team arrives, as long as you take that one with you." He flashed Willow a sarcastic smile. "I mean it. I don't care if this is an FBI scene..."

"No problem, Doc." Jackson gestured toward the door. "I need her anyway. She's in charge, and I need her approval on everything."

"Poor you," Dr. Johnstone said with a conspiratorial grin, turning back to the victims.

"You're an asshole," Willow said as they exited. "You know that, Agent Brooks?"

"Only when absolutely necessary," he replied. "I needed us out of there. We have a manhunt to conduct, and I know where to start looking." Finding people was his specialty. Well, Ruby's specialty, but they were a team...

Chapter Nine

Willow

Willow trailed Jackson through the throng gathered outside the restaurant. Gridlocked traffic and gawkers clogged the street, their conversations a cacophony of speculation about the victims and the grisly scene. Those discussing Rachel painted her in stark contrasts—either a saint or the devil incarnate. Given the brutality inflicted on her, Willow leaned toward the latter assessment.

The morning sun and the still air felt heavy with tension. Willow's skin prickled with unease as she caught snippets of conversation around her. "Did you hear? They say her face was…" "I always knew that Persie girl would come to a bad end…" The gossip swirled like vultures circling a carcass, feeding on the tragedy.

"Where are we going?" she called to Jackson's back as he wove through the crowd. He didn't respond, likely not hearing her over the din. Frustration bubbled in Willow's chest. She was used to being in control, to knowing the plan. This game of follow-the-leader grated on her nerves.

At the intersection of North Court and Tuscaloosa, Jackson slowed. He pulled a small brass tube from around his neck, put it to his lips, and gave a short blast. "Come on. We've got several blocks to go."

"What was that?" Willow muttered as Jackson took off down Tuscaloosa—opposite the direction he'd faced while blowing the whistle. Realization dawned. "A dog whistle. Shouldn't we wait for Ruby?" Again, no answer. Willow tamped down the urge to tackle the frustrating man. "Hey!" she bellowed. "Stop running!"

Jackson skidded to a halt and whirled to face her. "Are you a rookie who needs every action explained, or an agent who can figure out I don't have time for twenty questions? A man's life is at stake, and I'm wasting precious seconds explaining myself to you."

The rebuke stung more than Willow cared to admit. She was a seasoned agent, dammit, not some green recruit. But Jackson's intensity, the urgency in his eyes, gave her pause. There was more at play here than just solving a case. This was personal for him. "Fine. Go!"

Two sharp barks caught her attention. Ruby barreled down the street, seemingly oblivious to traffic. "Ruby, stay!" Willow commanded forcefully, as she'd been taught. The dog ignored her, continuing her headlong sprint. "She's going to get hit by a car," Willow yelled to Jackson. "Do something!"

Jackson didn't break stride.

Willow's heart raced, her eyes darting between the oncoming traffic and the golden blur of fur. She'd seen what happened when K9s died in the line of duty—the devastation felt by their handlers. She couldn't bear to see that happen to Jackson, no matter how infuriating he was. Her heart lodged in her throat as she watched Ruby reach the busy intersection. To her relief, the dog sat, waiting for the light to change before dashing across and racing past. Jackson was now a block ahead, his height the only thing keeping him visible in the crowd.

For six or seven blocks, Willow pushed herself to keep up with Jackson and Ruby. The pair seemed inexhaustible, never faltering. Meanwhile, Willow's blouse clung to her like a second skin, sweat stinging her eyes. She cursed her choice of impractical attire.

Her lungs burned, each breath a ragged gasp. Willow prided herself on her fitness, but this impromptu sprint was pushing her to her limits. The faces of passersby blurred as she ran, their startled expressions barely registering. All that mattered was keeping Jackson in sight.

At the next major intersection, Jackson veered left, vanishing behind a red-brick building. Willow gulped air and willed her burning legs to move faster. Her sensible shoes, while fine for short sprints, weren't meant for this impromptu marathon. She tried to regulate her breathing, but her hammering heart made it impossible. Logic told her to slow down, but stubbornness—honed by years of competing with five older brothers—propelled her forward. Their images, their taunts, their challenges, always pushing her to be faster, stronger, better. She'd be damned if she let Jackson outpace her now.

Rounding the corner, Willow scanned for Jackson and Ruby. No sign of them. They must have ducked into a building, but which one?

Sunlight glared off storefronts, obscuring the interiors. There wasn't time to check each one. They couldn't have gone far—she'd only been a block behind when they turned. A "Savings and Loan" sign caught her eye, but that seemed unlikely. Outside the next building stood two women with laundry carts. "Did you see a man with a Golden Retriever come by?"

"Sure did," the older woman replied. "They're in here. We got kicked out by some cop who said we couldn't stay."

"The man with the dog told you to leave?" Willow asked, puzzled. Jackson had insisted Levi was innocent—why would he think him dangerous?

"Nah, not him," the younger woman said, tossing her hair. "It was a cop. Flashed his badge when he came in. When I told him where to stick it, the prick pulled his gun."

Alarm bells sounded inside Willow's head. Why would a cop be pulling a gun in a public place over a simple dispute? Something was very wrong here.

"We were leaving anyway," the older woman added. "Just finished folding our laundry, but we didn't like how he was bossing us around, acting like he owned the place. If it weren't—"

"Thanks," Willow cut her off, unholstering her weapon. Someone had drawn a gun, and Jackson had walked in blind.

The scent of detergent and fabric softener hit her as she eased open the door. Sweat stung her eyes as she peered around the corner. Twenty feet in, Jackson stood behind a row of tables, hands raised. Ruby was statue-still at his side, coiled and ready to attack on command.

The scene before her was a powder keg, ready to explode at the slightest spark. Willow's training kicked in, her mind racing through possible scenarios, exit strategies, ways to defuse the situation without bloodshed.

"Put the gun away, Franklin," Jackson said. "You're only making things worse. Levi's innocent. There's no way he committed those murders. Give me a minute and I'll prove it to you."

"Prove what to me?" Franklin said. "What murders? I'm not here to arrest Levi. I'm here to kill him."

Willow stepped into view. A man in a light-colored suit had his service weapon trained on a bearded man wearing only a sleeveless undershirt and boxers—Levi. "FBI," she announced, aiming at Franklin. "Lower your weapon."

Franklin's head swiveled toward her, terror etched on his face. "I don't want to shoot anyone." His voice quavered. "But I don't have a choice. I can't fail. I just can't. My life would be... Sweet Jesus, I'm totally fucked." Despair replaced fear as he turned back to Jackson. "The photos. The video. It's all fake. None of it is me, but I'll be ruined if they come out. It won't matter that I'm innocent..."

Willow's mind raced. Photos? Video? What kind of blackmail was Franklin caught up in? And how did it connect to Levi and the murders?

"Franklin," Jackson pleaded. "This isn't the answer. Whatever it is, we'll work through it."

The next moments unfolded with nightmarish slowness. Franklin shook his head, eyes squeezed shut. His Adam's apple bobbed as tears tracked down his cheeks. "Sorry, Jax. I have no choice. I don't want to hurt anyone. Tell Winnie I love her." The detective lowered his weapon, pressed it under his chin, and pulled the trigger.

The gunshot echoed through the laundromat, deafening in the confined space. The acrid smell of gunpowder mingled with the clean scent of laundry, a jarring contrast that made Willow's stomach turn. As Franklin's body crumpled to the floor, time seemed to stand still.

Chapter Ten

Jackson

Jackson stared at the scene before him, his mind struggling to comprehend what had just transpired. Detective Franklin lay motionless on the floor, a pool of blood spreading beneath him. What drove him to take his own life? And why had he wanted to kill Levi?

"An ambulance is on its way," Willow said, her voice sounding distant and muffled.

Levi frantically pulled clothes from a nearby dryer, hastily dressing himself. "You've got to get me out of here," he pleaded. "It's all a setup. They're framing me for some murder I didn't commit, and they're going to kill me to make sure I have no say in my defense."

Jackson's brow furrowed. It was clear to him that the killer had dressed himself to look like Levi, but to what end?

"Agent Brooks," Levi continued, his tone measured despite the urgency in his words. "I need your help, and I need it now. If your friend called an ambulance, the police will be here soon. We have to leave before they arrive. My life is in danger—and yours might be as well. Franklin came here to assassinate me. Somehow, he knew I was here. He said he was sorry, but he was being blackmailed. Either he killed me, or his life and the lives of his family would be destroyed."

Willow holstered her weapon and approached the fallen detective, her face grim. "I'm Special Agent Willow Banks," she said, turning to Levi. "Why do you think your life is in danger?"

"Jackson, we don't have time for explanations," Levi insisted. "Get me out of here and I'll tell you everything."

Jackson's head throbbed, the ringing in his ears intensifying from the gunshot. Nothing made sense. Two homicides and now a suicide, all within the span of an hour—maybe less. He wasn't even sure how much time had passed since the explosion at the restaurant. Had it even been a bomb? There was no sign of blast damage. Franklin's final words echoed in his mind: 'I have no choice. I don't want to hurt anyone. Tell Winnie I love her.'

Ruby's sharp bark cut through the fog in Jackson's mind. "My truck is parked too close to where Tanner and Rachel were killed," he said, the reality of their situation sinking in.

"You're not serious?" Willow asked incredulously. "He's a wanted fugitive."

"I'm telling you," Jackson snapped, tension creeping up his neck and intensifying the throbbing in his skull. "He's innocent. You don't know me, Agent, but I'm asking you to trust me. Levi is right. The police are coming, and we have no time to argue."

"You can cuff me," Levi offered. "Take me into federal custody. Do whatever you think is necessary but get me out of here."

Willow's face reflected her disbelief. "You're willing to risk your career for a homeless man?"

Her skepticism grated on Jackson, but he didn't care if she understood. "For an innocent man. For a man who's already been railroaded for doing the right thing. Damn right I would risk my career for him."

A smile lit up Willow's face. "I'm going to like working with you, Special Agent Brooks," she said. Turning back to Levi, she continued, "Okay. My truck is parked at the hotel on East Tennessee, but I have no idea where that is from here."

"You have a room at the Gun Runner Boutique?" Jackson asked, relief washing over him. "That's barely three blocks away."

"Great," Levi said, buttoning up his pants. "Let's go."

"Go without me," Jackson said, his stomach churning at the thought of leaving Franklin's body alone. "Ruby and I will stay here to meet the ambulance. Someone needs to explain what happened."

"Where do you want me to take him?" Willow asked. "I don't know the city at all."

"My kennels," Jackson replied. "Get him there and I'll meet you as quickly as I can." Seeing Willow's arched eyebrow, he added, "Levi knows the way. Get him there and keep him hidden. Don't let anyone see him—including the vet, Dr. Simmons. I trust him completely, but the fewer people who know what we're doing, the better."

As Willow and Levi disappeared out the door, Jackson's face and shoulders sagged. He couldn't fathom what he'd gotten himself into. Florence wasn't crime-free, but events like this simply didn't happen here—at least, he'd never thought they did. His gaze fell to the fallen officer.

"Oh, Franklin," he murmured, resisting the urge to cover the body. "What did you mean, you didn't want to hurt anyone? Why did you feel you had no choice?" Ruby leaned against his leg, her soulful brown eyes filled with concern. "We've stepped in it this time, eh girl?"

The wail of sirens and flash of emergency lights announced the arrival of an ambulance and squad car. Jackson squared his shoulders and tried to calm his mind. How could he possibly rationalize what had happened here, let alone his decision to let Levi leave?

The laundromat door swung open as a paramedic entered, his demeanor jarringly cheerful given the circumstances. "Where's the patient?" he asked.

His casual attitude set Jackson's teeth on edge. "The dead police officer is right here," he said, gesturing to Franklin's body. "Show some respect."

A second paramedic, carrying a large medical bag, paused in the doorway. "Are you sure he's dead?"

"Oh shit," the first paramedic exclaimed, finally registering the severity of the scene. "Half his head is gone. What the hell happened here?"

Before Jackson could respond, two police officers burst in, guns drawn, shouldering past the stunned paramedic. "Hands!" one shouted at Jackson. "Show me your hands."

"Officers," Jackson said, slowly raising his hands, "I'm Special Agent Jackson Brooks, on assignment here in Florence. If you don't recognize my name, call Chief Wheeler. My badge is in my back pocket."

"I don't care who you say you are," the second officer snapped. "You were told to raise your hands, and now I'm going to tell you to shut the hell up." Ruby snarled, prompting the officer to level his gun at her. "If your dog moves, I'll shoot him."

"Ruby, settle," Jackson commanded. The Golden Retriever immediately dropped to the ground, laying her head between her front paws. Her gaze, however, remained locked on the officer threatening her. "This is FBI K9 Ruby," Jackson explained, his voice steady but firm. "Shoot her and you'll spend the next thirty-five years behind bars for shooting a federal agent."

The first officer lowered his weapon. "Put your gun away, Branden." When his partner shot him a questioning glance, he repeated more forcefully, "Branden. Now."

Reluctantly, Branden holstered his weapon, his jaw clenching visibly.

"Where's Levi?" the first officer asked. "Detective Franklin called in saying he had him cornered in here, and that Levi was armed and dangerous."

A bitter laugh escaped Jackson's lips. The accusation was so ludicrous it bordered on the absurd, yet it confirmed Levi's fears. They really were out to get him. "Levi was in his underwear," Jackson stated flatly. "He had no gun, or any other weapon."

"Are you calling Detective Franklin a liar?" Branden bristled, his hand drifting back towards his holstered weapon.

Jackson took a deep breath, forcing himself to remain calm. "Listen carefully, Officer..." he squinted at the man's nameplate, "Crampton, is it? I was here when Detective Franklin took his life. I suspect his actions are part of a larger federal investigation. Here's what needs to happen now: you and your partner, Officer Davidson, need to secure the scene. I assume you have police tape in your cruiser. There's a crowd gathering outside, and the press will be here soon. Get outside and do your job. I'm going to call the ME and let him know to come here after he's finished processing the other murder victims."

Officer Crampton's lips tightened into a thin line. "You don't have the authority to order me around."

"Actually, he does," Officer Davidson interjected. "Come on, let's secure the perimeter."

The paramedics, sensing the tension, had already retreated to their ambulance. As the officers exited, Jackson reached into his back pocket for his phone, only to find he was holding the confiscated phone from the selfie-obsessed girl at the restaurant. He considered whether he had broken any laws by keeping it, but reasoned that it was evidence that had never left his possession. He wasn't trying to conceal it, and there was no need to dust it for prints. While it might not be directly related to the crime, it could prove crucial in solving the case.

His thoughts drifted to Johnnie Walker, the eager journalism student who had been filming everyone at the murder scene. In hindsight, Jackson realized he should have taken that phone as well. Shaking off the regret, he slipped the girl's phone back into his pocket and retrieved his own.

"Hey Marcy," he said when the call connected. "Can you get in touch with Dr. Johnstone again? I need him to come to the Jukebox Laundromat. There's another body."

"Is it true?" Marcy whispered, her voice tense. "Rumors are flying around saying that Levi shot Franklin."

Fury burned in Jackson's chest. How had that rumor spread so quickly? It couldn't have been more than five minutes since Willow called in the incident. Had she mentioned Levi having a gun? "Levi had nothing to do with it," Jackson stated firmly. "Franklin shot himself. I was here when it happened. I saw the whole thing." He wanted to add that the detective hadn't been in his right mind, but something told him to keep that observation to himself. Nothing about this morning's events made any sense.

There was a prolonged silence on the line before Marcy spoke again. "Dr. Johnstone will be there as soon as he can. Sit tight. I'm calling the chief as well..." Her voice dropped to a barely audible whisper, as if she were cupping her hand around the receiver. "Take care of yourself, Jax."

"Thanks, Marcy. I owe you one." Jackson ended the call and surveyed the room, his gaze sweeping from floor to ceiling. His eyes locked onto what he'd been searching for—a surveillance camera. He traced the wire along the wall until it disappeared behind a solid door marked 'Private.'

That room likely housed the computer that stored the footage. Jackson tried the doorknob, but it refused to budge. He rapped lightly on the door. "Hello?" When no one responded, he pounded his fist against it. "This is Special Agent Jackson Brooks of the FBI. Open the door."

Time seemed to crawl as Jackson waited for a reply. Just as he was about to give up, a small voice called out from within. "Hold your badge up to the camera where I can see it."

Jackson complied, holding his badge aloft. The camera whirred and its lens spun, likely zooming in to verify his credentials. A moment later, the door cracked open, and a disheveled woman in her mid-to-late forties peered out. "Is it safe?"

"Ma'am," Jackson began, keeping his voice calm and reassuring, "were you watching what happened out here? Did you see the detective commit suicide?" The woman's face paled, and her body trembled as she gave a barely perceptible nod. "Ma'am, did you record the event?" This time, her nod was more emphatic. "Okay. Good. I need you to listen very carefully. I need a copy of that video. Right now. In a few minutes, this place will be crawling with police and I need that video before they get here. Can you do that for me?"

"Sure..." she replied, her eyes darting nervously to the picture window overlooking the street. Two news vans had already parked out front. "The videos are automatically backed up to the cloud, the hard drive, and a thumb drive." She gave a small shrug. "I'm just the assistant manager. Lots of crazy shit goes down during the night. I need to protect myself."

"You're amazing," Jackson said, a glimmer of hope rising in his chest. "Get me the thumb drive and please, don't tell anyone about the cloud backups. I'm guessing the police will seize your computer as soon as they come in. Do you understand what I'm telling you?"

The woman nodded and disappeared into the back room. Moments later, she emerged clutching a small red thumb drive. Her eyes widened as she saw two police officers entering through the front door, and she quickly closed her fingers around the tiny device.

Jackson, thinking fast, extended his hand as if for a handshake. "Thank you for your report," he said to the assistant manager. "Your assistance has been more than helpful."

"Anything for the FBI," she replied, shaking his hand and discreetly slipping him the drive.

Turning to the newly arrived officers, Jackson said, "She's got surveillance video. I haven't had a chance to see it yet. Hopefully it recorded the detective's suicide."

"Agent Brooks," one of the officers said, "we need you to come outside to get your statement."

"No," Jackson refused, stuffing his hands in his pockets and securing the thumb drive. "You can take my statement here. I'm first on the scene and I'm not relinquishing control without due authority telling me otherwise."

"Get outside or I'll put you in lockup and interrogate you there, Agent Brooks," came a gruff voice as Captain Sawyer stepped inside. His boots thudded against the linoleum. He looked Jackson up and down, his mouth twisted with disdain.

"Captain Sawyer." Jackson's voice was clipped. "You're here fast." Remarkably fast.

"Of course, I am. Florence is my city, and Franklin is my officer." His eyes narrowed. Like Jackson, he was struggling to maintain his composure. "I might ask you the same thing. We've got two murder scenes, and you were the first to arrive both times." His gaze moved from Jackson to the dead detective. "What the hell happened here? If I find out that you were involved—"

"I tried to stop him," Jackson said. He wanted to say more. He wanted to say how Franklin thought he was being framed and how his life had been ruined. He wanted to say that he was threatening to murder Levi. "He was out of his mind."

The captain's jaw clenched as he shook his head. He turned to his officer. "Take the woman to the station house. Bring her computers and any other evidence you see in her office as well. This is a local matter, and the FBI can go fuck themselves if they think they're going to push us out."

Because you want to cover this up like you do everything else... Jackson wasn't going to give up quite so easily. "Are you arresting her, Captain?" he challenged, feeling Ruby tense at his side. The dog's body was shaking with anticipation, clearly picking up on the captain's hostility. "If you're not, you have no right to detain her."

"If that's what it takes," the captain said. He motioned to his man.

"Lady, what's your name?" the officer asked.

"Jamie Maddison," she replied, her eyes pleading with Jackson for help. "I'm the assistant manager here."

"You're under arrest, Jamie Maddison," the officer declared. "Place your hands behind your back."

"What is she under arrest for?" Jackson demanded. "On what grounds?"

"On the grounds of shut your fucking mouth, Agent Brooks," Captain Sawyer snarled, jabbing his finger towards the exit. "Would you like me to arrest you as well? I told you to get outside. Don't make me tell you again."

"Come on, Ruby," Jackson said, accepting defeat for the moment. "We need to wait outside."

As he passed by, the captain dropped his voice to a whisper. "You know, Brooks. The city has eyes everywhere and you're not as invisible as you think. Eventually, whoever is covering your tracks will screw up and, I *will* get you. You can bank on it."

"I could say the same thing to you, Captain." Jackson didn't lower his voice. He pushed open the door and was immediately slammed by the warmth of the late-morning air. The intense sunshine did nothing to cool the anger boiling in his chest. Ruby pressed close against his leg, offering her much-welcomed support. The thumb drive felt like it was burning a hole in his pocket. He knew he was walking a fine line between following procedure and obstructing justice, but his instincts told him this evidence was crucial. Whatever was going on in Florence ran deeper than he'd initially thought, and he was determined to uncover the truth—no matter the cost.

Jackson paused and rolled the captain's words around in his head.

What did he mean, I will get you?

Chapter Eleven

Willow

Willow and Levi exited the laundromat, slipping down an alley. At Levi's sharp whistle, a small black and white dog materialized. They greeted each other briefly before ducking behind a building.

"We can stay hidden most of the way, but we'll have to cross Tennessee to reach your hotel," Levi said, his breathing labored. "I should stay out of sight. This area has cameras everywhere. It's risky for you to be seen with me."

"And an FBI agent darting out of an alley isn't suspicious?" Willow eyed Levi, noting his nervous energy. He stood silently, awaiting her next move. "What's your dog's name?" She needed a moment to think and to ease the tension.

"Boone," Levi said, running his hand over the dog's head. "He saved my life, in a way..."

"How?" Willow scanned the alley. There was no avoiding it. The cameras on East Tennessee would spot her as soon as she emerged. Her best option was to act natural, like she belonged.

"After I lost everything—my job, my fiancée, my home—I was suicidal. But Boone needed me." Levi's voice cracked as he scratched his dog's ears. "He gave me a reason to live. Through it all, he's been my one constant. He's never given up on me, no matter what."

Unexpected warmth blossomed in Willow's chest. Her eyes stung. Her partner Kate had often spoken of her connection with Ranger—how they relied on each other, would do anything for each other. Willow had dismissed it as typical dog owner talk. But Kate proved how much she meant it, taking a bullet for Ranger. That stupid, brave woman died so her dog could live.

Now, witnessing the bond between Levi and Boone, Willow understood. Their connection was real, profound. An unexpected pang of jealousy struck her. She had no time for, nor interest in, relationships. Outside of her family, there was no one she truly cared about—or who truly cared about her. It left her feeling empty inside.

"Alright," she said, her voice thick. She turned away, pretending to study the alley. "Let's get you out of here. I'll get my truck and meet you at the next block. Stay hidden. I'll come to you."

Levi's shoulders sagged with visible relief. "Thank you. I can't promise much, but I'll make this up to you somehow." His words rang with sincerity.

"I won't stand for law enforcement railroading anyone. I don't know why you're being targeted, but I'll find out." Willow paused, turning back to Levi. "And if you're playing me, I swear to Jesus Christ, himself, I will rain hellfire down on you."

Levi recoiled. "I'm not. I swear. But if I was, I'd expect nothing less. I'd do the same."

Willow wasn't sure if she liked his response. It almost sounded too sincere. As a former Deputy District Attorney, Levi had ample experience swaying jurors. She resolved to watch her words around him, even as she nodded and darted between buildings toward East Tennessee Street.

***

"Turn left here," Levi instructed, unwrapping Willow's new cell phone. They had briefly stopped for her to replace the one Ranger had destroyed. Levi hunched low in his seat; Willow's ball cap pulled down over his eyes. The pickup's tinted windows offered some protection, but a clear view through the windshield could still expose him.

"How far to the highway?" Willow asked, executing a sharp left turn. She enjoyed the cat-and-mouse game, but only when she was the cat.

"This road connects to Lee Highway. We'll take that out of Florence into Killen. About twenty minutes to Jackson's place." Levi inserted Willow's old SIM card into the new phone and handed it over.

"How long have you known him?" Willow probed. "Jackson, I mean."

"Since becoming homeless," Levi replied, his gaze fixed ahead. "But I've known his mother for years. She gave me Boone. That's how I know where Jackson lives. My ex knew him too, but she couldn't stand him. Rachel never had a kind word for the man."

"Rachel Persie? The woman murdered at the restaurant this morning?"

Color drained from Levi's face. He seemed to struggle to process her words, twice opening his mouth to speak before swallowing them back.

"Fuck. I'm sorry—I assumed you'd heard."

"How? When?" Levi wrung his ball cap in his hands. "Are you certain it was her?" He inhaled sharply. "This isn't good. God above."

"She was shot this morning," Willow said. She considered pulling over, wanting to fully observe Levi's reactions—especially the small, involuntary ones that couldn't be faked. "She was having breakfast with Tanner Montgomery. He was shot too."

Levi's grip on his hat tightened. "Tanner's dead as well?" He looked ready to fling himself from the moving vehicle.

"You knew him, too? Apparently, he and Jackson were best friends."

Levi shook his head but remained silent. They drove in uncomfortable silence for five minutes while he stared down at the crumpled hat in his hands. His leg bounced uncontrollably, and his jaw shifted, as if he were chewing over words he couldn't quite form.

"Were you still in love with her?"

Levi snorted. "No. At least, I don't think so. It's just..."

"A shock?" Willow said, finishing his sentence. Levi kept his face turned away, offering an almost imperceptible nod. "I'm sorry for your loss."

"She wasn't as awful as everyone claims," Levi said. "She could be sweet and kind... but her public persona was harsh. She was the daughter of a..."

"Politician?" Willow struggled to reconcile this. Public figures typically presented only their best selves. Anything else was career suicide. Levi grunted, still fidgeting with his cap. "Did she have enemies? Can you think of anyone who'd want her dead?"

Levi's laugh was bitter. "Rachel excelled at making enemies. Last year, she published her first novel. It was garbage, but her father poured money into it, and it made the New York Times bestseller list. She couldn't just enjoy the title—she had to flaunt it to her so-called friends. I used to overhear her Zoom meetings with other authors. The way she spoke to them was appalling."

"Jesus," Willow said, surprised by Levi's candor about his ex-fiancée. He might have loved her, but clearly harbored resentment, too. Not shocking, given what Rachel had done to him. "You really think someone would kill her for being self-centered?"

Darkness swept across Levi's face. He might resent Rachel, but he didn't seem to appreciate others criticizing her. "Turn right here."

Willow cut off a subcompact to make the turn. The woman crammed into the micro-sized car honked her high-pitched horn and flipped her the bird.

"Follow the highway until the speed limit hits sixty. Our turn is the next right." Levi turned away; his shoulders hunched up to his ears. The conversation was clearly over, at least for now.

They drove in silence. Willow realized Boone hadn't made a sound since entering the truck—a stark contrast to Ranger's incessant barking during their eleven-hour drive from Beaufort. She glanced back. The small Border Collie was curled up, sleeping peacefully.

"It just changed to sixty," Willow noted. "Next turn?"

"Yes. The turning lane's short, so slow down early."

A brief sixty-foot turn lane appeared. Willow braked hard and swerved. The tires skidded on gravel before finding purchase. Her heart raced at the maneuver.

"Told you," Levi said. "Stay on this road until you see Aqua Vista Drive. Turn right and continue to the end. That's Jackson's house."

"I thought we were going to his kennels. Why are we going to his home?"

"The kennels are on his property, down by the lake."

Satisfied with the explanation, Willow fell silent and followed Levi's directions. A large, weathered home came into view. "Is this it? Looks like it needs paint."

"It's not much to look at, but the structure's sound. For being over a hundred years old, I'd say it's held up well. Jax's parents aren't exactly flush with cash. Since his dad went missing, his mother's struggled. Somehow, she's kept the kennel going. No idea where the money's coming from. Jax's dad hasn't been declared dead, so she's not getting any pension or benefits from the police department."

Willow winced, wishing she could swallow her words. She'd never felt so small, so petty. Her lack of a verbal filter was a constant issue. The mention of Jackson's father offered a chance to change the subject. "His dad was a cop?"

"Former captain with Florence PD. Rumor was he and the chief didn't get along." Levi studied Willow as he spoke, seeming to gauge her reaction. "Before he disappeared, he was a legend in the DA's office. His arrests always stuck. Yet he kept getting passed over for promotions. The position of Deputy Chief has been vacant ever since Wheeler's promotion."

"You said Jackson's dad disappeared? What happened?"

"Nobody knows much, other than he went on a hunting trip and his entire group vanished without a trace." Boone, who had been silent the entire drive, suddenly unleashed a series of shrill barks. "One of his favorite places," Levi explained. "I'm surprised he stayed quiet this long." Before the truck fully stopped, Levi opened the door. Boone didn't hesitate, squeezing through the narrow gap between seats. He hit the ground at full speed, vanishing around the house in a heartbeat. "Like I said, his happy place." Levi hopped down and slammed the door. "Follow me, I'll show you the way."

Willow exited, locking up. In the distance, Ranger's distinctive barks echoed across the landscape.

Chapter Twelve

Jackson

Jackson bypassed the turn onto Aqua Vista Drive, the street that would have taken him home. Instead, he continued straight through to Tanner's childhood home. He had made many difficult visits in his career, but this one felt insurmountable. As he parked outside the Montgomery's house, he struggled to draw breath. What he wouldn't have given to not be the bearer of this news.

The late-morning sun and rising humidity beat down on him, making every step from his truck to the front door excruciating. A massive maple tree cast shadows across the neatly trimmed lawn, its limbs supporting a tire swing that spun in slow, lazy circles. Jackson tried to remember how many times he and Tanner had climbed this tree and played on that swing. The only memory that surfaced was watching the video of his best friend's life coming to an abrupt and violent end.

He walked slowly up the path, each step heavier than the last. He paused at the door, his sweaty hand trembling as it reached for the doorbell. Memories of Tanner laughing with his parents, their warm, inviting smiles, and the sound of his voice filled his mind. He pressed the doorbell and waited, his heart pounding.

The door opened, and Mrs. Montgomery stood there, her face lighting up with a smile that quickly faded as she took in Jackson's grave expression. "Jackson, it's so good to see you. Is everything okay?"

"Hi, Mrs. Montgomery," Jackson said. He struggled to maintain eye contact, afraid he might break down before he could deliver his horrific news. "Can I come in? There's something I need to talk to you and Mr. Montgomery about."

Mrs. Montgomery's smile faltered, replaced by concern. "Of course, come in," she said, stepping aside. She led him to the living room, where Mr. Montgomery was reading a novel. He looked up and smiled, but his smile disappeared as he saw Jackson's face.

"Jackson, what's going on?" Mr. Montgomery asked, his voice laced with worry.

Jackson took a deep breath, his eyes glistening. "Please, sit down," he said, gesturing to the couch. He waited until they were seated, then sat opposite them, leaning forward with his elbows on his knees. "I... I don't know how to say this," he began. He gripped his hands together to still their tremors. "Tanner... Tanner was killed this morning. He was murdered."

The room fell into a stunned silence. Mrs. Montgomery gasped, her hands flying to her mouth, while Mr. Montgomery stared at Jackson, his face pale and eyes wide with shock.

"No," Mrs. Montgomery whispered, shaking her head. "That can't be right. We spoke with him this morning. Tanner dropped off some paperwork for his father. He was going to have breakfast with that Rachel person. He said he'd come for a short visit later today before heading to see you." Her words faltered, and she turned to her husband. "Tell him, Jake. Tell him he's wrong. Tell him it wasn't our boy."

"Did he suffer?" Mr. Montgomery said. The muscles in his face were twitching. It was taking every ounce of his concentration not to break down.

Tears spilled over Jackson's cheeks. "No," he rasped, the word barely leaving his throat. "It was a single shot through the heart.

His death was near instantaneous." Mr. Montgomery's façade cracked. His eyes grew glassy and his lower lip quivered. "We're doing everything we can to find who did this. Tanner was one of the best people I've ever known, and he didn't deserve this."

Mrs. Montgomery broke down, sobbing uncontrollably. Mr. Montgomery wrapped his arms around her, his own tears falling freely. Jackson moved to sit beside them, placing a comforting hand on Mrs. Montgomery's shoulder.

"I swear on my life," Jackson said, his voice firm despite his sorrow. "We'll get justice for Tanner. I promise you that."

Mr. Montgomery's face twisted with rage. "I don't want justice. I want the sonofabitch who killed my boy. I want him dead. Do you hear me, Jax? Dead." Jake wrapped his arms around his wife and buried his face in her neck.

Jackson sat motionless, staring at the grief-stricken couple. They were two of the kindest people he'd ever known. They had always treated him like he was a member of the family. He couldn't do what Tanner's father asked. No matter how much he wanted to, Jackson believed in the justice system. He believed people should be given their day in court, and if convicted, be given an appropriate sentence.

Without saying another word, Jackson made his way to the front door. He glanced back at Tanner's parents, knowing their lives would never be the same. They'd never fully move on from their son's death, but maybe, someday, they could learn to live with it.

Jackson stood outside the doorway of the Montgomery's home, his chest aching. He paused on the front steps, taking a deep breath to steady himself. The image of Mrs. Montgomery's tear-streaked face and Mr. Montgomery's hollowed expression clung to him like a suffocating fog.

He walked back to his truck with slow, deliberate steps. It was all he could do to not let his legs buckle beneath him. He reached through the open window and scratched Ruby behind the ear. As he opened the door, she jumped into the passenger seat.

"Let's go home, girl," he murmured, starting the engine. As he drove away, Jackson's thoughts were a tumult of grief and anger. The drive was silent except for the hum of the engine and Ruby's occasional whine.

Jackson's unease grew as he neared his home. He didn't understand why, but Levi was at the center of this case. Someone was working hard to paint him as the murderer. He needed to see the laundromat video. Hopefully, it would shed some light on how the ex-DDA was involved. Jackson turned onto Aqua Vista Drive and pressed down on the accelerator. He sped into his laneway and skidded to a halt. He and Ruby were out the door and scrambling down the narrow pathway that led to the kennels in seconds. The Golden Retriever had disappeared around the corner long before Jackson reached the bottom of the stone stairway that had been cut into the cliff face overlooking Wilson Lake.

"Get Levi inside," he said as soon as Willow came into view. At the mention of his name, Levi appeared with Boone at his side.

"What's going on? Do they know I'm here?"

Ruby was standing by the gate that led into the kennels. Ranger was barking non-stop, leaping at the door to his pen. The three other residents, two shepherds and a mixed-breed hunting dog, were alert and interested, but otherwise quiet.

"No," Jackson said, dragging Levi towards the rickety wooden door that led into the kennel's tiny office space. "But I'm not taking any chances." He pushed open the door and flipped the light switch. Two bare bulbs sprang to life, filling the tiny room with a warm, pale-yellow light. The familiar scent of dust and dog food struck him full on. On the lone table in the room was an envelope with "Jax" penned upon it. It had to have been Jason's evaluation of Ranger. It would make for some interesting reading, but now wasn't the time. He folded the envelope and stuffed it into his back pocket.

"What the hell, Jackson?" Willow said as she followed the two men and the Border Collie into the small building. Ranger's barks punctuated the question. Repeatedly.

Jackson's head was throbbing. Too many things were happening too quickly. The entire drive home, his mind battled over grieving for his dead friend and desperately grasping for some reason behind the day's events. Images of Franklin's suicide kept playing over and over. The chief's insistence on bringing Levi in for justice, despite Jackson's insistence that the shooter was somebody else. And who was the homeless woman holing up in Levi's makeshift home? And Ranger's non-stop barking. Good lord. The Malinois might as well be driving iron spikes into Jackson's head. He threw himself into one of the four dinette chairs that surrounded the rough wooden table, taking up most of the space in the room. He pushed out another chair with his foot and motioned for Levi to sit. "Can you bring your dog in here please?" Jackson said to Willow. "I can't think with him carrying on like that."

"Try driving with him doing that in your ear for eleven hours from the backseat of your pickup truck." Willow stuck her fingers in her ears. "Earplugs haven't been invented that can block it out, nor is there enough ibuprofen on earth to dull the pain."

Jackson leveled her with a flat stare.

"I'll get him," Levi said.

"No. Stay inside. Special Agent Banks can get her own K9." Jackson fired a look that hopefully conveyed that he wanted a chance to speak with Levi alone. "Take your time."

"You could just ask me to step out." Willow returned Jackson's gaze, along with a heaping dose of 'you're being an asshole again.' Apparently, she could swear without speaking a word. "Fine." The woman yanked open the door and slammed it shut behind her, rattling its glass window.

"Levi, level with me. What is going on? Why did Franklin want to shoot you? Why would someone impersonate you and kill Rachel and Tanner?"

Levi knitted his fingers together and stared down at his hands. An unbearable knot twisted in Jackson's stomach as realization sunk in. The man was still in love with Rachel, and the wound her death left was deep and raw. "I'm sorry for what you're going through, but I need you to put on your DA face and push your emotions aside. We can mourn the loss of loved ones later, when we have a chance to breathe."

Boone whined and lay down at the broken man's feet. When he rested his chin on Levi's shoe, it all but shattered Jackson's heart.

"Why are you helping me?" Levi asked. "The world seems out to get me, but you've never turned your back on me."

It was a good question. One that Jackson had never taken the time to consider. There were other homeless people on the street, so why had he taken such an interest in Levi? Was it because of his dog, and that Jackson's mother had given Boone to him? "I don't like what happened to you, and I don't like that you're being framed for murders you didn't commit."

Levi's eyes darted to the door. "I know you're working with the chief but are you in league with the mayor as well? Is Willow? Her arrival seems a bit... well, let's just say, she shows up in town, two people get murdered and everyone is looking to lynch me for it."

He knew Levi had a right to be paranoid, but this was... too much. "Look, I know you've been put through the wringer," Jackson said. He couldn't piece together any meaningful rationale for what Levi was saying. "But you've lost me. Completely lost me. Agent Banks is here because her dog is out of control, and her boss thought I could help. Our proximity to the murders was coincidence. Nothing more."

Levi nodded slowly, but the doubt hadn't fully left his eyes. "I want to believe you, Jackson. I do. But after everything that's happened... I've seen too much in the last year. The corruption in this city is systemic, and there are people, powerful people, who can make shit happen, and they can make it stick. Franklin was scared shitless. He was a good man, and the mayor was going to ruin his life, just like he ruined mine. Can you blame me for thinking you and she are in league with him? I mean, you're tight with the Chief and he's got both hands deep in the mayor's pockets."

The door burst open.

"You need better kennels," Willow said, her face flushed, her breathing rapid. "Ranger scaled the fence like it was nothing. Eight feet isn't tall enough. And it needs a roof. I can't catch him."

"Did he run away?" Jackson asked, jumping to his feet. "Which way did he go?"

"He didn't run," Willow said. "He wanted to greet me and play with Ruby. The two of them are racing around the yard like maniacs." She locked eyes with Levi, as though they were sizing each other up. Perhaps she could sense the tension in the room. "Are you two finished talking about whatever it was that required privacy?" The Golden Retriever and the Malinois came trotting through the door, both looking pleased with themselves.

"I'm not sure," Jackson said, glancing between Willow and Levi. "Levi thinks you're here at the request of the mayor, and that we are somehow in league with him." Willow's face immediately screwed itself into a full-on WTF expression. She really could cuss without speaking a single word.

"Okay, okay," Levi said, throwing his hands in the air. "I get it. I'm sounding like a wackadoodle conspiracy theorist."

He clutched onto his head like it was about to come flying apart. "Damn it. If you two are in bed with the mayor, I'm dead anyway. What have I got to lose if I tell you the truth about... everything."

Chapter Thirteen

Willow

Willow pulled out a chair from the table that dominated the office space. The tension in the room was palpable as she positioned herself directly in front of Levi, studying his demeanor. Her investigator's instincts kicked in as she cataloged his micro-expressions, the way his eyes wouldn't quite meet hers, how his hands couldn't seem to stay still. He resembled a caged animal, torn between fear and acceptance of his life's shitty reality.

"Where to begin?" Levi said, his gaze finally settling somewhere over her left shoulder. "The mayor is running a fraud scheme of epic proportions. He's able to make it work because he's got the DA's office and high-ranking members of the Florence PD in his pocket."

"Like Captain Sawyer?" Jackson asked, leaning forward.

"Captain Josh Sawyer?" Levi's laugh held no humor. "He's one of the few righteous officers in the entire department." He groaned and blew out a long breath.

Willow shot a quick glance at Jackson, catching the slight tightening around his eyes. This contradicted everything he'd believed about the captain. Either Levi was lying, or they'd been masterfully played.

"Look," Levi said, his gaze continuing to skitter away from direct contact. "I was ousted before I could prove any of this, but there is too much circumstantial evidence. It all started when a local contractor approached me about the city's procurement committee. They had rejected his bid for refurbishing a city building, citing non-compliance. This wasn't his first rejection—it was his third. The pattern bothered him enough that he hired an outside firm to audit all three proposals. The audit revealed that his bids had met every requirement for compliance. In fact, based on price, materials, and projected timelines, he should have won two of those contracts outright. But here's where it gets interesting: in all three cases, the committee systematically rejected every bid except one. In each case, the winning company had bid nearly double the price of its next closest competitor."

The methodical precision of the scheme sent ice through Willow's veins.

"You think the mayor is taking kickbacks?" Jackson asked.

"I do now," Levi said, scratching at his beard. "At first, I figured it was the city manager, or one of the procurement officers running the scam, so I started digging into the bids and the awarded contracts. I kept it quiet, trying to not let on that I was investigating. I know a clerk in the city's finance department, and she was able to discreetly pull the files I needed. She got me the original requests for proposal, the bids that were submitted, and the contracts for the winning companies."

"I don't see how any of this information ties to the mayor," Willow said. She looked over at Jackson for confirmation, who gave her a perplexed look.

"It doesn't," Levi said. His voice carried a faint edge of irritation, but Willow let it slide. Considering the pressure they were all under, she figured he'd earned a little slack. After a pause to collect his thoughts, he pressed on. "What really caught my attention," he continued, his voice dropping as his eyes darted toward the door, "is that all these contracts were stamped *approved* by the mayor's office. And here's the kicker—none of the winning bids met the mandatory requirements. I mean, I'm no expert, but even I could see how non-compliant they were."

Willow leaned forward, her lips parted to fire another question, but Levi raised a hand to forestall her. "Hold on," he said, a shadow of a smile flickering across his face. "It gets better. The winning companies? They're all subsidiaries of a single holding company—Belladonna Enterprises."

"I'm sorry," Jackson said, leaning back in his chair. He scrubbed a hand over the back of his neck, his brow furrowing. "I still don't see how this means the mayor's on the take. But I'll admit, it's starting to look like someone in his office is neck-deep in fraud."

"Well," Levi said, his voice tight, his gaze flicking downward for a moment before meeting their eyes again. "What if I told you that Rachel sits on Belladonna's board of directors?"

A long silence followed the revelation. Jackson straightened in his chair, exchanging a loaded glance with Willow.

"That discovery was the beginning of the end for me." Levi's voice grew hollow, and his shoulders slumped. "I couldn't leave it alone. I should have, but..."

Jackson pinched the bridge of his nose and let out a slow, weary breath. "You confronted her about it, didn't you?"

Levi nodded, eyes closed. "I asked her about it. I thought she was going to blow a gasket. She screamed at me for five minutes straight. She called me every name in the book, and a few that I had never heard before."

Willow's eyebrows shot up. She knew love was blind, but apparently, it could also annihilate one's ability to reason. "How did you even survive in the DA's office if you couldn't recognize the sheer stupidity of discussing it with Rachel?"

"She was my fiancée." Levi's voice was laced with venom. "What was I supposed to do? I trusted her enough to spend the rest of my life with her. Why wouldn't I give her a chance to explain herself? I could have been completely wrong, and the whole thing could have been an unfortunate coincidence. But the day after I told her, the DA dragged me into his office and ordered me to stop looking into it. He said there was an ongoing federal investigation, and I was going to blow two years of undercover work."

A wave of sympathy washed over Willow. She had trusted her fiancé too, and like Levi, her trust had been misplaced. It was all too easy to put your heart in someone's hands, right up until he tossed it aside and took a roll in the sack with the first woman who showed off some leg. Jesus. She needed to focus. "You're suggesting the district attorney is in on this—whatever this is—as well?" Ranger moved in beside Willow and sat next to her, perhaps picking up on her increased stress. She gave him a scratch between his ears.

"I am," Levi said. "I stopped my investigation, or I made it appear that way. I used some back-channels to gather more details, and that's when I discovered some disconcerting facts. The DA personally oversaw over half the corporate fraud cases for the past three years. In every instance, the companies being prosecuted settled out of court for a fine that was well below what it should have been. I had asked him about it at the time, and he said the companies had deep pockets and protracted legal battles against them would have drained the department of its financial resources. He also alluded that closing the cases would help his bid for re-election, and he couldn't do good if he wasn't in office. He ran on a tough stance against white-collar crime in his last campaign and won by a landslide."

"It's not good," Jackson said, "but it's not the first time I've heard of DA's offices bitching over lack of funding, and it still doesn't prove the mayor's involvement."

"Is that why you broke up with her?" Willow asked. "Because you thought she was involved in some shady shit?"

A sour expression crossed Levi's face. "I never broke up with her. That's just the story she tells everyone. About a week after I confronted Rachel, I got a call from Judge Mayfield's clerk." Levi clenched his hands into tight fists. He looked ready to explode. "He had overheard the judge talking with the mayor, and suggested I meet with him at the Marriott's hotel bar. He didn't want to talk about it on the phone." He wiped his hands on his pant legs. "While I was waiting for him at the bar, an attractive redheaded woman started chatting me up. The next thing I know, I'm lying naked in bed with her. She wanted fifty thousand dollars for the compromising photos she'd taken while I was unconscious." The man's face crumpled. "I didn't have that kind of money. Even if I did... I wouldn't have paid it. I would never give in to extortion. In retaliation, the woman *supposedly* sent the pictures to Rachel, and she broke up with me the same day."

"Supposedly?" Jackson asked.

"Rachel's reaction when she showed me the photos..." Levi shook his head. "It was so... fake. My guess is, she's the one who set up the honey trap—or at the very least, she was aware of it. I think she was looking for a way to end our relationship, and she wanted me to come across as the bad guy."

"You poor bastard," Willow said softly, placing a hand on his shoulder. She'd never met Levi's fiancée, but the picture was becoming painfully clear—enough to see why her death had been so brutal. What struck Willow even more was the eerie parallel to her own past: the way a single, calculated betrayal had unraveled everything she thought she knew about love and loyalty.

"It got worse. The very next day the DA fired me, my landlord evicted me, and the mayor systematically dismantled my life." Levi turned to Jackson, his mouth drawn. "I had plenty of motive to kill her, but I wouldn't. I couldn't. Rachel had her problems but..." Levi's words trailed off as tears gathered in his eyes. He swiped angrily at his face. "Look what they did to me just for asking questions. What do you think they'll do to you both for actually finding answers?"

The question hung heavy in the air. Willow turned to Jackson, seeing the struggle play across his face. He'd lost his best friend to this conspiracy. Now they were learning that not only was the victim complicit, but the entire municipal government might be rotten to the core.

Ranger shifted against her leg, picking up on her growing unease. She absently stroked his fur, noting how his body remained alert but calm—a far cry from the aggressive and unstable animal she'd first brought to Florence. Her gaze shifted to Jackson, watching him process Levi's revelations. His professional mask had slipped, revealing the raw pain of learning his friend's death was entangled in something far darker than they'd imagined.

A sudden chill ran through her, despite the warmth of the room. They'd crossed a line here—one that put them squarely in the crosshairs of whatever conspiracy had claimed Tanner's life. Her hand drifted to her weapon, an unconscious gesture that didn't go unnoticed by either man.

"We need to get this to the US Attorney," she said quietly, but the words felt hollow even as she spoke them. One look at Jackson's face confirmed what she already knew—they were too deeply embedded now to simply hand this off. Whatever came next, they would need to trust each other completely to survive it.

Chapter Fourteen

Jackson

Jackson's head throbbed as he tried to reconcile Levi's words with his own findings. Nothing in his investigations suggested conspiracy outside of the police force. Levi had said that the mayor had high-ranking members of the Florence PD in his pocket. He'd also said that Captain Sawyer was one of the few righteous officers in the department. None of that lined up with the evidence he had on the man, iron-clad proof that he was on the take and involved in large-scale drug operations in Florence.

"Tell me about Detective Franklin and what happened at the laundromat." Jackson reached into his pocket. "I've got the entire thing on video," he said as he slid a thumb drive across the table. "So, I suggest you tell us the truth and don't leave anything out. Because, if you're lying to us, I'll arrest you myself."

"You witnessed it yourself," Levi said. "Franklin only showed up a few minutes before you. He came in waving his weapon at the two women who were in the laundromat with me. He yelled at them and told them to get out. As soon as they were gone, he pointed his gun at me." He held his arm out, imitating the detective's actions. "He was frightened. He could barely keep his gun steady, and the entire time, he kept apologizing, saying that he had no choice. He said he was being blackmailed. Someone had sent him a video showing children being forced to have sex with him, along with screenshots of a private bank account in the Cayman Islands with almost two million dollars in it. They had demanded he kill me, and if he refused, they would send the information to his wife and the local papers."

"But not the police," Willow said. "They knew the information would fail under close scrutiny, but once a person's reputation is destroyed—"

"There's no coming back from it," Levi said, finishing her thought. "That's when you two showed up. You probably saved my life, but to be honest, I didn't think he was going to go through with it. Franklin was a good cop and a good man."

"I don't know Detective Franklin outside of the police force," Jackson said, "but my experience with him was that he was as corrupt as Captain Sawyer and his partner, Detective Castor."

"You've got it all wrong," Levi said, his voice filled with frustration. "Chief Dawson Wheeler is the one you need to look out for. Sawyer's been trying to build a case against him since he took over for your father as captain of the FPD. Before I got shit-canned, he spoke with me often, sharing his information with me."

"We need to get him into WITSEC," Willow said. "There's no telling how far this goes. If the mayor has the DA, the chief of police, and most of the local PD in his pocket—"

"The police chief isn't involved," Jackson blurted out. "He can't be. My boss, Special Agent in Charge Savannah Greene, sent me here to work with the K9 unit. Since I've been here, I've noticed inconsistencies—things that don't add up. When I brought them up with Wheeler, he suggested I keep my eyes and ears open. The K9 units were often sent on raids or to sniff out drugs. It would give me a unique perspective on how the police officers were conducting themselves around large quantities of drugs, guns, and cash. The chief shared photos of Captain Sawyer meeting with several high-ranking fentanyl and cocaine dealers, but they didn't have enough to make the charges stick. SAC Greene was aware of the problem, and she was happy that I was willing to help. Now, if the chief was dirty, do you really think he'd invite an FBI agent into his department?"

"Sweet Jesus on a cracker," Willow said. "You liar. I knew there was something more to you being down here." The woman's mouth opened and closed without making a sound. "Is this why I was sent here? Did your SAC and my ASAC Alice Baldwin plan this out? She had said to keep my wits about me."

"Plan it out?" Confusion swept across Jackson's face as his head tilted to the side. "What are you talking about? And did you say *ASAC* Baldwin? When she was stationed in Birmingham, she was the SAC. Greene took her place when Baldwin transferred to Charleston."

"I've only ever known Alice as an Assistant Special Agent in Charge. If she was demoted, I wasn't told. But it never made sense to me why I'd be sent two states over for dog training." Willow's chest heaved, anger flaring. The idea that she had somehow been duped into returning to active duty pissed her off. When she got home, Alice was going to explain herself.

Jackson shrugged. "ASAC Baldwin sent you here because she knows my mother is the best K9 dog trainer. When I told her that my mother was ill, she asked if I could oversee Ranger's rehabilitation. I tried to talk her out of it. I was afraid it would seem like I was bringing in reinforcements and that it would blow my cover, but Alice insisted..."

"Jesus," Willow said. "Alice called you directly? How does she even know you?"

"She had worked with my father for a few years," Jackson said. "Back when Alice was the SAC in the Birmingham office, the two of them worked together on a joint task force of some sort. During that time, Alice and my mother had become close friends, but they haven't spoken since my father's disappearance. She was extremely upset to hear of her condition."

Willow wanted to press Jackson about his father but thought better of it. "I suppose that shouldn't surprise me. It explains why Alice sent me all the way out here to meet with a trainer."

Ranger's nose shot up, and his ears perked. His non-stop barking followed immediately after. Ruby and Boone hopped to their feet and sniffed the air. A moment later, the dogs outside in the kennels joined in, their barks adding to Ranger's.

"We've got company," Jackson said. "Get Ranger under control. Now! Ruby, guard." The Golden Retriever's body shifted into a ready position.

Willow snapped a leash on Ranger and looked out the window to see what the commotion was about. As far as she could see, there was no one in sight.

"I'm going to show you two something," Jackson said, "but you need to swear that you'll never disclose it to anyone. It's been a family secret for four generations." He seemed to be waiting for a reply, but all he got were blank stares. "I'm trusting you. Both of you."

Willow blew out a small whistle when Jackson pulled a panel off the wall. The bare lights hanging from the ceiling shone a short way down a pitch-black corridor.

"Get in," Jackson said to Levi. "You and Boone get in, move fifteen or twenty feet from the door, and keep quiet. Don't move around unless you have to. And for God's sakes, keep Boone quiet."

Levi hunched as he stepped through the secret door. Boone followed, his nose pressed hard to the wood-plank floor, snuffling his way into the room.

"Not a sound," Jackson said as he moved the panel back into its place.

Even though Willow knew exactly where the secret entrance was, the door blended into the woodwork and vanished. Ruby positioned herself in front of the panel and laid down.

"Sit," Jackson said, grabbing a binder off an old-school steel filing cabinet. "Start filling out these intake forms." He yanked out three pages and shoved them across the table. At the sound of approaching voices, Ranger's barks escalated into snarls.

"Now what?" Willow asked, mouthing the words.

"Ranger, settle," Jackson commanded as he stood at the door. The Malinois dropped to the floor and rested his head on his front paw. Ruby had never budged from her spot.

Out the window, four men came into view. All had their weapons drawn and there wasn't a friendly face in the bunch. Each had the bearing of ex-military. Three of the men had to be SWAT based on their tactical gear and the AR-15s they were carrying. The fourth, a burly man in his late forties, wore a suit that was at least one size too small for him. "Jackson Brooks? I'm Detective Brendan James, and I have a search warrant. Step back from the door. We're coming in."

"Easy, gentlemen," Jackson called out. "I have a skittish K9 inside, and I don't want him spooked."

The SWAT team's guns snapped towards Jackson as though he had threatened them, while the man in the suit remained stoic.

"I'm Special Agent Jackson Brooks, and I'm opening the door." Jackson pulled open the door and showed his hands. "Detective James, is it? Is there a development in this morning's murders? You could have just called me." The detective offered Jackson a stone-faced response. "It's funny, Detective. I've been working with the Florence PD for six months now, and I've never once heard your name mentioned."

James slipped his pistol into his shoulder-holster, pulled out his cell phone, and held it up for Jackson to see. "Whether or not you have heard of me is completely irrelevant. I have a warrant to search the premises. Back away from the door and allow us to do our jobs."

"Hold on," Jackson said. "If you don't mind, I'd like to read this first."

"I do mind," the detective in the sausage-casing suit said. "You'll step aside. Now. I'll show you the warrant when you've let us in."

Jackson stepped back, giving the men room to get past. The group came to a halt at the sight of Ranger and his formidable set of teeth. Willow got up from her chair and dragged Ranger by his leash, giving the men plenty of room to fully enter. "You might want to consider how many of you come through the door," she said while wrapping the leash around her wrist. "It's not a particularly large room." What she really wanted to say was 'come closer and my dog will eat your balls' but, despite their surly demeanor, they had every right to push their way into the room—assuming the search warrant was legitimate.

The detective had handed his phone to Jackson while he scanned the ten by fourteen room. He reached for the papers on the desk when Jackson told him to stop. "This warrant is for my home," he said, handing the phone back. "It doesn't mention outbuildings, which is what this kennel is. It also doesn't say anything about reading personal information. This warrant allows you to search my premises for Levi Benson, and that's all."

"The documents are in plain sight, and it is my assertion that it may be a part of a contractual agreement between yourself and Mr. Benson—and is therefore within the scope of the search warrant." The detective stared down at Ranger for several seconds. "But if you're afraid I'll find something... maybe I should call Judge Mayfield and request a wider scope?"

"Agent Banks," Jackson said, raising his eyebrows at Willow. "Is there any private information on your intake form that you don't want Detective James to see? I figure it's easier to let these officers do their work and not force them to bother Judge Mayfield—Mayor Persie's cousin."

Willow choke-coughed. "Wow. The mayor has a judge on speed dial." She picked up the first of the intake forms and held it up. "Detective Brendan James is welcome to look all he wants. All it has is my name—Special Agent Willow Banks of the FBI." She shook the paper to draw the man's attention to it. "Here you go, Detective. Fill your goddamn boots."

The detective glanced at the paper before turning his attention back to Jackson. "You two realize we're on the same side, right? Are you harboring a fugitive, Special Agent Brooks?"

"Do you see any fugitives?" Willow asked. She looked down at Ranger, who was sitting remarkably still at her feet. Ruby hadn't budged from her spot, keeping her eyes locked on the four intruders.

"Have you seen everything you came to see?" Jackson asked. "Or would you like to walk around in circles in here a while longer?"

Detective James smiled a cold, heartless smile. "I've been here long enough." The other three men who crammed themselves into the doorway all nodded. "Although, I'm not certain the search of the main house is complete. I think it's best we wait here for the all-clear from Lieutenant Spade."

Jackson's eyes narrowed. "Get out of my way and get out of my kennels." Ranger jumped to his feet and lunged, nearly pulling Willow's arm out of its socket. Ruby, too, jumped to her feet and put her impressive set of canines on display. Jackson didn't wait for the officers blocking the door to move. He looked something like a running back as he dropped his shoulder into the center man, sending him sprawling onto his back. The other two tried to subdue Jackson, but he was too fast for them. "If you harmed my mother..."

"Let him go," Detective James said. "And you—get those dogs under control."

Chapter Fifteen

Willow

"Why are you harassing an FBI agent?" Willow said while Ranger continued to pull on his leash. She was tempted to let him go, but she knew that it would end badly for everyone. "Ranger down. Ruby down."

Ruby flopped to the floor. Ranger completely ignored the command and continued lunging at the end of his leash.

"We're searching for the murderer of Rachel Persie." Detective James backed his way to the door. "We were told he was on these premises."

"Do you realize that the other person murdered was Agent Tanner Montgomery of the FBI?" Willow yanked on Ranger's leash. "He was SA Jackson's best friend. Do you actually believe he'd harbor the man who murdered his best friend?"

The detective's brow furrowed. "Tanner was the other vic?" He turned to the other three officers. They all shook their heads. The detective's face sagged. "I wasn't told. My instructions were to come here and arrest Levi Benson for the murder of Rachel Persie. I was told there were more than a dozen eyewitnesses and video of Levi Benson murdering her."

"And that same video exonerates Levi," Willow said. Ranger had stopped barking and lunging. His threat assessment seemed to have shifted. "Jackson saw the video. He saw that it wasn't

Levi—but he also saw the killer went to great lengths to look like Mr. Benson."

"You sound sympathetic to the murderer..."

Ranger's ears lowered, but his leash remained slack. "Are you trying to insinuate something, Detective? I suggest you tread very carefully before you speak another word. I might also remind you that you are stepping on the toes of a federal investigation. Any involvement you have in this case is at the discretion of the FBI. Do you understand my meaning?"

"I find the timing of your arrival very interesting, Special Agent Willow Banks. The very same day you arrive, we have a double homicide. Your proximity to the event was suspiciously close. It is also my understanding that you were present at the death of Detective Franklin."

Willow fought to mask her surprise. She had left the laundromat with Levi before the police arrived. How could he already know that she'd been at the scene? Had Jackson said something about her involvement?

"Are you planning on arresting me, Detective?" She tightened her grip on Ranger's leash. "If so, on what charges?"

"Can I see your credentials, Special Agent?" Detective James held out his hand. "I would like to see proof that you are who you say you are. Impersonating a federal agent is a felony offense."

Willow produced her badge and held it out for the detective to see. A sneer pulled at the corner of his mouth as he inspected her ID. "Would you like to see the credentials of K9 Agents Ranger and Ruby as well? They keep them in their mouth."

"There is no need to threaten us, SA Banks." Detective James smiled and turned towards the door. "We are supposed to be on the same side of the law. If I don't ask hard questions, I'm not doing my job."

Willow watched as the men left the kennel. It bothered her that the police already knew she was at the scene of Detective

Franklin's suicide. It also bothered her that she hadn't actually seen the video which supposedly exonerated Levi. She walked over to the hidden panel and leaned against the wall. "If you can hear me," she whispered, "stay put. The police have left but they might still be nearby. If you're playing me, Levi. If this is some sort of scam you and Jackson have roped me into, I'm going to rip off your balls and feed them to Ranger."

Her comments were met with silence.

Chapter Sixteen

Jackson

A mix of fury and concern spurred Jackson to climb the long set of stairs that led up to his home. His mother's home. She was frail and weak, and if they harmed her in any way…he couldn't think like that. He needed a cool head and a clear mind. Everything was happening too quickly, and people seemed to know too much. The mayor and the police were on the scene in record time, as though they had been tipped off. Sure, it was the mayor's daughter, and he was well connected, but… the thoughts faded away as Jackson rounded the corner, and the front of his home came into view. Three Chevy Tahoe SUVs and a Dodge Charger were parked in the laneway, blocking the exit of his and Agent Banks's pickup trucks. The nurse's Prius was parked on the street.

Jackson's heart raced as he took mental note of every detail of the intrusion. Another SWAT team member was standing out front, dressed in tactical gear and carrying an assault rifle. Beside him, perched on the edge of a rocking chair, was his mother. She looked so frail. "Mom," he called out, sprinting towards her. "Are you okay?"

The officer in tactical gear moved forward, holding his rifle in one hand while holding out his other for Jackson to stop.

"My mother is a cancer patient," Jackson yelled, "and you're putting her life at risk." The officer didn't budge. His facial expression didn't change one iota. The man pressed his palm against Jackson's chest as he tried to move past. "You're assaulting a federal officer, Corporal. Move aside or I will be forced to take action. Your warrant is to search the house for Levi Benson, and your team has already violated that order. Get out of my way."

Indecision flashed across the man's face. "Your mother is fine. She was treated kindly."

"She should be in bed, not out here. Where's her nurse? Why is she not out here caring for her?"

"The woman you claim to be your mother's nurse is in custody. She assaulted Lieutenant Spade." The man motioned with his chin towards one of the SUVs. The windows were heavily tinted, making it impossible to see inside.

"I'm pulling out my phone," Jackson said as he slowly reached into his back pocket. He pointed it at the officer and shot a pic. "You're going to release the nurse and allow her to care for my mother, or I swear to the almighty, I will see you behind bars for reckless endangerment of a geriatric citizen. Have I made myself clear, Corporal?"

"Crystal," the officer replied. He held Jackson's gaze for several seconds before relenting. While he headed towards their vehicles, Jackson stepped inside.

At the sound of a dish being smashed, he pulled out his FBI badge. Holding it and his camera in front of himself, he stepped through the vestibule and into the dining room. An officer was actively rummaging through the shelves of a curio cabinet. "I'm Special Agent Jackson Brooks of the FBI," Jackson said, startling the SWAT operator. When the man turned, Jackson snapped a photo of him. "I'm quite certain that Mr. Benson isn't hiding in my mother's crystal cabinet, Corporal." He looked down at the smashed dish on the floor.

"Give me that phone," the officer said. "You can't be in here."

"No," Jackson said, pulling his phone back. "I am the only one who actually belongs here. You are in violation of your search warrant, and I am ordering you to leave my house, or I will arrest you."

"What's going on here?" another SWAT operator demanded, stepping into the sitting room from a second doorway. His sidearm was drawn and aimed at Jackson's chest. "I don't know who you are, but you need to be outside. Now."

Jackson turned his badge toward the officer. His name tag read Lt. Spade. "I am Special Agent Jackson Brooks, and you are in violation of your search warrant, Lieutenant. That's who I am and that's who you are. How many more officers are in my house?"

"I told you to leave," the lieutenant stated, never bothering to lower his weapon. "Now, get outside or I will arrest you."

Jackson slowly raised his phone and took a picture. "I wanted to get a better shot of you. My in-home cameras might not have gotten a clean image. I want you and your cohorts out of my house. Now."

Lieutenant Spade lowered his weapon. "I expect you'll be in jail by end of the day, Special Agent." He holstered his gun and walked past Jackson, letting his shoulder bump him on the way by. "Maybe sooner."

"How many more of your people are in my home?" Jackson said. He was doing his best to keep his temper in check, but he'd had more than enough of their behavior. "Don't leave the premises. I'll be taking your names before you go. I want to make sure you're all personally named in the lawsuit I'll be bringing against the Florence PD."

The lieutenant whistled. "We're done here," he yelled, directing his voice to the second floor. "Everyone out."

"There was no sign of him," a female SWAT operator said as she came tromping down the staircase.

"Mrs. Brooks sure does take a lot of drugs," a male operator said as he followed. "Her medicine cabinet is overflowing with pill bottles. I'll bet we could get her on something, too, if we wanted." The two officers blanched as Jackson captured their faces. "What is he doing here?" the woman said. "Sir, you can't be in here. We're Florence PD conducting a court-ordered search warrant."

"Amy, shut it," the lieutenant said. "Get out. Now."

The woman gave Jackson the hairy eyeball as she stepped past. The man, the one who was suggesting they bring Jackson's mother up on charges, turned away as he stepped past.

"Nobody leaves the property," Jackson reiterated. "I want to see your IDs. Each and every one of you." He had to fight the urge to see how much damage the officers had caused, but more than anything, he wanted to check in on his mother. By the time he had stepped out the door, his mother's nurse was coming up the front steps.

"Do you need help getting my mother back to bed, Joanna?"

"Thanks, Jax," the woman said. "I'll take care of her." She glanced over her shoulder at the congregation of police officers. "I didn't assault any of them. They tried to manhandle your mother, and I intervened. That tall prick, the one with the mustache... he knocked me down and handcuffed me. I want to press charges." She leaned in close. "I'm sure it's all on the CCTV."

"I'm sure it is too." Jackson took a good look at the man. He was the officer who had rifled through his mother's curio cabinet. "I'm sorry this happened to you, but I'll make sure they pay for it. I promise."

Jackson felt a surge of protective anger course through him, his jaw clenching at the thought of these officers manhandling his mother and her nurse. He rolled his shoulders and stepped lightly down the six wooden stairs off his front porch. He eyed the ramp that had been installed for his mother's wheelchair. As he approached the four officers who had been in his house, Detective

James came around the corner with his three SWAT operators in tow. Willow was right behind them with Ruby at her side, and Ranger surging at the end of his leash.

"Roll out," the Detective called out. "We're done here."

"Not so fast," Jackson said. "I want to see your IDs. Each and every one of you. Produce them. Now." Satisfaction welled up inside when Lieutenant Spade's throat bobbed. "Hold them up so I can get a picture of your face and your ID."

"You're making a mistake, Mr. Brooks," Detective James said. "You're going to piss off the wrong people."

"I've made a career of pissing off the wrong people, Detective. And the next time you address me, you will call me by correct title—FBI Special Agent Jackson Brooks." He held up his phone, ready to snap the picture. "Your ID, please. You can choose to not smile if you're not in a good mood."

Willow snorted and covered her mouth, failing to hide the grin on her face.

Jackson got his photos, and the officers departed. The adrenaline that had been coursing through his veins was subsiding, leaving him shaky and ill at ease. "I'm going to check on my mother. Go back to the kennels and I'll meet you there." He moved close enough to whisper. "Let Levi know that he's safe, but don't let him out just yet."

"What the fuck is going on?" Willow asked. Her obvious annoyance was back and in full color. "An FBI agent and the mayor's daughter were executed. Cops are committing suicide. An innocent man is being railroaded for a murder he didn't commit. Judges are issuing search warrants on a whim. And the local PD is sending SWAT to raid your house."

"Don't forget an FBI agent and her K9 having been conveniently sent my way." Jackson folded his arms over his chest and cocked an eyebrow.

"Are you suggesting I'm somehow involved in this?" Willow crossed her arms over her chest as well and cocked an eyebrow. "Detective Fuckwad had a similar notion."

Jackson's unexpected snort broke the tension. "Why in the world would I think you're involved? I'm simply happy you're here. You have a stellar reputation, as did Ranger before your partner's death." Jackson watched Willow's expression, looking for her reaction to what he'd said. It was small, but her body relaxed ever so slightly. "If it's okay with you, I really would like to check on my mother. Can I meet you at the kennels in ten minutes? Please."

"Ruby, come," Willow said as she turned to head away.

"Actually, I want Ruby to stay with me. I've found that she has innate calming affect with my mother." Truth was, she also helped keep Jackson's anxieties in check as well, but that wasn't something he needed to share. Not yet, at least.

"Sounds good," Willow said. She gave a tug on Ranger's leash, and he immediately complied. They had walked a few steps when she turned back. "Can I ask you something? Before I got here, Ranger was a mess. But his behavior has already changed dramatically."

"When you got here," Jackson said with casual air, "you were a bundle of nervous energy. Your dog picked up on it, and he was trying to protect you. You're calmer now, and so is he."

Willow rolled her eyes and silently made her way to the kennels. Jackson watched the woman and her Malinois head off. Truth was, Ranger's inconsistent behaviors were something of a mystery to him, too, and he was looking forward to figuring it out—right after he checked on his mother and locked up his best friend's murderer.

Chapter Seventeen

Willow

"What have we gotten ourselves into, Ranger?" Willow looked down at her dog and ran her hand over his head, letting her fingers brush his silky ears. "I wish Kate was here with us." She sighed and stared out at the water. The tranquil scene before her stood in stark contrast to the turmoil within. Things had been so chaotic that Willow hadn't taken time to notice the scenery. The stairs down to the kennel overlooked Wilson Lake, a widening in the Tennessee River sandwiched between two dams. It supposedly was one of the best fishing spots for bass and catfish in the lower states. Then again, pretty much every state boasted that they had the best fishing places. She doubted she'd have time to test the hype. Even if she did, it had been at least five years since the last time she had drowned a worm. Her partner, Kate, had taken her. They'd spent a full day out on a small aluminum boat getting fried under the South Carolina sun. They hadn't caught a thing all day, but she didn't care. They had shared stories, and laughs, and more than a few beers. She pushed the thought aside. The tear in her heart was too fresh, too raw. Every time Willow looked at Ranger, Kate's face swam into view.

"She died for you. Do you understand that? I lost my partner and my best friend..."

Ranger whined and stared up at Willow, his big brown eyes a reflection of the pain she felt. His empathetic gaze seemed to pierce through her defenses, touching the raw wound of her grief. She wanted to hate the dog, but she couldn't. On countless missions, Kate and Ranger had worked side by side, and every time the situation grew dire, Ranger never backed down. He would have willingly given his life to protect his handler. Without hesitation. How could she blame her partner for doing the same thing? How could she fault Kate? It had been on Willow. It had been her brash behavior that had put Ranger in danger. She clutched her chest and buckled over; the all-consuming grief of her loss was unbearable.

Jesus. You need to pull yourself together. Now is not the time to dwell on the past.

Before the wave of emotion completely overwhelmed her, Willow took a deep breath and forced herself to regain her composure. She forced the pain down, locking it away where it couldn't hurt her, at least not right now. She straightened up, blinking back the sting in her eyes. The lack of sleep was catching up to her, and the adrenaline that had been keeping her going was gone. She yawned, sharp and sudden, and wiped a hand across her face, forcing herself back to the present. She pushed open the kennel door as another yawn took hold, much larger and more intense than the last.

With a huff, she dropped Ranger's leash and plopped herself on a wooden chair. She scanned the intake form that Jackson had asked her to fill out. Maybe later. Her eyelids were getting heavier by the second.

"It won't be much longer," she said to the panel that hid Levi. "Jackson will be here shortly."

Willow folded her arms on the table and rested her head in the crook of her elbow. She wished she was home and in bed.

***

Voices and the smell of fried chicken roused Willow from her sleep. The aroma wafted through the air, teasing her senses and pulling her from her impromptu nap. Her mouth tasted like the bottom of a boot. Jackson and Levi were seated at the far side of the table, each with a plate of food in front of them. Good god, it smelled like heaven.

"Feel better?" Jackson asked. "Sorry if we woke you. We tried to let you sleep."

Willow rubbed her eyes. They still felt like they were full of sand. "What time is it?"

"Nearly six," Levi said.

"Six?" Something was different about him. "Holy shit, you shaved off your beard."

Levi nodded and pushed a basket of rolls towards her. "I guess it's not much of a disguise," he said with a grin. "You saw right through it."

"There's chicken in the basket," Jackson said. "And some potato salad." He pushed a dinner plate towards Willow. There was a rolled red napkin laying on top of it. "Ranger's in the dog run. He's been fed and walked too."

"Jesus, I'm sorry." Willow was struggling to clear the cobwebs muddling her brain. "I didn't mean to..." She pulled the plate closer and reached for the basket of chicken. "You ordered out?"

Jackson's face reddened. "No. I cooked." He glanced over at Levi. "You were fast asleep, so we let you be. Levi got himself cleaned up and I made chicken."

Willow pulled back the red and white checked cloth that covered the chicken, releasing an aroma that set her mouth to watering. She grabbed a piece and didn't bother to put it down on her plate. She took a big, crunchy bite and moaned. "Holy shit," she said, unfolding the napkin on her plate. She wiped at the juice running down her chin. "You made this?"

The lanky man shrugged. "My mom taught me. She figured cooking was a skill all men should have. My dad taught me how to hunt, and fish, and track—and my mom taught me everything else."

She took another bite of chicken and snatched a roll from the basket. It was still warm.

As Willow ate, Jackson pulled out an envelope from his pocket. "Do you remember Dr. Simmons, the behavioral vet who had looked after Ranger? He gave me his analysis. I've already read it, and... well, I think it's pretty significant."

Willow set down her chicken, wiped her fingers, and carefully unfolded the letter. As she read through Dr. Simmons' assessment, her expression shifted from interest to concern. She paused occasionally, glancing up at Ranger in the dog run, then back to the letter.

"Canine PTSD?" She muttered, looking up at Jackson. "I didn't even know that was a thing."

Jackson nodded solemnly. "It's not uncommon in working dogs who've been through trauma. What do you think about his observations?"

Willow skimmed through the letter again, her eyebrows knitting together. "It makes sense, I suppose. The way Ranger's been acting... but this part about loyalty transference, that's unexpected."

"I thought you might find that interesting," Jackson said. "Ranger's strong connection to you explains why we've seen the shift in his behavior since you've arrived. He is tuned to your emotions, and when you're stressed, he feels it and reacts to it."

Willow set the letter down, her mind racing. She looked out at Ranger again, seeing him in a new light. "So, what does this mean for Ranger's future? And mine, for that matter?"

Jackson leaned back in his chair. "That's something we need to discuss. Dr. Simmons believes Ranger can potentially return to duty, but it will likely require extensive training for both of you. Are you willing to consider that?"

Willow was silent for a moment, her eyes drifting to the dog run where Ranger was. "I... I don't know, Jackson. I'm not a K9 handler. I never wanted to be." She paused, thinking about Kate, about the bond she'd witnessed between her partner and Ranger. "But if it's what Ranger needs... I owe it to Kate to at least consider it."

Jackson nodded, understanding in his eyes. "Take your time to think it over. There's no rush to decide right now."

Willow nodded, her mind still processing the implications of the letter. She turned back to Jackson, ready to refocus on the case at hand. "Alright, let's set that aside for now. Let's assume that Levi's conspiracy theory is accurate, why go through all this effort to frame him for murder? From what he said, the mayor had already ruined him."

Jackson turned to Levi and raised his eyebrows.

"I have no clue," Levi said. "I didn't do anything to him recently, at least, not that I'm aware of."

"Okay then," Willow said, taking another bite of her roll. As she chewed, her mind raced, trying to process the overwhelming amount of information she had taken in. "Let's start with the murders and see where that takes us." She swallowed her food and thumped her index finger on the table. "Whoever killed Rachel hated her with a passion, it was classic overkill. What about the dead agent? Was he just an innocent bystander, someone at the wrong place at the wrong time?"

Jackson looked like he was ready to puke. The idea that Tanner had been collateral damage clearly didn't sit well with him. Willow wasn't accustomed to pussyfooting her way through an investigation, but here she was, dealing with a double homicide, and the two people helping her were carrying a shit-ton of associated emotional baggage.

"Here's footage of the murders." Jackson slid a cell phone across the table. "Some of the answers you're looking for might be in this video. It's a recording of... everything, from beginning to end."

Levi lowered his eyes and turned away.

Willow blinked and stared at Jackson. "Where did you get that?"

"From Charlie, the selfie-girl who was more interested in making a social media splash than caring about two murdered people. I took it from her on the scene." He gave Willow a crooked smile. "I guess I forgot to turn it in."

For the next three minutes and twenty-seven seconds, Willow watched in detached horror as a man dressed up to look like Levi brutally murdered two people. Neither of the victims saw it coming. "Rachel called her killer by name. She called him Levi. No wonder everyone is after you." She struggled to understand how the woman couldn't see through the disguise. "How long has it been since you and Rachel split up?"

"Almost six months," Jackson said, placing a hand on Levi's forearm. "It happened shortly after I was assigned here."

Willow nearly choked on the news. "You've been undercover for six months, and you haven't made a case yet?"

"I've made my case." Jackson's eyes turned to steel. "I have enough to bring corruption charges against Captain Sawyer and at least four of his officers, but there are others pulling his strings. I'm sure of it. Every time I feel like I'm making headway, the leads dry up. This isn't an official investigation, so I'm pretty much on my own."

"You couldn't get help from the anti-corruption task force? If the situation is as systemic as it sounds, there should be more than a single agent working on the case."

"I agree, but I wasn't allowed to involve anyone else, at least not officially." Jackson got a pained expression on his face.

"Holy shit," Willow choked on her dinner roll. "Tanner was helping you, wasn't he? What was his role?"

"Financial forensics," Jackson said. He let out a sigh, his chin dipping toward his chest. "He was pulling together the money trails. I asked him to help when my own leads were drying up." Jackson's expression soured. "If you're suggesting that he was the target... it's impossible. Nobody but the SAC knew he was helping. She insisted that nobody else know about it."

"Why?" Willow couldn't wrap her head around it. "What possible benefit could there be to compartmentalize your investigation?"

"None that I could think of. But I've known the SAC since I joined the FBI. She was my SSA when I was first posted to the Birmingham office." Jackson shrugged. "She's as good as they come. If she wanted our investigation kept quiet, it was for a worthwhile reason."

That answer still didn't sit well with Willow, but it would have to wait. She turned her attention back to Levi. "You need to think of a reason you'd be set up like this. I know you said you have no clue, but that's not good enough."

"Jackson," Levi said. "Do you have a place for me to sleep? I'm exhausted."

Jackson paused.

"Boone and I can sleep in a kennel. In case the PD comes back for a double-check."

"It's not even seven o'clock yet, and you're not sleeping until you've finished answering my questions," Willow said. "I need to understand your involvement in this case. Someone went through a lot of effort to make you their patsy. You can sleep after you answer my questions."

"Not everyone just woke up from a nap," Levi said.

"You don't need to sleep in the kennels." Jackson blew out a breath and stared at the ceiling. "I just... my mother's not well."

"Jesus, Jackson. I'm sorry. See? That's how tired I am. I'm not thinking straight."

"Forget about sleeping." Willow said. "We need to figure out why you're being targeted."

"There is plenty of room for both of you," Jackson said. "But I don't want my mother knowing you're here. She doesn't need the extra stress."

"Concentrate!" Willow slammed her palm on the table and glared at Jackson, imploring him to shut up. "You can sleep when we have something solid to work on. Right now, we've only got theories and suppositions. Meanwhile, two people are dead and we're harboring a fugitive."

"I'm fine in the kennels," Levi said. He stood up, making ready to leave. "Boone and I have slept in much worse."

"No." Jackson's voice turned firm. "You're not sleeping in the kennels. You and Boone can have a place inside, but for tonight, you'll need to share the room with Willow and Ranger."

"I'm not sleeping with him!" Outrage burned in Willow's chest. "And I'm not sharing a room with two dogs either. What is wrong with you two? We've got a double homicide to solve, and you want to go to sleep?" The two men stared at Willow. They were both barely holding on. They weren't her. They weren't the type who threw themselves into their work when life fed them a shit sandwich. She craved the hustle and bustle. She needed the distraction. If she could, she'd never sleep, and she'd never slow down. "I'm not ready to call it a night. I'm going to take Ranger for a walk. It's about the only thing he and I do well together."

"You can go for a walk after I get your room set up..." Jackson leveled his gaze at Levi. "The room I'm putting you in has two double beds, but more importantly..." He pressed his lips together. He had something to say, but he desperately didn't want to say it. "You need to share a room in case we get another surprise visit. If we have four rooms with messed up beds, they'll know Levi was here. That's why you're going to be sharing the room, along with the two dogs. It creates a plausible reason for an empty bed to be mussed."

Willow bounced her forehead off the table. She wasn't going to get anything more out of these two, but she also wasn't quite ready to let it go. A sudden yawn gripped her. She covered her gaping mouth and stretched.

"Can we pick this up tomorrow?" Jackson said. "I really would like to check in on my mother, get you two settled, and hit the hay. We all need some sleep."

"Sure," Willow said. "We're clearly not solving this is one day."

Chapter Eighteen

Jackson

Jackson pinched the bridge of his nose. Good Lord, he was exhausted. The food had provided some relief, but not knowing who to trust gnawed at him. While he had no reason to doubt Willow, Levi, and Savannah, beyond them lay a murky sea of potential deception. He trusted Chief Wheeler, yet Levi was adamant about the man's dishonesty. Conversely, Jackson possessed concrete evidence of Captain Sawyer's misdeeds, but Levi insisted on his integrity.

The mayor's relentless efforts to pin his daughter's murder on Levi seemed, on the surface, a natural reaction. His hatred for Levi, stemming from past events, made him an easy scapegoat—especially since the murderer had gone to great lengths to look like him. In the heat of the moment, even Rachel had believed it was him.

"How are you going to get Levi into your house?" Willow asked, her fingers combing through her wavy blonde hair as if to stimulate thought. "It wouldn't surprise me if there are officers hanging around, hoping to catch you harboring a fugitive."

"There's a secret passage," Jackson replied, his gaze fixed on the wall. He hesitated, weighing the implications of revealing more. "It leads to another hidden door that opens into a series of rooms and corridors that lead up to the house."

"Why?" Willow said.

Jackson approached the wall and removed a panel. "My great grandfather built this house. To say that he was paranoid would be the understatement of the year—at least that's how my grandfather described him. He'd go on and on about how the man was obsessed with the notion that the government was out to get him." He peered into the darkness of the hidden room before continuing, "In the twenties, he used the secret rooms to make moonshine."

"During prohibition?" Levi asked, incredulous. "Your great grandfather was a booze runner?"

"According to my dad, my great grandfather ran a thriving business. Almost everyone who lived on this street helped. It was the only thing that kept some of the families alive. The depression hit the area hard. Running bootleg booze helped ease the pain."

Concern creased Willow's forehead. "He's lucky he didn't kill himself. Running an indoor still? There'd be no place for the vapors to escape. He could have died by explosion, toxic fumes, or carbon monoxide poisoning."

A smile played on Jackson's lips. "My great grandfather was paranoid, but I think he was also an engineering genius. There are a series of baffled vents that create a basic air exchanger. My dad explained it to me once, but if I'm being honest, it was so far over my head that I barely understood a third of it." He exhaled deeply. "None of that is important right now. What matters is, there are pathways and ladders that lead up to the house. More specifically, it leads to the bedroom you two will be sharing. Willow and Ranger will come with me through the front door, and you and Boone will use the secret passage and remain hidden."

Jackson studied their faces, relieved to see no objections. It was a small victory, but he'd take what he could get. Now, all he needed to do was guide Levi and Boone past the second hidden door and escort Willow upstairs—without his mother, Maybelle, making a fuss about a woman spending the night. Who was he kidding?

Getting past his mother would be like trying to slip a steak past a ravenous dog. All he could do was brace himself for the awkwardness that was sure to come.

***

"You could have let me carry some of the leftover food," Willow grumbled as they climbed the stairs. "I don't put up with this helpless female shit..."

"You're far from helpless," Jackson countered, struggling to balance six large Tupperware containers. "But I don't know how Ranger is going to react when you try to bring him into the house. I want you to have full control over him." While not entirely false, it wasn't the whole truth either. The reality was that if he wasn't carrying everything, his mother would seize the opportunity to embarrass him in front of Willow, lecturing about being a good host and how a proper gentleman treats a lady. Worse still, if Willow objected or challenged his mother's perspective, Maybelle would unleash the full force of her southern matriarchal disapproval.

"What are we going to do tomorrow?" Willow asked, absently patting Ranger's head. The dog's gaze remained fixed on the Tupperware, clearly hoping for a chance at the treats within. "I mean, where do we start?"

"We'll start at the morgue," Jackson replied. "I want to see the ME. He should have the preliminary autopsy results by tomorrow morning. I expect Dr. Johnstone is being forced to work through the night on it. I'll text him first thing to set up an appointment. From there, we'll head to the SBI building. According to my SAC, she's setting up a command center there. I expect there will be at least a half-dozen agents assigned to this case. Savannah's going to oversee the entire operation. She wanted to come here tonight but I put her off until tomorrow."

Willow scoffed. "Local PD, the SBI, and the FBI all working together to solve two murders? It's going to be a total shitshow. Throw in the political issues and the media frenzy..." She bugged out her eyes and made an explosion gesture with sound effects.

"Maybe," Jackson conceded. "I expect Savannah will keep everyone in line. She has a knack for dealing with sensitive situations, and a presence that commands respect."

"Wow!" Willow clutched her heart, grinning. "Do you think you could put her on a higher pedestal?"

"Oh, grow up. I respect her, okay? She's an amazing agent, but she's got higher aspirations."

"Like she wants the director's position?"

"Maybe." Jackson paused at the stairs leading up to his house, a nervous knot twisting in his gut. Ruby, sitting in front of the door, barked as if to urge him forward. "She spends a lot of time cultivating relationships, particularly with the media. That tells me she's got her sights set on something bigger than heading the Birmingham field office. My gut tells me she's looking to make a move into politics."

"Be careful of her then," Willow warned. "She wants to make an example of this case and wrap it up as quickly as possible. Like I said, there's going to be a media frenzy, and if she's looking to run for public office, she'll milk every drop out of it."

"Cynical much?" Jackson remarked as he climbed the stairs.

"It doesn't take a cynic to see what she's up to." Willow rushed forward to open the front door. Ranger remained silent and showed no resistance. "Special Agents in Charge do not take direct involvement in an off-site investigation unless there are extenuating circumstances. In this case, I'm guessing it's publicity. Lots and lots of publicity. Mark my words, Special Agent Brooks. Your SAC is going to take every possible opportunity to put herself in front of the cameras."

Jackson stepped into the house and toed off his shoes. "If you don't mind. My mother gets upset if people track mud in from outside." He glanced at Ruby and Ranger, rolling his eyes. "Dogs are the exception to the rule. They can be covered in muck from head to toe, and she'll welcome them with open arms."

Ruby whined, her gaze flitting between Jackson and the door leading out of the front vestibule.

"Go," Jackson said. "You can let Ranger off his leash. I don't expect him to misbehave."

Willow unclasped the leash, and the Malinois skidded around the corner, trying to catch up to Ruby.

"You know," Jackson said, "you're the reason he's struggling right now."

"Excuse me?" Willow replied, pressing her fists against her hips. "I'm the reason he's on the verge of being put down for being too violent?"

"No... it's not that. Not exactly." Jackson wondered why he had broached this topic now. It was just that, for the last few hours, Ranger had been behaving exactly as his training had taught him to behave. And...

"Jax," his mother's frail voice called out. "Who does this dog belong to, and why are you lurking in my foyer?"

"We're not finished discussing this," Willow said, flashing a feral look that could scare snakes. "He's mine, Mrs. Brooks."

Jackson fought the urge to flee, to hop in his pickup, and drive until he hit the Pacific Ocean... and then keep on driving. This was going to be a trying night, and he lacked the energy to deal with it. He expected he'd still be apologizing when the sun broke over the horizon.

Chapter Nineteen

Willow

"Good evening, Mrs. Brooks," Willow said. Jackson's mother was a wisp of a woman who looked as if she'd shatter from too firm a hug. "I'm SA Willow Banks. Your son is helping me fix Ranger."

A scoff escaped the frail woman's parched lips as she scrubbed the Malinois' ears. "If you think your dog is broke, the problem is likely at the other end of the leash."

The comment made Willow's ears burn.

"Momma." Jackson stretched out the word like a six-year-old pleading for a treat. "Be nice." His intervention only intensified the heat in Willow's ears.

"Don't be so dramatic, Jax." Mrs. Brooks rolled her eyes and turned back to Willow. "My name is Maybelle. You can either call me that, or May, or Momma." The woman might have looked like a twig ready to snap, but she made up for it with attitude and spunk.

"Yes, ma'am," Willow said, instantly regretting her choice of words. "I mean, Maybelle." She paused, carefully selecting her next words. "Why do you think I'm broken? I am, after all, the problem at the other end of the leash." It irked her that Jackson had said the exact same thing moments ago.

Maybelle examined Willow from head to toe with the precision of an FBI interrogator. Without speaking a word, she knocked

Willow off balance. "Well, since you asked so nicely, I get the impression from you that you don't like dogs all that much. I think you see them as a tool, and not as a companion."

"Momma, please!" Jackson scrubbed his hands over his scalp.

"She asked," Maybelle said, feigning innocence. "I could have said more."

More? Willow didn't like the sound of that. It unsettled her that the woman's instant assessment was so accurate. The question 'why?' hovered on her lips, but she chose to swallow it down. The quirk in the corner of Maybelle's mouth suggested she saw far more than the average person.

"Look at your hand," Maybelle said. "Look how you've wrapped your dog's leash around your wrist. I'm assuming that's how you were holding Ranger before you released him. You don't trust him, so he doesn't trust you. Jax said his previous handler was killed in the line of duty. He said that she died protecting her dog. That, deary, is what love is all about, willingness to sacrifice for the other, no matter the cost." She paused to cluck her tongue. "My guess is, Ranger here is afraid you'll die too. He doesn't want to be left alone. He may not fully trust you, but you're all he's got."

The words hit Willow like a physical blow, practically knocking the wind out of her. Never had she considered the emotional impact Kate's death might have on Ranger. Why would she? He's just a dog.

"Momma," Jackson said. "I'm going to show SA Banks to her room. She's going to be spending the night with us."

"She doesn't seem tired to me, Jax." Maybelle shot her son a pointed look. "Are you going to deny me the opportunity to talk with someone new? All I've got is the same old gossip from the same old biddies." Jackson's mother flashed her a smile. "Are you tired, SA Banks? Or would you like to chat?"

Jackson groaned.

"I would love to sit with you, Maybelle," Willow said, patting her hand. Jesus. It was ice cold and her skin clammy. The scent of sickness clung to her. "But I'm afraid that your son and I have an early morning ahead of us."

"What could be so important—?"

"Momma," Jackson said, cutting Maybelle off mid-sentence. "I've got some bad news to share." He glanced at Willow. A deep sadness had crept into his brown eyes. They looked exactly like Ranger's the day her partner had sacrificed her life to save him. "I don't want to upset you but..."

"Oh, for the love of God," Maybelle said. "Spit it out. If you don't tell me, I'll call Grace, and she'll tell me everything anyway. If it's bad news, I'd prefer to hear it from you."

"Tanner was murdered this morning. Rachel Persie too."

"I see," Maybelle said. Her chest rose and fell in rapid succession before settling into a constant rhythm. "Are you okay? How are Jake and Louise? They must be devastated."

"They're in shock," Jackson said. He stared up at the open-beam ceiling and swiped at his eyes.

Sympathy, along with a debilitating sadness, swept through Willow. She understood what he was going through. Kate's death had felt like her heart had been ripped out through her bellybutton. She, too, had been the one to break the news to her partner's parents. When the elderly couple broke down, Willow had wished she had been the one who'd died, if only to spare them the pain they were living through.

"Do you have any suspects?" Maybelle asked, changing the subject. The woman was at death's door, but she was indomitable. "I'm assuming you've already processed the crime scene."

"They're blaming Levi." Jackson's demeanor shifted. Discussing the case snapped him out of his funk. Willow could relate. She also used work to avoid her feelings. If she was busy solving crimes, she wasn't thinking about how much her heart hurt. "It wasn't him, Momma. But someone was trying to make it appear like he was the one who did it."

"Jackson," Willow said, shaking her head. "I don't think it's appropriate to discuss the case."

"Please, child." Maybelle leveled Willow with a haughty glare. "I've been helping Brooks men with their investigations before you were even born. I see things with a unique perspective, as my late husband used to say. Even when I don't have something meaningful to add, I can offer a direction to look in."

"Tanner was killed with a single shot to the chest," Willow said. "And Rachel was shot three times in the face." She studied Maybelle, sizing up her reaction to the details. It wasn't like she wasn't sharing public knowledge. Witnesses had recorded the entire murder, anyway. "The murderer used a flashbang grenade to help with his escape."

"A flashbang?" Jackson said. "How do you know that?"

"Didn't you hear it?" Willow tilted her head and frowned. "It's a distinctive sound. We use them all the time when we are breaching a room with armed perps. By the time they come to their senses..." Memories of her raids with Kate and Ranger flooded her mind.

"Did you work SWAT?" Maybelle asked. "Jax didn't tell me that about you."

"No, ma'am—I mean Maybelle." Willow raised an eyebrow at Jackson, questioning why he was discussing her with his mother. "My partner and I worked in the Violent Crimes Unit. SWAT often accompanied us on our missions."

"My Jax used to work in the VCAC unit." Maybelle's chest puffed up as she spoke of her son. "I told him he wasn't cut out for that type of work, but he insisted."

"Jesus Christ. Seriously?" Willow's hand went to her mouth. "I thought you were Search and Rescue. Holy shit. I can't imagine dealing with victimized children." Guilt crept up her throat. She hadn't looked into him very carefully before coming to Alabama. What was worse, she had listened to office rumormongering.

"Are you a God-fearing woman?" Maybelle asked, her tone sharp and incredulous.

"Excuse me?" Willow looked over at Jackson, who was actively rolling his eyes. "A God-fearing woman?"

"I don't appreciate your language, young lady. Foul language is the sign of a weak mind, one who is easily influenced by Satan." Maybelle sounded like a Sunday preacher thumping out a sermon from her pulpit. "Up until now, I didn't take you for a weak-minded individual. Did I misjudge you, SA Banks?"

"No." Willow said. "I am neither a God-fearing woman, nor am I weak minded. I speak how I choose to speak, and when I choose to speak. I'm sorry if my use of language offended you. I will do my best to speak more respectfully in your presence, if that's what you'd prefer."

Maybelle pursed her lips and stared at Willow. She held that pose for several seconds before a sly grin widened her mouth. "You could do worse, Jax." Her grin morphed into a toothy smile. "I like her, even if she isn't a God-fearing woman. Now, off to bed. Both of you. I'm tired and I need to think on what you've told me. Something is afoot, but I can't quite see it yet. Off with you now." A shadow of confusion crossed her face. "Did you come all the way here from Beaufort without a change of clothing?"

"No." Willow looked down at her feet. "I brought clothes. I left them in my truck. I'll be right back."

"You'll stay put, young lady." Maybelle looked over at Jackson. "A proper gentleman doesn't let a woman fetch her own bags. I raised you better than this, Jax."

"Keys please," Jackson said. He looked like a little boy. A six-foot-three ten-year-old whose mother had just admonished him.

"I say what I want, and I do what I want, Maybelle." Willow fished the fob for her truck out of her pocket and tossed it to Jackson. "I don't need a man to look after me. But out of respect for you, I will allow your son to bring my bags into your home."

"Bags?" Jackson asked. "How many did you pack?"

"Just three," Willow said. "I didn't think I'd be here for too long. And bring my laptop too if you don't mind."

"I like her, Jax." Mischief sparked in Maybelle's eyes. "Treat her properly. Do you hear me?"

Jackson grumbled, lowered his head, and shuffled toward the front door.

"And don't forget about the kennel, Jax," Maybelle added. "Tommy can't come tonight, and I'm not up to looking after the dogs myself. He said he'll walk and feed them at first light."

"Got it," Jackson said. "I'll bring Willow's bags, and laptop, and then I'll get the dogs settled for the night." He whistled for Ruby, who bolted after him, her tail straight up in the air.

As the door closed, Willow watched Ranger sitting like a perfect gentleman beside the elderly woman. "Are you sure you don't mind me staying here, Maybelle? I don't want to be an imposition."

"You're here to work with your dog, right? Well, if your dog is staying in my kennels, then you're staying in my house. If I'm going to fix your problem with this Malinois, I need to get to know you."

Willow swallowed hard. Nothing had gone the way she'd expected—not even remotely close.

Chapter Twenty

Jackson

Jackson winced as the medical examiner's morgue doors slid open. The sharp scent of chemical disinfectant did little to cover the metallic tang of blood and the lingering odor of decay. The mixture created an unsettling combination that clung to the inside of his nostrils. His gaze was fixated on the bodies of Tanner Montgomery and Rachel Persie.

"Hey, Doc." Jackson swallowed down his gag reflex. No matter how many times he'd visited the county morgue, he simply couldn't get used to its peculiar stench. "What have you got for us?"

Dr. Johnstone's gaze tracked to the doors that Jackson and Willow had just stepped through. "Sorry, Jax. I can't say anything about the case to you... or *her*. I got word that all information was to go directly to your supervisor."

"Excuse me?" Willow said, her eyes wide, and her lips pressed into a thin line.

Dr. Johnstone glowered at Willow while he snapped off his latex gloves and tossed them in a waste pail.

"Sorry, Doc." Jackson tentatively stepped closer to Tanner. There was a large hole directly over his friend's heart. "I think what SA Banks meant to say is, why can't you tell us what you found?"

"I'm sorry that you made the drive out here, Jax," Dr. Johnstone said. "But I received instructions just minutes ago. Had I known sooner, I'd have saved you the effort. If you don't mind, I'm going to head home and get some sleep. I haven't been to bed in over twenty-four hours."

"Hold on, Doc. I don't report to Captain Sawyer," Jackson said. He hustled across the room, cutting off the doctor's progress. "This is official FBI business, and the captain has no authority."

"It wasn't the captain to whom I was referring." Dr. Johnstone pulled off his blood-splattered white smock and tossed it into a large plastic bin. "The message came from SAC Savannah Greene. I believe you know her."

"Yes, I do." Jackson's brow crinkled. "She runs the Birmingham field office. My field office. She told you not to tell me anything?"

"Not specifically you," Dr. Johnstone said. He stepped past Jackson and made his way to a sink. He pumped out a good supply of soap and began washing his hands. "She said, and I quote, 'You are not to share the details of your autopsy with anyone other than myself.'" He scrubbed his hands together, forming a thick lather. "So, unless you can prove that you have clearance from her..." He rinsed off his hands and shook them dry. "Sorry, Jax. I know all about your relationship with Tanner. I wish I could help but my hands are tied here."

"I don't give a shit what you've been told, Doc," Willow said. "I don't report to SAC Greene, and this is my case. By not providing me with your findings, you are obstructing justice. I know you're tired and want to go to bed, and if you continue to stonewall me, I will make sure you have a most uncomfortable and sleepless day."

The ME flashed Jackson a *please save me* look. Under other circumstances, Jackson might have even complied. But, right now, he didn't care what SAC Greene said or thought, he wanted the information as much as Willow did. "I'm sorry for Agent Banks's behavior, but she's not wrong," he said. "This is her investigation and, until she's told to stand down, she is in charge. Not to mention, every minute wasted is time for the killer to get away."

"You're going to get me fired, Jax."

"It seems to be the lesser of two evils," Willow said. "A federal penitentiary is no picnic."

"Yes, ma'am" the doctor said. "I will cooperate fully with the FBI. You're kicking a hornet's nest. You know that, right?"

Willow shrugged and grinned. "It won't be the first time I've been stung, but I have questions for you, and I'm not a terribly patient person."

The waves of animosity flowing off the doctor were palpable. "I live to serve." He spoke the words with calm civility, but his stiff posture suggested he wanted to say something completely different.

"What can you tell me about the ammunition used?" Willow said. It was clear that she didn't care what the doctor thought of her.

"I've got a copy of my autopsy report right here," the ME said as he made his way across the room to a computer covered with a plastic drop cloth. "Just give me your FBI email address and I'll forward it to you."

"I'd prefer a printed copy," Jackson said. "If you don't mind, can you make one for each of us?"

The doctor offered a grunt in response.

"Does your report discuss the specifics of the ammunition?" Willow asked. "That's what I need to know right now."

The doctor ignored Willow's question and sat himself in front of his computer. He clicked a few buttons, stood, and gave the two agents a flat-mouthed stare. "The printer is in the office next door. If you'll follow me, I'll hand them to you."

"It's okay," Willow said with a condescending note. "We'll wait here for you. I have things I want to discuss with Special Agent Brooks. Private things."

The doctor didn't respond. His eyes remained distant, his expression neutral. When the automatic sliding door whispered shut behind him, Willow moved closer, her voice dropping to a low, predatory tone. "Don't you ever do that again."

Jackson flinched and took a small step back. "I have no idea what you're talking about."

"Don't you ever apologize for my behavior." Willow glanced at the exit to the morgue. "The man is frightened, and I don't know why. What I needed him to understand was, SAC Greene isn't the only alligator swimming in his small pond."

"I'm well aware of what you were hoping to accomplish with your aggressive behavior," Jackson said through clenched teeth. "Except you don't know the man. More importantly, you don't know his wife. She is hell on wheels, and now he has an irrational dislike for any woman who he believes is emasculating him. If he's your friend, he'll do what he can to assist. If you make him your enemy, he will stonewall you at every turn—especially if he feels it's to his benefit. I intervened to make sure he knew I was on his side. Remember our agreement? You're in charge, but I know these people, and I know how to deal with them."

"You're right," Willow said, clenching her eyes tight. "I need to treat you better. It's no excuse, but I didn't get much sleep last night which means I've been awake for the better part of forty-eight hours. Ranger insisted on sharing my bed with me, and both Levi and Boone snore."

The idea of her sharing a bed with Ranger made Jackson smile on the inside. He had a king size bed, and Ruby still managed to take up the majority of it. Willow's bed was only a double, which meant Ranger likely spent the night lying on top of her or smooshed up against her. Either way, it was good for their bonding.

Willow nudged Jackson, letting him know the ME was about to return. He had a manila envelope tucked up under his arm. "I've informed your Special Agent in Charge that I was forced to give you these reports," Dr. Johnstone said as the doors closed behind him.

The ME clearly struggled with strong women, and Savannah was one of the most forceful people Jackson had ever met. The doctor also seemed pleased that he was indirectly making Willow's life as difficult as possible. "Ms. Greene sounded particularly annoyed that there was an out-of-state agent on the case. I expect you're going to have a very bad day, Agent Banks."

"Doctor Johnstone," Willow said, inclining her head slightly. Her voice was contrite and subdued. "I need to apologize for my behavior earlier. As you can understand, the death of an FBI agent has me on edge, and like you, I'm horribly sleep deprived. However, neither are an excuse for my treating you in any manner other than respectfully."

"Um... thank you." The ME stood taller. "We all have our jobs to do." He took the envelope out from under his arm and handed it to Willow. "Everything I know about the murders is in here."

Something in the way he said '*know*' suggested that he wasn't being completely honest. Judging by Willow's expression, she had picked up on the same thing.

"What isn't in the report?" Jackson asked. "It sounds like you held some information back."

"There is no tox screen and no ballistics report." The ME still sounded like he was being cagey. "The labs haven't sent me the results yet."

"Seriously?" Willow asked. "I'd have expected the labs would have pushed everything aside to make this case a top priority."

"I only just sent them my samples a few hours ago," the doctor said. "The murder scene was a jurisdictional nightmare. The Florence PD were securing the scene when the SBI showed up. While they were arguing over who had authority, I went to the laundromat to deal with Detective Franklin's death. I ended up having to wait there for the CSI team to show up, which took over three hours. Apparently, they couldn't spare anyone because they were busy at Yumm. By the time the SBI met me, I found out that they were told to back off and wait for the FBI CSI team to arrive. I wasn't able to collect the bodies of Ms. Persie and Mr. Montgomery until well after midnight. Your SAC has been riding my case all night long, insisting I get my job done. Meanwhile, I've got the mayor screaming at me, saying, and I quote—'Fuck the FBI. Get the samples to my people at the SBI.'" The poor man was about to explode. "I follow protocols, Jax, but I also serve at the pleasure of the mayor. I've got too many masters."

"Jesus, Doctor," Willow said. "I'm really sorry that I added to your already horrific day. But if you could help us out, I'm certain the mayor would appreciate it. Can you please tell us what you didn't include in the report?"

Jackson watched in amazement at how Willow was pandering to the man. In mere seconds, she had turned an adversary into a cooperative ally. It was interesting how she was leveraging the ME's relationship with the mayor, leaving Savannah completely out of the conversation.

"I'm not a ballistics expert," the ME said, "but I'm going to guess that, unless there were multiple shooters, the murderer used two different bullets in his gun. I've been doing this for a long time, and I've never seen that before."

"What do you mean?" Jackson asked. "I can guarantee there was only one shooter and one gun." He thought back to the video. Rachel had been shot three times, but only a single bullet penetrated her skull.

"The bullet that killed Mr. Montgomery was a hollow point. Given the size of the entry wound, I'm guessing it was a nine-millimeter." Dr. Johnstone motioned to Tanner's body. "When the bullet struck his ribs, it flattened out and fragmented. His internal injuries were catastrophic. I am guessing that it killed him instantly." He turned to address Rachel. "Ms. Persie was shot in the mouth and through both of her eyes. The bullet to the mouth struck her upper teeth. Like the bullet that killed Mr. Montgomery, it was also a hollow point. It fragmented heavily and changed direction on impact, destroying her palette and traveling up into her cranial cavity. Based on the patterns of the damage, I believe this was the first shot. The second shot, also with a hollow point, went through her left eye. The bullet obliterated much of her brain and flattened out against her occipital bone." He tapped the back of his head to show where he meant. "The third and final bullet was full metal jacket, or something similar. It passed through her eye, through what was left of her gray matter, and out her skull. The exit wound was relatively clean, considering." He looked directly at Willow as he finished. "I didn't include any of this information in my findings because it is conjecture, and I was told by SAC Greene to only include what I could prove in court."

"Did she not think your professional opinion was important?" Willow asked. "Surely, your expert conjecture would be meaningful to her."

The doctor pressed his lips into a thin line that suggested that the SAC had no interest in his expert opinion.

"Where did you send the bullets and the testing samples?" Jackson asked. "I'm assuming that SAC Greene insisted they be sent to her."

"She did," the ME said, raising his eyebrows. "Unfortunately, I had already couriered them to the SBI. The mayor had beaten her to the punch. I took additional tissue and stomach samples and sent those to Ms. Greene along with a note that said she'd need to get the ballistics report from the SBI."

"Well," Jackson said. "I guess we should be heading over to the labs if we want to see the forensic reports."

The ME nodded and motioned towards the exit. "If there is nothing more that you need of me, agents, I really would like to get home and get some sleep."

"Thank you, Doctor," Willow said. "We appreciate your help."

The ME didn't reply. He quietly exited the room, leaving Jackson and Willow to their own devices.

Jackson watched the doctor leave, his mind already racing with the new information. The use of different bullets was unusual and could be a crucial clue. He felt a surge of energy. They were making progress, and every piece of evidence brought them closer to arresting his best friend's killer.

Chapter Twenty-One

Willow

"Have you ever heard of an unsub using two different types of ammunition in the same gun?" Willow asked as she slid into the passenger seat. Jackson had been quiet as they'd exited the building.

Jackson shielded his eyes from the morning sun streaming in through the windshield. Without a word, he put his truck into gear and pulled out of the parking lot.

"Well?" Willow prodded.

"Sorry, no," he said. "I've never heard of someone loading different rounds into their weapon. Maybe the shooter was out of full metal jackets and hollow points was all he had left." He reached into his pocket, pulled out a small metal box, and took out a pill, which he dry-swallowed.

"That sounds unlikely," Willow said, resisting the urge to inquire about the pill. "The killer was too methodical and calculated in his assault. I'm certain the different bullets were loaded intentionally."

"Likely, but I can't for the life of me imagine why." Jackson slowed the truck at a stop light. "So, you didn't sleep well? You didn't mention that during breakfast or while we were walking the dogs."

"I'm not much of a talker in the morning," Willow said with a snort. "I live alone and typically spend my mornings drinking a half gallon of coffee while reviewing whatever case I'm working on."

"Yeah," Jackson said as the light turned green, accelerating smoothly through the intersection. "That's all going to change. Having a dog will disrupt everything in your life, but in the best way possible."

Maybe life with a dog wouldn't be so bad. Willow thought back to her morning walk, and the companionable silence she'd shared with Jackson and their dogs.

"Your mom's amazing," Willow said, changing the subject. "I bet she was a force to be reckoned with in her youth."

"She still is. I suspect she'll be that way until the moment she passes to the afterlife."

"Was it true?" Willow asked. "Did she really help you and your father with your cases?"

"She's remarkably insightful." He rubbed the back of his neck. "When I was growing up, I used to listen to her and my dad discuss his cases. My dad had a stellar reputation, and I expect she was a major contributor to his success. She tried to help me as well, but I didn't like discussing my VCAC cases with her. I didn't want her to know the level of evil people could sink to. I wish I had never known."

"I'm sure she already knows," Willow said, rubbing her arms to shake off the dirty feeling that came with thoughts of human cruelty. "I don't think much gets past her."

"No," Jackson said, anger seeping into his voice. "People think they know, or they think they can imagine what it's like... but they can't. Nobody wants to truly know just how—"

"We don't need to talk about it," Willow interjected, placing her hand on his forearm. He was gripping the wheel like he wanted to rip it from the steering column. Something had happened to him, something so bad that it had forced him to leave the task force. Special Agents didn't typically stay in the VCAC for more than five years, but his reaction suggested there was something significant that had caused him to change to Search and Rescue.

"If you don't mind me asking," Jackson said, "how do you know ASAC Alice Baldwin? I have to say, I was surprised to get a call from her asking for my help."

"Through my partner," Willow replied, realizing she hadn't considered how her meeting with Jackson had been set up. "Kate and she were... close. They had been living together for a few months when Kate was killed."

"Well, that explains a lot." Jackson nodded as he spoke. "When she asked me to help you, she spoke of Ranger like she knew him well. And she spoke very highly of you. She also thought you'd benefit from having the dog in your life. My guess is, she thought it would help you heal."

A debilitating wave of sorrow washed over Willow. She became despondent, struggling to draw a breath. She couldn't fathom how, in the midst of her own grief, Alice's thoughts had turned to her and Ranger. It made Willow feel small. After Kate died, the only person she thought of was herself. Her family had tried to reach out to her, to console her, but she wanted no part of it. She was angry at the world, but mostly, she was angry with herself. She had been the cause of her partner's death. It had been her own hubris that had cost Kate her life. She had told Willow to hold her position, but she couldn't stand the idea that the perps might escape. All she cared about was making the collar. It was because of her actions that Ranger was put into a perilous position that had forced his owner to protect his life. A teardrop fell onto her hand, snapping her out of the memory. She was clutching her chest while bawling her eyes out. "Jesus, Jackson. I'm sorry. I..."

"Don't be," he said, his voice filled with caring and concern. "Believe me when I say, I understand. If I wasn't still numb from Tanner's death..." Jackson barely choked out the words.

"How's about we talk about something different, okay?" Willow said, wiping the tracks of her tears from her cheeks. "We can't show up at the crime labs looking like a pair of sad sacks."

Jackson blew out a long breath and shook his shoulders, as if trying to rid himself of his grief. "Sure. What do you want to talk about?"

"Why did she call you? I mean, what made her think of you to help me with Ranger?"

"Alice and my dad worked together for a few years. Apparently, we met when I was a young teen while she was visiting the house." Jackson grimaced. "I have no memory of it. None whatsoever."

"I imagine you were too busy chasing girls to notice your parents' friends. Do you have a wife or a girlfriend back home in Birmingham?" Willow instantly regretted asking the last question. She wasn't even sure why she had. Well, she knew why. The man was tall, and handsome, and as kind as anyone she had ever met... but still, it's not like she was going to have a relationship with him. She was staying until the case was over, and she got the training she needed for Ranger. After that, she'd drive home to her sad little one-bedroom apartment.

"No, I'm not married, nor do I have a girlfriend. Ruby and I are on the road a lot, and there was no way I could be in a serious relationship, especially while I was on loan to the VCAC."

"On loan? You weren't permanently assigned to the task force?"

"No. Ruby and I were brought in to help track some missing children that were being held captive in a remote cabin. She was so effective that they kept calling us in to help." Jackson's brow furrowed. "Saving the kids was the only thing that kept me coming back. Each case I worked stole a piece of my soul, but how could I say no to helping children?"

"So, what made you leave then?"

Jackson's throat bobbed. "I needed to be with my mother. When I heard of her condition, I put in for a leave of absence.

Savannah refused to grant it, but she said she could send me here on assignment to help with the city's K9 unit."

"And when you got here, you discovered the corruption in the PD?" When Jackson didn't respond, Willow pressed harder. "Did it occur to you that she did it intentionally, to put you in a perfect position to *discover* the corruption?"

Jackson paused to navigate a corner through a crowd of pedestrians crossing against the light. "I hadn't considered that. Savannah showed me pictures, videos, and even some bank records that proved the captain was dirty. She insisted that it wasn't enough to take him down. She was certain there was a long list of officers who were a part of the stink. She said she'd support me remotely while I built a case against the department. Savannah worked out all the details with the chief."

"And now Levi is saying the chief is dirty and the captain is a righteous man." Willow rubbed her hands over her pant legs. "Kind of makes you wonder, doesn't it? Someone's lying. The question is... who?"

Jackson seemed irritated by the question, although Willow thought it had everything to do with the contradicting evidence. Levi had provided no concrete proof that the captain was a good man or that the chief was corrupt. Then again, photos and videos don't lie.

"We're here," Jackson said as he hit his signal light.

Chapter Twenty-Two

Jackson

The heavy tires of Jackson's pickup rumbled over the grate marking the entrance to the parking lot of the Alabama State Bureau of Investigation. He pulled up to the gate and lowered his window. A rotund rent-a-cop emerged from his small guardhouse, his gray-blue shirt straining at every button. "Good morning. How can I help you today?"

Jackson extended his FBI badge with a smile. "Special Agents Brooks and Banks. You can help by letting us pass."

The man stepped closer, requesting to inspect the badges. His nameplate read Robert Roberts.

"Is there a problem, Bob?" Willow interjected from the passenger seat, earning herself a scowl.

"No problem. I'm doing my job, ma'am." Bob returned Jackson's badge. "If you don't like the way I'm conducting my business, you're free to take it up with my supervisor." He motioned for Willow to hand over her credentials.

"Mr. Roberts," Jackson said, his patience wearing thin. "We're in the middle of a double homicide investigation. The FBI has set up a command center here. I would appreciate your cooperation in this matter."

Bob ignored Jackson completely, his beady black eyes locked on Willow with obvious contempt. "Your badge. Now." When he held out his hand with the entitled impatience of a small man drunk on what little power he had, it became clear that things were about to escalate.

"Do you really want to fuck with me, Bob?" Willow clipped her badge to her waistband, refusing to relinquish it. "I've already shown you my badge, and you've inspected Agent Brooks's. I don't need to speak with your supervisor, not when I can have you thrown in jail for impeding a federal investigation. Now, open the gate and get back to your breakfast burrito, or whatever the fuck is dribbling down your belly."

Rather than acquiesce, the guard's face reddened, bubbles forming at the corners of his mouth. His eyes narrowed as he leaned towards the open window. "I'm not doing a goddamn thing to prevent you from doing whatever investigation you want to be doing. What I'm doing is preventing you from entering a state-owned employee parking lot. If this patch of pavement is part of your investigation, bring me a warrant and I'll gladly lift the gate for you. Otherwise, get off this property, or I'll call the police."

"Special Agent Jackson Brooks for Chief Wheeler," Jackson said into his cell phone. "Wait, Marcy, before you do, can you send a squad car to the south parking lot of the SBI complex? I need the security guard taken into custody."

The passenger door slammed, and Willow yelled for the guard to raise his hands. Jackson watched through the windshield as she drew her weapon. Bob flailed like an overweight wacky waving inflatable tube guy. "You can pass. You can pass. Jesus Christ. I'll open the gate for you!"

"Against the wall," Willow commanded. "Do you really think you can treat federal agents like this and get away without repercussions?"

"I was only doing as I was told," the guard pleaded, practically throwing himself against the guardhouse. "My boss left explicit instructions not to let anyone who wasn't an employee into the parking lot. The place has been overrun with news crews and reporters... I swear to Jesus, I was only doing as I was told."

"What do you say, Special Agent Brooks?" Willow wore an evil grin, reminiscent of a Disney villain relishing someone else's pain. "Should we give this man a break? After all, he was only following orders." She had already holstered her gun and was returning to the passenger side.

"Mr. Roberts," Jackson said, his tone stern but measured. "If you would be so kind as to open the gate. You have already wasted far too much of our time today."

The man spun around, his eyes bulging as they jumped between the two agents. "You're not going to arrest me?"

"I'll give you a pass," Jackson replied. "Next time, when federal agents suggest you do something, maybe apply a bit of critical thinking before falling back on 'I was told to do it.'"

Bob scurried into his cramped guardhouse and slammed his palm on the button to raise the barricade.

"I can't believe you pulled your gun on him," Jackson said as he parked his truck. "He's a parking lot attendant. Did you really believe he was armed?"

Willow responded with a loud snort. "Did you really call for backup?"

Jackson pressed his mouth into a thin-lipped smile and exited the truck. They walked in silence until rounding the corner to the front of the SBI building. Four news crew vans were parked out front, with at least two dozen reporters held back behind barricades. Two police officers managed crowd control. One reporter called out Jackson by name, sparking a chorus of pleas for interviews. Jackson placed his hand on the small of Willow's back, guiding her past the throng, towards the building's main entrance.

"SA Brooks," a familiar voice called out. "I need to speak with you."

Jackson scanned the crowd, searching for the source. He cocked an eyebrow upon spotting Johnnie Walker struggling to push his way to the front.

"Don't you dare get us pulled into that frenzy," Willow warned. "If you engage, we're going to spend the rest of the morning dealing with these jackals."

"Agent Brooks," Johnnie called again, using his stocky body to shove aside a cameraman. "I need to speak with you."

Jackson hesitated, torn between the need for potential evidence and the urgency of their task at hand. Johnnie had filmed everyone coming and going from the restaurant. It wasn't unheard of for killers to linger nearby, watching the chaos they'd sown. Like arsonists watching their fires, murderers often observed the aftermath—sometimes to gloat, other times to gauge how the police were handling the case. Based on the crime scene and the killer's brazen behavior, Jackson pegged him as a narcissist, likely a psychopath. The use of the flashbang grenade was as much a statement as it was a tactic. The obscene overkill used against Rachel, and the up-close attack on Tanner... they didn't fit in Jackson's head. One was an act of passion, the other calculated and deliberate.

"We need to talk to that reporter," Jackson said, pointing to Johnnie. "He was at the scene filming outside. He might have caught the killer on camera."

"Not now," Willow insisted, grabbing him by the shirt and dragging him forward. "Find him later, when he's not in the middle of a feeding frenzy."

She was right, and Jackson knew it. But still, his gut screamed at him to speak to Johnnie. As Willow pulled him toward the building, Jackson sought out the student. When they locked eyes, Jackson tapped on his watch, raised his hand in a brief apologetic wave, and shrugged helplessly. The disappointment in Johnnie's eyes was immediate and intense. Their connection wasn't lost on several nearby reporters, who converged on the young man, obscuring him from sight.

"I have to ask," Willow said after they were well away from the crowd. "If you knew he had footage of the scene, why didn't you secure it the same way you did selfie-girl's?"

Jackson glanced back over his shoulder. "I was kind of busy at the time. I took the girl's camera because she was corrupting the murder scene."

"Well, you can kiss that tape goodbye then," Willow said. "The mayor has already confiscated all the cell phones. If Levi's right, and the mayor is dirty, those cell phone videos will never see the light of day."

"I don't care if the mayor's corrupt or not. The man's daughter was murdered. I can't see him doing anything to obstruct the investigation. Not intentionally at least. My guess is, he wanted to make sure they were sent to the SBI for processing."

"Why?" Willow shot Jackson a questioning look. "He doesn't trust the FBI's forensic teams?"

"You'll see in a minute," Jackson said, sprinting up the grand staircase leading to the building's entrance.

Chapter Twenty-Three

Willow

Willow failed to keep pace with Jackson as he took the stairs leading up to the office building four at a time. By the time she stepped through the revolving glass doors, the special agent was already in conversation with the building's rent-a-cop. Her tennis shoes squeaked as she crossed the marble-tiled floor. The opulence of the surroundings struck her immediately. It seemed that everything was glass, marble, and granite, and it all gleamed to shiny perfection.

"Savannah's set up a command center on the fourteenth floor," Jackson said as Willow neared. She was still taking in the pristine surroundings. "I want to start at the ballistics lab though."

Willow was relieved that the security guards inside the building weren't giant asshats like the man guarding the parking lot. "Which floor?" she asked as they stepped into the all-mirrored elevator.

"Ten."

As the door closed, light instrumental jazz music filled the space. Jackson was clenching his jaw, while his hands fidgeted by his side. "Expecting problems? You look like you're ready to crawl out of your skin."

"No…" he said. He shook out his hands like he was trying to force himself to relax. "A bit. Something about this case is making me uneasy, like there is a storm over the horizon. Everyone seems to be at odds with each other."

All Willow could do was shrug. She felt the same way, but she couldn't quite put her finger on what it was that left her feeling uneasy. Before she could say anything more, the elevator dinged, and the doors slid open, along with her lower jaw. She gaped at the office accommodations. The Alabama State Bureau of Investigation seal was crafted into the floor as a glass mosaic. Beyond the emblem was a massive mahogany desk with three receptionists dressed in matching dark-blue uniforms wearing headsets.

"Jesus Christ," Willow said as she continued to gawk. "Is your federal building in Birmingham anywhere near this nice? This place makes the Charleston office look like a backwater slum."

"How may I help you?" the perky, redheaded receptionist asked. Her gaze was firmly fixed on Jackson as she tucked a lock of hair behind her ear.

"FBI Special Agents Brooks and Banks," Willow said, holding up her badge. "We're looking for the ballistics lab. Can you point us in the right direction? It's the first time we've been here."

The receptionist's lust-filled smile faded. She looked Willow up and down and, with a hint of a sneer, pointed to her right. "Follow the signs. You can't miss it." She adjusted the mic on her headpiece and pressed a button on her switchboard. "Two FBI agents are heading for the ballistics lab."

"It sounded like she was calling ahead," Willow murmured. "It feels like we're being announced at a five-star hotel or something."

"The SBI receives a lot of private funding," Jackson said. "It was a part of the mayor's push to fight crime in Florence. It resulted in substantial donations over the past years."

Willow scoffed. "And nobody questioned why private individuals were funding state-run institutions. That's got to be seen as a conflict of interest."

"Supposedly, third party commissions dug into it all, along with the DA." Jackson shrugged. "There didn't seem to be any sign of corruption or quid pro quo." He placed his mouth close enough that Willow could feel his warm breath on her ear. "I thought nothing of it, but if Levi was right about the mayor and DA being dirty... how easy would it be to make this sort of thing appear legit?"

"If the chief is a part of this, too..." Willow's thoughts fell away as she caught sight of a man in a rumpled blue suit strolling towards them. His expression was a mixture of relief and regret when his eyes fell on Jackson.

"Jesus, Jax. I'm so sorry," the man said. He held out his arms, inviting the much taller Jackson in for a hug. The two men embraced for several seconds, slapping each other's backs. When they pulled away, both had glassy eyes.

Jackson cleared his throat. "Willow, this is Special Agent Thomas Crenshaw from the VCAC unit. He's one of the best I've ever worked with."

Thomas thrust his hand towards Willow. "Ah, you must be Special Agent Willow Banks. I'm pleased to meet you. I hear you brought your K9 with you. We'll take all the help we can get in tracking down Levi Benson."

Willow wanted to bitch-slap the man. "Why are you conducting a manhunt for an innocent man? There is video evidence that Levi was at the laundromat up the street."

Crenshaw's brow knitted into a tight V before he turned to Jackson. "What is she talking about? There were over two dozen eyewitnesses at the murder scene. One of the murder victims even called him out by name."

"Is your boss intentionally tanking the investigation?" Willow said. "I understand the mayor has a hard-on for Levi, but what's the SAC got against him?"

"If you're referring to the video evidence from the laundromat," Crenshaw said with an overly dismissive gesture, "it doesn't exist. We've been through the hard drives and the cloud storage. Either the cameras didn't work, or they simply weren't set to record."

"How about that the two of us were there," Jackson said. "Is our word good enough for you?"

The agent's pissy expression melted into confusion. "You were both there?" He cracked the knuckles of his left hand. "Savannah said it was only you, and that we should take your version of events with a grain of salt."

"And why would she say that?" Willow asked. She couldn't fathom why Jackson had put his SAC on a pedestal when it seemed she was either incompetent, or she was so fixated on her political aspirations that arresting anyone was better than arresting the right one.

"Follow me," the agent mumbled. "SAC Greene is in the ballistics lab right now. You two can ask her yourself." Crenshaw spun about and marched away, his footfalls heavy and deliberate.

"I thought you said he was the best you'd ever worked with," Willow whispered.

"I lied," Jackson mumbled back to her. "What was I going to say, here comes Thomas Crenshaw, the worst agent I've ever worked with? That's not fair of me. He's not a bad agent, but he doesn't think outside the box. If it's not directly in front of him, he won't see it. But in the field, the man is fierce and utterly fearless."

The pair followed Crenshaw through the maze of corridors and cubicles until they arrived at another set of glass doors etched with the word "Ballistics". Beyond the doors, in an all-glass office, was a furious-looking woman in a blue blazer and a matching pencil skirt, two men in non-descript black suits standing behind her, a frightened-looking man in a white lab coat and a large, beefy man with a crew cut who appeared to be taking the brunt of the woman's wrath. Off to the side was a squat, heavy-set man in a suit standing in front of two Florence PD officers.

"We're late to the party," Willow said as she peered through the glass door. "This is going to be a humongous clusterfuck."

When Crenshaw pushed open the door, a din of voices came pouring out. A second later, they all silenced. "I think most of you know SA Brooks. This is SA Willow Banks from the Charleston office. She was first on the scene and has been working with Jackson."

Outside of the severe-looking blonde woman striding forward, everyone else barely even acknowledged their arrival. She was a couple of inches shorter than Willow with narrow hips and a nearly flat chest. "Well, well," she said, her tone cutting. "Look who finally decided to grace us with their presence."

"Good morning, Savannah," Jackson said. He checked the wall clock and winced. No wonder he felt famished. It was well past 1:00 p.m. "I mean, good afternoon. I'm surprised to find you here."

"One of my agents was murdered, Jax," Savannah replied. The woman's voice was deep, rich, and exuded power. "Where else would I be?" Her deep blue eyes shifted to Willow. "I'm guessing you're the one who took it upon herself to assume the lead in this investigation."

"I am, ma'am," Willow said. She approached SAC Savannah Greene and extended her hand. "I'm SA Willow Banks, and I'd like to know why you've prevented two on-site agents from accessing critical, time-sensitive information."

Savannah eyed Willow's outstretched hand with disdain before returning her attention to Jackson. "I've got a binder set up for you in the war room. It's got all the forensic analysis, autopsies, and a complete dossier on our prime suspect, Levi Benson." She turned back towards the man in the lab coat. "I'm just waiting for this petty functionary to hand over the rest of our evidence."

"The petty functionary is doing his job," the beefy man with the crewcut said. "Like I said, SAC Greene, as soon as we're finished with our analysis, you are welcome to have the bullets and our reports. Until then, they stay with us."

"And like *I* said, SSA Marsden, this is a federal investigation and the SBI holds no standing. I'm demanding you hand everything over right now."

"Produce a federal warrant, and I will happily comply." Marsden's eyebrows shot up while he waited for Savannah's retort.

"I want them within the hour," Savannah said. She pushed past Jackson and swept out the glass doors. Crenshaw and the two non-descript agents followed.

"Agents Brooks and Banks," Marsden said, offering his meaty hand in greeting. "SSA Jeff Marsden. I was hoping to speak with the two of you."

The heavy-set man in the suit came over with his pair of uniformed police officers. "Special Agent Brooks," he said to Jackson as he approached. "Are you here to feed the storm?"

"Castor," Jackson said with a curt nod. "This is Special Agent Willow Banks. Willow, this is Detective Castor. He was Franklin's partner."

The heavy-set man's face crumpled at the mention of his partner's name. The sight of it made Willow's heart ache for him. "Detective," Willow said, extending her hand. "I'm sorry for your loss."

Castor accepted her gesture and gave her hand a firm shake. "Why are you protecting him, Jackson?" he said. The moment of grief in the detective's eyes vanished. "Levi did it. We found his gun and a suppressor tucked away in his hovel. As soon as the SBI are finished with their analysis, we'll know for sure that it was the weapon used in the murders."

"Jesus Christ, Castor," Marsden said. "Stop fixating on Mr. Benson. How many times do we need to go over this? He was at the laundromat. Captain Sawyer confirmed it himself. There were multiple witnesses that saw him washing his clothes at the time of the murders."

Castor threw his hands in the air. "Do you not think it's convenient that the laundromat security tapes show nothing? The cameras all mysteriously stopped recording at midnight last night."

"And all the videos taken at the restaurant have blurry faces," Marsden yelled. "There is no definitive proof that Mr. Benson was in the restaurant."

"Yet you continue to ignore the fact that there were dozens of eyewitnesses who saw him there," Castor shot back.

"What do you mean the videos all have blurry faces on them?" Jackson asked.

Willow's mind raced, trying to piece together the conflicting information. It bothered her that she hadn't seen the laundromat video, but she did see selfie-girl's. There was no doubt in her mind that the murderer was not Levi, but evidence was piling up against him. The situation was becoming more complex by the minute, and she couldn't shake the feeling that they were missing something crucial.

Chapter Twenty-Four

Jackson

"Explain to me again about the restaurant videos," Jackson said. "How are their faces blurry?" At SSA Marsden's request, the group had moved to a small conference room to continue their discussion.

"I don't know how or why they're blurry," Marsden said. "My IT guys are having a go at them. As a goodwill gesture, I gave half the phones to your SAC to let her techs also have a crack at it."

Jackson squeezed his eyes tight, doing his best to not bellow at the SBI agent.

"I don't think that's what he was asking," Willow said, her voice cutting through the tension. "He wanted a better description of what you meant by blurry faces."

"Every video," Castor said, dragging out the words for effect. "The faces are impossible to make out, yet the rest of the images are crystal clear." He finished the statement with an eye roll.

"I've always known you to be a good detective," Jackson fired back at Castor. "Why are you ignoring the evidence and letting your emotions guide you instead?"

"Fuck you, Jax," Castor said. "You're harboring a known fugitive. That's another charge I'll add to your list."

"Harboring a fugitive. Are you insane? We saw the whole thing," Willow said, earning herself a sharp glare from Jackson. "We have a video of the murders. Every face is perfectly clear, and the killer is definitely not Levi. I compared them myself."

"Goddamnit!" Marsden slammed his hand on the table. "So, Castor's been right all along. You do have Mr. Benson." His gaze bored into Willow. "That's the only way you could be so sure. You were gone from the laundromat by the time the paramedics arrived, but witnesses saw you and Levi leave together."

"Levi's being railroaded," Willow said. "I got him out of there before something bad happened to him." Her face tightened in concentration. "I don't get it. Castor insists Levi did it, and you say it couldn't be him."

"I'm not changing my mind," Castor said, pacing as he ticked off the points on his fingers. "The evidence against Benson is rock solid. One: his ex-fiancée called him out by name in the restaurant. Two:"—he held up a second finger—"his blood-covered boots match the tread at the scene. And three:"—he stopped pacing and tapped the desk—"his gun, which ballistics should confirm fired the bullet we recovered. After that, it's just tying the boots to Benson through DNA and the blood to Miss Persie. It all adds up, and I don't see how it won't."

Willow scoffed. "That's completely circumstantial. I'm telling you; he couldn't have been there."

Jackson watched the two men closely. Their faces gave nothing away, but a quick glance between them told him they were holding something back. He didn't know the SBI agent, but he knew Castor well enough. Based on Jackson's investigation so far, all indications were that Castor and Franklin were the captain's number one and two in his crime ring.

"Okay, SA Brooks," Marsden said, filling the silence after Willow's remark. "You've made it obvious that you have Mr. Benson tucked away somewhere, which is fine for now. It's a federal case, and it's within your prerogative to hold him in your custody. But you're making yourself look more and more like an accessory to the murders, and you're dragging SA Banks down with you."

Willow's face flushed as she pressed her palms on the table. She looked ready to launch herself at the SBI agent. "Are you kidding me? You think he's involved in this? You think he had his best friend murdered?"

"Why are you in Florence, Jackson?" Castor asked, his voice smooth and menacing. "The PD didn't need a K9 trainer. Our unit was doing just fine before you got here. All the while, you've been poking into Captain Sawyer. For what? To discredit his investigation into the Chief?"

Jackson struggled to keep up. The constant change of topic was an interview tactic, one that he had put to good use over his career. The idea that the captain was investigating the chief was laughable. The evidence that Jackson had collected made that clear. It painted Captain Sawyer as the mastermind behind systemic corruption in the PD. And yet, Castor's words lined up with Levi's assertion that he was a righteous man.

"Where is all the money coming from?" Marsden said, never giving Jackson a chance to answer Castor's question. "How are you paying for everything? I know how much you and your mother make. And yet, you're living in a waterfront house, you run a charity kennel, have a private nurse, and you're putting your mother through experimental cancer therapy."

Jackson's jaw slackened. The questions and accusations continued like rapid-fire blows, each one striking him harder than the last. They knew too much—about the house, the kennel, and his mother's condition. Was she really enrolled in experimental cancer therapy? If she was, why hadn't she said anything to him about it? He'd accompanied her to all her doctor's appointments, except when work got in the way. Her nurse... he never considered how she was being paid. His mother simply told him not to worry about it and to concentrate on doing his job.

"Are you expecting us to believe you didn't know about your mother's treatments?" Marsden stood from his chair and leaned over the table like a predator about to devour his prey. "You never noticed the tens of thousands of dollars being deposited into your mother's bank account? She went to the bank once a month and deposited huge sums of cash. Always cash."

Jackson's mind reeled, trying to reconcile this new information with what he thought he knew. Despite his being home for the last six months, he didn't monitor his mother's every move. She had her nurse to manage her day-to-day needs. Had he been so wrapped up in his assignment that he was oblivious? Had he been too scared of losing her to see the truth?

"You're as corrupt as the chief," Castor declared, his tone icy. "You're going to go to jail, and your mother is going to spend what's left of her life wondering if you're getting shanked in gen-pop. Dirty cops, especially feds, don't tend to last long in state prison."

"If you've got all this evidence," Willow said. "Why are you talking about it with Jackson and not arresting him? Because it's all bullshit. That's why. A steaming pile of crap."

Castor and Willow looked like they were about to go to blows. Jackson wanted to intervene, but he was still neck-deep in trying to process the news of his mother's experimental therapy. "How do you know so much about my mother's condition and her treatments?"

"We've seen her medical reports," Marsden said. "It was a part of our investigation into you."

"The SBI is investigating me?" Jackson barely got the words out. "What? Is that why the captain said he was out to get me?" His mind and body went numb when Marsden dropped that nuclear bomb on his head. Tension clamped down on his neck like a hound dog on a bone. He scrambled for his meds. His hands were shaking so badly he dropped the case, spilling its contents across the floor. While he stared down in disbelief, Willow dropped to her knees and gathered up the pills.

"The floor's pretty clean," she said. Her blue eyes were filled with sympathy. "They're probably okay."

Two pills were in Jackson's mouth before he even considered how dirty they might be. Both got stuck in his throat. His mouth had gone bone dry making it impossible to swallow. "Do you have any water?" he asked, tapping his throat as he did. Neither Marsden nor Castor moved.

"Jesus Christ," Willow said. She kicked the back of Castor's chair as she walked past him. "What the hell is wrong with you people? You're going to let him choke?"

"The kitchen is to the left," Marsden said. "There are water bottles in the fridge."

"I don't know how you're linked to all of this," Castor said. "But we're going to prove it, and we're going to bury you so deep that you'll never see the light of day as long as you live."

"How did you get my mother's medical records?" Jackson asked. Castor's threats meant nothing to him, but he wanted to know why they were investigating him. On what grounds were they able to get a warrant for his mother's personal information? Before either of the men could speak, the answer came to him. "Never mind. I know how. You got a court order from Persie's cousin, Judge Mayfield. It seems the mayor's reach is longer than even Levi knew."

"What's that supposed to mean?" Castor said. "What does the mayor have to do with this?" The questioning look he shot at Marsden suggested Jackson had struck a nerve.

"Are you charging me with anything?" Jackson asked. "If not, I would like to leave now." He stood from his chair and cocked an eyebrow at the SBI agent. "I didn't think so. But I have a question for you, SSA Marsden. Who asked you to investigate me?"

Before Marsden could answer, the sound of quick footsteps in the hallway caught Jackson's attention. He turned towards the door just as Willow reappeared, a water bottle in one hand and a slight smile playing on her lips. Behind her trailed a petite woman in a lab coat, clutching a red file folder to her chest.

"We're under no obligation to tell you anything," Castor said, his eyes darting between Jackson and the new arrival.

"And I find it curious that you never bothered to ask me about what happened to Franklin," Jackson said, giving Willow a curt nod. He was on a roll and had no intention of slowing down. "If my partner committed suicide, I'd want to know everything about it, and yet, you're asking about my mother's financials. And more so, how did Franklin get to the laundromat so quickly? I'm guessing he wasn't there to do his own laundry. The only reason for it was because he knew Levi would be there. From what I saw, he wasn't there to arrest him. He was there to murder him." Then it dawned on him. "That was the personal business that Marcy had told me about. When I requested you two at the murder scene, she said Franklin was busy with personal business."

"Fuck you, Jax," Castor said. "I think it's convenient that the person we're investigating is the only witness to my partner's death."

"He wasn't the only witness," Willow said. "You already know I was there, as was the assistant manager. Your captain even interviewed the woman."

"What are you doing here, Betsie?" Marsden asked. The woman in the lab coat held up a red folder and shook it lightly.

"She's got the entire set of lab reports," Willow said as she tossed Jackson a bottle of water. "I ran into her on the way back here. It looks like we might get some answers after all."

Jackson caught the water bottle and unscrewed the cap. While he guzzled the contents, he tried to consider everything he had just heard. It had to have been a mix of truth and lies. He hoped the lab reports might help shed some light on which was which.

Chapter Twenty-Five

Willow

Willow pulled out a chair for Betsie and retook her seat. "What can you tell us?" Willow asked.

"Not a word," Marsden said to Betsie, holding up his hand like a stop sign. He turned back to Willow. "Get your information from your own forensics team. Our findings are a part of our investigation, and we have no obligation to share those with you."

"Sweet Jesus." Willow leaned back in her chair and stared at the ceiling. When she'd told Jackson the investigation was going to be a clusterfuck, she hadn't realized just how massive it would be. "You understand this is a federal investigation, SSA Marsden?" Willow continued to stare up at the acoustic tiles. "By refusing to give us access to the information, you are essentially committing obstruction of justice. You know full well that you are the only ones who have the bullets." She leaned forward and blew out a long breath, making clear her frustration. "Do you truly believe that either of us is involved in the murders? What possible motive could Jackson have?"

"He hated Ms. Persie," Castor said. "Word is, he's hated her since his college days."

"So, you're thinking he killed his best friend to get back at the mayor's daughter?" Willow barked out a laugh. "You can't possibly believe that's true, not if you're the solid detective that Jackson thinks you are."

"I didn't hate her," Jackson said. He had his hands wrapped behind his head while his forehead rested on the conference table. Willow wondered if he was in the midst of a full-on migraine. "I didn't hate her, but I didn't like her. She was an egocentric prima donna who didn't care who she hurt, not if she thought it benefited her. Rachel took great pleasure in humiliating others. She believed that it made her appear bigger if she made those around her look smaller."

"Where's Mr. Benson?" Marsden asked. "Show us that you're not involved by telling us where you're hiding the killer."

"Do you have a laptop?" Jackson asked, his eyes bloodshot. "I uploaded the video to the cloud, along with all the pictures from the murder scene, the laundromat footage the assistant manager gave me, and shots of the SWAT team that raided my house. I haven't checked the laundromat video yet—it might be blank like the others."

Marsden opened a cabinet and pulled out a laptop. "SWAT raided your home?" he asked, disbelief clear in his voice. Jackson nodded, and Marsden grunted as he returned to his seat. "Alright, what's the URL?"

Jackson quickly tapped on his phone before reading off the link. "I made the videos public. No password needed."

Castor had insisted the video from the laundromat be played first. But, as Willow had feared, the recording went blank at exactly 12:01 a.m. It might have been a coincidence, but in her experience, coincidences were as rare as albino alligators.

Marsden opened selfie-girl's murder video and for the next few minutes, they watched the murders of Rachel Persie and Tanner Montgomery. Marsden had projected the video on one of several large-screen monitors around the room.

Willow kept a close eye on Jackson. It broke her heart as tears fell down the man's cheeks while he was forced to relive his best friend's death, yet again. "I sent the killer's photo to Quantico," she said. "They ran it through every known database, and it came back negative—including Levi Benson. The long hair, scraggly beard, and facial dirt all obscured the killer's features, making it impossible to get a positive match. That's how I know he didn't do it." She dug her phone out of her pocket. "I've got the results here, if you feel the need to fact check me."

"Well?" Marsden asked of Castor. "Is that good enough for you?" When the detective didn't respond, Marsden pressed him harder. "Do I need to get Sawyer on the phone?" Castor gave him a one shoulder shrug like he was beyond caring anymore.

"Come on, boys," Willow said, keeping her tone friendly. "I showed you mine. It's your turn to show me yours." The comment made Betsie snigger.

"Go ahead, Betsie," Marsden said. "Let's hear it."

The petite woman cleared her throat and flipped open her file folder. "Ballistics reports confirmed that the bullet extracted from wall at the crime scene was fired from Mr. Benson's Berretta M9. What is most curious to me is that it was a solid brass, monolithic full metal jacket. It all but guaranteed that the bullet would remain intact."

"It's almost like the killer wanted the bullet to frame Levi," Jackson said. He was staring directly at Castor when he spoke. "Monolithic bullets also tend to have clearer striations on them, making them ideal for ballistics testing."

"I'll leave the sleuthing and conjecture to you folks," Betsie said. "If I may continue, the remains of the other fragments sent to us by Dr. Johnstone of the State Medical Examiner's office were too degraded to make a positive identification. We had a rather heated debate over the probability of two distinctly different types of ammunition being used in the same clip, but after having watched the very disturbing video, there is no doubt."

That answers one of my questions.

Willow chose to keep that thought to herself, not wanting to further interrupt the flow of Betsie's presentation.

"Next," Betsie said as she turned the page. "The only prints we found on the murder weapon belonged to Mr. Benson. It would take a more detailed analysis of the video I just watched, but I'm guessing the killer was wearing clear latex gloves. Otherwise, his prints would have been present. While we examined the other videos, we calculated the killer's height to be approximately five-foot-nine, which takes into account the one-inch heel boots he was wearing. Based on our calculations and DMV records, the murderer is the same height as Levi Benson."

"Whoever this man is," Willow said, "he's gone to great lengths to make it appear that Levi was the killer. The question is why? What did Levi do to warrant such a thing? I mean, holy hell, he lost his fiancée, his job, and his home." Truth was, she knew why. Levi had been gathering incriminating evidence against the mayor and the district attorney. She doubted the mayor would have taken part in his daughter's murder, but the DA was a possibility. She put the man at the top of her mental list of suspects.

"What about Levi's shelter?" Marsden asked. "Was your team able to gather any DNA evidence to identify the woman Agent Banks saw?"

"I'm afraid the only DNA we pulled from Mr. Benson's *home* belonged to Mr. Benson himself." Betsie screwed up her mouth like she was solving a puzzle. "Like the bullet, I found that very odd. People shed skin and hair all the time. Even though we found the suspect's DNA, there was hardly any of it as well. It was as though the space had been meticulously cleaned by someone who knew exactly what they were doing."

Willow immediately thought of the police officer who had been sent to process the scene, the one Jackson said had been specially trained in CSI procedures. Judging by the concerned look on his face, he might have come to the same conclusion.

"Fucking hell," Castor said. "Dawson processed Levi's hovel. When we're done here, he and I are going to have a *discussion*."

"Don't bother," Marsden said. "If he did tamper with evidence, it's already been destroyed. If you bring it up, it's only going to let the killer know we're onto him. But if it's true, if he did tamper with the evidence, it means the killer has an in with the PD."

A silence fell over the room while everyone seemingly considered the ramifications of this discovery. This was no longer a case of a single individual. There was a conspiracy underway, one that needed either Rachel Persie or Tanner Montgomery, or both, permanently out of the way.

"I also have the tox screen results from the victims' bloodwork and stomach contents," Betsie said, "if anyone's interested." She waited a moment, and when no one objected, she pressed on. "Ketamine was found in the blood stream of both victims. Ms. Persie's levels were higher than Mr. Montgomery's. Neither of them had any food in their stomachs at their time of death, but they both had significant amounts of coffee." Betsie paused while she looked to each person in the room. It seemed that the petite woman with black hair and pale skin had a penchant for the dramatic. "The coffee in Ms. Persie's stomach content was loaded with the dissociative drug. Mr. Montgomery's was at a much lower concentration, and yet, the caffeine content in both his stomach and bloodstream was significantly higher."

"Are you suggesting that Tanner drugged Rachel?" Jackson said. His jaw tensed, and his hands clenched into tight fists.

"I'm not drawing any conclusions, sir," Betsie said. "As I mentioned, I leave that in your capable hands. I am merely sharing the results of my department's forensic analysis." She looked over at Marsden. "Do you want me to continue, or am I finished here?"

"Continue," he said. "I'm sure SA Brooks will keep his thoughts to himself from now on."

"We haven't finished processing the samples of food and drink we took from the restaurant. There was a lot of it and my people worked around the clock to get what we have..."

"We'll take what you have, Betsie," Marsden said. "I appreciate your team's efforts."

"Well," she said, sitting up straighter, "we didn't find any trace of ketamine in the food samples we processed, but we did find significant amounts of amphetamine, dextroamphetamine, and methamphetamine. It appears that their breakfasts were designed to provide a mental boost. All these drugs can contribute to increased focus and wakefulness."

"The place was filled with college-aged kids," Jackson said. "And it is exam week at the university. The use of stimulants isn't unheard of."

"But," Betsie said, holding up her hand. "That wasn't all. We also found significant amounts of benzodiazepine in the coffee and orange juice at most of the tables. As you likely know, benzos are anything but a stimulant. They're the exact opposite, in fact. They're a depressant that directly affects the nervous system and can cause sedation, drowsiness, and impaired cognitive function. It can also reduce the body's overall response to stress."

"What about the ketamine?" Willow asked. "If they both had similar amounts of coffee, why were Tanner's ketamine levels lower?"

"Their carafe of coffee had a high concentration of ketamine." The lab tech sighed. "Look, I don't like to draw conclusions, that's your job, but based on the amount of ketamine we found in the carafe, and the amount in Agent Montgomery's stomach, I have to assume that he had drunk about thirty-two ounces of coffee before arriving at the restaurant."

"Jesus," Marsden said. "Do you think the restaurant was selling drug-laced food?"

"It sure as shit looks that way," Castor said. "I need to loop Sawyer in on this. He's going to blow a gasket."

"Why the captain and not Chief Wheeler?" Willow asked. Jackson trusted the chief, but not the captain. Levi's opinion of the two officers was the polar opposite.

"Because the chief is good friends with Brock Ainsly, the owner of Yumm," Castor said. "It doesn't implicate the chief, but having a drug dealer for a friend is yet another strike against our boss."

"You can't tell Sawyer," Jackson said. "I'm telling you. The man is dirty. I've got a ton of proof to back that statement up."

"That's impossible," Castor said. "I've known him for years, long before he replaced your father as captain. He is as straight as they come."

Jackson's jaw tightened, the mention of his father stirring old wounds. "Not surprising you'd defend him," Jackson said. "I've got enough to indict you as well."

Castor leaped from his chair and threw himself at Jackson. The special agent caught the detective mid-air and threw him across the room. The detective slammed into the wall with a thud before tumbling to the floor.

Before Castor could get back to his feet, Marsden put himself between the two combatants. "Enough, both of you!" he bellowed. "Neither of you is thinking straight. You both lost people close to you, and you're both looking for someone to blame. Now, sit down and shut up, or I'll have you both restrained."

"I don't know where you're getting your information, Jax," Castor said from his place on the floor. He rolled over onto his hands and knees before pushing himself back to his feet. He ran his hands over his rumpled suit, likely to smooth out his bruised ego.

"I'm guessing that whatever you have is the same as the deep-fake AI bullshit that Franklin was being blackmailed with. He showed me a disgusting video of him violating children. He also showed me the letter that had come with them, saying that if he didn't get on board, the video would be sent to his wife and the newspapers."

"They were some of the best fakes I'd ever seen," Betsie said. Considering the tussle that had just taken place, the tiny woman was completely unfazed, and Willow was already taking a liking to her. "I ran the photos through multiple tests. At first, everything looked normal, including the metadata and the camera details. But when I dug deeper, small inconsistencies started to show up. During my analysis of the image's layers and lighting, I noticed tiny differences in the compression ratios and pixel patterns around Detective Franklin's face. I mean, they were barely off, but they were off."

"Did you run your photo and video evidence through such rigorous testing?" Marsden asked.

Jackson massaged the back of his neck. "No. No I didn't." The poor man looked defeated, like his entire world had been pulled out from under his feet.

"Where did you get the photos?" Willow asked. She didn't want to dog-pile on him, but things were at play here. Big things. And that didn't sit well with her.

"They were from a CI," Jackson said. "I don't know who the person was, only that he was in the captain's inner circle. Savannah thought I could use my connections in Florence to get to the bottom of it."

"And the FBI couldn't be bothered to validate the photos?" Castor said. "Pretty fucking convenient."

"Why would they?" Willow said. "Do you do a deep dive into your CI's evidence? Nobody does."

"I've never seen this much misdirection in my entire career." Marsden said. "I'm not sure how we can trust anything we have.

Whatever is going on, the FBI is neck-deep in it as well. I was convinced that Agent Montgomery was collateral damage. I mean, look at the way the vics were killed. With the level of violence inflicted, I was certain Ms. Persie was the primary target, but now I'm not so sure."

"We need the name of the CI," Castor said. The color in his face had returned to normal, and his body language suggested he had let go of his anger. Jackson, on the other hand, looked like a rattlesnake ready to strike.

"The task force will never give him up," Jackson said. "Not without a federal warrant."

"Good thing we've got a friendly judge then," Marsden said. "But I've got a big ask. I don't want you to share any of this with your SAC. I fear her political aspirations are clouding her judgment. The woman wants Mr. Benson's head on a platter, and she wants to serve it up to the media and make a big name for herself. According to my source, she's about to announce that she's throwing her hat into the political ring, and finding the killer would make for a terrific sound bite.

"What's she running for?" Willow asked.

"State Senator," Marsden said. "It's my understanding she's got strong backing across Alabama, but what she's missing is the governor's support. That might be why she's so hot to get the credit for solving this murder. Mayor Persie and the governor are long time friends."

"Is there anyone the mayor isn't connected with?" Willow asked. She took in the opulent surroundings of the office space. "Based on the SBI's funding, I'm guessing he's got connections with the SBI's director as well. This place is ridiculously nice."

"Not that I'm aware of," Marsden said. "But that's above my pay grade."

"What are your thoughts on this?" Jackson asked Castor. "You've been awfully quiet."

"I'm thinking," he said, glowering at Jackson. "I'm thinking this is the most fucked up case I've ever worked on."

"And I'm thinking we're all on the same side," Willow said. "Whether we like it or not, we're going to need to trust each other. You guys work Detective Franklin's case, and we'll work the double homicide. I can't help but think the deep fakes are somehow at the heart of this. We can share our findings and compare notes."

"I don't trust Jackson," Castor said. "How do I know he's not at the heart of this?"

"Jesus Christ!" Willow had had quite enough of his bullshit. "If you think he's involved, you had better investigate me, too. For that matter, I suggest starting with ASAC Alice Baldwin in the Charleston field office. She's the one who sent me here. After you've wasted your time, maybe you could yank your head out of your ass and concentrate on the facts of this case."

"We need to put Mr. Benson into protective custody," Marsden said. "If you're looking after him, you're not working the case."

Willow and Jackson ignored the SSA's request and headed for the door. "It was a pleasure to meet you, Betsie," Jackson said. "If you don't mind, can you send us a copy of the forensic reports?"

Jesus. The woman practically sprinted across the room to hand Jackson her business card. Heat rose in Willow's chest as the lab technician flashed a flirtatious smile.

Fuck, Willow. What's wrong with you?

She blinked a few times, surprised by her reaction.

It's been a couple of long days, and you need a proper night's sleep. Exhaustion. That's all it is.

Chapter Twenty-Six

Jackson

Jackson peered through the glass doors of the makeshift FBI command center. Agents were huddled around a large table, their faces illuminated by the glow of laptops and the harsh fluorescent lights above. SAC Greene paced back and forth, gesticulating wildly as she spoke to the group. The senior agent's obvious agitation concerned Jackson. His reluctance to share information with Savannah gnawed at him. Despite his respect and admiration for his boss, her insistence on prosecuting Levi left him uneasy.

"You ready for this?" Willow asked, glancing at Jackson.

He pressed his lips together and nodded. "As I'll ever be."

They pushed through the doors, and an abrupt silence fell over the room. Everyone looked their way, a mix of curiosity and concern on their faces. SAC Greene halted mid-sentence, her piercing gaze focusing on Willow. "I have no idea why an agent from South Carolina is here, and I don't care. What I do care about is your direct interference with my investigation, and if I have my way, you'll face disciplinary action for insubordination."

"Ma'am," Willow said, edging closer and looking down at the SAC. "I mean no disrespect, but I don't report to you, and it's you who's impeding *my* investigation. If my SAC wants me to stand down, he'll tell me so. Until then..."

Greene's eyes narrowed. "My office. Now."

As they followed Greene to a small, glass-walled room adjoining the boardroom, Jackson felt his colleagues' stares burning into the back of his head. The tension in the air was palpable. He was grateful for the extra pill he'd taken earlier, but Savannah's evident hostility suggested it might prove insufficient.

Once inside, Greene shut the door and confronted them. "What the hell, Jax? Tanner was your best friend. Why are you protecting his killer?"

"Ma'am," Jackson began, his voice steady despite the pressure, "Levi Benson isn't the killer. I have video evidence proving his innocence, and he has a solid alibi. He simply couldn't have done it."

Greene's eyebrows shot up. "And the twenty-three people in the restaurant are all mistaken? Ms. Persie identified the killer by name." She scoffed. "I don't trust video evidence. It can be manipulated, just like all the videos from the crime scene with conveniently blurred faces. And this alibi you mention means nothing. There's no proof Benson was in the laundromat during the murder. He could have easily slipped away in the chaos and gone straight there. What better way to remove blood and gunshot residue?"

"With all due respect, ma'am," Willow countered, "that doesn't align with the evidence. We've also reviewed the forensic reports—"

"You what?" Greene interrupted, her voice rising. "We just received those reports from the SBI. How did you access them?"

Jackson intervened. "That isn't important, ma'am. The point is, the evidence doesn't support Levi as our killer. We need to refocus our investigation."

Greene's jaw clenched. She paused, her eyes darting between Willow and Jackson. Finally, she spoke, her voice low and controlled. "I don't trust the SBI. You know as well as I do that the entire Florence PD is corrupt, and the SBI is too cozy with the mayor and his wealthy friends. We'll wait for the FBI labs to conduct their analysis. Then I'll determine who is and who isn't a person of interest. Meanwhile, I want Benson brought in. Immediately. I don't care if you think he's innocent. You're harboring a fugitive."

"A fugitive who's innocent," Willow interjected.

"That's not for you to decide," Greene snapped. She took a deep breath, visibly trying to compose herself. "Look, I appreciate your... initiative. But this isn't how I run investigations. You will bring Benson in, hand over all evidence you've collected, and fall in line with the rest of the team. Is that clear?"

Willow and Jackson exchanged glances. This wasn't proceeding as he'd hoped. Willow's phone chimed. She checked it, smiled briefly, and put it away.

"Something amusing, Agent?" Savannah's tone was sharp, bordering on sarcastic.

"Not amusing," Willow replied. "But Levi Benson's situation is out of our hands. If you want to speak to him, you'll need to consult the DOJ. He's under US Marshal protection."

Savannah stiffened. Her nostrils flared as she struggled to maintain composure. "You got Benson into WITSEC?" Her mouth twisted into a bitter smile. "You're fucking with the wrong person, Agent. You think I don't have connections in the DOJ? You believe Benson is beyond my reach? I'm telling you that Benson is guilty, and he's going to pay for his crimes."

"Ma'am," Jackson said. He stepped forward, his voice pleading. "Levi is innocent. I'm certain of it. His life is in danger. Detective Franklin told me everything. He wasn't at the laundromat to arrest Levi. He was there to kill him. Franklin was being blackmailed, and he would have gone through with it if SA Banks and I hadn't intervened."

"Detective Franklin?" Savannah said, her tone incredulous. "Are you shitting me? You believe the word of a corrupt cop over me?"

"Yes," Jackson said without hesitation. "Right now, I do. None of this adds up. Franklin was terrified, and he chose to take his own life rather than subject his wife and family to ridicule."

"You're suspended," Savannah said through clenched teeth. "This is your last day with the bureau, Special Agent Brooks. I'll file the necessary paperwork with the Office of Professional Responsibility by day's end, and you'll be permanently dismissed within the month." She held out her hand. "Gun and badge. Now."

A surge of disbelief crushed Jackson's spirit. He was doing his job, following the evidence. Savannah's reaction indicated someone pushed beyond her limits. He almost felt bad for her. Almost. Slowly, he removed his badge and placed it in her palm. "You know I don't carry a gun. Not since..." His hand shook as he withdrew it. "Don't do this, Savannah. You know me. I wouldn't take this stance without cause."

Savannah's eyes flickered with uncertainty. She glanced at the badge in her hand, then back at Jackson. Her rigid posture slowly softened, and she let out a deep sigh. "Christ, Jax. I'm sorry." She extended the badge back to him. "I'm not myself today. Tanner's death is affecting me more than I realized. Please, accept my apology."

Jackson reclaimed his badge, returning it to his pocket. "I'm sorry too, Savannah, if you feel we've overstepped in this investigation. Everything's unfolded so quickly and... I need to find Tanner's killer. I hope I'm not wrong about Levi, but every instinct tells me he's innocent."

"Your instincts have always been reliable, Jax. Let's get back to the war room. I want you to review the information we've gathered. It might provide a new perspective for you and SA Banks." The mention of Willow still carried a bitter edge. Jackson hoped that as they worked together, they'd recognize each other as dedicated agents pursuing a common goal.

"Give them full access," Savannah instructed as they rejoined the group around the boardroom table. "SA Banks is leading this investigation. Understood?" As the agents exchanged bewildered looks, the SAC strode out, marching her way to the elevators.

"Where do you think she's going?" Jackson asked. "I expected her to stay with us."

"She's off to contact her DOJ connections," Willow said. "She recovered well, but I thought she was going to explode when I mentioned Levi going into witness protection."

"I can't believe the Marshals approved that so quickly. They usually take weeks to clear a new WITSEC entry."

"They do," Willow confirmed. A sly smile tugged at her mouth. "The message was from my brother, Colton. I'm an aunt again. Baby boy, seven pounds, eleven ounces. Named Cole."

"You lied to her?" Jackson struggled to process this. Willow exuded such confidence and self-assurance. She'd stood up to an SAC and crafted her tale without hesitation. He wasn't sure if he respected Willow for it or feared her because of it.

"The woman was losing control, and she needed to calm her tits." Willow chuckled at her phrasing. "I provided that. Free of charge. Now, introduce me to your colleagues, and let's get some food. I'm famished."

Chapter Twenty-Seven

Willow

Willow shook Agent Thomas Crenshaw's hand. She recognized him from the ballistics lab, recalling Jackson's assessment that he wasn't a good agent. This made Willow question why the SAC would include him if he wasn't among her best. The team needed solid investigators, not door-kickers. "What new details do you have to share with us?"

"Not much, I'm afraid." Crenshaw wrung his hands together. "We just got the forensics from the SBI, and we haven't heard anything from our own guys. We only shipped the samples out to them a short while ago, so it might be a day or two before we hear back from them."

Willow suppressed an exhausted sigh. "Hopefully you'll act on the SBI findings until the FBI labs get back to you."

Crenshaw looked down at his shoes. "We're going to evaluate the information we received from them. SAC Greene has doubts as to the accuracy of the reports. She thinks if we can poke holes in it, we can prove that the SBI is somehow complicit in the coverup of Benson as the murderer."

"Bloody hell," Willow said, stifling a scream. Her frustration threatened to boil over. She wanted to chase after SAC Greene and shove her white tennis shoe up the woman's tight, skinny ass.

"I'm going to tell you to stop doing that and help us identify the murderer. It wasn't Levi and to suggest otherwise is ludicrous."

"We can't do that," Crenshaw said. At this point, every agent in the room was staring at Willow, and she couldn't have cared less. "We were given explicit orders to find fault with the SBI findings."

"And SAC Greene said that I am running this investigation, and I'm telling you to stop."

"Technically," a chubby female agent said as she neared, "what we're doing is not a part of the investigation, and even if you are in charge, we don't report to you. Savannah said for us to give you access to what we find. She didn't say for us to be your underlings."

"And who the fuck are you?" Willow said.

"Agent Beverly Thomlinson," the woman said, sticking her chins out at Willow. "Cyber Crimes Division."

"Cyber crimes?" Jackson said. "Why would Savannah want IT techs on the case?"

"Because much of the evidence being collected is digital in nature, and Alex is convinced that it's all been doctored. He's currently overseeing the configuration of a secure cyber center down the hall."

"Alex? SSA Alexander Mitchell is here?" Jackson was perplexed.

Agent Thomlinson smiled a cold smile and nodded. "As soon as the secure hard lines are established, we'll be moving our operations there. We're going to rip Agent Montgomery and Ms. Persie's electronic devices apart and go through them byte by byte."

"Why?" Willow asked. "What are you hoping to find?"

"Is this your first time investigating a murder, Agent Banks?" Agent Thomlinson snorted. "To find any possible links between the murder victims and their killer. We might know who the killer is, but we have no idea why Benson did what he did. If we're going to make our charges stick, we need details. If you don't already know this... then I don't understand how you can possibly lead this investigation."

Willow's hand clenched into a fist. She wanted to punch the fat bitch in the face.

"Hey," Jackson said. He slipped his hand over hers. It was warm, and comforting, and it was the last thing on earth that she wanted him to be doing. "We're not going to make any headway here. I'm embarrassed to say, this is not my office's finest hour."

"Save your sanctimonious bullshit for your admirers, Agent Brooks." Agent Thomlinson folded her arms over her ample breasts. "None of us are buying what you're selling. Go back to your dogs and leave the real work to the professionals."

"That's Special Agent," Willow said. "If you disrespect my partner again, you and I are going to go round and round, and you won't last five seconds." She'd had enough of this bitch's attitude and stepped closer, lording her significant height advantage over the woman. A sense of personal satisfaction warmed her belly when Agent Thomlinson's face paled. She was all bluster, but when push came to shove, she backed down like so many bullies. Willow surmised that Thomlinson was accustomed to being a keyboard warrior, fighting her battles from behind a screen, using distance and anonymity as her shield.

***

"Well," Willow said as the elevator doors closed, "it looks like the SBI are the only people who don't have their heads crammed up their assholes."

"I don't know what's what," Jackson said. "I've known Savannah for years, and she's the best agent I've ever worked with. Is it possible that we're the ones blind to what's happening?"

"Really?" Willow resisted the urge to grab him by the shoulders and give him a thorough shaking. "We saw the killer. It wasn't Levi. How can you possibly doubt that?"

"What if it was faked somehow? What if it really was Levi and he somehow made the video look like someone else?"

The elevator dinged, and the door opened to the main floor. Willow grabbed Jackson by the front of his shirt and dragged him away from the bank of elevators. "Sure. It's possible. In some science fiction movie where super computers are taking over the world. The girl took the video. You took her phone. And it's been in your possession ever since. What you're suggesting is im-fuck-ing-possible."

"It's easier for me to believe that this is the work of some super-hacker than the idea that Savannah is somehow disregarding the facts."

"Listen to me, Jackson." The turmoil in the man's eyes was gut-wrenching. He was loyal to his SAC, and Willow respected that, but he was reacting emotionally, and not with his head. "It's been a tough couple of days. Neither of us has had much sleep and we've both been put through the wringer. It's coming up on two, and I'm starving. My stomach is growling so hard that I can barely think. How about we get some food, take a mental respite, and get back at it when we both have full bellies and clear heads?"

Jackson looked like a little boy the way he stared down at his feet and nodded. "There's a BBQ joint not far from here. It's got some of the best smoked pork in northern Alabama." He lifted a shoulder. "I know you're right about the video, but..." He squared his shoulders and raised his chin. "I'm sure the SBI techs are already verifying the validity of the girl's video. We'll likely know for certain by the time we're finished lunch." He got an earnest look about him. "Thank you for keeping me grounded. Tanner's death has me all busted up inside. I'm glad you're in charge."

Willow had taken a leave of absence after her partner's death. It hadn't been enough, but she needed to work to keep her mind from slipping into oblivion. Had it not been for Ranger's bad behavior, and his necessity for rehabilitation, she'd likely be neck-deep in her tenth bottle of bourbon.

"BBQ sounds perfect." She placed her hand on the small of Jackson's back and guided him forward. "For shits and giggles, we can harass the parking lot guard on the way out."

Jackson chuckled at her comment. His laughter sent reverberations through his body, making his back muscles tense beneath Willow's hand. She quickly pulled it away and tucked it into her pocket.

Chapter Twenty-Eight

Jackson

Jackson rubbed his belly as he surveyed the remains of his lunch. "I'll need to go for a long run if I'm going to burn off this meal." He appreciated that Willow never brought up his mother's experimental treatments while they ate. She seemed to understand which boundaries not to cross. He observed the woman sitting across from him as she finished off the last of her food.

"I've got to admit," Willow said. "I know you said the BBQ was amazing here, but if I didn't know this place, I'd have driven right past and not given it a second look."

"Yeah," Jackson said as he gathered up the various containers and bits of packaging off the heavily weathered picnic table. "Bunyan's is something of an institution here in Florence. Rumor has it they sell out every day."

Willow licked her fingers before wiping them with the remains of her napkin. She balled it up and tossed it in the large garbage can. "I don't doubt it," she said as she walked to the truck. "Where to now? I'd really like to talk with the owner of Yumm. The man is selling drugs right out in the open. He'll be pretty easy to lean on, I'm guessing. The threat of serious jail time is one of the best ways to loosen lips."

"He's friends with the mayor," Jackson said as he slipped behind the wheel of his truck. He started it up and put the AC on high.

The spring temperatures hinted at a brutally hot summer ahead. He waited until Willow was seated before continuing his thought. "If we take a run at him too early, he's going to turtle, and the mayor's going to protect him. Even if he's dirty, we need the mayor on our side, and to do that, we need to bring Persie a solid lead on his daughter's killer."

"He's fueling the fire to put Levi behind bars. That's for sure." Willow turned to Jackson and raised her eyebrows. The sun streaming in through the windshield ignited the gold flecks in her eyes. "Where do you want to go then? After talking with SSA Marsden and Detective Castor, we've got plenty of doors to kick down."

"I want to go to the university," Jackson said. "The kid we saw out front with all the reporters, he's a journalism major. He said he took video of everyone coming and going at the restaurant. If he's smart, and I think he is, he didn't give up his phone to the cops. He might have shared the video with them, but he'd have kept the original for himself."

"To what end?" Willow cocked her head to the side. "You've already got a complete video of the murder. What more are you hoping to see?"

A flicker of uncertainty crossed Jackson's face. Truth was, he didn't know what he was hoping to find in the pimple-faced kid's video. It was unlikely the killer had an accomplice. "No clue. Not exactly, anyway. I liked the guy. He was a go-getter, and he wants to succeed. At no point did I get a whiff of dishonesty, but he was aggressively recording everyone who was at or near the restaurant. There must be a reason why he was there."

"Sure," Willow said. A playful smile tugged at the corner of her lips. "Let's add more doors to the kick-down list."

***

"I was wondering how long it would take for you to come see me," Johnnie Walker said. He stood as tall and proud as his overweight five-foot-six frame would allow. "Did you know the Florence PD confiscated my phone shortly after the mayor arrived on the scene? That's why I needed to talk to you this morning."

Jackson's hopes deflated. He really didn't know what he had hoped to gain from seeing the student's recordings, but now he'd never know.

"You seem to be a sharp kid," Willow said. She shifted her weight to one leg to accentuate her hip. "I'm guessing you didn't give them the only copy of your recording."

Johnnie raised his chin and smiled. "What's in it for me? The officers who took my phone made it pretty clear that if I had a copy of the video and shared it with anyone..."

"What do you want?" Jackson asked. "With the way things are going, there isn't much we have to offer."

"I want first crack at information," he said. "Exclusive."

"We can't share information of an ongoing investigation, Johnnie," Willow said. "Surely, you already know that."

"You can give me non-sensitive information that has yet to be made public." Johnnie's eyes narrowed. "You can also share certain tidbits that, if they were leaked, might help with your investigation. And you can promise to let me be the first journalist to interview you after the case is wrapped up. But you have to give me access right away. You can't let it linger to the point where your information becomes stale."

"I won't do anything dishonest." Unlike Willow who was actively using her feminine attributes to her advantage, Jackson was using his substantial size advantage to make his point of view crystal clear. "I don't care if it's the difference between finding the killer or not, there are some lines that I won't cross."

The young man took a step away from Jackson and held up his hands. "I wouldn't break the law either, and I certainly wouldn't try to coerce someone else to break the law." A grin pulled up the corners of his mouth. He looked like a cat that had just swallowed a canary. "But, let's say… hypothetically… that a public figure was getting in your way, and that if… oh, I don't know… you gave me a bit of info on said public figure, like he was behaving in an untoward sort of way… if I knew that, I might be able—through the power of the press—convince said public figure to… stop getting in your way."

"What do you know?" Willow asked. She stepped in close and lorded her own height advantage over the man.

This time, Johnnie Walker didn't even flinch, except to crane his neck up to get a better look at the agent. "I suspect many things," he said. His smile never waned. "But I don't know very much. I do suspect that there is at least one more copy of the video I took at the murder scene. Do we have a deal?"

"I can't promise you anything," Jackson said, "but I will give you a limited-scope interview as soon as the murderer is convicted. Not arrested. Convicted."

"But you'll consider my other requests?" Johnnie's eyes brightened. "You'll give me what I asked for, if it's to your benefit?"

"Sure," Willow said. "We'll consider it."

Johnnie pulled a business card from his wallet. "Call me." He looked at both agents, waiting for someone to take his card. "I'll give you the URL where you can get the video."

"You can't just give it to me now?" Jackson was growing weary of the games.

"Sure. Give me your number, and I'll text it to you."

"Didn't the police take your phone?" Willow said.

"They took *one* of my phones. The idiot cop just said, 'Give me your phone.' He didn't say which phone." His comment made Willow snort-laugh.

"Can't you just give me the phone with the video on it?" Jackson asked. "I could compel you to give it to me."

"You could," Johnnie said, lifting his shoulders, "but then you wouldn't get access to what else I know. Quid pro quo, Special Agent Brooks. Quid pro quo."

"Is the video complete and unedited?" Willow asked. "If you send us anything but the complete original, I'll arrest you for obstruction, and I'll make it stick."

"It is the complete video," Johnnie said, "but as a show of good faith, I'll give you my phone and all the raw footage I took. Can you promise me I'll get it back? All of it?"

"You have my word," Jackson said, holding out his hand. He was surprised when the wannabe journalist handed it over. "Is there a passcode?"

"90210" Johnnie blushed. "Like the TV show."

"Got a pen?" Jackson asked.

"Really?" Johnnie's forehead scrunched up. "You can't remember that?"

"Do you want my cell number or not?" Jackson slipped the young man's phone into his pocket.

"Um..." Johnnie patted his pockets and grimaced.

"You can use mine," Willow said, reaching for her pocket.

"No need," Johnie said, waving away the offer. "I'll remember. Part of being a good journalist is having a powerful recall."

Jackson rhymed off his digits and made the young man repeat them back to him, forwards and backwards. It was a memory trick he'd learned when he was young.

"How many phones do you have?" Willow asked.

"Three," Johnnie said. "Well, only one now, I suppose."

"What's the number?" Willow pulled out her notepad and waited until the young man recited his tertiary number. "Have it with you at all times. If we need you, you'd better damn well pick up."

"Thank you for your help," Jackson said. "I appreciate it."

As the pair walked back to Jackson's truck, Willow had her nose stuck in her phone. "You know," she said, "there is someone I think we need to chat with sooner than later." She bit her lower lip, like she was waiting for Jackson to prod for details. When he raised his eyebrows, Willow smiled. "You said we should leave the owner of Yumm alone for now, at least until we have a solid lead, but I have another person who might be more helpful."

"Who's that?" Jackson said as he pulled open the passenger side door.

"Am I driving?" Willow asked while Jackson held the door open. "Because unless you're getting in on this side, I don't need you opening the door for me."

Jackson's cheeks flushed. "Sorry," he said. He let go of the handle like it was on fire. "It seems my mother's training runs deep."

Willow patted Jackson's chest. "Well, if you put it that way, I guess I'll give you a pass."

His pulse quickened as he waited for Willow to climb onto the seat. Once she was settled, he shut the door and sprinted around the front of the truck. By the time he got inside, his face burned with embarrassment. "You were saying?" The words came out shriller than intended. "Someone else you want to visit?"

Willow held her phone for Jackson to see the picture of a portly Thai man holding two thick-bladed knives across his chest. "Chef Kamon Suwan," she said. "He's the head chef at Yumm. If the food's being laced with narcotics, there's no way he wouldn't know about it."

"Sounds good," Jackson said, his heartbeat gradually returning to normal. While he backed out of the parking spot, Willow gave him the chef's address.

Chapter Twenty-Nine

Willow

Willow knocked on the flimsy screen door and straightened her jacket. Jackson scanned the street, his gaze moving from house to house. The neighborhood was lower middle-class. With few exceptions, the homes appeared to have been constructed in the mid-to late seventies. They all looked tired and in desperate need of a facelift, but the yards were clean and well-maintained. The residents here didn't have money, but they took pride in what they had.

The squeal of rusty hinges pierced the afternoon quiet, drawing Willow's attention to the sallow-faced man in the doorway. "We're looking for Mr. Kamon Suwan?" The homeowner appeared confused, so Willow held up her ID. "I'm Special Agent Willow Banks, and this is Special Agent Jackson Brooks. We'd like to have word with Mr. Suwan."

The man squinted at the badge. "FBI?"

"Yes, sir," Jackson said. "Does Kamon Suwan live here?"

"I am Kamon." The man stood a bit taller. "How can I help you?"

"If we could have a few minutes of your time, we'd like to ask you about the murders at your restaurant."

"Yes, of course." Kamon blinked rapidly and backed into his house. "I still can't believe what happened."

Willow led the way, moving into the living room positioned directly off the entrance vestibule. While the exterior of the home was tired, the interior was well-appointed and impeccably tidy—unlike any bachelor's home she'd ever encountered.

"You're the head chef at the restaurant?" Willow asked, taking a seat on a stiff-backed living room chair. Jackson sat on the couch and surveyed the room. "You look different from the photo I saw of you online."

"I'm the executive chef," Kamon said with an air of superiority. "I was much rounder before I came to Florence. I've been working for Mr. Ainsley for almost three years now. The restaurant's popularity has nearly tripled since I took over the kitchens."

"Particularly with the younger crowd," Jackson said. He was staring at a framed photo on the wall. "On the morning of the murder, your restaurant was slammed. Do you always have so many guests for breakfast?"

"It was a particularly busy morning." Kamon slumped. "It seemed that Tanner Montgomery's reservation had somehow become public knowledge." He knitted his fingers together and lowered his head. "He was a hero. I can't believe he was killed. I just can't." He pulled his hands apart and wiped them on his pant legs. The afternoon sun reflected off the crystal of his Rolex.

"Are you selling drugs at your restaurant?" Willow asked. She liked double-teaming a suspect with rapid-fire questions. It threw them off balance and subconsciously encouraged them to choose the path of least resistance. "Is that how you can afford the twelve-thousand dollar watch you're wearing?"

Kamon covered his watch with his hand. Perhaps he thought she'd forget about it if the Rolex was out of sight. "Me... selling drugs? God, no! My sister OD'd on fentanyl five years ago. I hate drugs."

"I understand." Willow leaned closer and offered a sympathetic nod. "When you lose someone so close to you, it changes your perspective on things. I lost a brother. It's why I work so hard to uncover drug dealers. Ever since Mason died, I've made it my life's mission to put as big a dent in the drug trade as I can." She wiped at a non-existent tear and frowned. "I don't just take down the bosses. Other agents only care about the top-dogs, but me... I want everyone involved. Without the foot soldiers, the shot-callers wouldn't get anything done. The little guys, the street dealers, they're just as much to blame." Her gaze turned feral. "Even if someone knew about what was going on, and chose to keep quiet about it... I'd pin those bastards to the wall and make sure they get the maximum penalty. I don't really care if they're afraid to testify. Do you get me, Mr. Suwan? I. Don't. Care."

Sweat glistened along Kamon's hairline. The hand covering his watch now clutched onto his wrist like it was a life preserver. All she needed to do was stay silent and wait. Jackson stood and strolled across the room. He practically pressed his nose against a photo on the wall. It looked like the picture was of Kamon and Mayor Persie, standing in front of Yumm. Jackson turned back to the suspect and smiled.

"It's the sous chef!" Kamon hopped to his feet. He looked like a rabbit caught between two coyotes, unsure which to escape first. "Sam Wellington. He's the guy you want. He's the one bringing the drugs into the restaurant. I wanted him to stop. I said I was going to report him but..." The poor guy was white as a sheet. The beads of sweat that had broken out along his hairline were now dripping over his eyes and down his temples.

"Mr. Suwan." Jackson rushed to the chef's side and guided him to a chair. "If you help us, we'll put in a good word with federal prosecutor. I can't promise you anything, but I swear that I will do what I can to help you. Despite my partner's zealous pursuit of those involved in the drug trade, I'm certain I can convince her that it's in everyone's best interest that you are not held accountable for other people's actions."

Willow suppressed a grin, pleased with their unplanned good cop, bad cop routine. She had not discussed any of this before coming through the door. All she'd asked was that she led the questioning. At Jackson's words, the suspect's breathing slowed, and the color returned to his face.

"Did you know that Ms. Persie and Mr. Montgomery's coffee had been spiked with ketamine, Kamon?" Willow kept her voice quiet. She barely moved a muscle as she spoke. The executive chef's eyes widened, and he violently shook his head.

"Jesus Christ!" Kamon grabbed his stringy black hair like he was about to yank it out by the roots. He turned to Jackson. "Like you said, we were slammed. My line cooks couldn't keep up. I was helping them. I would never..."

"Who serves coffee?" Jackson said. He placed a comforting hand on Kamon's shoulder. "We understand. You wouldn't do that, but you'll help us figure out who did—won't you?"

"Evelina Rainier." Kamon grasped onto Jackson's hand. "She's the head waitress. It doesn't matter how busy we are in the morning. Her job is to deliver coffee and chat up the patrons." The man's face twisted while he tried to solve the puzzle. "She works mornings from eight to ten, and she's the highest paid employee in the restaurant. I always thought she was banging Mr. Ainsley. I mean, the woman is smoking hot... and..."

"Did it occur to you that she was selling drugs to the patrons?" Willow raised her eyebrows. "If you are so against drugs, I would have expected you'd have noticed such an obvious thing."

"I do my best to not see anything." Kamon lowered his head. "It's why I've lost so much weight since coming to Alabama. I'm trapped. I earn a decent wage at the restaurant, but if I was to ever leave, Mr. Ainsley said he'd tell prospective employers that he fired me for being a thief. I'd never get another gig. Ever. At least, never at any place worth working at. I've been the executive chef at

Yumm too long to leave it off my resume. I'm an excellent chef." He drew a shuddering breath. "I am so royally fucked, aren't I?"

"Not if you cooperate," Jackson said, taking a knee next to the frazzled man. "I promise. Do you hear me? I promise I will do everything I can to get you out of this. Just sit tight. Don't do anything out of the ordinary. Don't talk to anyone about our visit. Don't be stupid." Kamon was busy examining his feet and nodding when Jackson winked at Willow. The minuscule action made Willow's heart stutter. "If you do something stupid, I doubt there is anything I can do to stop Special Agent Banks from crucifying you."

Kamon lifted his head and swallowed. Hard. "I swear, Agent Banks. I'll do everything I can to help you, and I won't do anything stupid." He turned back to Jackson. "If I help... is there anything you can do to get me out of this? Like witness protection or something? These are bad people... Powerful people."

"I can't promise anything," Willow said. She stood from the chair and ran her hands over her pant legs. "But I've got some friends in the Marshal's office. They've got pretty strict criteria on who they let into WITSEC... but if you help us, I'll help you. You have my word."

Kamon looked like he was ready to prostrate himself and kiss Willow's feet. "Anything. Anything to get me out of this. Sweet Jesus sent an angel to look over me."

"Thank you for your cooperation," Jackson said. He handed the chef two business cards and a pen. "Give me your phone number. Keep the other card in case you need to reach me."

The man whipped out his wallet and produced a business card. It was heavily battered, but still legible. "One other thing," he said. "Something that might be important." He paused while his gaze jumped to each of the agents. "We have an app that the college crowd uses. It lets them order items that aren't on the menu, if you get my meaning. If anyone wants a special meal, they have to use the app. No exceptions."

"How do you get this... app?" Jackson asked. "Can I get a copy of it from Google Play or the Apple Store?"

"No." Kamon shook his head vigorously. "You need to download it from Yumm's on-site server. It's the only way. There's some sort of... I don't know what the hell they call it. I mean, I don't really get how all the tech stuff works, but it's something like this: the students download what looks like a normal app for the restaurant, like the kind where you check out the menu and order your food, right? Except this one has some secret menu items—they order those, and they get their drugs mixed in with the food. But here's the creepy part... as soon as they step foot inside the place, their phone automatically connects to the restaurant's system. It's like the app takes over their phone the second they walk through the door. Ever since I learned this, I removed the software. I had to do a factory reset on my phone to get rid of it. Now, I always put my cell into airplane mode before I go to work. Who knows what weird shit that app was doing?"

"We should be going," Willow said, motioning with her head to Jackson. She strode to the front door, replaying the chef's words in her mind. "Remember what we said. Don't change your routine and don't do anything stupid."

"This is messed up." Jackson slammed the truck door as he got behind the wheel. "Have you ever heard of anything like this before?"

"Never." Willow clicked her seatbelt. "I wonder if anyone thought to pull the server. If not, we need to get IT guys down there and bring it in."

"If anyone can figure it out," Jackson said, "it'll be SSA Mitchell. The man's something of an asshat, but he's one of the best in the country. I heard the NSA tried to lure him away, but he didn't want to leave the Birmingham office."

"I don't know." She had never met the man before, but the chubby agent who worked for him gave Willow the creeps. "I'm worried that if Savannah gets her hands on it, the information it contains will never see the light of day—unless she determines it will further her agenda."

"Look," Jackson said, his tone defensive. "I don't know why she's being like this, but if Savannah wants to make headlines, she'll move heaven and earth to solve these murders. She's powerfully motivated, and when it comes to dogged determination, she's tops."

The way he praised the woman grated on Willow's nerves. "Earlier, I said you put her on a pedestal. Now it sounds like you've raised her to deity status."

"Do you not have people you've met over your career that you look up to and respect?" Jackson didn't sound angry. He sounded hurt. "I've had three in my lifetime. Savannah, Tanner, and my mom... and my dad."

That was four people, but Willow didn't need to point that out. She pulled out her phone and tapped out a message. "I've asked Marsden to put an agent on Kamon. If these people are as bad as I think they are, they may have someone watching his house. If they saw us visiting him, his life might be in danger." She squirmed in her seat. "I also told him to collect the server at Yumm, but I didn't say why."

"I can't believe you trust him more than you do Savannah." Now Jackson sounded pissed. "Do you think she's dirty?"

"No." Willow threw up her hands in surrender. "I believe it when you say she's the best. I have no doubt. But until she lets go of Levi being the murderer, I doubt she's going to spend her resources anywhere but on him."

The anger drained from Jackson like air from a tire. "You're probably right." He massaged the muscles in the back of his neck and groaned. "This shouldn't be this hard. We've got people who could help, and we don't seem to fully trust any of them."

"I trust you," Willow said. Jesus, the words sounded cringe-worthy, but the way Jackson nodded, and his obvious relief made her feel a little less self-conscious about it.

"Likewise," Jackson said. He checked the time on the dashboard. "It's a little after three-thirty. What do you say about paying Evelina Rainier a visit?"

"Sure thing." Willow tapped at her phone. "I'll see if I can pull up her address."

Chapter Thirty

Jackson

Jackson parked his truck on the street, two blocks from Evelina Rainier's home. According to Willow's research, she lived in a semi-detached two-story house in Muscle Shoals, a small city neighboring Florence. The building stood in the center of the town's hottest music and restaurant district. Rent here had to be astronomical, corroborating Eugene's story about the woman's wages.

"Come here much?" Willow asked as they passed a bar. Light jazz rolled out the door, inviting everyone to relax and unwind. "I'm guessing this place is hopping when the sun goes down."

"Not as much as I'd like." Jackson held little interest in trendy tourist attractions, but he did enjoy good music. Muscle Shoals was renowned for its rich music history. The Fame Studio had recorded the likes of Aretha Franklin, Little Richard, and Wilson Pickett. Since the early 60s, it seemed every famous R&B, soul, or country artist had come to make music in this quaint little city. "I used to spend a lot of nights out here when I was younger. When I wasn't in training, anyway. I mean, I still came out to enjoy the music, but alcohol was off limits."

"What were you training for?" Willow's intense stare made Jackson's stomach flop.

"Football." Jackson looked away, his cheeks burning. "I played with Tanner at UNA. I was on a full-ride scholarship, and I wasn't going to risk being ousted for showing up to practice with a hangover."

"What about Tanner? Did he abstain?"

Jackson snorted at the thought of his friend passing up an opportunity to party. "No. Not at all. Tanner was the golden boy. He was a natural athlete in every sense of the word. When he showed up for practice during his freshman year, he put his cannon of an arm on display. Tanner sent me on a fly pattern—basically, I was to run straight downfield, and he'd throw the ball. I half ran the first fifty yards. When he launched the ball, I had to sprint full-out. From where he threw the pass, to where I caught it, measured seventy-eight yards. With that one display, he got us both onto the first-string roster. Freshmen never made the team. He told Coach that he needed me, and that I was the only receiver he could truly trust."

Jackson's throat constricted, and his eyes watered. He hadn't thought much about Tanner's death. There hadn't been time. He would grieve when his killer was behind bars.

Willow gave Jackson's hand a gentle squeeze. "I'm sorry. I really am, but it's time to put those emotions to use. You go in the front. I'll take the back." Willow pulled her Glock and gave it a quick check. "Where's your firearm?"

"I don't like guns." Jackson shrugged. "I usually have Ruby with me, anyway. If I get in a fire fight, she's doing her thing. I'm not going to risk her getting hit with friendly fire."

"She's not here now. You need a weapon." She held out her Glock. "Take mine. I'll use my backup." She pointed at the bulge at her ankle.

"No." Jackson refused. He didn't want to take a life, even if it meant losing his own. Never again would he shoot someone. "I don't need a gun. We're just asking the woman some questions."

"She's a drug dealer, and possibly a murderer." Willow pushed the gun at him. "If you get shot, I'm... You're taking the gun, and that's all there is to it. Do you hear me Special Agent? Take the weapon or... Jesus, man, just take it."

A wave of conflicting emotions washed over Jackson. He had his reasons for refusing to carry a firearm, but the agent standing in front of him had just lost a partner. She had her reasons, too. "Fine." He took the weapon and stuffed it into the back of his pants. Nausea gripped him. The last time he handled a gun, a child died. Jackson yanked out his shirt and pulled it over the gun, hiding it from sight. He stuffed his hands in his pockets to keep them from shaking.

"Thank you," Willow said as she pulled her Ruger LCP from her ankle holster. "It's small, but it shoots straight. If necessary, you had better shoot straight, too."

Anxiety coiled in Jackson's stomach as he climbed the stairs. He wanted to toss Willow's gun into the bushes. The cold metal pressing against his back made his knees weak. The door opened before he had a chance to knock.

"Hello?" A diminutive woman in her early twenties appeared, her brow knitted tightly together. She brushed her long, platinum blonde hair from her eyes. "Can I help you?"

"Yes..." Jackson froze. He wasn't ready to question her yet. He had been fixated on his traumatic memories and not on the task at hand.

"Are you okay? Are you lost?" The woman held out her hand, perhaps in an attempt to steady Jackson. "Do you want me to call someone for you?"

How could this be a drug dealer? Nobody who'd dose someone could possibly be this caring. "I'm Special Agent Jackson Brooks with the FBI. Are you Evelina Rainier?" His focus returned, and he stood a bit straighter.

The woman smiled. It was sweet and innocent. Jackson found himself whispering a little prayer that this not be the woman.

"Oh, heavens no. I'm her housekeeper." She stepped into the house and invited Jackson inside. "Ms. Rainier is getting dressed. She'll be down in a moment. Can I get you a glass of water, or maybe some lemonade while you wait? It's dreadfully warm out today." Jackson shook his head in a silent reply. The housekeeper looked out onto the street before closing the door. "I was expecting the delivery man." She dropped her voice to a whisper. "Ms. Rainier's going to give him an earful. He's over thirty minutes late."

Blood pounded in Jackson's ears. He had walked in on a drug deal. He was certain of it, and he had to let Willow know. He also needed to get the housekeeper out of harm's way. "Ma'am... I've changed my mind. I would very much like that glass of water." He hoped the kitchen was at the back of the house.

The housekeeper waved her hand in a dismissive manner. "I'm happy to get it for you. Wait here. I'll be right back."

As soon as she was out of sight, Jackson pulled out his phone and texted Willow. "Drug delivery imminent. Get out front."

Jackson stood in the hallway, acutely aware of the Glock pressing against his back. It was a cold reminder of his past, and how a gun and a single bullet could destroy the lives of so many people. Sweat tickled his back as a droplet ran down his spine. He hated guns. Never again would he pull a trigger. He couldn't. The sound of the fridge door closing reminded him of the sweet young woman in the kitchen. If things went sideways, she might be caught in the crossfire. What if Willow hadn't read his text message?

The memory of Tanner's easy smile crept into his consciousness. His childhood friend, the best friend he ever had, had been murdered. The drug-pushing woman who lived here had a hand in it. She helped assassinate one of the best people Jackson had ever known. "For you, buddy." He adjusted his shirt, giving himself ready access to the gun in his waistband.

A car door slammed outside. Any second, the delivery man would be darkening the doorway. The man would be armed and dangerous. Of that, Jackson was certain. Even still, he didn't want to draw his weapon. In this moment, he had the upper hand. In the same way the housekeeper had surprised him, he'd do the same thing to whoever was coming up to the door.

Jackson's heart raced as he placed his hand on the cool brass doorknob. He wished that he was home with Ruby. A shadow appeared in the front-door's opaque textured-glass window. Jackson flung open the door, startling the delivery man. "You're late! Evelina's throwing a hissy fit."

With his left hand, Jackson grabbed the wiry man by his shirt and dragged him inside. With one smooth motion, the agent twisted his body and used his lead leg to trip the delivery man and send him hard to the ground. The man's face hit the hardwood with a sickening thud. The satchel he was carrying tumbled across the floor, spilling bags filled with pills and tightly wrapped opaque packages.

Jackson grabbed the man's wrist and twisted it behind his back, pressing it up high between his shoulder blades. Using his body-weight, Jackson kneeled into the small of his prisoner's back, ensuring he wouldn't move.

"Get the fuck off me," the downed man said. "You're a fucking dead man. Do you hear me? You're fucking dead."

"I'm Special Agent Jackson Brooks with the FBI, and you're under arrest. You have the right to remain silent. Anything you say can and will be used against you. You have the right to an attorney. If you cannot afford an attorney, one will be appointed to you. Do you understand these rights as I have explained them to you?"

This man likely had nothing to do with Tanner's murder—at least not directly. It still felt good to apprehend him. Long hours of training had kicked in. Every movement was instinctual. Jackson hoped Willow would show up soon. He couldn't hold the guy like this indefinitely, and Evelina appearing at the top of the stairs with a gun was a real possibility.

That exhilaration of apprehending a suspect vanished, replaced with the gut-wrenching need to draw his weapon. Jackson's stomach churned as he reached behind his back, his hand gripping the cool polymer handle of the Glock.

"Don't do it, Mr. Brooks. Put your hands in the air and get off Zeke."

Jackson lifted his head. The housekeeper was standing in the hallway, pointing an enormous handgun at him. It might have been a Desert Eagle, but he couldn't be certain. All he could see for sure was the huge bore of the barrel.

"Shoot the motherfucker, Evelina," Zeke said. "I can't go back to prison."

Chapter Thirty-One

Willow

Willow had known special agents who, after twenty-five years in the bureau, never once fired their weapon. She doubted any of them were apprehensive about carrying their firearms, and yet, Jackson wasn't just wary of it. The gun seemed to terrify him. He had alluded to it during his conversation with SAC Greene, but Willow hadn't paid much attention. In hindsight, his comment about not carrying a gun had softened Savannah's stance. Whatever had happened in his past, it had to have been traumatic. When Willow had looked up his service history, she saw nothing that would have red-flagged him.

She waited, out of sight, while Jackson stood on the sidewalk. "Come on, Jackson. Pull yourself together. Don't leave me hanging." Her words were barely a whisper. Trusting he'd do his part, Willow rounded the corner and stepped into the narrow alleyway between Evelina's house and the neighboring property. An eight-foot chain-link fence with a padlocked gate blocked the way to the backyard. There were no windows on this side of the house. At least she wouldn't be seen while she scaled the fence.

As Willow continued down the alley, her breath left her lungs in a whoosh. There were two well-hidden security cameras on the wall of the neighboring house. Hopefully, they wouldn't call Evelina if they saw her breaking into her backyard. It was a long-shot, but Willow holstered her gun and pulled out her FBI badge. She held it up to the camera before sprinting towards the eight-foot barrier.

After a decent vertical jump, Willow latched onto the fence. The toes of her sneakers easily found purchase between the links. Keeping her body flat against the mesh, she scaled her way up. There were no barbs, but the twisted wires that held the links together were sharp. Getting over unscathed was worrisome.

She climbed as high as she could, gripping the cold metal links tightly. Reaching over with her right hand, she steadied herself and pushed off with both feet, propelling her body upward. As she cleared the top, she twisted to avoid the sharp, twisted edges of the chain links.

Her left hand caught the fence, bearing the sudden weight of her body. She tried to hook her toes against the links to take the strain off her fingers, but her footing slipped. A sharp, sickening pop shot through her left hand as pain exploded in her middle finger. Her body slammed against the fence, and she hung there for a moment, dangling awkwardly and breathing through the sudden jolt of agony.

The pain didn't pass. If anything, it worsened. She must have dislocated her finger. Climbing down one-handed wasn't an option. With a push of her feet, she launched herself away from the fence and landed somewhat gracefully on the stone walkway below.

The middle finger of her left hand was bent at an obscene angle. It looked like it was dislocated, but it might have been broken. She took a deep breath and prepared herself for the jolt of pain she knew would follow. If her finger was broken... well, shit—this was going to be bad. Willow carefully took hold of the obtuse finger and gave it a yank.

Stars burst into her vision and the world swam. "Sweet Jesus," Willow said through gritted teeth. She wanted to bellow the words at the top of her lungs. When her stomach settled and the pain eased to a dull throb, she took a tentative peek. It looked okay. Mostly. It was already swelling and on its way to a brilliant shade of purple. She swallowed down the bile in her throat and made a fist. It hurt, but it was bearable. At least it wasn't broken.

There was no time to waste. Jackson was likely already talking to Evelina by now. Willow pulled her gun and dashed into the backyard, skidding on the slick flagstone walkway. She was approaching the steps that led up to the back door when her phone binged. Whoever was sending her a text message would have to wait.

She pointed her gun at the solid wood door. If Evelina ran, she wouldn't be escaping this way. The steady beat of the agent's heart marked the passage of time. What if it had been Jackson who'd texted her? Her phone was in her left back pocket. Retrieving it was going to be… difficult. Holding her breath, preparing for the pain that was certain to come, Willow reached into her pocket, doing her best to use her thumb and index finger. Her pants were tight, making it impossible to get a firm grip on the slick phone. She switched her gun to her left hand and grimaced as pain flared in her swollen finger. Reaching around with her right, she easily slipped the device from her pocket. After taking a quick glance at the door, she checked her text message.

Oh shit!

There was no way she could get back over the fence. Coming through the back door was her only hope. If the door was locked… things were going to go from bad to worse. Willow's mind raced, replaying the events that had led to her partner Kate's death. Despite being cleared of any wrongdoing by IA, she carried the burden of knowing that her actions were instrumental in the tragedy. Had she not been so brash… Had she paid closer attention to her partner's instructions… The circumstances here were different, but what did it matter? If Jackson was in danger, it would be her fault that she didn't get there on time to back him up. Why had she forced him to take her gun when he clearly didn't want to? Why did she send him through the front door knowing he was apprehensive about being armed? Worrying about how she got into this mess wasn't going to help. What would help was if her partner used his training and did what was necessary.

Jesus, Jackson. You had better be using my gun.

With the gun still in her left hand, Willow pocketed her cell phone and climbed to the top of the stairs. She wrapped her fingers around the brass handle and gently turned it. Or at least she tried to turn it. She took a step back and examined the door, hoping she could breach it. There was a large window to her right, but it was at least nine feet off the ground, and it was too far away to leap for. Besides, with her dislocated finger, there was no way she was going to be able to hold herself by the ledge while opening the window. Worry clawed at her chest, making it difficult to breathe. Willow lowered her gaze and shook her head. She needed a way inside and she needed to do it now. Under her feet was a thick wicker mat. Colorful yellow and orange flowers surrounded the word 'Welcome' which was woven into the ratan strands.

What did she have to lose? Maybe the woman who sold drugs wasn't the brightest light on the Christmas tree. Low-level criminals weren't renowned for their massive intellects. With her gun trained on the door, Willow bent down and lifted the mat. She recoiled as a handful of earwigs skittered off, leaving behind a single chrome key.

Thank God for stupid people.

Willow slipped the key into the door handle's center-cut keyhole and turned. Both the key and the doorknob turned with ease. She gave a gentle push, opening the door just far enough to clear the latch. After switching the pistol to her dominant hand, Willow crouched low and eased open the door.

Nobody was in sight.

The door opened to a bright yellow galley-style kitchen. With her gun at the lead, Willow stood straight and slipped inside. The room was empty, with two doorways on the far side. One led to a dining room where fancy wood chairs could be seen. The other likely led to the front hall. Raising her gun, she moved forward. A man's voice that Willow didn't recognize halted her in her tracks.

"Get the fuck off me. You're a fucking dead man. Do you hear me? You're fucking dead."

"I'm Special Agent Jackson Brooks with the FBI, and you're under arrest. You have the right to remain silent. Anything you say can and will be used against you. You have the right to an attorney. If you cannot afford an attorney, one will be appointed to you. Do you understand these rights as I have explained them to you?"

Atta boy, Jackson.

Willow picked up her pace. She was about to round the corner when a third voice broke the moment of silence. A female voice.

"Don't do it, Mr. Brooks. Put your hands in the air and get off Zeke."

"Shoot the motherfucker, Evelina," Zeke said. "I can't go back to prison."

Her pulse raced as adrenaline surged through Willow's veins. She forced herself to take a steadying breath before creeping forward to the doorway. She stepped around the corner with her finger poised over the trigger guard. Everything moved in slow motion, her brain working overtime to process the entirety of what was happening.

Jackson was kneeling on the back of a downed man, forcing his arm in a chicken-wing hold. He held out his free hand like a traffic cop telling a car to stop. A tiny woman with platinum blonde hair was facing Willow's partner. It was impossible to tell for certain, but the way her arms were raised, she had to have been holding a gun.

"Evelina," the man on the ground said. "Behind you."

The barrel of the fifty-caliber gun swung around. In the millisecond that passed, Willow processed the situation. Her training was to shoot the girl, aiming for her center mass. That might have been the safest choice, but at this range, her Ruger LCP would likely kill the suspect. If Ranger were here, he'd already have the woman by the wrist and would be wrestling her to the ground. Instead of shooting, Willow took three long strides, closed the gap between her and Evelina, and pistol-whipped the girl across the side of the head. The butt of her handgun met with the girl's temple, and a deafening blast echoed through the house.

Chapter Thirty-Two

Jackson

Jackson's ears rang. Willow and Evelina both dropped to the floor, while Zeke struggled against his bonds.

"Agent Banks?" Jackson wanted to run to her, but he couldn't release his prisoner. "Willow? Are you okay?"

Willow rolled onto her back, gripped her neck, and let loose a long string of unintelligible curses.

"Are you hit?" Jackson craned his neck for a better look. It was a stupid question, but in the heat of the moment, they were the only words that came to mind. Zeke thrashed and nearly escaped. Jackson planted his free hand behind his prisoner's head and ground the man's face into the hardwood floor.

"Holy shit, that stings." Willow pulled her hand away from her neck, revealing a small amount of blood. "The stupid bitch winged me. Are you okay?"

"Me?" Jackson asked, leaning into his prisoner. "Yeah. I'm fine. Are you sure you're okay?"

Willow grabbed the Desert Eagle from Evelina's hand and pushed it out of reach. "Yes, except for the burning in my neck and my swollen purple finger." She holstered her pistol and grabbed Evelina by the hair. The petite woman was a rag doll, out cold from being smacked on the side of her head. Willow slapped her across the face. "Wake up!"

"We need to call an ambulance." Jackson didn't like the amount of blood seeping from Willow's wound. She said the bullet grazed her, but he wasn't so sure. His partner ignored him. She was too busy trying to rouse the woman who shot her, but Evelina was out cold. "Willow, call an ambulance and then look for something to tie this guy up. I can't let go of him."

Willow's brow knitted into a tight V. "What do you mean, tie him up? Just cuff him."

A groan crept up from Jackson's belly. He had used his cuffs to detain selfie-girl, and he never bothered to get them back. He flashed an apologetic grin. It was mostly out of embarrassment. What else could he do?

Willow reached around her back and pulled a set of handcuffs off her belt. "What sort of special agent doesn't carry handcuffs?" she asked as she tossed them at him—much harder than was necessary.

While Jackson handcuffed his prisoner, Willow continued her efforts to wake up Evelina. "She's breathing, right?" He couldn't handle another death, even if it wasn't by his hand. "Did you have to hit her so hard?"

"It was either knock her out or shoot her." Willow laid Evelina on her back and pressed an ear to her chest. "And yes, she is breathing, and her heartbeat is strong and steady." Blood dripped from Willow's neck onto the unconscious woman's chest.

With his prisoner fully secured, Jackson pulled out his phone and dialed 911. He requested an ambulance and police backup to their location. As soon as he hung up, he called Savannah and filled her in on what was happening. "She said she'd request a warrant and send two agents over to conduct a search of the premises."

Willow nodded and pressed her hand over the wound. She didn't want to let on, but it was clearly bothering her. "While we're waiting, you need to clear the upstairs. I'll stay here with these two."

Jackson looked at the wooden banister that led to the second floor. He wished that Ruby was here. If there were any perps hiding, she'd know it long before she climbed the stairs. His palm was slick when he reached behind his back to draw Willow's Glock. If there was anyone laying in wait, they'd have the advantage.

As his foot touched the first step, a memory struck him—*Hiding in a closet. The trembling hand of a frightened young teenager gripping a gun. The sheer panic on the boy's face...* A desperate urge to vomit wracked Jackson's body. His legs became leaden. He glanced over at Willow. She was leaning against the wall, clutching at the wound on her neck. Her shoulder was now covered in blood, and her face was deathly pale. He may have been struggling with his own demons, but he couldn't allow his fears to endanger the life of his partner. He couldn't be responsible for the death of another innocent. Not again.

The stairs groaned under Jackson's weight. Each step announced his ascent. With his gun at the ready, he pressed his shoulder against the wall. Stairwells of any kind were dangerous. With no place to duck and hide, they were a kill zone. He took another step, allowing him a better view of the second floor. All he could see was a wall covered with cat paintings. The cute, fluffy portraits did nothing to ease his anxiety. As he tightened his grip on his pistol, a wave of regret crashed into his consciousness.

"Drop the gun," Jackson had shouted. The boy was fourteen at most—bone-thin, wearing only a pair of white briefs. Dark circles highlighted his bright blue eyes. The kid was terrified. He stared directly at Jackson's face, his eyes unseeing.

A cold chill ran up Jackson's spine as he continued up the stairs, step by step. He didn't stop until he reached the hallway. Tucking his gun close to his body, he took a quick peek around the corner. His heart rate was much too fast. His palms were far too sweaty.

Brandon Caldwell was the boy's name. Jackson only learned that days later. He had been one of twenty-three children who had been abducted and forced into...

Jackson shuddered. He didn't want to think about it. Not now. Not ever. The poor boy had been so scared, but like a beaten dog, he had found a way to fight back.

The upstairs hallway had four doors. Two to the left and two to the right. The first door, the one nearest the top of the stairs, was likely the bathroom. It was a popular design choice in these older homes. The door was closed. If someone was behind it, they could be waiting, holding a gun, ready to shoot the first person who came into view. Sweat bloomed under Jackson's arms and down his spine.

Ruby had alerted him to the closet that day, her low growl barely audible over the hammering of his own heart. He remembered the way she had frozen, with her focus locked on the door. Jackson had called out and demanded the person inside surrender, but there was no response. He threw open the closet door, revealing the terrified young teen hiding in the darkness. The boy hadn't wanted to hurt anyone—he just wanted his own pain to end. If only Jackson had known he was a victim and not another abuser, he wouldn't have surprised the child.

With his finger on the trigger, Jackson nudged the door open, his pulse quickening. The bathroom was long and narrow, the dim light casting shadows that made it feel smaller. It seemed empty, but his eyes darted to the tub. A powder blue toilet sat against the far wall, just beside a tub with its shower curtain drawn tight.

"I'm Special Agent Jackson Brooks... You're safe." The wide-eyed boy stood alone in the dark closet. His body trembled while he pointed a thirty-eight at Jackson's chest. He hadn't heard Jackson's words. He didn't see the agent as a savior, but as another abuser ready to denigrate and torture him further. The child's finger twitched, and a gunshot rang out.

Anger and frustration filled Jackson. It pushed him forward. He was holding his gun low when he threw open the shower curtain. He didn't care if someone was hiding there, or what they might do to him. Whatever happened, he likely deserved it. His mother's church preached that God was loving and filled with forgiveness, but that didn't line up with what Jackson experienced in his lifetime. A loving god wouldn't let children be abused in the ways that they were. A forgiving god wouldn't have put him in a situation where he would be standing face to face with a frightened child holding a gun.

Jackson wheeled around and exited into the hallway. The next door was open. He didn't slow as he entered the room. Everything here was a nauseating shade of pink, like a bottle of Pepto had exploded and nobody bothered to clean it up. The closet was a pair of mirrored sliding glass doors. One side was open, showing off an array of dresses. Unlike the pink that filled every corner of the room, the clothing appeared to include every color of the rainbow.

"Sit still and shut up!" Willow's words echoed up from the first floor. Her voice snapped Jackson out of the funk that had crept into his soul. Other people's lives were at stake here, not just his own. He needed to focus on the task at hand and stop dwelling on a past that could never be changed.

Standing to the side, Jackson pulled the pair of closet doors. They slid with minimal effort. He raised his gun and stepped in front. The closet was empty, except for more dresses hanging neatly from their hangers. He blew out a breath and centered himself. He had two more rooms to go.

Approaching sirens calmed Jackson's nerves. Despite the corruption in the Florence PD, there were plenty of good cops. Those who were on the take were in the minority—at least he hoped that was true. He should wait for backup, but clearing the top floor was something he needed to do. For himself and for his wounded partner.

With his gun leading the way, Jackson entered the next bedroom. Unlike the obnoxious pink room, this space was tiny and paneled with dark wood. A writing desk and chair filled most of the space. A laptop sat closed on the glass surface. There was no closet and nowhere to hide. He took a step back and turned toward the last room.

Jackson sucked air through his nose and pushed open the final door. Sunshine blinded him as it streamed through a wall of windows. Instincts kicked in, and he dropped into a crouch, making himself as small as possible. His eyes adjusted, giving him a better view of the room. It looked more like a library or a reading room. Floor-to-ceiling bookcases crammed with books of all shapes and sizes covered every wall. A red velour couch was arranged by the windows, with a small table standing next to it. On the table were a stack of paperbacks. On the daybed was another book featuring a bare-chested man on the cover. *Lover's Quarrel* by Rachel Persie.

Chapter Thirty-Three

Willow

Willow winced as the paramedic applied antiseptic ointment to her wound. "You're very lucky," the exceptionally large woman said. The EMT's physique suggested she could bench-press a bus.

"How's the perp?" Willow asked. "Is she going to be okay? I gave her a rather hard rap on the noggin."

"My partner is with her, but since he's not calling me for help, I'm going to assume she's fine." The paramedic leaned closer. "I'd have shot her. She was carrying a cannon."

"I need to talk to her." Willow lifted her chin, allowing the paramedic enough room to place a bandage over the wound. The ointment's analgesic properties had already begun to alleviate the pain. "Are we done?"

"Since you won't let me splint your finger…" The paramedic shook her head in annoyance. "I guess so." She handed Willow a tube of ointment. "Remember to change the dressing on your neck twice a day for three days. Don't use this sparingly. You'll be thankful for it."

Willow tucked the salve into her pocket and glanced over to where the second EMT was strapping Evelina onto her gurney. "I'm coming for the ride to the hospital." She didn't wait for a response. Before the ambulance doors closed, Willow pushed her way past and climbed on board.

"You can't be here," the paramedic said. He was young, geeky, and looked completely out of his element. "Excuse me... ma'am... you can't ride along."

"I'm an FBI special agent, and this woman shot me." Willow flashed her badge and used it to point to the wound on her neck. "Your partner says I need to go to the hospital, and since you're the only ambulance here..."

The burly female paramedic closed the doors, locking Willow in with her suspect along with the other EMT, who looked ready to jump out the back. When the engine rumbled to life, Willow stuck her head through the passageway to the cab. "Take your time, okay? No lights. No sirens." She glanced over her shoulder. "And your partner might want to sit up front with you. I'll let you know if your patient is showing any signs of distress."

The big woman chuckled and called her partner up front. After a brief but futile objection, the young man squeezed himself into the passenger seat.

"I'm guessing this isn't how you expected your day to go." Willow poked Evelina in the shoulder. "We can add the attempted murder of a federal agent to the conspiracy to commit murder charges you're already going to be saddled with. Add that to the litany of drug charges, and I'm thinking you'll be sitting in a federal penitentiary for about thirty-seven years."

Evelina remained silent, keeping her eyes closed and pretending to be unconscious. The beads of moisture on the woman's upper lip betrayed that she'd heard everything Willow had said.

"Do you think your boss, Mr. Brock Ainsley, is going to give a shit if you spend the majority of your life doing hard time? I'm betting he's already filling your position with the next little bitch who will kiss the ring and do his bidding... or should I say... bedding."

The last comment made Evelina flinch. The threat of prison didn't faze her, but the idea that her boss might find comfort in the arms of another... *Stupid little girl.*

"Who told you to spike the coffee with ketamine and benzos? Was it Brock? Was it that cheating, two-timing sonofabitch?"

Evelina turned away from the questions and briefly struggled against her restraints.

"You're tied down and handcuffed. Where do you think you're going to go? Tell me who ordered you to dose the coffee. I'll put in a good word with the AUSA. They might even be able to offer you immunity if you give me enough details to put away whoever murdered Rachel Persie and Agent Tanner Montgomery."

"My paramedic lent me his phone, and I called my lawyer. He told me to talk to nobody but him." Evelina continued to face the wall, doing everything she could to turn away from Willow. "So why don't you just shut the fuck up."

Willow sat on the side of the gurney and placed her hand on Evelina's thigh. "It's your right to an attorney, but you can't stop me from talking. You don't need to say a word, but I recommend you listen to what I have to say." Willow waited for several seconds to let her words sink in. "Whether I recommend attempted murder charges for shooting at me depends on what happens here. Right now, we have no proof that you are the one who slipped the drugs into the coffee. I might be incentivized to take my investigation in another direction... one that doesn't ever shine a light on you and your involvement. The alternative is, I'm going to put every ounce of my energy into locking away the woman who tried to kill me."

The ambulance bumped and rattled down the street. All the while, Evelina remained silent.

"We're about ten minutes from the hospital," the big EMT said from the front.

"That's how long you have to give me a reason to not put you away for the best years of your life." Willow applied a bit of pressure to the woman's leg. "I'm guessing lover boy isn't going to wait..."

Evelina's head snapped back to Willow. She pulled her lips back in a snarl. "You broke into my house. I had every right to defend myself." She looked away again, seemingly confident that she had struck a winning blow.

"Do you truly believe that your attempt to kill me was justified? What about my partner? Had he broken in as well?"

"He was hurting my friend." Evelina didn't bother to face Willow. "I was protecting him."

"Whoever your lawyer is, you'd better hope that he's a miracle worker... because now I can add another five years for lying to an FBI agent to your list of crimes." Evelina turned back and flashed an incredulous look. "I shit you not. I know. It's crazy, but it's true. You can ask him about it." She scooted closer to the top of the gurney and whispered. "I'm going to make your life a living hell."

"Brock had nothing to do with it. A delivery guy dropped off the drugs along with five grand and a note that said, *Dose Rachel Persie and Tanner Montgomery's coffees with ketamine. Everyone else gets the benzos. Make sure this happens, and if things go well, there is another ten thousand dollars in it for you.*"

"Did you get the ten grand?"

Evelina rolled her eyes and shook her head. Of course, she didn't. Why would an anonymous person bother to follow up? The deed was done.

Willow almost felt bad for the young woman. Pretty and gullible was not a winning combination. "What company did the delivery man work for?"

"Company? It was some punk on a bike."

"What did he look like? Would you be able to pick him out of a lineup?"

"I don't know what he looked like. It was dark and why would I care what some kid on a bike looked like?" Her expression darkened. "He told me it was a subpoena, and that I had been served. Had he not said that I'd have thrown it in his face."

"He was a process server?"

"A what?"

Jesus, how dim is this woman?

Willow suppressed a sigh of frustration. "Never mind that. Do you still have the note?"

Evelina rolled her eyes and shook her head. "I threw it out with the trash. It was like a week ago when I got it." The woman's eyes lit up. "I'll bet it was the homeless dude that was behind it. The one who shot Rachel and the other guy."

"Wow." Willow pressed her hands to her cheeks, feigning shock at the insightful revelation. "You figured that out all on your own?"

"Can I get something for the pain?" Evelina called out. "My head is killing me."

"We're pulling into the hospital," the male EMT said. "Someone will take care of that right away."

"Last chance to give me something that can help you," Willow said.

"I've told you everything." Evelina started thrashing against her bonds. "I swear. I told you everything except..." She met Willow's gaze, her eyes wide and brows slightly raised. It was her last-ditch attempt for sympathy. "Brock is selling drugs through the restaurant. The students order special meals..."

"And Mr. Ainsley is there while this is happening? Was he there the morning of the murders?"

"No, he's never there. He doesn't want to be *connected* to them, if something goes wrong."

"But he doesn't mind that you might be implicated? Afterall, he's made you his drug mule."

Evelina's face soured.

"We're here," the EMT called.

"Will you testify in court?" Willow asked. "Will you tell a jury what you just told me?"

"If it keeps me out of prison, and puts that motherfucker behind bars... I'll do whatever you want."

The ambulance doors flung open, and the big paramedic looked inside. "Is everyone ready, or do you need a minute?"

Evelina's eyes were wide. Her desperation was palpable. "Yes," Willow said, patting the girl on the leg. "So long as my friend here doesn't have a memory failure, I expect she's going to live a long and happy life."

"I'm ready to go," Evelina said. "I want some pain meds. My head is really throbbing."

Willow held up a finger to the paramedics. "Don't speak to anyone," she whispered. "If you do what you promised, I'll take care of you."

"I'm Ms. Rainier's attorney, and I demand you to stop talking to my client," a tall, hawkish man said. He was dressed in a suit that had likely cost more than Willow made in two months.

Chapter Thirty-Four

Jackson

Jackson vaguely remembered having left Evelina's library when the paramedics had arrived. He watched from the veranda as the ambulance carrying Willow and Evelina disappeared around the corner. His breath came in short gasps, his legs trembling beneath him. For months, he had buried his trauma, pushing it deep down until it only resurfaced in his nightmares. His therapist had insisted that confronting these repressed memories would alleviate his migraines and set him on the path to recovery. But Jackson knew better. There was no coming back from killing a child—a frightened, abused boy who had only wanted to escape his captors. Savannah had called it tragic but unavoidable. Kill or be killed. Jackson's minister had claimed it was a service, speeding the boy into the loving hands of Jesus Christ, our lord and savior. He'd said the boy would have lived a tormented life, potentially ruining everyone who loved him.

Jackson believed Savannah understood his burden, but he thought the minister was a moron. Nobody deserved to die for wanting to live. It was never better to be dead than alive. The memories flooded back with crystal clarity: the scars on the boy's wrists, the cigarette burns on his arms and chest, the .38 trembling in his hands. The child hadn't seen the FBI letters emblazoned across Jackson's windbreaker. His vision had been obscured by tears and months of physical, psychological, and sexual abuse.

"I'm going to need to take your statement," a voice said, barely registering in Jackson's consciousness. It sounded a million miles away. "SA Brooks," the voice repeated, louder and more forceful. "SAC Greene wants a full accounting of what happened here." Agent Thomas Crenshaw leaned closer. "Are you okay, Jax?"

Jackson nodded. He wasn't sure when Crenshaw had arrived. He was suddenly aware he was still clutching Willow's gun. He breathed a word of thanks before tucking it into his waistband. "Sure," he said. "Walk with me. I want to take a look around."

"Umm..." Crenshaw paused, struggling for words. "No can do. You're..."

"Savannah doesn't want me searching the house?" Heat rose in Jackson's chest. "Are you kidding me?"

"She thinks..." Crenshaw shook his head. "I don't give a flying fuck what she thinks, Jax. It makes no sense to me what she's doing. Well, other than... did you know she's going to be announcing her candidacy for the State Senate? I swear, she's been off her game for a couple of months. It all started when she got a visit from the governor and the Alabama GOP party leader. It's like all she cares about these days is making arrests. When the Assistant US Attorney couldn't make the charges stick, she publicly attacked the man. I mean, holy hell, Jax. We arrested people with almost no evidence against them. It was only after we had them in custody that we started finding reasons to incarcerate them. Three court cases were thrown out because the evidence the AUSA presented, evidence that the FBI had supplied him with, was deemed inadmissible."

"You're right," Jackson stared across the street, his eyes unfocused. "That's not like Savannah at all. She had the best conviction rate of any agent I've worked with. The US Attorney's office loved her. When she made an arrest, she brought solid, actionable evidence, that the prosecutors could easily make stick."

"Come on, Jax" Crenshaw said. "Give me the details of what happened while you look around, but if anyone asks, I'm going to say you forced your way inside. By the way, where's Ruby? I can't recall the last time I've seen you without her... well, except for yesterday at the SBI. Is she okay?"

Jackson pulled open the door and invited the agent to take the lead inside. "She's fine. Ruby's at home, keeping an eye on a new arrival."

"I have no idea what that means," Crenshaw said, "but I'm happy to hear she's still with you. She's one of the best dogs I've ever seen. You can't help but smile when you meet her." A middle-aged woman with heavy makeup and short black hair moved closer. She noisily cleared her throat, spurring Crenshaw to introduce her. "Ah, Jax. I don't believe you two have met. This is Olivia Tate. She works in the crime lab."

"By my estimation, there was over sixty grand worth of drugs in that satchel," Olivia said, skipping over any pleasantries. She was busy affixing a seal to an evidence bag containing Evelina's Desert Eagle. She held up another clear plastic bag that contained an Uzi with an extended cartridge. "This was in the bag as well. The delivery man's name is Zeke Small, at least according to his driver's license. He refused to say anything other than *lawyer*."

"Where is Mr. Small now?" Jackson asked. He hadn't seen him leave.

"Agents, you're going to want to see this," someone called from upstairs. "I didn't touch it."

"Small's in the dining room," Crenshaw said, "and I can guarantee that idiot touched whatever it was he said he didn't touch."

"Who's up there?" Jackson said. "Savannah said she was sending two agents to search the premises. Has a search warrant even been issued yet?"

"It's the two Florence PD officers who arrived on scene…" Crenshaw tilted his head. "Are you okay, Jax? They walked right past you while you were standing on the porch."

A knot gripped Jackson's neck, directly at the base of his skull. He pulled out his medication and popped another into his mouth. He knew he was exceeding the recommended dosage, but he couldn't let himself be sidelined because of a debilitating headache. "I remember them," he lied. "I just didn't expect them to be wandering around an FBI crime scene."

"They're performing a secondary search, making sure nobody else is hiding." He glanced at the other FBI agent, a young woman who Jackson didn't recognize. "I don't think Olivia had the nerve to go up by herself. She's a new lab tech, but she's doing a good job of bagging and tagging evidence."

"And what's your excuse for letting them go up?" Jackson pinned Crenshaw with an accusatory stare. "I've watched you kick down doors when you knew there were armed perps on the other side."

"I was trying to get Mr. Small to talk," he said with a shrug. "I told them to only look, and not touch *anything*."

"Agent Crenshaw," the officer said. He had come down a few stairs to see what the hold up was.

"Don't get your panties in a bunch, we're coming." Crenshaw grimaced at Jackson, stretching his mouth to comical proportions.

Jackson's heart raced as he ascended the stairs, sweat beading on his brow. He systematically touched his thumb to each finger as he tried to remember five things he'd seen while he was clearing the second floor. As he listed off his memories, the book written by Rachel Persie came to mind. The novel had been sitting next to the reading chair in the library. He doubted it had anything to do with the case, but Jackson hated coincidences.

"What's got you so excited?" Crenshaw asked. When the police officer pointed to an air-conditioning grate across from the bed, he pursed his lips and motioned with his head for them to take a closer look.

Jackson, who was a good head taller than his counterpart, craned his neck. "A hidden camera pointed at her bed. Classy lady."

"Can't wait to see who she's got on tape," Crenshaw said. "I'll bet it's going to be em—barr—assing!" When Jackson cocked a questioning eyebrow, the agent shrugged. "The only reason to keep a secret camera in a bedroom is to catch people in compromising positions."

He wasn't wrong, and the thought of it made Jackson's stomach churn. Too many times he'd conducted raids on abusers' homes, only to find massive video libraries of their crimes against humanity. It wasn't enough that they tortured and demeaned children, they also wanted to watch themselves do it or sell their despicable recordings to other sick individuals. Knowing there was a market for such things... he couldn't think about it. If he did, he might slip into that dark place, the one he feared he'd never come back from. It was another horror that he had managed to keep compartmentalized and buried deep in his subconscious.

While Crenshaw and the other two police officers were busy speculating about who might be on the videos, Jackson made his way to the library. He wanted to see Rachel's book, the one he'd noticed when he had been clearing the room. Neither the FBI agent nor the police officer noticed when he slipped out of the room. As he stepped into the reading room, Jackson focused on the scarlet couch and the book laying open, face-down upon it. A sneer pulled at the corner of his lips. The bare-chested man adorning the cover was Levi. From out of the darkness that surrounded the central figure, the outline of a woman could barely be seen, and in that woman's hand, was a knife. Only then did Jackson notice there was no barcode on the back cover. This could only mean that it was a private printing and not an officially published novel, suggesting that Rachel and Evelina were likely friends. How else could she have gotten an early-release copy of the book?

Jackson pulled out his camera and took a photo. He flipped through a few pages, stopping when he saw a hand-written note scribed on the title page.

To Evelina, my best friend and my biggest fan. You always stood by me, no matter what others said. Rachel.

Jackson put the novel back where he found it and snapped a pic of the books neatly stacked on the end table. Based on the titles, *Hot like Me, Billionaire's Harem*, and *Mr. Big's Last Date*, it was clear that Evelina liked her stories spicy. There was one title at the bottom of the pile didn't fit with the rest. *Of Kings and Wizards* sounded more like epic fantasy than contemporary romance. The author's name was JT Mitchell. It made Jackson chuckle. It was the same name as the head of the cyber crimes division.

With his camera at the ready, Jackson reviewed the shelves and the hundreds of books that were stuffed into every shelf. As he snapped photos, he noticed many repeats. The author's name printed on the spine, EV Rainier. He didn't know Evelina's middle name, but he was certain these were her novels.

"Whatcha doing?" Crenshaw asked. "I thought you had slipped out without giving me your accounting of what happened."

Jackson cringed. He'd forgotten all about it. "Did you find the computer the camera was connected to? I'm assuming you searched for it."

"Couldn't tell for sure," Crenshaw said. "Not without touching things. I called Savannah. She said the electronic warrant should be here before six. By the time I finish getting your story, I hope to have it. We can tear this place apart, just like the old days, before you traded in the VCAC for whatever the hell it is you're doing here. The rumor mill suggests you needed a break after..."

Jackson's shoulders slumped, the memories pressing down on him. It was bad enough that he had to live with what he'd done, but to be the center of the coffee-room's gossip clutch…

Crenshaw's face reddened. "Jesus, Jax. I'm sorry." He ran his fingers through his hair. "I… I can't imagine what you're going through. Fuck the idiots who have nothing better to do than… I'm going to stop talking now. How's about you tell me what happened here, and we forget how I can be an insensitive twat-waffle."

"Forget about it," Jackson said. More than anything, he wanted to change the channel. Giving Crenshaw the details of what had happened was the simplest escape plan. With meticulous detail, he recounted everything that had happened. Well, almost everything. He skipped over the part that included his having to borrow Willow's service weapon. Since neither he nor Willow had fired a shot, it wasn't relevant to the narrative. He didn't need to feed the gossipers and rumormongers.

By the time he was finished, the search warrant still hadn't come through. His thoughts immediately shifted to Willow, wondering how she was doing. He checked his phone for messages, but there was nothing. A unexpected pang that started in his belly and worked its way up to his heart caused Jackson to suck in a breath. It worried him that he hadn't heard from her, and his mind couldn't help but jump to the worst conclusions.

Are you okay? Please get in touch. He typed out the message and hit send. As the seconds ticked past, anxiety crept into Jackson's consciousness. What if the wound had been more severe than it had looked? What if something had happened on the way to the hospital? Surely, if all was well, she'd have already let him know. With each new thought, his worry deepened.

"I've got to go," Jackson said. "I need to check in on SA Banks. Keep me posted on what you find once the search warrant arrives. Give me the full details, not the redacted version I fear Savannah will want to share."

"Sure thing, Jax," Crenshaw said with a quirky smile. "Go be the pretty agent's white knight. Maybe you can kiss her booboo better."

Good Lord. Was he overreacting about the state of Willow's health? "Ha ha," he said by way of an incredibly weak retort. "She took a bullet to the throat, and I haven't heard from her since she left with Ms. Rainier."

"Admit it, Jax. You like her. I can't remember the last time you've been on a date." Crenshaw lifted an eyebrow. "I don't think I've ever heard you talk about being out with a woman. Do your predilections go in a different sort of direction?" His knowing wink made Jackson want to punch him in the face.

"Just because I don't advertise my personal life, doesn't mean I don't have one," he said. Crenshaw's snigger suggested there was going to be a new topic around the water cooler when he returned to the Birmingham field office.

"Go, Lover Boy! Save the damsel. Be the hero." Crenshaw slapped Jackson on the back.

Jackson would have strenuously objected to the joke had he not been running down the stairs, taking three steps at a time.

Chapter Thirty-Five

Willow

Willow noticed Jackson's growing frustration. During the drive home from the hospital, he had been silent and visibly awkward, reminiscent of a teenage boy on his first date—completely unsure of what to say or do. When he arrived at the hospital, he had burst through the curtains of her emergency room bay. His expression was a mixture of concern and relief, and for a brief moment, Willow thought he was going to hug her. Instead, he stuttered and blustered and babbled like an idiot before saying he was glad that she was okay. She found his awkward concern for her to be charming and endearing.

Jackson's silence broke when they turned into the laneway. Levi and Maybelle were sitting on the porch deep in conversation while the three dogs laid at their feet. They lifted their heads as Jackson threw the gearshift into park. By the time he had opened his door, they were at the truck. Ranger was leaping up at Willow's window while Ruby and Boone were weaving their bodies around Jackson's legs.

"Momma!" he shouted as he stormed toward them. He'd called his mother's name, but his eyes were locked on Levi. "You..." It seemed his anger had left him lost for words. "Levi..."

"She came into my room when Boone barked at a squirrel trying to claw its way through the window." Levi threw up his hands as if trying to ward off Jackson's fury, but all he ended up doing was giving him something to grab on to. Jackson yanked Levi out of his chair and dragged him down the stairs. Boone took offense to the way his owner was being handled and threw himself at Jackson's legs. Ruby, who looked ready to eviscerate the much smaller dog, nipped at the Border Collie's hindquarters. To Willow's surprise, Ranger stayed out of it. The entire encounter came to an abrupt end before any serious injuries were sustained.

"You can't be outside, and my mother can't be climbing staircases." Jackson was clearly trying to keep his voice low as he spoke through clenched jaws, but he was failing miserably.

"Your mom's doing better than she lets on." Levi said. His voice dropped too low for Willow to listen further, but the way the men had turned and looked at Maybelle suggested they were still talking about her.

"It seems your son doesn't think you're capable of deciding what physical activity you're up to doing," Willow said. The memory of how he had come charging into her hospital ward popped into her head. "He's got an overprotective streak in him, doesn't he?"

"Oh," Maybelle said, waving off the notion. "He's got a heart the size of Texas, and he'd fight to the death to protect the people he loves. I'm sure you'll see that in time." The words made Willow's pulse race. Had he developed feelings for her? Is that why he'd come crashing into her room? They'd known each other for barely more than a day, but she couldn't deny the attraction she felt towards him. Jesus. She gave herself a mental shake. It had been an exhausting forty-eight hours. She decided her feelings were a mixture of sleep deprivation and a need to fill the hole left by her partner's death. Neither was a good reason to dive into a relationship. She glanced at the man who now had his finger pointed into Levi's face.

He does make for a pleasant distraction, though.

Willow's phone buzzed, rescuing her from her meandering and inappropriate musings. She swiped the little receiver symbol and pressed her cell to her ear.

"Agent Banks," her contact in the US Marshal's office began as he apologized for the delay in getting back to her but was regretful to inform Willow that he was unable to get Levi into WITSEC. Based on the information she had provided, the risk to his life didn't rise to the level required to get into the program. He did go on to say that if he testified against Mayor Persie or the District Attorney, he would qualify for whistleblower status, and that he might be able to afford him some additional protective services. She wanted to argue her case, but Willow knew better. The decision wasn't his, and she'd have better luck finding whiskey in a bottle of wine.

"Bad news?" Maybelle asked. "You look like you just sucked a lemon."

"Yeah…" Willow took a seat next to Jackson's mother. "I wanted to put Levi into WITSEC."

"But the DOJ had other ideas?" Maybelle tutted. "If everything Mr. Benson told me is true, I'm afraid you've stepped into a bear's den."

"How much did he tell you?" Willow was becoming more and more fond of the woman. She was the calm at the eye of the storm.

"Plenty. It took me a while to break through his protective shell, but once I did, the man wouldn't shut up. He even told me about how the SBI were investigating my Jax for his part in the mayor and Chief Wheeler's… indiscretions. I tell you what, I put that part to rest. But if he's only half right about what Persie and Wheeler are up to… Lord, save us all. Those two men need to be exposed, prosecuted, and stuffed into a jail cell until they're worm food."

"The rich and powerful always seem to find a way past the rules," Willow said. "It's fucking disgusting, but it's also the truth." Maybelle pressed her lips into a thin line, clearly annoyed with Willow's use of vulgar language. "I'm sorry for the way I speak. I know you don't appreciate it, and I'll do my best to curtail it."

"I know I'm an old prude at times," Maybelle said. She rolled her eyes. "I suppose my daddy's switch across my backside has ingrained certain sensibilities that I can't shake. You speak the way you want, and I'll react the way I want, and neither of us will let it color our view of the other." She stuck out her bony hand. "Deal?"

Maybelle's grip was surprisingly strong as they shook on their ladies' agreement.

"Momma, tell me Joanna didn't see Levi," Jackson said as the two men and three dogs drew near.

"No," Maybelle said, her voice overflowing with sarcastic annoyance. "I didn't let her see him. Some days, Jax, I swear you don't even know me."

"Some days I don't think I do," Jackson said. Willow cringed. She knew exactly where the conversation was headed. "Maybe you can explain these experimental treatments I just found out about. What the—" Maybelle tilted her head to side and pursed her lips, catching her son before he cussed. She had trained her son well, like a good dog. "Why didn't you say anything to me?"

"Because I know you'd have disapproved," Maybelle said. There was a dire challenge in her tone that said, in no uncertain terms, that this was not her son's decision to make. "I was either going to go out quick, or I was going to get better. But the last thing I wanted was to waste away and be a burden on you."

"How can you possibly afford this?" Jackson dropped to a knee in front of his mother. "Tell me you didn't mortgage the house." Ruby pushed her way into the conversation and dropped a chin on the woman's lap.

"I didn't borrow money," she said, taking her son's hands in hers. "Grace gave it to me. With her husband passing, she wanted to do something good with his fortune. I became another one of her projects."

"Is that the woman I met in the diner with the Chihuahua?" Willow asked, thinking back to her first meeting with Jackson.

"The very same," Jackson answered. "She's an old friend of the family."

Levi let out a big breath, like the news of where the funding had come from had lifted a weight off his shoulders. Like SSA Marsden and Detective Castor, Levi had been concerned about where the funds had come from, fearing that, perhaps, Jackson was on the take.

"How are the treatments progressing?" Willow asked. She took a seat beside Jackson's mother. Based on Jackson's expression, she had asked the very question that had been burning in his mind. He almost looked to be praying that the prognosis would be favorable.

"The cancer is in complete remission," Maybelle said. Jackson's face lit up at the news, but the sagging corners of Maybelle's mouth suggested there was a darker side to the revelation. "The treatments have severely compromised my kidneys. In time, they will fail completely." She stuck out one of her legs. "Apparently, swelling in my ankles will be an early indicator."

"How long?" Jackson croaked. "Are you on the transplant list?"

Maybelle raised a shoulder. "The specialist couldn't say. The drugs are too new to fully understand how aggressively my kidney failure will progress. It might be a couple of months. It might be a couple of years. Because I'm not critical, the national transplant list won't accept me."

Jackson dropped to the floor and sat cross-legged. He looked so much like a lost little boy that it nearly shattered Willow's heart. Maybelle clearly saw the same thing, and her face became etched with concern. "We're dwelling on the darkness, Jax, when we should be praising God for the miracle he has given me. I am in complete remission and, very soon, my strength will return. Our Lord never gives us more than we can handle. Never forget that Jax.

We have faced adversity our whole life, and we have always dealt with whatever trials we've had thrown in front of us."

Maybelle's indomitable spirit almost convinced Willow that faith in a higher power was the path to true happiness. Almost. Then again, Jackson had worked with the VCAC, and he seemed able to maintain his faith in God and humanity. The thought that she could not do the same left her feeling small and more than a little empty inside.

"I don't know about you three," Maybelle said with a bright smile, "but I'm starving. Do you think you can whip us up some food, Jax? I would really enjoy some of your crispy catfish and okra. Al dropped off a six pound blue cat this afternoon. It's in the fridge." She turned to Willow. "Al and Christine run a charming Air B&B up the street. If Al's not fixing something around the house, he's out fishing. They are two of the nicest people you'll ever want to meet."

"I doubt either of those are good for you, Momma," Jackson said. "But if that's what you want…"

"It is," Maybelle said. She looked to the west and tutted. "You're going to go for a walk before you lose the last of the light. Willow needs to spend more time with Ranger."

"I'll get the rest of the dogs, too," Jackson said. "I'm sure they could use the exercise as well."

"No need," Maybelle said. "Tommy came by a while ago. He took the dogs, including Boone, for a long walk and a swim."

"He took Ranger?" Willow asked. "Holy shit." She regretted her choice of words. "I mean, that's incredible." Her pathetic attempt to correct herself made Maybelle smile.

"No," Maybelle said, her smile never waning. "I wanted Ranger to spend time with *you*. Levi and I gave him some scent training to give him a job and keep his mind busy. If Mals don't have a job, they become bored, and boredom leads to destructive behaviors. Now, you two need to get your dogs and get going. You should douse yourselves in bug spray, too. The mosquitoes are going to be out in full force before long."

Chapter Thirty-Six

Jackson

Jackson's brow furrowed as their walk led them down Echo Lane, a narrow, hilly street that followed along the water's edge. He was carefully watching Ruby and Ranger. Both seemed to be on alert, their heads high and their ears perked. There might have been a bear nearby, but they were likely picking up the scent of the large family of deer that lived in the area.

"Seek," Jackson said, whispering the word into Ruby's ear. The command was generic in nature, telling the dog to find whatever was out of the ordinary, like human remains. The Golden Retriever, as a part of her search and rescue job, was trained as a cadaver dog. Without hesitation, the dog trotted ahead, her nose in the air.

"Jesus, Ranger," Willow said, her voice laced with equal parts frustration and annoyance.

Jackson looked back to find Ranger surging at the end of his leash, and Willow struggling to restrain him. "You're still wrapping his leash around your hand. When you do, you're sending the wrong message to your dog." Jackson stuffed his hands into his pockets to stop himself from taking over.

"Because he's strong, and I've only got one hand to hold onto him," Willow said, showing off her still-swollen finger. She wrapped another loop around her wrist. "If he decides to run, I don't want him to get away."

"So, you're afraid for him?" Jackson kept his eyes forward. He didn't want to be influenced by facial expressions or body language. He was listening for the tone of Willow's responses.

"No," she said. The single word dripped with sarcasm. "I'm worried what he'll do to someone if he decides they're a perp."

"What?" Jackson stepped in front of Willow and stopped. "Has he ever done that before? Attacked a civilian without cause?"

Ranger sat by Willow's side and locked his gaze on Jackson. One ear swiveled, listening for any threats. Even on a country-road stroll, the dog's training burbled to the surface. K9's didn't take breaks. Especially Belgian Malinois. To them, everything was either an exercise or real life. They rarely had an off switch, even when they slept.

"Well… no." Willow averted her eyes, refusing to meet Jackson's gaze square on. A frown pulled at the corners of her mouth. After several seconds, she turned forward. "He almost punched his ticket when he bit an FBI handler. He's the last remnant of my partner… Kate." Ranger whined and leaned against her leg.

"Interesting." It was clear to Jackson that, despite the woman's lack of dog-handler skills, the Malinois had attached himself to her. He shared her pain. Willow pinned Jackson with a furious stare. The gold flecks in her eyes caught the light of the setting sun. "Sorry." He turned away and started walking on unsteady legs. "I didn't mean anything by it. Nothing bad, anyway. It's just that… I think you're both trying to deal with the loss of someone you cared deeply about, and you're both trying to protect the other from harm. I think that's why Ranger fought to keep you out of the restaurant the day we met. He picked up on your fear of what was beyond the doors, and he did his best to save you from it."

"Really?" Willow squeaked out the word. She took a knee beside Ranger and ran her hand over his head, scrubbing his ears. The dog leaned into the small display of affection.

"You need to show him that you trust him." The sight was breaking Jackson's heart. The idea that the FBI might have destroyed the dog because he was in a state of grief was more than he could take. "But he also needs to know that you're in charge."

"I try to." Willow's voice was defensive. "I use a big voice when I speak. I keep my commands short and precise—exactly as I was taught, exactly as Kate did."

"That's good, but there is more to it than how you speak to him." Jackson held out his hand for the leash. "You need to show him through your body actions, your demeanor..." He thumbed his hand over his heart. "He needs to feel what you feel. In here. They're far more intuitive than most people give them credit for. It's the things you do subconsciously that he picks up on. Big words. Strong actions. They're secondary to who you actually are. On the inside. Your emotions leak out without you realizing. Subtle things, like your breathing and heart rate. Clenching your hands like you're doing right now."

Willow immediately relaxed her hands and blushed.

"You can't *will* these things to happen." Jackson said, taking a deep breath to center himself. He was getting preachy, and he knew it... but he believed this philosophy down to his core. It was something taught to him by his mother, a woman he respected more than anyone, but it was their dogs that confirmed it. He had witnessed their behavior. They were the ones that confirmed his mother's teachings. "When you spend time training with the dog... you learn each other's rhythms and thought patterns. Ranger will learn from you, and you from him. He already loves you more than you realize. You just need to learn how to love him back. Not because he was your partner's dog, but because he's your dog." He flexed his fingers, asking for the leash again.

Willow unwrapped the leather from around her hand and placed the lead in Jackson's. "I'm afraid to love him." The woman's granite-like exterior cracked. She swiped at a tear that had gathered at the corner of her eye. She wrapped her arms around her belly and shuddered.

"I understand," Jackson said. He hated to see people cry. Not for any reason other than it made him cry, but right now, he needed to not let that happen. "Not for the same reasons as yours, but I understand all the same." He took a steadying breath. "I grow very attached to my dogs, even the ones I'm boarding. But my dogs, the ones that I spend practically every minute of every day with... they become a part of me. A piece of my soul. When they pass, it's like a piece of my heart has been ripped from my body. The pain never really goes away. I just learn to live with it. When I get a new dog... my first instinct is to protect myself. To not let them get too close. But it's impossible. They just have a way about them..."

Jackson bent down and unclipped Ranger's leash. He needed a moment to gather himself. "Your dog doesn't know me. He doesn't love me. But even though we've hardly spent time together, he respects me. He can feel that I am in charge." Jackson sniffed, wishing he had a Kleenex. His nose always ran when he got upset. He stood and walked briskly down the street. Head high. Shoulders back. Ruby was nowhere in sight. "Ranger, heel."

The sound of four feet came pattering up beside him. The dog went into lock step with him. He took a dozen or so paces before turning in towards Ranger, using his body to help guide the dog into the turn. They walked back toward Willow and stopped in front of her. Ranger sat at Jackson's side and looked up to him for his next instruction.

"This dog is amazing." Jackson handed Willow the leash. "He is extremely well trained, and he is on permanent alert. He is craving a leader." Jackson scrubbed the back of his neck, wiping away a thin sheen of sweat. "Not everyone believes that dogs would rather be led than be in charge—but I do. It's easier on them. They don't need to make decisions. Their leader does it for them. They thrive on routine, and it's their leader that provides it." Jackson winced.

"Am I making any sense? I kind of get into a fanatical headspace when I talk about dogs, and training them, and living with them…"

Willow smiled and nodded. "You're quite remarkable. Your passion comes through without sounding like a crazy person." The smile faded. "But I don't know how to do what you say. I don't know how to be his leader."

"Sure, you do," Jackson said. He turned around and started walking. "You're a natural leader, and I can teach you how to adapt that to leading your dog." His head turned left and right, feigning that he was searching for Ruby. He wanted to give the impression that there was a problem and that he was worried about his dog's safety. Jackson ran thirty yards up the street, pressed his fingers to his lips, and gave two short, sharp whistles.

Willow came jogging up beside Jackson with Ranger at her side. "Where'd Ruby go?"

"Did you tell Ranger to heel?" He raised an eyebrow. "He wants you to give him direction. All the time. As soon as you don't, he needs to decide on his own."

Willow pressed her lips into a thin line. She rolled her eyes and scratched Ranger's head. "Sorry, Boy. Don't hate me. Okay?"

"It would be almost impossible for him to hate you. Like I said, he already loves you, and when a dog commits like that, it's a near-unbreakable bond." Jackson flashed a quick smile before pressing his fingers to his lips to give two more sharp whistles.

"Is everything okay?" Willow searched the area. "Where did she go?"

Jackson didn't answer. He pulled the dog whistle from around his neck and gave two sharp blasts. Ranger sprung to attention and barked. "Tell Ranger to search for Ruby. Use the word *find*."

"Where is she, Boy?" Willow gave the command, sort of. She saw Jackson's disapproval and groaned. "Ranger, find Ruby!"

The Malinois sniffed the air, gave a sharp bark, and took off at a steady run up the street. After traveling a hundred yards or so, he made a sharp turn to the left and disappeared into the forest.

"Call him back," Jackson said. "Keep it simple. Just 'Ranger, come.' Hurry, before he's too far away."

"Ranger, come!" Willow called. She was sucking in a breath to yell again, but Jackson shook his head. The Malinois appeared from the forest's edge, his ears alert.

"Praise him and call him to you. Right away. You need to mark his good behavior."

Willow did as Jackson instructed, and Ranger came bounding back to her. He unleashed a series of excited, ear-piercing barks.

"Keep praising him," Jackson urged. "Make his coming back to you as fun and happy as you can manage." He watched with amusement as the woman and dog bounced around each other. "How did you feel before you called him? When he had disappeared into the woods, how did you feel?"

"What?" Willow froze. Her hands were across Ranger's back, mid pet. "What do you mean?"

"Were you happy, frightened...? What emotion were you feeling?"

"Um... concerned, I guess. I was worried about Ruby. I was afraid she was in trouble." She gave Jackson a flat stare that suggested he might be a bit dim.

"Excellent." Jackson smiled at her. "You were worried about someone else. Not Ranger. You sent him out on a potentially dangerous assignment, and your concern was for his target. Not him."

"So?" That same 'Are you stupid?' expression etched into her face. The expression melted away and her eyes widened. "I treated him like my partner..."

Jackson gave a small nod. "And when you called him back to you? What emotion were you feeling?"

Willow's brows knitted together. "I have no idea. I was doing what you told me to do."

"Were you worried that he was out of sight?"

"At first. A little, but when you said to call him back." Her eyebrows shot up. "I was really worried because I thought you were worried."

"Your fear was in your voice. Did you notice his reaction when he came out of the woods? He was looking to you for more instructions. He could see you were in no danger, so he didn't know why you were frightened earlier. Calling him to you and praising him fulfilled his need."

"Okay. Now you're just screwing with me. Every single word you said was pure bullshit." She was watching Jackson like she was interrogating him. He held her gaze, never backing down, and giving no clue about his true emotions. "It was bullshit, right?"

"It might be," he said, raising his shoulders slightly. "But I believe it's true. In my experience, dogs pick up on things that nobody else can… except maybe horses. Not that I'm a horse expert by any means. But they do seem acutely aware of the people around them."

Willow looked up the street to where Ranger had disappeared to. "Where is Ruby, anyway? Aren't you worried she didn't come when you called her."

"Nope." Jackson walked away. "I told her to hold. One whistle blast is for her to come. Two is to stay where she is." He turned back. "They are the most important commands a dog can learn. Sit. Down. Place. They're all good, but come and stay can save her life. I wish trainers would focus more on those commands and less on the others." Sometimes he couldn't help himself when it came to talking about dog training. "I want you and Ranger to find Ruby. Again, guide him, tell him what you expect of him. This time don't let him get too far ahead of you. Having him stay near while he guides you forward can be critical in dangerous situations.”

A peculiar look crossed Willow’s face, as though his words had physically harmed her.

“Are you okay?” Jackson said. “You’re looking a bit ill.”

Willow sniffed and waved him off. “It’s nothing. Let’s go. Tell me how I ask Ranger to lead while he stays beside me.”

“Sure,” Jackson said. Whatever it was that had affected Willow wasn’t nothing, but if she didn’t want to talk about it, he wasn’t going to press her. “If Ranger gets farther ahead of you than you’d like, you can choose to say *easy*, which tells him to slow, or you can say *come*, and tell him to return to you. They serve different purposes, but they’ll both keep the dog from getting away from you.”

Willow looked skeptical when she told Jackson she was ready.

Chapter Thirty-Seven

Willow

"Heel" Willow said. She took off at a dead run with Ranger at her side. Jackson had sprinted ahead and disappeared into the woods. By the time they made it to his entry point, the man was nowhere to be seen. The dying light of the day didn't help at all. She wished she had a flashlight on her. "Don't let me go the wrong way. We need to follow him."

Ranger looked up with his big brown eyes while one ear swiveled about. It reminded Willow of a directional mic trying to pick up a signal. While she fought to not get tangled in the mass of branches, the dog slipped through narrow openings with ease. "Don't you leave me behind." Willow groaned. She had already failed at giving the dog the correct commands. "Easy, Ranger. Easy."

The dog slowed, keeping himself within visible range while he followed Jackson. Willow was doing exactly what she had been told not to do—to let the dog make the decisions. This had to be different, though. There was no discernible path through the bramble, and she had no idea where she was going. The sight of Jackson crouched behind a tree sent her pulse racing. While she was still thirty yards away, he held a finger to his mouth, making a shush sign.

Ranger raced forward, leaving Willow behind. When he got beside Jackson, he laid down, his eyes and ears focused on something in the distance.

"There are three men on ATVs," Jackson whispered as Willow slipped in beside him. "They have Ruby."

The texture of the polymer handle of her Glock felt good against the palm of Willow's hand. She had the weapon drawn before she realized what she was doing. "Why would they take your dog?"

"I don't think they did." Jackson cocked his head toward where Ruby was. "I think she found them, and when I told her to hold... she obeyed. Now she won't leave them alone."

"You take Ranger and flank them," Willow said. She slipped her gun behind her back and removed her holster. "I'll come straight at them, pretending I'm lost and looking for my dog." She grabbed a handful of leaves and crushed them into her long, wavy blonde hair. "If I'm in trouble, you come in guns blazing."

Jackson got a sheepish look about him. "You know my view on carrying a gun."

At some point, Willow would find out why he had an aversion to guns. She couldn't even imagine how he'd be allowed to be on active duty if he wouldn't carry a side arm. "Okay then, if I get into trouble, send in the hair missile." Her lips pulled into a smile. "I like that nickname, even if you stole it from a TV show." Willow searched the area, hoping for an indication of where Ruby was.

"She's that way," Jackson pointed. "About forty yards. There is a clearing just past those pines."

"You saw them? How do you know that?" Willow squinted. She couldn't see jack-shit.

"I lived here my whole life. I've run through these woods a thousand times."

His annoyed exasperation got Willow's blood up. How was she supposed to know that? She pushed down her desire to defend herself and sucked a breath through her nose. "How long do you need to get into position?"

"Don't wait for us," Jackson said. He pulled his dog whistle off from around his neck. "If Ruby's in trouble, blow once. Make it short and sharp. She'll come to you."

Willow slipped the whistle over her head and crept out from behind the tree. She took extra care to not step on any fallen branches, which was no easy task in the increasingly dark and dense underbrush. She glanced over her shoulder and muttered to herself. Jackson and Ranger were already gone, and she hadn't heard them leave.

After taking forever to skulk forward, Willow peered through the heavy bows of an ancient pine tree. It might have been a spruce. She never really understood the difference. She heard the voices before she saw who she was looking for.

"What's with this damned dog? If he doesn't take off, I'm going to shoot him."

Willow poked her head through the thick evergreen branches, risking exposing herself. She needed to get a better look at what she was about to run into. There were three men in tactical camo gear and three ATVs. One of the assholes had his handgun pointed at Ruby, who was sitting and watching.

Why isn't she running away, or attacking, or doing something? Her hand went to her Glock, checking to make sure it was still safely stowed.

"Put the fucking gun away, Ramsey," a heavy-set man rocking a buzz-cut said. "The dog likely escaped from the FBI guy's kennels. Where the hell is our video feed? We've been feeding the mosquitos for over an hour and we're still blind here."

"How can I get anything ready?" said a geeky-looking fellow with a laptop, swatting at flying insects hovering around him. "Between the snakes and the swarm of"—he paused long enough to swat at a bug—"whatever the hell these things are, I can't get my bird in the air." Only then did Willow notice the large drone on the ground.

"I don't like it," Asshole said. "He won't stop staring at me."

"First off," Drone-guy said. "She's a girl. Second, if you shoot her, everyone within a two-mile radius will know we're here. Marsden will shit a brick if we fuck up again. Do you two want to spend another month working the complaints desk?"

"It's better than sitting here feeding the goddamn mosquitoes," Asshole said. "I mean, what's the point of this, anyway? You said your drone has a five-mile range. We can watch the video feed from our truck on the highway."

"Because we're here to watch Brooks's residence, and we won't have time to respond if we have to drive ten minutes to get to the house," Buzz-cut said. "Jesus Christ, I'm not going to tell you again. Put your fucking gun away."

Asshole adjusted the grip on his gun and leveled the barrel directly at Ruby. "I don't like the way *she's* looking at me. Maybe she's got rabies."

Ruby's head snapped to the right, away from where Willow was hiding. Her tail was wagging, vigorously sweeping the dirt.

Asshole turned his gun towards the forest, in the direction Ruby was looking. In an instant, Willow's world crashed down around her ears. The circumstances of the situation mirrored what happened when her partner was killed. Kate had moved out from cover, desperate to focus the enemy's attention on her rather than Ranger. Willow feared that Jackson was doing the same thing. Refusing to allow him to become the target, she drew her gun and slipped out from the pine tree. With her free hand, she put the dog whistle between her lips and pulled out her badge. A single blast on the whistle was all it took for Ruby to spin and launch herself towards her.

"FBI," Willow called out with a clear and steady voice. "Drop the gun and show me your hands." Asshole's head turned to his right, preceding his weapon. Before he had a chance to take aim, Willow repeated her order. Only when Asshole was facing her head-on did she notice the yellow letters stitched over his left breast. SBI.

Too bad for Asshole, Ranger couldn't read. The hair missile was mid-flight when he latched on to his arm. Willow had seen the K9 do this a dozen times before. The seventy-pound dog spun his body, using his size and momentum to twist the man's arm and fling him to the ground. A loud blast followed. The drone operator howled in agony as he gripped his thigh and toppled over.

Buzz-cut drew his gun and pointed at Ranger and Asshole as the two tumbled across the ground.

"FBI. Drop your weapon," Jackson bellowed. He was sprinting towards the last man standing, his long arms and legs pumping in rhythm. Ruby appeared from out of nowhere, latching onto the gunman's ankle. While the Golden Retriever hit him low, Jackson hit him high, putting his shoulder into the man's chest.

A second crack split the air.

***

"What the hell were you thinking," Willow asked as she wrapped a sterile bandage around Asshole's forearm. The man flinched as she tightened the strip of gauze. She was treating his bite wound, but she was directing the question at Jackson. He was busy applying a bandage to his shoulder. Buzz-cut's bullet had grazed him. It was barely a scratch, but like her neck wound, it was bleeding like a son of a bitch.

"I was thinking I didn't want to see your dog get killed." Jackson shot her an incredulous look. "I'm surprised you didn't shoot him yourself."

With the memory of her partner's death still on her mind, Willow had been asking herself the same question the whole way back to Jackson's house. It didn't matter if the man was an SBI agent, he was threatening the life of an FBI K9. Her K9. It would have been a mountain of paperwork, and possibly a criminal conviction for having killed the man... but none of that factored into her decision. She had frozen, and the thought of it settled like a boulder in the pit of her stomach.

"What were you doing surveilling Special Agent Brooks's home?" Willow asked. She pulled the bandage tighter, making Asshole yelp.

"Doing our job," Buzz-cut said. He was busy inspecting his ankle where Ruby had bitten him. Outside of a few red dents in his skin, he didn't appear any worse for wear. He frowned at his partner, who was stretched out on the couch. He had a thick sterile pad over his leg wound, held in place by a copious amount of gauze. "You attacked us."

"Agent Asshole was brandishing his gun like a maniac," Willow said, her gaze boring a hole through the man's face.

"The name's Jenkins," Asshole said, "Agent Jenkins."

"Like I give a shit," Willow said. "I'll ask you again. Why were you there? Under whose authority?"

"Under the authority of *it's none of your fucking business*," Buzz-cut said.

"SSA Marsden sent us to keep an eye on your residence," Drone-guy said. Jackson had cleaned and dressed his wound first. The bullet had passed through his upper thigh. After applying pressure, the bleeding slowed. Despite Jackson's assurance that no major blood vessels had been hit, he packed the wound with gauze and bandaged it tightly. Unlike Asshole and Buzz-cut, he was coping with the pain like a champ. "He said you had a man under federal custody, and he doesn't think you can protect him on your own."

Willow had her phone out and was dialing the SSA. The man answered before the second ring. "This is SA Banks. Did you send three idiots to guard Jackson's house?" The question was met with silence. "Marsden?"

"Yes. They're my guys." Marsden sounded exasperated. *"I wasn't confident that SWAT wasn't going to pay you another visit. If they did, I wanted to know about it. They were supposed to sit back and observe. They weren't supposed to go anywhere near the house."*

"If you want their report, you're going to need to meet your men at the hospital. Dog bites and self-inflicted gun-shot wounds. The ambulance is on the way. The Florence PD will be coming too, I imagine. Tough to call in an ambulance for two shooting victims without the local police making an appearance."

"If it's all the same to you," Marsden said, "I'd like to hear your side of the story first. I'll call Captain Sawyer and let them know I'm taking over the case. We're going to look like a clown show if the media gets wind of this."

"Thanks," Willow said. She wasn't certain that she trusted the police captain, but she trusted Marsden. "Do you think you could hold off coming this way until tomorrow? I don't really have the energy to deal with this shit tonight."

Marsden didn't respond, which meant he wasn't going to wait.

"Fine, have it your way." She ended the call, stuffed her phone in her pocket, and addressed Jackson. "Their story checks out, assuming they didn't concoct this beforehand. But you know what? If Marsden was looking to snatch Levi, he wouldn't have sent this circus. And, judging by his reaction to the news, he didn't send his A-team."

"Tell me about it," Drone Guy said. "My first field assignment, and I got saddled with these two."

"Fuck you, Dave," Asshole said. "If you spent more time outside and less time playing video games in your mom's basement, you'd have had your bird up in time to see these two coming our way."

"I'm a remote drone operator," Dave said. "I wasn't hired to do field work. What's your excuse? You two are the *special agents*, and from what I've seen of you, you're both some kind of special."

The wail of approaching sirens brought the conversation to a halt. Willow hoped there'd be more than one ambulance coming, otherwise these three were likely going to come to blows in the tight quarters.

Chapter Thirty-Eight

Jackson

Jackson watched the last ambulance pull away. He was weary to his bones. In less than four hours, he and Willow had both been shot. Strangely, it was clearing Evelina's house that was on auto-repeat inside his head. Having to check the closets... It didn't matter that his shooting incident was eight months ago. It remained fresh in his mind, and the memory of it continued to bubble up to the surface. If he was back home in Birmingham, he'd be making an appointment to see his therapist.

"You should have let them dress your wound," Willow said. She lightly brushed her fingers over his shoulder. "I'm afraid the blood has seeped through to your shirt."

"I wanted them out of the house." Jackson's gaze never left the street. "I'll change the dressing after I make us some dinner. I don't know about you, but I'm starving." He wasn't. Not really. But cooking was an outlet, a place where he could focus on the details of preparing the food. When he was in the kitchen, the world seemed to fade into the background.

"Does it hurt?" Willow asked. "I've got plenty of analgesic ointment. It really helps take away the sting."

"Maybe after dinner," he said, turning to face his partner. "I don't want Momma to have to wait."

"And I don't want your blood in my food," Maybelle said. "The dressing needs changing. Unless you want your momma to do it..." She flashed Willow a brief smile. "You can change her dressing as well while you're at it."

"Come on, Big Guy," Willow said, taking Jackson by the wrist. "It won't take but a moment, and you can get back to cooking us up a feast. I can't wait to find out if your catfish is anywhere near as good as your fried chicken."

He didn't fight it, but Jackson felt like he was being ganged up on. He was happy that Willow and his mother got along, but their ability to double-team him was worrisome.

"Pull off your shirt," Willow said. "I'll get the new dressing ready."

A flash of shame ripped through Jackson. He liked the idea of being in her bedroom and undressing for her. He liked it far more than he should have. His breath hitched when Willow turned back to face him, bandage in hand. The instant flush in her cheeks made Jackson's heart race.

"I put on a good amount of salve," she said. "It should make you more comfortable."

Make him more comfortable? That would be great, because right now he was about as uncomfortable as he'd ever been. Unable to hold her gaze, Jackson turned his attention to the medical tape holding his gauze pad in place. With a quick pull, he yanked it off, sending a jolt a stinging pain through his shoulder.

"Ah, Jesus," Willow said. "You've opened it up again. You might need stitches."

It was bleeding badly. Jackson pressed his old bandage back over the wound. "There's a first aid kit in the bathroom under the sink. Do you think you can stitch it for me?"

"You want me to do it?" She looked at the doorway. "Seriously?"

"The kit's got everything you'd need, but if you're not comfortable..."

"No," Willow said. She seemed to be looking for somewhere to place the ointment covered gauze she was holding. "It's not that. I've hemmed pants before, but I've never…" She gave a half shrug. "Nurse Ratchet at your service."

In no time, she had retrieved the first aid kit, cleaned the wound with iodine, and put in two stitches. She had offered to use some of her ointment to numb the area first, but Jackson had refused. When she stuck the hooked needle into his shoulder, he wished he hadn't tried to play the tough guy. It took every ounce of his willpower to not flinch.

Willow blew on the wound after she tied off the last knot. "It's supposed to make it feel better," she said with a playful grin. "I can kiss the booboo, if you'd prefer."

The offer made Jackson's ears burn. His bare torso suddenly made him feel completely exposed.

"You're blushing, Agent Brooks." She lightly punched him in the chest. "Are you sweet on me?"

"If you have to ask, Agent Banks," Jackson said, his heart pounding in his chest. "Maybe you're not as good a detective as I believe you to be."

"Oh, I'm plenty observant, Agent Brooks," Willow said, carefully taping down the fresh bandage. Her fingers lingered a moment longer than necessary. "I notice how you deflect attention when you're uncomfortable. How you cook when you're stressed. I especially notice how your eyes linger when you think I'm not watching." She stepped back, her professional mask sliding back into place, though her eyes still held a glimmer of amusement. "Now put your shirt on and go make us that catfish. Your mother's waiting."

"Not so fast," Jackson said. "You need your dressing changed as well."

"Should I take off my shirt as well?" She moved in close enough that her body warmed Jackson's exposed skin. "I mean, it seems only fair."

We like strong, take-charge men—wild stallions that ain't been broke yet... that's what Violet, the owner of Trowbridge's, had told him. It was completely out of character, but Jackson decided to give it a try. "Quite right, Agent Banks." He wrapped his arms around Willow's waist and drew her close. "It seems fair to me, too. But that would likely lead to one thing or another, and I've already promised to cook you a catfish feast. So, maybe we'll keep our clothes on while I bandage your booboo. If you ask nicely, maybe I'll even kiss it better for you."

Willow draped her arms over Jackson's shoulders and pressed her body against his. "That does sound tempting, but I'm too hungry to think about anything other than crispy fried catfish and okra." She pushed him onto the bed and raised her chin. "Get dressed and get cooking. Maybe after dinner I'll let you kiss my booboo better. Maybe I'll even return the favor."

Jackson propped himself onto his elbows and watched Willow exit the room. When she was gone, he covered his face and fell back onto the bed. "What are you doing, Jax?" he muttered to himself. "She's going to go home, and you're going to be broken hearted."

The mattress bounced and a warm tongue raked over his belly. He pulled his hands away to find Ruby straddling him, her tail spinning in circles.

"Not quite what I was hoping for," he said, scrubbing her ears and neck with his fingers. "But I can always count on you to make me smile."

Ruby pounced on him and gave Jackson's face a thorough tongue bath. After a moment she paused and sniffed his bandage. The dog sneezed and hopped from the bed. She sneezed a second time before bolting from the room.

"Abandoned again," he said with a chuckle. He pulled his t-shirt over his head, taking note of how the pain in his shoulder was completely gone. The analgesic cream was powerful stuff.

Butterflies filled Jackson's belly as he bounced down the stairway. The third last stair squeaked when he stepped on it. Maybe after everything had settled down, he'd finally take some time to fix that. Then again, that stair has been that way for as long as he could remember.

Maybelle grinned at him when he passed by on his way to the kitchen. "Do the double-thick batter, Jax. You know the one I mean. It means it will take a bit longer, but waiting makes it all the sweeter."

Jackson was certain she wasn't talking about food.

Chapter Thirty-Nine

Willow

"You know," Willow said as she licked a bit of crispy fish batter off her thumb, "if you ever decide to leave law enforcement, you'd have a promising career as a chef. Damn, boy, you can cook." She had spent the evening listening to Maybelle talk about her son's youth while Jackson cooked up a deep-fried feast. "His father taught him how to hunt and fish," Maybelle said, "and I taught him how to make it tasty." The elderly woman dabbed the corners of her mouth with a simple cloth napkin. "But I could never cook like this. Jax has a God-given knack for it." An impish grin highlighted tiny dimples in her cheeks. "Nothing better than a man who knows his way around the kitchen."

Jackson got up and grabbed his laptop off the side table. Willow was certain he was trying to hide his reddening cheeks. She couldn't blame him. Had the tables been turned, and it was her brothers giving her the gears, Willow would have wanted to turn to goo and slip through the floorboards. Even still, the big guy was cute when he blushed.

"If it's all the same to you," Maybelle said. Levi rushed to her side as she stood from her chair. She shot him a glare that told him, in no uncertain terms, to back off. "I'm going to go to bed and catch up on my reading. Ambulances and gunshot victims are more than a bit tiring."

"Okay, Mom," Jackson said, tucking his laptop under his arm. "We're going watch a video, and then I'll check in on you." Jackson plopped his laptop on the table and attached Johnnie's phone to it.

"I'll put a pot of coffee on," Levi said. "Right after I clean up here." As he gathered up the dishes, Ruby, Ranger, and Boone popped to their feet and scrambled over to him. The way they were sitting shoulder to shoulder, and their tails brushing the floor warmed Willow's heart in a way she couldn't have anticipated. Levi slipped Boone a small piece of fish, drawing pathetic looks of dismay from the other two dogs. "Not to worry, you two," he said, picking up larger pieces of fried fish. "I've got some for you, too."

"What do you expect to find on the video?" Willow asked as she watched Levi hand feeding the dogs. They were remarkably gentle, which was surprising to her, but the large pools of drool collecting on the floor beneath them was disgusting. "You've already got video of the killer, and it really wasn't all that helpful."

"No clue. But I don't think spending an hour or two reviewing the video is going to..." Jackson was about to fast forward to the time of the murder when the image of Tanner walking up to the restaurant came into view. "He's by himself."

"And he looks annoyed," Willow added. "He keeps checking his watch."

"Rachel's late, I'm guessing." Levi gave an exasperated sigh. He had moved in behind Jackson and was watching the video over his shoulder. "Rachel was never on time. It's like she thought the world needed to wait until *she* was ready. Not one of her more endearing qualities."

"Check the timestamp," Willow said. "It's 8:31 am—about twenty minutes before the murders. Why do you think Mr. Walker was filming this? He locked his camera on Tanner and nobody else."

"Because he's a fan boy?" Levi added. "I mean, Tanner's a big deal in the city." He tossed the dogs more of the catfish.

"There is no way that pimple-faced nerd is going to swoon over an ex-jock," Willow said. "He's there for a reason."

The trio continued watching the footage of Tanner and his ever-growing annoyance at being stood up. While the seconds ticked by, Willow kept picking at the food. Levi hadn't gotten very far clearing the table. "Good god, this stuff is like peanuts. I can't stop eating it." She pushed the serving dish half filled with deep-fried catfish and okra. "I thought you were going to clear the table?" Willow smiled at Levi. "If you don't get this out of my reach I won't fit into my jeans in the morning."

Levi scooped up the bowl of fried goodness and fed the remainder to the dogs. "There. Temptation gone. I'll clear the table in a sec."

"Tanner! Here I am!" The video immediately panned up the street to Rachel Persie. She held her chin in the air as she strutted past the people on the sidewalk, forcing several to move out of her way. She waved at Tanner like she was the queen of England.

"You're late. The email you sent me suggested this was urgent."

Willow could only assume that was Tanner because Johnnie's camera was still locked on Rachel. As she neared, she turned towards the camera and flashed a bright smile. "Well, that explains what nerd-boy was doing there. Either he was stalking the mayor's daughter, or he's her videographer."

"Email I sent?" Rachel appeared perplexed. *"You're the one who sent me the email inviting me to breakfast. I canceled a spa day to meet you."* She turned towards the camera and mouthed the words *Thank you.*

"I'd say she knew Mr. Walker was going to be there," Jackson said. "I wonder what other videos he had been taking for Ms. Persie. It might have been helpful if he'd shared this bit of info with us."

"Come on," Rachel said. *"It doesn't matter. We're here, and I called ahead to reserve your favorite table. Let's eat breakfast and get to the bottom of this."* She linked her arm with Tanner's.

"I don't have time for this, Rachel." Tanner looked ready to take the woman's head off. *"You made me drive all the way here from Birmingham. I want to know what this is about."* He pulled out his cell phone, tapped a few buttons, and read it aloud. *"I have information on your 'special' case that I can only share in person. Meet me at Yumm this Wednesday at 8:30 a.m."* He turned the phone to Rachel for her to see. *"You sent it to my work. Do you have any idea how stupid that was?"*

Rachel's eyes bulged out of her head. *"Keep your voice down."* She looked left and right, perhaps fearful of who might be listening in on the conversation. When she caught sight of Johnnie still filming, her face turned a brilliant shade of red. *"Put that fucking phone away! Now's not the time."*

The video stopped and restarted. Johnnie was holding it up to the window, trying to get more video but the reflection off the plate-glass window made getting a clear image impossible. The camera panned away from the window, catching the back of the killer stepping through the front door.

Headlight beams raked across the walls, announcing SSA Marsden's arrival. Jackson paused the video and moved to the window to get a good look. All three dogs were by his side, doing the same thing. "Levi, get out of sight. Even if Marsden believes you're here, you don't need to confirm it for him."

"He's right," Willow said. "We don't know for certain what side Marsden's on. And take Boone with you. I'm sure the agent would know he's your dog."

Levi blew a sharp whistle and Boone raced to his side. The dog's butt slammed to the floor while his eyes were locked on his owner's. Without a word, man and dog disappeared into the kitchen.

When the screen door slammed shut, she surmised that Levi had chosen to take Boone outside.

"Sorry to have taken so long," Marsden said as he stepped into the foyer. "I got a phone call from Agent Peele. He wants to press charges against you two and the FBI. He wants your dogs destroyed."

"Who's Agent Peele?" Willow asked. "Is he the asshole who shot your drone guy, or was he buzz-cut prick who shot Jackson in the shoulder? Don't forget, it was Asshole who started the whole thing, threatening to shoot FBI K9 Ruby."

Marsden spun around to face Jackson. "Jesus Christ. Are you okay? Why aren't you at the hospital getting that checked?"

"Come on in," Jackson said, leading Marsden into the living room. "It was just a scratch. Nothing a bit of antiseptic and a bandage couldn't take care of."

"And who do we have here?" Maybelle said. The woman was dressed in a robe with her hair tied back in a tight ponytail. "You didn't mention we had company coming over."

Jackson inclined his head toward the agent, "Momma, this is Jeff. He's helping us with our case."

"I'm sorry if I woke you, Mrs. Brooks. Truly, I am." The SBI supervisory agent held out his hand in greeting. "SSA Jeff Marsden of the Alabama State Bureau of Investigation. It's an honor to meet you."

Maybelle's head snapped back. "An honor, you say? I can't for the life of me think why you might say that." She lightly gripped the proffered hand and gave it a shake.

"Ma'am," Marsden held her hand for several long seconds like he was in awe of the woman. "Your address on The Power of Community and Service, the one you gave at Brooks High School... my eldest daughter was there. I swear to Jesus, you changed her outlook on life. The way you shared your experiences of balancing family life, your involvement in the church, and the positive impact of giving back to the community... she still talks about it."

"You have a high school named after your family?" Willow closed her mouth, fearing it was hanging open.

"Jackson's grandfather," Maybelle said. "He was a pillar of the community, and he generously gave his time for the local youth."

"Momma," Jackson said. "Didn't you say you've got some reading to catch up on?"

She blew a raspberry. "I know when I'm not wanted." She gave Willow a wink and disappeared back into her makeshift bedroom.

He comes from good stock. No wonder he is who he is.

Chapter Forty

Jackson

Jackson offered Marsden a seat in the living room. "Can I get you something to drink? I'm afraid I don't have anything stronger than coffee."

"No, thank you. I'm good." Marsden's gaze was fixated on the dining room table. "Dinner for four, I see. I hope I didn't interrupt." He raised an eyebrow at Jackson, practically daring him to deny that Levi was at his house.

"Would you like to hear our account of the incident with your men?" Jackson did his best to deflect the conversation away from Levi's place at the dinner table. "I'm guessing your guys' recounting of the incident is going to vary slightly from ours."

"No need. I've already put my agents on administrative leave and quashed the lawsuit." Marsden harrumphed. "It looks like I'm going to need to find something more distasteful than working the complaints desk. Do you need any help mucking the kennels? They could keep on eye on your place while doing something useful."

"Your men are already drawing too much attention," Levi said. He was standing at the entrance to the kitchen, leaning against the door frame. "The cops had given up on my being here. They searched the house and kennels top to bottom, and they came up empty."

Jackson's jaw clenched, his fists curling at his sides. He took a step toward Levi, his movements sharp and deliberate, as though restraining himself took physical effort. His glare could have drilled a hole through the wall. How could he have been so careless? It was one thing to risk his own life by making his presence known, but if anyone came looking for him, it might, in some way, endanger Jackson's mother as well.

"Easy, Agent," Marsden said. "Benson's presence here only confirms what I already knew. I've got more details for you, if you're interested. One way or another, I'm going to prove to you that I'm not against you."

"Like maybe you can tell him that I was working with you?" Levi said. "Cards on the table, Jeff. I'm now certain that Jackson isn't working with the Chief. The excess money you were worried about came from Grace Foster. She's been funding Mrs. Brooks's medical treatments, as well as the kennels."

"What the absolute fuck?" Willow yelled. "You're not homeless, and you've working with this asshat the entire time?"

"Oh, no," Levi said. "I am definitely homeless. After the hatchet job the mayor and the DA did on me, I was lucky they didn't decide to break my thumbs and kneecaps as well. Jeff offered to let me stay at his house, but I thought it was better to keep up the appearances. You'd be surprised how much information homeless people glean from the public. If I ever make a comeback from the gutter, my top priority will be making their lives easier."

With his fingers knitted behind his head, Jackson pulled it down until his chin was resting against his chest. This stretch helped ease muscle tension, but right now, it served as an excuse to keep his focus away from anyone else in the room. Holding that pose, he took slow, deliberate breaths. "You could have saved us a lot of grief if you had just told us the truth."

"Listen to me," Levi said. "The corruption is systemic, and it goes to the highest levels. The mayor and the DA are actively ripping off the people of Florence, but what they've been able to accomplish over the past few years... they have help. Chief Wheeler wasn't always this way. He used to be a good man who worked tirelessly for the city. There has always been low-level corruption in the PD, but we knew who they were and, because they're not the brightest of criminals, their behavior helped lead us to a number of significant convictions. Captain Sawyer has been instrumental in making those cases."

"How do you explain all the evidence I've got against the captain then?" Jackson asked. This wasn't the first time Levi had stood up for the man. "I've got photo and forensic accounting evidence that proves the captain wasn't just on the take, he was masterminding the entire operation. I've got more than enough proof to put him away for evidence tampering, collusion with the local drug trade, extortion, and falsifying warrants. He's accumulated in excess of two million dollars in his offshore bank accounts."

"Did you ever attempt to verify the data?" Willow asked. The question was a complete gut-punch. "Did it line up with your personal investigations?"

"Why would I?" Jackson asked. "The intelligence came from FBI analysts inside my field office." The question would have been ridiculous, if it hadn't been Willow asking. If she asked the question, then she had a reason for it. A damn good reason most likely. She was staring at him with her eyebrows raised, prompting him to think it through. The world was shifting under Jackson's feet, and it was making him queasy. Truth was, he never was able to corroborate any of the intel, but he had always assumed it was because the captain was an intelligent and capable criminal. Jackson had been able to gather plenty of evidence on other members of the police force... but he consistently came up blank on the captain. It dawned on him who Willow was referring to, and as it did, the shifting ground turned to quicksand and threatened to swallow Jackson whole. "You think Savannah's behind it."

"No," Willow said, "I don't specifically believe she's the ring-leader, but you're so blinded by the woman, you've put her so high on a pedestal…" She left the words hanging.

"I'm not saying I think she's behind this," Marsden said, "but it would explain a lot. I mean, think about it." Marsden had the same expression on his face that Willow had when he stared at Jackson. "The chief is dirty, and the captain has been trying to build a case against him since…" He left the phrase hanging.

"Since when?" Willow asked.

"Since he took over the position from my father, after he disappeared." Jackson might have come to terms with his father likely being dead, but a small part of him clung to the hope that he was alive. Until his body was discovered, there was always a possibility.

"Captain Brooks was building a case against the chief," Marsden said. "He told me that he couldn't leave it to internal affairs. He was certain they were in on it, too." He scratched at his cheek. "It was all too convenient. Captain Brooks disappears, and FBI SAC Baldwin gets demoted and shipped off. I never got the details of their investigation, but it was clear that they were working anti-corruption. After Greene took over as the SAC, the investigations stopped. Not long after Captain Sawyer took over, he pulled me aside. He said that he couldn't put his finger on it, but too many things felt off." Marsden looked ill. "Shortly after that, Jackson was assigned to work with the PD, and he almost immediately began an investigation into Sawyer. What else were we supposed to think? In our mind, he was working with Chief Wheeler and SAC Greene was likely a part of it."

"She didn't send me here," Jackson said. He knew he was sounding defensive, but he didn't expect to be interrogated in his own home, and he hated that the agent was so quick to impugn Savannah's reputation. "I came to be near my mother. I thought she was dying. The idea that SAC Greene is dirty… it's laughable."

"You told me," Willow said. Her tone was soft and caring, as though she was taking pity on Jackson. "You told me that she wouldn't let you come unless you helped with the police's K9 unit. I think Savannah saw an opportunity, and she jumped at it. You were desperate to come home, and you were more than willing to accept whatever task she gave you, so long as it gave you what you wanted."

"And the chief took you in and put you in charge." Levi's eyes had glazed over. He was deep in thought, likely trying to put the pieces together. Jackson didn't need his help. He could see the connections, plain as day.

"It looks bad," Jackson said. "I get it, but why would she care what was happening in Florence? What does any of this have to do with the murders of Tanner and Rachel Persie? Tanner was one of her best IT analysts and I'm guessing she'd never even heard of Rachel. Whoever killed her knew her. Intimately. It was classic overkill, and that's something fueled by hatred."

"You said that Rachel was on the board of the company receiving special treatment from the DA's office," Willow said to Levi. "Belladonna Enterprises, if my memory serves."

"I'm sure there's a connection to the corporation," Levi said. "But I've never been able to directly tie either the DA or the mayor to them. Not in a significant way, at least."

"If the FBI is running interference," Marsden said. "There's no way you're going to. Even as the deputy district attorney, your reach is limited compared to theirs."

"Jesus," Willow looked ill. "I have no doubt that SAC Greene is involved in this. I mean, I have no proof, but my gut is screaming at me that she's the linchpin here. She's leaving the FBI. On that fact, everyone seems to agree. To break into the political world, she needs funding. Heavy funding. What better way than to have her claws dug into a conglomerate?"

"What about Alice?" Jackson asked. Bile rose in his throat as he asked the question. He was entertaining the notion that a woman he knew and respected was somehow linked to the death of his best friend. "Maybe she can do some digging for us?"

"Not without significant proof," Willow said. "She's not going to open an investigation into one of her own with nothing more than a hunch, and right now, that's all we've got."

"Okay," Jackson said. "If digging directly into Savannah is problematic..." He turned to Marsden, reluctant to openly voice his distrust. "We need to look at what she's given me. If I share the evidence I was given on Captain Sawyer, do you think your team can verify its authenticity? I'd rather not send up a flare that we're investigating my boss."

"Without a doubt," Marsden said. "Any photo or video evidence you have... my techs can tear them apart pixel by pixel if necessary. Digging into offshore accounts will be trickier, but I'm not without my own international contacts. Which reminds me, when I arrived, I said I have information to share with you."

"I was wondering when you were going to get around to that," Willow said.

"I know why all the videos taken at the restaurant have blurry faces..."

Chapter Forty-One

Willow

Willow waited for Marsden to get on with his explanation. It annoyed the shit out of her that he was drawing it out for so long.

"Every phone we looked at had an app installed on it," Marsden said. "According to my IT guys, the app integrates directly into the phone's operating system. It creates something like a filter on the camera that automatically blurs the faces of anyone they film."

"You'd think the kids would have noticed that a long time ago," Jackson said. "From what I've seen, these young adults are entirely dependent on their phones. If they didn't let them take videos of people, they'd likely trash it and buy another."

"My guys had the same thought," Marsden said. "They're working at disassembling the software directly to figure out how it works. They're guessing that the feature is either connected to the server at Yumm, or that it's remotely activated, or both."

"Is that all the software does?" Jackson asked. "If so, why would everyone in the restaurant have it installed?"

"Oh," Marsden laughed, perhaps embarrassed by his oversight. "The app is their menu. If you want to order food, you have to do it through their software. There are no printed menus available."

This bit of news lined up perfectly with what the head chef had said. Willow couldn't help but admire the cleverness that the owner showed here. The restaurant catered to a younger crowd, people who lived and died by their cell phones. They wouldn't think twice about being forced to install the restaurant's app to place their orders.

"They have tablets, too," Jackson said. "I've eaten there quite a few times, and I've never been forced to install an app on my phone. If I had, I would have gone elsewhere."

"But you're not buying drugs from them," Willow said. "I'm guessing the app gives them access to items not on the standard menu."

"Okay," Jackson said. He was rubbing the back of his neck again. Based on the late hour, it was either simple fatigue, or he was working on another migraine. "We're not any closer to knowing who the murderer is."

"Not entirely," Levi said. "We know that Rachel and Tanner were set up." When Marsden's eyebrows shot up, Levi quickly filled him in. "Jackson has a video of when the two victims met outside the restaurant. It seems that Rachel believed Tanner had initiated the meeting, and Tanner believed it was Rachel. The man was some pissed that he had driven all the way here for a meeting that didn't exist."

"Fuck me." Willow closed her eyes tightly and groaned. "We know for certain that Rachel said she had received an email from Tanner, and yet..." She stared at Marsden. "You're saying you found nothing on her emails. Someone is hacking into devices and cleaning the evidence before we can look at it."

"Just like Detective Dawson did at Leroy's encampment," Jackson said. "There may have been a single shooter, but this is looking more and more like a conspiracy at every turn."

"Let me deal with Dawson," Marsden said. "We need to get Captain Sawyer involved. I'm certain that, between the two of us, we can get what we need from the detective."

Willow raised an eyebrow at Jackson, prompting for what he thought of Marsden's suggestion.

"Sure," he said. He seemed reluctant to give up his hunt for the captain's guilt. "Bring Sawyer into this. I just hope we're not inviting the fox into the henhouse."

"Can you get your team to revisit Rachel's email accounts and such?" Willow asked Marsden. "Emails are notoriously difficult to completely erase from the net once they're sent."

"Why didn't I think of that?" Jackson said. "I've gotten details on child pornography rings all because of email trails. Whenever one is sent or received, they go through a litany of servers, backup servers, routers… and they all keep record of what passed through. It's a place to start at any rate."

"We can't get into her account data," Marsden said. "At least, not yet. We're waiting for a warrant to compel the email provider to give us *all* her data. The judge seems to be dragging his feet in issuing the order."

"Do you think the mayor's blocking it?" Willow asked. It didn't make any sense as to why the mayor might do that, but there were so many layers to this investigation it was impossible to know. "I mean, the judge is his cousin, and it seems he's been more than willing to issue warrants on a whim."

"Because they likely hold information about Persie's guilt," Levi said. "Think about it, Belladonna Enterprises is funneling money to the mayor, and Rachel sat on the board. You can pretty much guarantee that there have been some compromising communications between them. If we had access to everything, we'd likely find a gold mine of evidence against them."

"There was no record of emails to or from Agent Montgomery," Marsden said, "But we discovered that she had hired a ghost writer to write her next novel. *Lover's Quarrel*, or something like that. We looked the girl up. She sells her services on Fiverr, if you can believe it. The mayor's daughter is flush with cash, and yet she hires someone through a discount service."

That was interesting. The murderer had said that Ms. Persie was a fraud. It made Willow wonder if that's what he had been referring to.

"I saw that book," Jackson said. "At Evelina Rainier's house. She appeared to be reading it, along with a number of others." He paused for a moment. "Savannah was waiting on a search warrant to go through Ms. Rainier's home. I should call Agent Crenshaw to see what they found."

"Are you certain you can trust him?" Willow said.

"I believe so," Jackson said.

He sounded defensive, and perhaps rightly so. Anytime people from his field office came up, Willow had gone on the offensive. She didn't like doing that to him, but she still wasn't convinced that he was willing to accept that the woman he revered was potentially guilty as sin.

Jackson pressed his hands against his thighs. "God save us. Crenshaw might not be a critical thinker, but the man is utterly fearless. More importantly, he cared about the children we were helping, and he never hesitated to put his life at risk for them." He scrubbed the back of his neck again. "While we were waiting for the search warrant for Evelina's house, he confided in me. He said he didn't trust Savannah, and that she'd been acting off ever since he heard she was planning to run for Senator."

"And the DA is going to be running for Attorney General this summer," Levi said. "Let's assume for a second that SAC Greene is in on this. What do you think she'll be able to get away with if she can influence state-wide legislation, if she's teamed up with the chief prosecutor, and if she's got the support of one of the richest men in northern Alabama?"

"Even if it's true," Jackson said. "Even if she is as evil as you all seem to think she is, the mayor isn't going to sanction a hit on his daughter."

"Rachel's the wildcard in this," Willow said. "Tanner was the target. I'm certain of it. Look at the efficiency in which he was killed. A single shot to the chest with a hollow-point bullet. It was clean. It was neat. And the killer made sure he killed him first." Excitement burbled up in her gut. This was the first time since this horrific ordeal started, that she felt like she had a handle on the why. "Jackson, you said Tanner was an IT forensic genius, right?"

The conversation about Tanner had struck Jackson hard. He seemed to have shrunk after Willow had suggested that he had been the primary target. "He was. Tanner was gifted. He saw things in a way that nobody else did. He could identify patterns in chaotic data unlike anyone I'd ever known."

"What was he working on?" Marsden said. "Before he died, what case was he on?"

"What case?" Jackson scoffed. "He never worked just one. He often had six or seven on the go. How he could shuffle through the sheer volume of intel was beyond me."

"We need his files," Willow said. "I still don't think I've got enough to get Alice to open an investigation on Savannah, but I doubt she'd balk at getting the details of what Tanner was working on at the time of his death."

"It might raise suspicion," Marsden said. "I'm going to guess that any inquiries into Agent Montgomery is going to set off warning bells."

"I'll call her," Willow said. "I'm sure Alice can manage this without alerting anyone."

Marsden looked at his watch. "Look, it's going on ten. It's too late to be bothering anyone with queries, so why don't we call it a day and touch base in the morning. I'm thinking it might be best if I take Levi with me. I've got a safe house I can set him up in, one that I doubt either the FBI or the local PD know about."

"I'm staying here," Levi said. "I'm perfectly safe, and except for you, nobody knows I'm here. I've got four federal agents to watch over me while I sleep. I can't believe there's a more secure location for me than right here." Boone, who had been sleeping under the dining room table with Ruby and Ranger, lifted his head and whined. "Correction, four agents and an overly sensitive canine companion."

Willow groaned inwardly. She'd have preferred to not be sharing a room, at least not with that man. Her head turned toward Jackson, who appeared to be deep in thought. Jesus, she needed to keep her head in the game. "I'm going to take Ranger for a quick walk, grab a shower," *a cold shower,* "and then hit the sack. I can't recall the last time I was this tired."

Chapter Forty-Two

Jackson

The overnight frost clung to the grass as Jackson stood on the front porch steps, his breath visible in the unexpectedly cool air. He wrapped his hands around his steaming coffee mug, grateful for its warmth. With detached amusement, he watched Levi and Boone romp across the crunchy lawn. Ruby lay flopped on her side, content to be a spectator, while Ranger vibrated with pent-up energy, desperate to join in.

Jackson had argued against Levi being outside, but his mother insisted that he was being overprotective. She also said that she'd gotten the *neighborhood watch* involved, which was code for 'every busybody from here to Highway 72 would be on the lookout for any suspicious people or vehicles.' They could warn Jackson if they spotted anyone out of place.

He took a sip of coffee and shifted his gaze to the Malinois beside Willow, his coat ruffled by the crisp morning breeze. "He's going to explode if you don't let him go... Willow? Did you hear me?"

The special agent had headphones on, and a laptop folded across her knees. "That's one mystery solved," Willow said as she pulled off her headset.

"Willow?" Jackson pointed at her dog. He was half lying down, half standing up, and one hundred percent ready to launch at

Levi and Boone. The woman heard him, but she wasn't listening. "Willow, you need to release Ranger before he explodes."

"What?" she said. She cocked an eyebrow until she saw her dog's behavior. "Oh. Right. Ranger, break!"

The Belgian Malinois accelerated from zero to Mach-1 in less than a heartbeat. His paws thundered as he streaked towards Levi and the ball he was holding. Ranger changed direction and nearly toppled over when the orange rubber ball flew across the home's expansive front lawn. As fast as the K9 was, he was no competition for the wiry Border Collie. Boone used his little body to cut the larger dog off before snatching the ball on its second bounce.

"He's not going to hurt him?" Willow said. "I don't know if Ranger even knows how to play. All he does is work."

"Boone might wear Ranger out, but I doubt he'll hurt him." Jackson grinned, knowing that wasn't what she was talking about. "They're playing. The competition is good for both of them."

Willow ran her hands over the laptop's cover, once again lost in thought.

"You said the mystery is solved?" Jackson was still grinning. "You know who the murderer is?"

"No," Willow said. She was biting on her lower lip; a nervous tic Jackson had never noticed before. "But thanks to Marsden's IT team, we know that the photographic evidence against Captain Sawyer is entirely bogus. It's extremely good, but bogus, nonetheless. The team had to have been working all night to figure it out."

"I take it there's nothing on the financials?" Jackson didn't know why he was even asking. That information was going to take time, and he already knew what they were going to say—it was all fake. The thought that he was a patsy in someone's master plan burned, and he continued to struggle with the idea that Savannah was involved. He needed to keep his eyes wide open and be extra careful where his SAC was concerned.

"Nah," she said. "No mention of them." Willow was gazing into Jackson's eyes, and it was incredibly unnerving. "Can you do it? If the evidence leads to SAC Greene, can you put aside your admiration for her long enough to cuff her?"

The question was difficult to answer, and it forced Jackson to turn away. "It's a hard thing to do, turn off your feelings for someone." He drank deeply from his mug and sighed. "But I'm going to have to. Even if there's nothing definitive, it sure looks like she's involved, and I need to treat her like any other suspect." He nearly spilled his coffee when Willow placed her hand over his.

"I'm sorry that you're going through this," she said. "If you want, I can handle all the interactions with Greene. Afterall, I'm running this investigation." She squeezed his hand and chuckled. "I mean, she already hates me for leaving boot prints on her scalp when I went over her head to begin with."

"If you take lead with her..." Jackson didn't pull his hand away when Willow's lingered, "she'll know something's up. Savannah and I have been friends for years. If you start in on her, she'll throw up her defenses, and we'll likely blow any chance of catching her."

Willow's hand slipped away, brushing over his skin as she did. It sent tingles up Jackson's arm, and his stomach fluttered. If he had been standing, the sensation might have actually made him weak in the knees.

"While Marsden's doing his thing," she said, "what should we be doing? I mean, we can't use our FBI resources to dig into Savannah. She'd know immediately."

"We're going to need to do the legwork," Jackson said. "But first we need to check in with the rest of Savannah's task force. If we don't, it's going to seem awfully suspicious. Besides, I still want to talk to Crenshaw. I want to know what they found at Evelina Rainier's house. I saw some interesting things while I was there. She had a stack of books on her reading table, along with Rachel's new novel *Lover's Quarrel*." His eyebrows shot up. "Speaking of that novel, Rachel had written a note inside the book. She said Evelina was her best friend and biggest supporter."

"They were best friends, and yet Evelina dosed her with ketamine? If I was a gambler, I'd lay odds that their friendship was entirely one sided."

"That would make sense," Jackson said. He pulled out his phone and opened his photo gallery. "Take a look at this and tell me if anything looks... well, interesting."

Jackson held up a photo that showed the stack of books on her reading table. Willow moved closer. Her head was practically resting on his shoulder as she examined the image. Her proximity was intoxicating. "That name looks familiar," she said. "Mitchell... isn't that the last name of the cyber crimes guy? Do you think it's the same person?"

Jackson blew out the breath he was holding when Willow pulled away. "Unlikely, but anything's possible. I don't know what his middle name is, but the man's first name is Alexander."

Willow chuckled as she tapped furiously on her phone. After a few moments, she paused typing and smiled. "Alexander Jebediah Mitchell, Supervisory Special Agent, Unit Chief, Cyber Crimes Division." She waggled her phone at Jackson. "I'd say it's more than a likelihood that AJ Mitchell and Alexander Mitchell are one and the same person."

"What do you think that means then?" Jackson said. "It would be very interesting to see how he fits with all of this. I think we need to talk with Evelina again. I'd like to know how she got a copy of his book."

"And I'd like to hear what she has to say about Rachel having hired a ghost writer for her new book." Willow popped to her feet. "Do you think she's back home yet? She had a high-priced lawyer in her corner, so it wouldn't surprise me if she's out on bail awaiting her hearing."

"I doubt she spent any time behind bars," Jackson said. He pulled out his cell phone to check the time. "It's too early to go see Evelina, but Savannah will be up by now. We really should check in with her." A thought crossed his mind. "I want to ask her about Tanner's emails."

"You're not worried that will tip her off?"

"It's a legitimate question for us to be asking her. Besides, I want to hear her reaction."

"Put in on speaker," Willow said. She moved closer until their shoulders were pressed together.

Jackson swallowed hard and tapped on his phone. "Hey, Savannah." Jackson was happy that she'd picked up on the first ring. His ploy bordered on juvenile, but that's what made it such a good idea. It was too simplistic to be a trick, and he hoped his boss would see it the same way. "Did the cyber guys go through Tanner's devices? Agent Banks and I are hitting a dead end here, and I'm looking for anything that can get us back on the trail." The SAC paused for a moment before confirming having received the report from the cyber team. "Can you forward them on to me, please? I'd like to check something out." Again, there was a pause.

"Yes. I've got them back, but I haven't looked at them yet. Come by and I'll give you a copy of the report." Savannah's voice sounded distant, like she was talking away from the phone.

"Can't you email them to me?" Annoyance bubbled up, leaving a sour taste in Jackson's mouth. There was another long pause. "Savannah?"

"Yes, sure." The SAC paused again. "Sorry, Jackson. I'm juggling a dozen things at once right now. I'll have them sent out to you within an hour. On second thought, I don't want to email them. There's something very odd going on, and I... just come in. I'll see you soon." The line went dead. Jackson tucked his phone away and scrubbed the stubble on his chin. He needed to shave. He also needed an antacid.

"It sounded like she wanted you to come pick up a hard copy." Willow sounded as perplexed as Jackson. "She doesn't trust using a secure email server?"

Tension crept up the back of Jackson's neck, and he reached into his pocket for his meds. He popped open the container, noting that he only had four left. He needed to call in a refill.

"You're taking an awful lot of those," Willow said. "What are they?"

He popped one of the pills into his mouth and dry-swallowed it. "Sumatriptan."

"My partner was on Imitrex," Willow said. "I think it's the same drug, but a different name. I remember her saying it can have some serious side effects if you over medicate."

"Whatever they are," Jackson said. He stood up and brushed the dust from his backside. "It can't be as bad as the effects of a full-blown migraine. Besides the pain, I get extreme sensitivity to light and sound." It had been a while since he had experienced the full gamut, but he remembered it all too clearly.

"Don't say I didn't warn you."

The sing-song way she said it made Jackson smile.

Chapter Forty-Three

Willow

Willow grumbled at the crowd gathered outside the SBI building. At least eight news vans lined the street, and hundreds of people crammed the area. Jackson pulled into the parking lot, greeted by the same attendant they had encountered on their first visit.

"Good morning, agents," Robert Roberts said, slamming the button to open the gate.

"Good morning to you, too," Jackson replied with a nod. "What's with the crowd? It's even larger than it was yesterday."

"Hard to say for certain," Robert said, stepping out from his guard station to investigate. "I think someone is holding a press conference. I could hear a woman's voice over a loudspeaker. There was a lot of shouting. Impossible to know if they were happy or angry. They both sound the same to me when people get riled up."

Willow didn't need to get closer to know it was Savannah. She was using the crime as an opportunity for a campaign speech. "Is the rear entrance open to the public? We don't want to fight our way into the building."

"It's employees only," Robert said, leaning into Jackson's window. At the sight of Ranger, he jerked back. "I'll call ahead to let the guard know you're coming."

"Well," Willow said as Jackson drove to the rear of the parking lot. "Any doubt what Savannah is doing out there?"

"I had the same thought. My guess is, she's announcing her run for the Senate, and she's saying she's caught the murderer."

"Do you think your little buddy would like an inside scoop on it?" Willow liked the idea of using Johnnie to put pressure on SAC Greene. "I'm guessing he's there anyway, but I'll bet he'd like to hear that Savannah's jumping the gun."

Jackson pulled into a parking spot and slammed the gear shifter into park. "I'm completely in favor of the idea, but we can't call him based on conjecture. We need to know for sure it's what she is doing out there."

"Fair enough," Willow said as she hopped down from the truck. She clipped her leash on Ranger and invited him out of the back seat. Today was a field test for the Malinois, an attempt to see how he was without Ruby's calming presence.

"Remember," Jackson said as he stepped out into the morning sun. "Loose leash. Project authority. Praise him when he behaves the way you want."

"Is every outing with the dogs a lesson?"

"Not just outings," Jackson said. "Every minute of every day is an opportunity for you and Ranger to work on your connection. It will become instinctual, eventually, and you'll continue doing it without even thinking about it."

Willow considered his words. Kate had been the same way, forever working on her Malinois' behaviors. As she closed the truck door, Ranger stared up at her, eyes alert and ears perked. He wasn't just waiting for her command. He was eager for it. Willow resisted the urge to wrap the leash around her wrist. Instead, she slipped her hand through the loop and kept her mind and body relaxed. She took a step toward the building and told Ranger to "Heel." The dog went into perfect lockstep, his gaze fixed on her.

As they neared the rear of the building, Willow paused long enough to give Ranger a back scratch and a *good boy*. The dog responded by leaning into her leg.

"Keep the same energy as we approach the entrance," Jackson said. "You're doing great."

His words of praise warmed Willow's heart, and she wondered if they were the equivalent of receiving a *good girl*. She gave him a crooked smile but came up short of leaning against him—not that she'd have minded. The warmth in her heart spread into her cheeks. "Heel," she said and marched forward.

The solid steel rear door opened as they approached. "Good morning," an elderly man in a guard's uniform said. "I was expecting you." The man's face blanched slightly as his gaze fell onto the Malinois. He looked like he was about to object, but managed to hold his tongue.

"Good morning," Willow replied. She glanced down at Ranger, who was staring intently at the man holding open the door. As Jackson had instructed, she kept her head high and her shoulders straight, and she entered the building without any concern for herself or the dog. *Maintain neutral emotions*, Jackson had said. *If you're calm, the dog will be calm too.* The pair entered the building without incident. "Good boy," she whispered. Her throat tightened. For anyone else, having a dog follow them into a building was simple and normal, but for Ranger, this was huge.

Willow continued with her confident approach as they climbed into the elevators. Again, Ranger behaved like a perfect gentleman. Not once did he pull, and not once did he resist. When the door closed behind them, Willow pressed fourteen and breathed out a sigh of relief. She looked down at Ranger, who was sitting calmly at her left side, his eyes on her.

The elevator binged, announcing their arrival. When the doors opened, Agent Crenshaw was waiting for them. "Good morning," he said, his eyes locked on Ranger. "I'm glad you made it past the gong-show out front. Savannah's giving a press conference. She announced that she is officially running for State Senate, and then followed it up by saying she has identified Rachel Persie's killer, and that his arrest is imminent. The crowd ate it up."

Willow palm-slapped her forehead. "Sweet Jesus. What is wrong with her? Does she not even care that the real killer is still running around out there?"

"Apparently, Alex has definitive video evidence," Crenshaw said, shaking his head. "It makes no fucking sense, but he was able to unscramble the videos from the restaurant. They clearly show Levi Benson was the murderer. There's no doubt. She's called DOJ, demanding he be pulled from WITSEC."

Jackson shared a knowing look. Apparently, Savannah had completely bought into the lie that Levi was under the protection of the US Marshals Service.

"*No doubt?*" Willow said, her annoyance with the situation getting the better of her. A low growl rumbled in Ranger's chest. "Except that we can personally verify that he couldn't have been at the scene of the crime. It's a good trick to be in two places at the same time." The leash went taut as Ranger stepped forward.

"Willow," Jackson said. "Calm yourself and call Ranger back to you." His voice was firm and authoritative, and completely out of character.

"Ranger, heel," Willow said. The dog immediately backpedaled until he was at her hip. "Sit." Again, the dog complied. That same feeling of warmth spread through her chest as she scratched his head.

"Apparently they were able to get street-cam footage of Benson racing through the back alleys immediately following the shooting." Crenshaw shrugged. "Alex's team pieced footage from multiple sources, and they show him sprinting all the way to the laundromat."

Jackson, for the first time since Willow met him, showed doubt in his eyes. "Can we see the footage? If Levi played us, I'll deliver him to Savannah myself."

"I figured you'd want to see it," Crenshaw said, leading them to the back of the office space. "Alex has everything set up in the war room. I have to admit, it's damning stuff."

"You must be Agents Brooks and Banks," a small but fit man said. He couldn't have been any more than five-six, even with his platform shoes. "I was able to undo the filter on the video footage taken at the restaurant. It took me a minute to get past the algorithm the software employed, but once I did, it was just a matter of running it through a reconstruction program to reverse engineer the video. I then used open-source footage of Mr. Benson during press conferences and his online media to create a baseline for my facial recognition programs. All three confirmed he was the killer with up to ninety-seven percent confidence."

"You're wrong," Willow said. "I don't know who you are, but whatever software you're using, it's faulty and inadequate. Use your eyes and compare the images. It's not Levi."

"I'm SSA Alexander Mitchell, Cyber Crimes Division," the much shorter man said, lifting his chin in defiance. "My friends call me Alex, but we're not friends... yet. I can assure you that I have taken every precaution to ensure that my software *only* provides complete and accurate estimations to identify a criminal." His gaze ping-ponged between Willow and Jackson. "While we're working together, I will allow you to call me Alexander. Savannah likes to keep things casual during a high-profile investigation. We're already under enough stress as it is, and the chip on your shoulder is doing nothing to improve things. So, like Savannah said, get on board or get out of here. Kapeesh?"

Ranger took offense at the man's aggressive tone and pinned back his ears. Willow gave him a sharp correction with the leash, but her K9 remained hyper-focused on Mitchell. "Just play the video for us," Willow said. She dragged Ranger to a chair and took a seat. It was difficult to keep an open mind when she knew fake evidence had already been fabricated.

"You'll show me some respect, SA Banks," Mitchell said. "I am your superior, and I don't give a shit who you've got in your corner. Right now, you're a guest in my meeting, and I won't hesitate to throw you out on your ass."

Ranger was up in an instant. He pinned his ears back and bared his teeth, but he never left her side. Willow swiveled her chair towards the little man with the Napoleon complex. "I'm waiting."

"We both are," Jackson said as he took the chair nearest to her. Where Ranger appeared ready to disembowel the man, Willow did her best to remain calm and completely indifferent.

"I'll play the goddamn video when I say I will."

Willow was turned towards the oversized monitor, but she was certain the little man was stamping his feet.

"No," Savannah said as she strolled into the room. "You'll play the video when I say you will." She gave Jackson a head-bob for a greeting and completely ignored Willow. She tucked her pencil skirt under herself and took a front-row seat. "You may begin."

The room was in complete silence as the video played. The images being shown were from a different angle than what Jackson had shown Willow, but everything was otherwise exactly the same. When the camera met Levi full on, the image was not the disheveled version she had seen before. The man was well kempt, his beard was neat, and his hair was combed and tidy. Willow glanced over at Jackson, who was leaning forward, his attention fully locked onto the flatscreen.

"Pause," Savannah demanded. She swiveled her chair to face Jackson, showing off a triumphant smile. She brushed non-existent lint from her suit jacket and raised her eyebrows. "Any doubt now, Agent Brooks?"

"None," Jackson said. His chin lowered to his chest. "None whatsoever."

His look of defeat devastated Willow. She was torn between wanting to console him and racing home to strangle Levi. The bastard had lied to her. Right to her face. And Marsden, the low-life scumbag, had backed the weasel up, insisting that they were working together to bring down the mayor and the DA—and she had taken the bait like a spring catfish in spawning season.

"Where is he, Agent?" Savannah said. Her joyous expression shifted to predatory. "Tell me where you're hiding him, and maybe I won't tank your career over this." Her head turned on her neck like a hoot owl, only stopping when her gaze fell on Willow. "As for you, Agent Banks. I've contacted your supervisor insisting you be recalled. Immediately. If I see you and your bleach-blonde hair in my state again, I'll have your badge."

"There is no need to threaten Agent Banks," Jackson said. He regained his composure as he stood. "She'll call her friend in the US Marshal's office to let them know that Mr. Benson is no longer under witness protection."

I'll what?

She had told Jackson that Levi didn't qualify for WITSEC, so why was he suggesting that he was already in the program? Willow turned towards the monitor and stared at the paused image. What did he see that she had not? She turned back to Jackson, bewildered by the way he was standing at attention like a tin soldier. Jesus, he was doing what he had taught her to do… to project confidence. She had never received a more cryptic message in her entire life.

"Sure," Willow said, pulling her cell phone from her back pocket. She put her phone on speaker and dialed a number she knew by heart—one that she knew would go directly to voicemail.

A robotic voice immediately answered: "You've reached 555-0199. This number is not monitored, and messages will not be returned."

Willow waited for the beep, then spoke clearly into the phone: "Hey, Betty. It's Willow. Can you give me a call back when you get this message? I need to talk to you as soon as possible. There's been a development in the investigation, and I need Mr. Benson brought to the SBI building immediately. I know this is extraordinary, but I need him out of WITSEC."

She ended the call and turned to Savannah with a shrug. "Sorry. She never answers right away, but she'll get back to me as soon as she can." She prayed that, if Jackson was paying attention, he'd know that she hadn't called the Marshal's office. Her contact was a man, and not a woman as everyone would have overheard. If he missed it, Jackson didn't let it show.

"My mother has an appointment with her oncologist," Jackson said. He rolled his head and gripped the back of his neck. "If it's okay with you, Savannah, I'd like to head home. She's not been well, and I want to take her myself."

"Unless there is something more you need from me, SAC Greene," Willow said, "I'll take my leave. But make no mistake. I'm not going home. I'm in Florence to have my K9 trained, and there is no way I'm leaving until he's right in the head."

The obvious rage that was consuming Savannah nearly made Willow smile.

Chapter Forty-Four

Jackson

Jackson could hardly breathe when he started the truck's engine. Willow had kept silent during the walk but the way her arms were pumping at her side suggested that she had a lot to say. No sooner did they both close their doors, than she let into him.

"What was that all about? Jesus Christ. You saw the footage. There's no way it wasn't Levi."

"I know," Jackson said. He held up a finger to his lips, signaling Willow to remain quiet. "He made me look like an idiot." He pulled out his phone and powered it down. Willow raised an eyebrow, prompting him for an explanation. "I hope he gets the death penalty."

Willow clearly didn't understand, but she followed Jackson's lead.

He mouthed the word *bugs* while he ran his hands along the underside of the dashboard, doing a quick search for any devices. He motioned with his head for Willow to do the same on her side. When she found nothing, she checked under her seat and in the back of the cab.

"Why are you killing our phones?"

"So they can't be used as listening devices," Jackson said.

"Seriously? Why are you suddenly so paranoid? Do you think Levi's listening in on us?"

"Not Levi." Jackson pushed his head into his headrest. "Mitchell. He's in on it. I don't know why or how, but he's a part of this."

"You think SSA Mitchell is the killer?" Willow shifted in her seat to fully face Jackson. "You know it can't be him, right? Not unless he was wearing platform shoes during the murder. He's way too short. I'm afraid your friendship with Levi is clouding your judgment. You saw the videos. He killed Tanner and Rachel and ran directly to the laundromat to create his alibi."

"Except that it wasn't him," Jackson said. He slammed the truck into reverse and stomped on the gas. The back tires screeched as they spun on the pavement sending Ranger into the foot well. He jammed the brakes and pushed the shifter into Drive. He waited for the dog to return to the back seat. "There was no stain on his shirt. It was a fake. Someone threw coffee on Levi that morning. He had a huge stain down the front of his shirt. That's why he went to the laundromat. Mitchell fabricated the videos, but he didn't know about Levi's stain."

"Fuck me." Willow squeezed her eyes tight. "I've got to loop Alice in on this. She going to shit a cinderblock." She looked down at her disabled cell. "I can't believe that he's hacked into my phone. It's brand new. I bought it yesterday after Ranger destroyed mine. There's no way he could know the number."

"The man's got access to resources." Jackson eased off on the gas, intent on making the ride smoother for Ranger. He already felt bad enough for tossing them around. "I wouldn't doubt that he was able to latch onto our phones when we walked into the meeting room. It's called a baseband attack. I can't tell you how it works, but my VCAC task force used them to hack into perps' phones."

"If you think that's true," Willow said as she popped the back off her cell. "Pull the SIM cards, otherwise they can remotely activate them too. Just because they're powered down, it doesn't mean they're completely off." She held her hand out for Jackson's phone and disconnected his as well. "The real question is—what are we going to do now? We are on our heels and completely outgunned."

"We'll pick up some burners for now." Jackson waved to Robert as he opened the exit gate from the parking lot. "Hey," he called out, waving the attendant to come closer. "I need something from you..."

"However I can help," the man said. He was red-faced and far too eager for Jackson's liking. Then again, ever since Willow had pulled her gun on him, his entire demeanor had changed towards them.

"If anyone follows us out," Jackson said. He looked over his shoulder as though they were in peril. "Delay them. I don't care how you do it, just give us time to get ahead of them."

A grin split the fat man's face. "No problemo. The gate's been acting up this morning. In fact, it might be completely broken after you leave."

"Much appreciated," Willow said as she leaned over Jackson to get a better view of their newfound ally. "You have yourself a blessed day."

They drove in silence for several minutes until Jackson pulled into a strip mall. He parked in front of an ATM and hopped out. "I won't be long." He inserted his bank card into the ATM and withdrew five hundred dollars. Mitchell was likely monitoring his credit cards, and this was a less-than-awesome countermeasure, but it did allow him to make some purchases without the FBI immediately knowing about it. He grabbed the wad of cash and sprinted down the walkway toward the far end of the mall. When he got to the mini mart, he pulled open the door and slipped inside. "Prepaid cell phones?" he asked of the clerk who hadn't bothered to look up from his comic book. "Do you have any?"

"End cap. Aisle three," the dispassionate kid said, never bothering to raise his eyes. "Stay away from the Nokia knockoffs. They're complete shit. Spend the extra five bucks and get the T-Mobiles.

They're basic, but they work. They come fully charged and ready for use. Pop in the SIM card and go. No activation required."

Jackson looked over the selection and took the kid's advice. He grabbed four phones, paused, and grabbed two more. At forty bucks a pop, he was burning through his small cash reserve at a horrific pace. Then again, he had no plans to buy anything else. He paid the kid and left him a good-sized tip for his help. In moments, he was hopping back into his truck.

"Jesus," Willow said as Jackson tossed the bag of cell phones onto her lap. "How many calls are you planning to make?"

"One for each of us," he said. "One is for Levi, because I don't want him using my mother's phone. I also want to give one to Marsden. I'm guessing his work phone is well encrypted, but I'm not risking it."

"That adds up to four, not six." Jackson didn't respond, so Willow ripped off the clamshell casing of her phone and popped open the back. She slipped in the SIM card, reassembled it, and hit the power button. "I'm calling Alice," she said. "She's got an encrypted sat phone. It's nearly impossible to hack into."

Jackson's head was spinning. Driving helped, but he couldn't shake the feeling of betrayal. Someone in his own office had a hand in killing his best friend. It made him sick to his stomach. How was he supposed to catch Mitchell? The man could fake evidence and cover his tracks with frightening ease.

He considered bringing his findings to Savannah, but doubt continued to whisper at the edges of Jackson's mind, persistent and unwelcome. He didn't want to believe she was involved. Sure, she was ambitious—maybe too ambitious sometimes—but at her core, she was an exceptional agent. She'd put in years of solid work, and she genuinely cared about justice. And yet, too many things didn't add up. The convenient evidence, the timing, her insistence on steering the investigation to focus on Levi... If it had been anyone else, Jackson knew he'd be suspicious. Hell, he'd probably already have them under surveillance.

He shook the thought away, clinging to what he wanted to believe: Savannah wasn't that kind of person. Mitchell, though? That man was another story. Jackson could see it clearly now—Mitchell had the tech skills and the authority to pull this off. He'd been manipulating Savannah, exploiting her drive and keeping her in the dark about what was really happening.

If Savannah made a mistake, it was by being too focused on her goals to see what was right in front of her. But being blind didn't make her guilty—it made her another victim in Mitchell's elaborate scheme.

Jackson exhaled slowly, forcing himself to let the suspicion go. Until there was hard proof, he'd keep believing in Savannah. Anything else felt like a betrayal, and Jackson didn't betray the people he trusted.

"It's gone to voicemail," Willow said. "Alice, it's Will. Call me at this number. You sent me into a viper's nest here, and I need your help. My regular phone is powered down. Don't contact me on any device that isn't completely secure. The FBI are involved... Jesus, Alice. I need Agent Montgomery's case files, as quickly as you can get them. I think he was looking into internal corruption in the bureau... Outside of yourself, I don't know who I can trust. We're certain that SSA Mitchell is involved, but it's impossible to prove." She ended the call and turned to Jackson. Her eyes were wide and glassy. "This is fucked up, Jackson. I mean... sweet Jesus. What a goddamn mess."

"You go by Will?" Jackson asked. It was a stupid question, but he wanted to break the ice and lighten the mood. Breaking fixation on a negative emotion was one of his therapist's many suggestions for dealing with an emotional crisis. "I like it."

"Yeah." Willow tucked a wayward lock behind her ear. "I won a precision rifle competition a couple of years back. Kate gave me the nickname Willliam Tell—you know, the guy who shot an apple from his kid's head? She thought the name fit because of the whole 'perfect aim under pressure' thing. Alice latched onto it too, and they'd been calling me Will ever since."

"What distance?" Jackson asked. "I once took down a buck at six-hundred yards."

"I don't like bragging," Willow said. "But six-hundred yards wasn't even the competition's starting distance. We needed to put three in the black at eight hundred, just to get in."

"I'm guessing that's from a prone position," Jackson said. "I mean, who can't do that if you're all nice and comfortable. I was free-standing when I shot my buck."

"I call bullshit," Willow said. "Unless you were resting against a tree, there's no way you did that."

Jackson shrugged. "When we're out of this mess, I guess we'll just have to see who can do what." He turned to face her. "Are you always this competitive?"

"I grew up with five older brothers," she said. "Of course, I am. It's pretty much an ingrained response for me. Much the same as you can't help being a southern gentleman." Willow turned to face the windshield. "Not that I mind. A proper gentleman is a nice change from most of the men I've had to deal with in the bureau. A nice change indeed."

Butterflies erupted in Jackson's belly, which was immediately followed by a wave of guilt. He had no right to feel joy. Not now. "Call my house," he said. "We need to let them know what's happening and that our cell phones are compromised." The words had barely left his mouth when a new problem dawned on him. "Wait...what if they're tapping my home phone?"

A grimace crossed Willow's face. "I have no idea how, but I'll figure a way to warn them without tipping off anyone who might be listening."

Jackson was doubtful, but they didn't have much choice. Willow started tapping out his home phone number as he rhymed off the digits. Just before she made the call, Willow paused.

"You don't trust me?" she asked. "You look ready to crawl out of your skin."

"Of course I trust you, but I'm a worrier. What can I say?" He flashed an apologetic smile.

While Willow made the call, Jackson pulled out the small tin and popped another pill. Everything he believed was unraveling, his trust in Savannah twisting into something unrecognizable. The thought of her being tied up in this mess refused to let go. It didn't make sense—not yet—but too many pieces seemed to point her way. A knot tightened in his gut, a sickening mix of doubt and dread.

He blindly made a right turn and nearly clipped a pedestrian. He needed to stay focused on driving and not let his mind wander aimlessly.

"Jackson," Willow said. "You need to get home. It sounds like Ruby's got someone cornered down by the kennels."

Chapter Forty-Five

Willow

Willow's shoulder slammed against the truck door as the vehicle skidded around the corner. She had wanted to call the police, but Jackson had refused. He didn't want to give them another excuse to search his property. They barely swerved around a car that had stopped short. The maneuver sent Ranger tumbling into the back seat footwell.

"If you get us into an accident," Willow started to say. She stopped when her partner glared at her. He looked angry, but she knew fear was motivating his actions. Fear for his mother. Fear for his dog. Fear he was going to be too late.

Willow's phone chimed a lighthearted tune.

"You didn't turn off your phone?" Jackson glared at Willow and nearly slammed into the back of a car.

"Eyes on the road," Willow said. She leaned close to Jackson while she fished it out of her back pocket. "It's my new burner. Relax." She pressed the small device hard against her ear. It was nearly impossible to hear anything over the roar of the truck engine. "Hello?"

Jackson kept glancing over while Willow said nothing. Each time, the concern on his face deepened.

"It's Castor," she finally said. "You can ease up. Apparently, Ruby has secured the detective, but you're going to need to chase down the dogs you're boarding. They've all escaped. Levi also mentioned that the neighborhood watch worked perfectly, whatever the hell that means."

Even though the situation no longer warranted it, Jackson never let up on the gas. The twisty, hilly road that led from Highway 72 to his home felt like a high-speed rollercoaster. Only when the truck pulled into the laneway did he hit the brakes.

"Give Ranger clear instructions. Don't leave anything up to him." Jackson's instructions came out in rapid fire. "If the situation warrants, unleash him and tell him what to do. Do you know his commands?"

Willow nodded and clipped the leash onto her dog. She'd been in these situations a hundred times, and she'd seen how Kate handled Ranger. She wanted to pull her gun, too, but her left hand was incapacitated, making holding the leash and a weapon an impossibility.

"Easy," she said. The dog had immediately tried to drag her around the back of the house. "Ranger, heel." The Malinois was vibrating, but he complied perfectly with her instructions. With Jackson bolting on ahead, Willow did her best to keep pace. Sprinting down the narrow stone staircase to the kennels proved tricky while holding onto the leash. As they neared the bottom, the kennels came into view. Castor was inside, clutching onto a badly bleeding forearm. Ruby was on the other side of the eight-foot gate, her hackles raised and her impressive set of teeth on full display. Only then did Willow notice the gun in the detective's hand.

With Ranger pulling on the lead, it was difficult to unsnap the leash from his collar. The moment he was free, Willow ordered her K9 to "Hold!" While he raced toward the kennel, she drew her Glock. "Drop your gun," she demanded as she raised her weapon.

Castor stumbled backward, trying to get away from the K9 who had slammed himself into the gate. Ranger was barking, and snarling, and carrying on like he wanted to eviscerate the man in the kennel.

When the detective pointed his gun at her dog, Willow issued her order a second time. "Drop your gun or you're a dead man. Do it, Castor. Now!"

"Get Ranger under control," Jackson said.

"Drop your weapon!" Willow repeated. Ranger's behavior was the least of worries. She kept her weapon trained on Castor; her eyes locked on his. "Don't make me shoot you."

"I wasn't doing anything," Castor said, letting his gun fall to his feet. "Get that fucking dog away from me."

"On the ground!" Willow yelled. "Face down, hands behind your head." Her words went unheeded. The detective was too busy focusing all his attention on the snarling set of teeth standing in front of him.

"Call off Ranger," Jackson said. "Willow. Do it now."

She wanted to smack her partner upside her head. Even if the detective was secured, he was still within arm's reach of his weapon. But the expression on Jackson's face said, in no uncertain terms, that keeping her dog under control was critical. "Ranger, heel," she said, following it up with a short whistle. The action was nearly instinctual. It was what Kate had done every time she called her dog back.

Ranger broke away from the gate, dashed over to Willow, and sat next to her.

Praise the dog. Jackson had made it clear that good behavior needed to be reinforced. "Good boy," she murmured. Ranger's gaze was focused on her and only her. His eyes were bright, his ears erect. Jesus, it felt good seeing him respond to her this way.

"You best do what Agent Banks said," Jackson said as he opened the gate. Ruby still looked ready to rip the man to shreds, but she never moved from her spot. "One word from her, and Ranger's going to rip your face off."

Castor flopped to the ground, wrapped his hands around the back of his head, and interlaced his fingers. Willow holstered her gun and tossed her cuffs to Jackson. If the detective was going to get a chance to plead his case, he'd do it fully restrained. Only when he was secured did she holster her weapon.

"What are you doing here?" Jackson asked, hoisting the man off the ground by his arm.

"I need to go to the hospital," Castor said. "Your dog attacked me."

"What are you doing here?" Jackson repeated. "I'll call an ambulance after you explain yourself."

Before the detective had a chance to speak, Willow's phone buzzed in her pocket. She pulled it out and checked the caller ID. It read *Private Number*. It didn't matter. She knew who it was. "Hey, Alice," she answered, keeping her voice low. "Can you hold for a second? I want to make sure this perp is secure." She waggled her cell at Jackson. "I've got to take this. All good?"

Jackson's raised his chin, silently questioning who was on the phone.

"A friend from back home," Willow said, hoping that he'd understand.

"You can talk with her in the office," Jackson said. "I'm going to have a chat with the detective."

He understood. They had already found a rhythm, something that had taken her and Kate months to establish. The thought of it made her chest ache. "Hey, I'm back."

"We need Agent Montgomery's files," Willow said, as she closed the door. While walking to the kennel's office, she had briefed Alice on the events over the past three days. "I'm certain he was killed over what he's been digging into." When Alice didn't respond a lump formed in Willow's throat. "Alice? Why aren't you talking to me?" Several excruciating seconds passed by. "Alice? What's wrong?"

"Sorry, Will," she whispered. She sounded winded "I've been trying to find someplace I can speak without being heard. I'm in one of the secure rooms now. Let me start off by saying, I'm sorry. I... I don't know how anyone got wind of what Montgomery was up to. He'd been keeping his work behind an iron curtain. Oh, bloody hell. Is Jackson okay? How's Maybelle?"

"Iron curtain?" It sounded like something from a cold war era movie. "What was he working on?" The question was met with silence. "Alice? What the fuck?"

"Will..." Another long silence. "While I was the SAC in Birmingham, I was working on an anti-corruption case. Jackson's father and Agent Montgomery were a part of the team. Travis was convinced that Chief Wheeler was working with DA Beauregard to cover up crimes, specifically drug related crimes."

"Who's Travis?" Willow asked. That was the question that came out of her mouth, but what she really wanted to ask was *Why didn't you tell me any of this before you sent me here?*

"Jackson's father, Captain Travis Brooks. He reached out to me... it was, I don't know, a year and a half ago. Maybe longer. He didn't know how to build a case against his boss without him finding out. Travis was certain there were several high-ranking detectives involved as well, but the evidence against them..."

"Dried up? Vanished? Does this have anything to do with the captain's disappearance?" A thought popped into Willow's mind, a thought that rocked her. "Does Jackson know anything about this? From everything I've seen, he was very close to his father."

"No," Alice said. "Travis insisted that his son be kept out of it. Jackson was already doing work for the VCAC, and his dad didn't want him distracted. He didn't want me to let Tanner get involved either—because he and Jackson were so close—but I needed him. The guy's abilities were... uncanny. And yet, he couldn't pin anything down. He was certain that someone in the FBI was involved. Multiple people, most likely."

"Like SAC Greene and SSA Mitchell?" Again, Willow's question was met with silence. It was pissing her off, and it was making her think that Alice was holding back on her—feeding her only enough information to appease her. "Alice? What aren't you telling me?"

Alice muttered something that Willow couldn't make out. "Why do you think Mitchell is involved?" she asked. "What makes you think he's a part of this?"

"Because we caught him doctoring videos." Willow switched her phone to her left hand to wipe the sweat from her right. Her dislocated finger throbbed. She had been babying her hand since she injured it. At first opportunity, she needed to get it checked out. "He manipulated video evidence to make it appear that Levi Benson was the shooter."

"Fuck. Fuck. Fuck." Alice scream-whispered into the phone. "I knew it. I *knew* Mitchell was involved in this. I had my suspicions about him from the start. I thought Savannah might be the mole, but Mitchell was too close to everything. He was working with the DEA on a case targeting a Mexican cartel. When I asked him to help me get past some encryption issues, I also confided in him about my concerns with Savannah. Jesus, I thought he was going to explode. He shut me down immediately. He said he was too busy and that I was a fucking moron if I thought Savannah was involved. Then, less than a week later, I got demoted and shipped off to Charleston. The bastard must have gone straight to Savannah with what I told him. Between the two of them, they dismantled my career. Savannah claimed I was involved in the same corruption I was investigating, that I couldn't make charges stick because I was in bed with Captain Brooks. She even produced 'proof' that I was helping him facilitate drug flow in northern Alabama."

"And you took it up the ass?" Willow wanted to smash her phone. "You just bent over and let them ream you?"

"They wanted to bring me up on criminal charges. The deputy director stepped in and saved my career. He suggested that I take the demotion and the relocation, and that I drop it. He also said that he'd take over the investigation, and that he would clear my name."

"Obviously that never happened." The rock that had settled in the pit of Willow's stomach turned into a boulder. "Do you think the deputy director is involved? Was he a part of the cover up? Jesus Christ. If he's involved... this is completely fucked. We're completely fucked."

"I refuse to believe it," Alice said. "I mean, if he was involved, he'd have let them bury me. I was a cunt-hair away from spending the rest of my life in federal prison." She blew out a long breath. "Listen. I've got to go. Watch your back, Will. Savannah's dangerous, and if she's got Mitchell helping her..."

"What about Jackson's dad?" Willow pressed. "You didn't say if his disappearance was a part of this."

"Leave him out of it, Will. Do you hear me?" The line went dead.

Willow stared at her phone for a moment, her mind racing with the implications of Alice's revelations. If the corruption went as high as the deputy director... She quickly pulled out her notepad and fired off a text to Johnnie Walker: "Updates as promised... Phones compromised. SAC Greene intentionally pursuing wrong suspect. Real killer still out there. More details soon." She hesitated, then added, "Watch your back."

She'd promised him an exclusive, and right now, they needed all the allies they could get—especially ones with platforms to expose the truth if things went sideways.

Chapter Forty-Six

Jackson

Jackson flopped onto the couch and scrubbed his face. After bandaging Castor's forearm, which wasn't as bad as the man had said, Jackson drove him to his car and sent him on his way. Willow didn't buy the detective's story despite Agent Marsden corroborating it. Castor had said that no one answered when he rang the doorbell, but he couldn't explain why he had gone to the kennels. If he had been to the house to drop off information, why had he left it in his car and parked at the other end of the street?

"If Castor is dirty, we sent him back to his handler with nothing of interest," Jackson said. "He never saw Levi, and my mother was at her doctor's appointment with Joanna. We've said that Levi was in the DOJ's hands, and now it looks that way to Castor, too."

"This is messed up," Willow said. She sat next to him, their shoulders touching. Her proximity made it difficult for Jackson to think, but he didn't want her to be anyplace else. "I need to tell you about my conversation with Alice."

She took Jackson's hands in hers, sending his pulse racing. Her eyes were locked onto his. There was an intensity to them he'd never seen before.

"When Alice was the SAC in Birmingham," Willow continued "she was working with Tanner and your father on an anti-corruption case. Specifically, they were investigating Chief Wheeler and

DA Beauregard's facilitation of drugs being brought into northern Alabama."

The excitement of sitting next to Willow evaporated. Tension crept up his neck and settled at the base of his skull. He wanted to reach for his pills, but he only had two left. He should have called in a refill.

"Their investigation kept hitting dead ends, so Alice went to Mitchell, asking if he could help get her access to information that was beyond her reach. He refused. Shortly after that, serious charges were laid against Alice. The deputy director kept her from being prosecuted so long as she left the Birmingham office and took a demotion."

"That's the same time as when my father disappeared," Jackson said. "Did she say that Mitchell was behind that?"

"No." Willow tightened her grip on his hand. "She wouldn't say anything about your dad. When I pressed her on it, she hung up. But there's something else. Alice said, at the time, Mitchell was working with the DEA, helping them make a case against a Mexican cartel."

Pieces were fitting together, but Jackson didn't like the picture it was presenting. "Do you think this is all about the cartel? It explains all the drugs in Yumm, and it also explains why every bit of damming evidence against Captain Sawyer was related to the drug trade. With everything that Levi had said, it sure looks like Mayor Persie is involved in this too." He stared at his hands for a moment. "Why didn't Tanner tell me? I was right here. I could have helped."

"Maybe he was trying to protect you," Willow said. "You had been through a lot, and this was his way of keeping you safe."

The familiar creak of the staircase brought the conversation to a halt.

"Levi?" Willow called out. "The coast is clear."

Boone led the way as Levi entered the room. Ranger and Ruby scampered to meet their little buddy, resulting in a play-fueled tussle. "Did you forget about me, or were you two looking for some quiet time? It's been over an hour since you sent me to hide in your secret bunker. If I hadn't come to check, you'd have left me there all day."

The jest made Jackson's ears burn. "Sorry about that," he said, scrubbing his hands down his face. "After I dropped Castor off at his car..."

"Forget about it," Levi said, taking a seat on the couch next to Jackson. "Why was he here?"

"He said he was dropping off information," Willow said. "Except he forgot it in his car and decided to snoop around."

"What did he bring?" Levi asked. "You said he had information for you."

"Along with the rest of the lab reports, it had the definitive proof that Savannah's intel on Captain Sawyer was all fake. Every bit of it. I guess he wanted me to see it in black and white." The dogs' play was escalating, becoming louder and more aggressive. "Ruby, settle," Jackson said. The Golden Retriever immediately broke away, leaving Ranger and Boone to continue the battle on their own. "Call Ranger to you," he said to Willow. "Get him to disengage."

Willow rolled her eyes. "Ranger. Come." She gave the command perfectly. Clear. Concise. And without emotion. The Malinois obeyed, but Boone wasn't making it easy on him. The little Border Collie followed him back to Willow, nipping at him the entire time.

"They're bored," Jackson said. "They need to be exercised or they're going to tear the house apart." He rubbed the muscles in his neck. "Are you up for a run?" he asked Willow. "It will give the dogs a chance to burn off some of their energy, and you can work on your connection with Ranger in the open."

"Sure," Willow replied, albeit not too enthusiastically. "If you plan on taking me through the forest again, I'm going to put on something more suitable. When we get back, I'll take a shower, and you can cook us up something tasty. We skipped lunch and I'm running on fumes."

***

The mid-day sun had raised the temperature. Sweat stained Jackson's chest, back, and armpits. His breathing was free and easy, and a slow jog through Mother Nature was exactly what he needed. He glanced over at Willow. Her long blonde hair was tied back in a messy ponytail. She had put on a tank top and fitted compression shorts. Her runners had started off looking glittering-pink and pristine. Now they were a dingy brown. Her skin was glistening, and her tank top was plastered to her slim form.

"You're staring," Willow said. "What's up?"

Jackson's cheeks burned. Hopefully he was already red-faced from exertion. "I was just wondering if you do much long-distance running." He motioned over to Ranger whose tongue was lolling out the side of his mouth. Ruby and Boone were both panting, but they looked like they could go all day. "I'm thinking your dog needs to do this more often."

"I run at the gym," Willow said as she leaped over a tree root protruding from the path. "I'm scared shitless I'm going to turn an ankle here. The ground is treacherous."

"It's a risk," Jackson said. He stepped onto a boulder and launched himself into the air. "But it's a lot more fun than spinning your wheels and going nowhere all day."

"I suppose, but if you go down hard, there is no one to help you. Maybe we should take a break. Ranger looks like he's going to drop dead."

"He'll be okay for a few more minutes. There's a small river up ahead. The dogs can jump in and cool off."

"You're not worried about snakes and gators?" Willow glanced at Jackson, her lips pressing together as if she wasn't quite sure she believed him. "It's part of the reason I don't do nature runs." It was her turn to blush. "To be fair, it's the only reason."

"Outside of a reserve that is a hundred miles away, there are no gators in Wilson Lake. We've got snakes, but not where we're going. I've been taking my dogs here for over twenty years and I've never seen a single one." Jackson's insistence that they'd be perfectly safe clearly didn't assuage Willow's fears. Not one iota. "The water here is shallow, fast, and the ground is covered with small rocks. There is no vegetation in the water until late summer. Even then... Just trust me. Okay?"

As they crested the next hill, Ruby bolted forward. Boone followed close behind her. Ranger whined.

"Ranger, break!" Willow said. Despite the dog's obvious exhaustion, he sprinted forward and disappeared over the ridge. The sound of splashing dogs suggested they were only a few feet from the water's edge.

"Race you," Jackson said before breaking into a sprint. The promise of cool springtime water urged him forward. When he got to the sandy beach, he barely slowed long enough to kick off his runners. Socks and all, he barreled into the frigid water. When the water hit thigh-deep, he dove in. He choked on the water when his head broke the surface and he came face to face with Willow, water cascading over her bright blue eyes. The sight made Jackson's heart race.

"If you're wrong about the snakes and the gators," she said, swimming closer. "I expect you to protect me."

Jackson swallowed hard and nodded. He moved closer, his pulse pounding in his ears. Willow's playful smile nearly made his heart stop.

"We best be heading back," she said, placing her hand on Jackson's chest. "I'm way too hungry, and we've still got work to do. When we've got more time..." Willow winked and swam for shore.

Thank God for the cold water.

Chapter Forty-Seven

Willow

Willow popped another nugget of homemade granola into her mouth. "The ham and cheese sliders you made were fantastic, but this bag of fruit and nuts and whatever else you put in it... I could eat this all day, every day."

"I'm guessing it's the dates and molasses," Jackson said as he pulled into a parking spot out front of Evelina's house. "I swear, they make everything irresistible."

With a smile, Willow tossed another handful into her mouth and sealed the bag. She was starting to feel like a hog at a trough the way she'd been shoving the food into her mouth. "How do you want to handle this?" she asked between chews. "I've already got a bit of a rapport with her. I'll play good cop, and you play bad cop?"

"I don't think we'll need to play anything," Jackson said. "Evelina's looking at a long list of drug charges, plus conspiracy to commit murder. If she doesn't want to spend her youth behind bars, she'll need to be an extremely cooperative witness."

"You think the State's Attorney would saddle her with conspiracy?" Willow climbed out of the truck. "It seems a bit of a stretch."

"Her actions were directly attributable to the death of two people, including an FBI agent." Jackson said as he joined Willow on the sidewalk. "I'm guessing the bureau is going to want to toss her in prison and throw away the key. I expect she was an unwitting accomplice, but I don't think that matters."

"Okay," Willow said. "You hit her with the threats, and I'll throw her a lifeline. I don't believe the woman is stupid, but I think she relies on her pretty face and perky tits to get by."

"I think you've got her wrong," Jackson said, inviting Willow to take the lead up the stairs to the semi-detached home. "I think Evelina's shrewd, conniving, and manipulative. Her looks are a distraction that she chooses to use to great effect. And, based on the camera in her bedroom, I think she's using her body to ensnare her victims."

"Let's find out," Willow said. "I don't think it will take us too long to see her true colors." She peered through the front door's sidelight window and pressed on the doorbell. She tilted her head side to side, hoping to get a better view but there was too much reflection from the midday sun off the windowpane. She was just about to give up hope when she saw movement on the staircase. Unsure who it was, Willow unsnapped the safety strap on her Glock and gently placed her hand on its grip. When a pair of fuzzy pink slippers came into view, she pulled her hand away from her weapon.

"You can't ask me questions without my lawyer," Evelina said as she threw open the door. Despite it being late in the afternoon, the young woman was dressed in slippers and a short fluffy robe that did nothing to hide the GPS monitor strapped to her ankle.

"We're not here on official business," Willow said. "If we ask you anything you don't feel comfortable answering, you can refuse. No pressure."

"You brought the asshole who beat up Zeke? Do you know his arm's in a cast? We're going to fucking sue. My lawyer said your abuse will be worth millions."

"It is, of course, your right to bring charges against me and my partner, or against the FBI as a whole," Willow said with a shrug.

She cocked an eyebrow. "I wonder how well that's going to help your plea deal. I'd imagine that you're facing a long list of felony offenses."

"Including conspiracy to commit murder," Jackson added.

Evelina harrumphed in response. "Yeah, and my lawyer said he'll beat all the charges in court, and I'll come out a rich woman."

"And if your lawyer fails? What happens then?" Willow pointed to the ankle monitor. "You'll go to prison for the rest of your life while your lawyer will still get paid for defending you, and then he'll go home and laugh about how foolish you were while he sips on some hundred-dollar bottle of Scotch."

The cocky smirk melted away from Evelina's lips. "If I don't sue, and if I help you, you'll still get me a good deal with DA's office? Any chance I can get complete immunity?"

"The DA won't be involved in this," Jackson said. "You helped kill a federal agent. You're going to go to federal court, and your lawyer will have no sway. There will be no friendly prosecutor or judge to help him out. You'll to be convicted, and you'll spend the rest of your days in a maximum-security prison."

Evelina's eyes were wide as they flitted between the two agents.

"I can't make any promises for what the United States Attorney will do, but I can promise that if you help, I'll do my very best to see you get the best deal possible."

"I'd be tried in federal court?" Evelina said, wilting at the news. "My attorney never told me that. He said he had an in with the DA."

Willow pressed her lips together and shook her head.

With a sigh, Evelina rolled her eyes and stepped back into her house. "I'll do what I can to help. You two can come in."

"Would you like to record the conversation?" Jackson said. "I know you are represented by a lawyer, so if you feel you are being pressured in any way..."

Evelina glanced at Willow.

"It's entirely up to you," she said, "but I really don't think it's necessary."

Jackson cleared his throat. "I'd like to ask you some questions about the books I saw in your study."

"It's a library," Evelina said. "It's where I do my reading and writing, and nothing else."

"You're an author?" Willow asked, feigning interest. "What genre do you write?"

"Adult fantasy, or *romantasy,* if you prefer." The scared woman vanished as she practically danced from foot to foot, clearly excited to have someone showing interest in her books. "I've published three. One's an alpha werewolf story, one's a vampire lord story, and the last one is a reverse harem where the heroine gets her pick of shape-shifting men." She fanned her face and made a swooning sound. "It's extremely spicy. Like, five red-hot chili peppers spicy."

"I'll have to check that out," Willow said. Inside, she wanted to puke. Pandering to the woman was nauseating. "I love that sort of stuff." She glanced at Jackson who was failing to hide his boyish grin.

"Oh, you'd love the books written by the other authors in my writers' guild. We all write similar styles of stories, except for AJ." Evelina made a tutting sound. "He writes young adult fantasy and believes that sex doesn't belong in books targeted for teens. Pfft. Like the majority of them are not already having sex. We've all told him he'd sell a lot more if he gave in to the dark side."

"Who's AJ?" Jackson asked. "Is that AJ Mitchell? I saw one of his novels in your library."

"One and the same," Evelina said. "He's actually very good, but he and Rachel never got along."

"Rachel Persie?" Willow asked. "She was in your guild, too? Why didn't they get along?"

"Because Rachel was being a bitch, and she never let up on him." Evelina covered her mouth with her hand, a mortified expression crossing her face. "Oh, Jesus. I don't mean to speak ill of the dead, but when Rachel got into one of her high-and-mighty moods, well, she could be difficult to take. Her books were trash, and I mean really badly written, but she hit the New York Times Bestseller List." She leaned in closer to Willow and whispered. "Because her rich daddy and his friends spent nearly one hundred thousand dollars buying up copies of her books." She pulled back and laughed. "That drove AJ insane because we all knew how she got the award, but she flaunted it like she had earned it through grass-roots social media campaigns."

"It seems that you didn't think much of Ms. Persie," Jackson said. "And yet, in the signed book she gave you, she called you her best friend and biggest supporter."

Evelina rolled her eyes. "What else was I going to do." She blew out a breath. "She was so mean to everyone in our writers' group... our tribe, as she called it. When we had our weekly meetings, all Rachel wanted to do was talk about herself. It was supposed to be a support group, a way to cheer each other on, but all she wanted was to brag. As soon as anyone else started talking she would get bored and fiddle with her phone, or she'd attack them, or belittle them. She was the worst with AJ because he wrote YA fantasy. Rachel thought it was a waste of time, and that people only read smut."

"If you didn't approve of her behavior, why support it?" Willow imagined herself pistol whipping the woman again.

"Because Rachel had money and that could open doors for me." She almost sounded remorseful. Almost. "All the other members in the group are never going to go anywhere. I want to succeed, and I'll do whatever it takes to get there. She paid me a huge pile of money to ghost write her next novel, but nobody knew anything about that. Well, except for AJ. I told him the last time he was here."

"AJ Mitchell came to your house?" Jackson asked. "Why?"

"He'd slip in, from time to time," Evelina said. "If you get my meaning. I don't know how, but he helped keep the cops off my ass if I let him… you know."

"Did you know he works for the FBI?" Willow asked. "Are you sure he wasn't, you know, *pumping you* for information?"

The comment made Evelina laugh. "Yes, I knew he was a fed. When he came over, we didn't do much talking about anything. He only ever had one thing on his mind. I knew from the first time I met him in our Zoom meetings that he had a thing for me."

"What about Brock Ainsley?" Willow asked. "I though you and he…"

"I like him," Evelina said. "He's not ripped like AJ is, but he's not hard on the eyes, and the man is fucking loaded. Do you think I could afford a place like this in downtown Muscle Shoals without some help?"

"When was the last time you saw AJ?" Jackson asked.

"I don't know. Maybe a couple of months ago? I thought I'd see him earlier this week, before all hell broke loose, but he never showed. He said he was coming into town on business."

"What business does he have in Florence?" Willow asked. "Besides you, I mean."

"No clue." Eveline wrapped her arms around herself. "Like I said, we don't talk much when he stops by." She leaned to the side to look past Jackson. "Did I answer everything okay? Will you help me stay out of jail?"

"Expecting someone?" Willow said, noticing how the woman seemed fixated on what was happening outside.

"Brock said he'd check in on me. I'm not allowed to leave my property."

"Have you ever recorded him talking about being in the drug business?" Jackson asked. "We found your hidden camera in your bedroom."

Evelina's eye twitched. "You weren't supposed to see that. It's private."

"But he did see it," Willow said, "and now he wants to know if you've captured any incriminating evidence on Brock, or anyone else for that matter. Do your *visitors* know they're being recorded?"

"I don't know," Evelina said. She looked away, seemingly unable to look either agent in the eye. "I use it for my books. I write my sex scenes from a voyeur's point of view. I set the scene, and the cameras record the action."

"Cameras?" Willow said. She raised an eyebrow at Jackson. They had only found a single camera in the air duct.

"I've got four," Evelina said, her cheeks reddening. "Well, five, really. I have one in the air duct, but it's phony. In case I get raided, or something, the cops would find that it isn't attached to anything."

"Where are the other cameras?" Willow asked. She was coming to believe that Jackson had pegged her perfectly. Evelina was smart, manipulative, and extremely dangerous.

"Three are built into the bed posts, and one is in the light in the shower." She looked at Jackson with hungry eyes. "I want to make sure I get every possible angle when I'm fucking their brains out. If you'd like, I'll give you copies of my books. You can read all about how I turn men into quivering bowls of jelly."

"I want those videos," Jackson said. "All of them."

"I'll bet you do," Evelina said. She tugged at the edge of her fur-lined housecoat.

"You can't help yourself," Willow said. She wanted to throttle the woman. "Do you really think trying to seduce a federal agent is going to help you?"

Evelina's sultry demeanor shifted to predatory. "Not at all, but I wanted you to witness the effect I have on men. My videos are worth millions and I'm not going to just hand them over. The only way you're going to get access to them is with a warrant, and by the time you get one, the hard drives that hold the videos will be fried. You bring me a written promise of full immunity from the US Attorney, and I'll give you a copy of everything I've got. And I'm going to want to be put in witness protection too. Someplace nice. With lots of money to keep me in the style to which I've become accustomed. If I give up these videos, I'm as good as dead, and I plan on growing old and wrinkly."

"You think you'll get full immunity?" Jackson said with a mocking laugh. "The way I see it, you're going to prison for a very long time—plenty of time for you to grow old and wrinkly. The question is, do you want to spend your time at the minimum-security women's prison in Aliceville, or the maximum-security prison in Hazelton, West Virginia?"

"Either way," Willow added. "You're likely going to end up being someone's bitch. Come on, Jackson. You were right. She's too stupid to understand just how much trouble she's in."

"You said you'd help me, bitch!" Evelina yelled. "You act all kind and understanding, but you're just another fucking liar like the rest of them."

Willow wheeled around on the young woman and used her size advantage to back her into a wall. "I said I would help you if you helped me. But that wasn't good enough for you. You needed to push it and ask for the moon. I don't care who you've recorded, and I don't care what they said. If you think you can extort me, then you're not nearly as smart as Agent Brooks gives you credit for. I said you were stupid and that you get by on your looks. I'd say I had you pegged perfectly."

Evelina cringed, her eyes shifting from side to side. "I... I have the names of the people bringing drugs into Florence. Brock. He talked about them a lot. He said he was terrified of them but..."

"But what?" Willow said, applying more physical pressure by closing the distance between them further.

Evelina's eyebrows pinched together. "They're from Mexico, I think. I don't know who they are, but Brock sounded like he was going to shit himself whenever he talked about them. AJ... he said they were businessmen and that I was safe as long as I didn't cross them. That's why I want immunity and protection. If I give you these tapes, and these fuckers find out that I did... I don't want to die. Given the choice, I'd rather go to jail."

"I'll talk to the US Attorney," Willow said. "You give us the hard drives, and if they contain the information that you say they do, then I'll do everything I can to make sure you get what you want."

"No way," Evelina said. "You bring me the immunity deal. You can put in a provision that what I told you is true, because it is all true, and I'll hand them over. Maybe you'll be able to figure out who the frigid bitch was who killed Rachel and Tanner."

"What do you mean by that?" Jackson asked. "Are you saying their killer was a woman?"

"Fucking right it was," Evelina said. "You didn't know that? I mean, she was dressed up to look like a dude, but I know a woman when I see one. She tried to act butch, but I saw right through it."

"Holy shit," Willow said, turning to Jackson. "We never considered it could be a woman."

"We need to leave," he said. "Now."

"You'll bring me my deal?" Evelina said. "I told you. I can help you. You need me."

"I'll make the call right away," Willow said. "We'll be back tomorrow, and you better be ready to give us everything we need."

Chapter Forty-Eight

Jackson

Jackson flipped the venison steak on the BBQ, sending up a sizzling waft of smoke. He couldn't shake what Evelina had said. Had the woman in Levi's encampment been the killer? Had Willow been within arm's reach and let her go? He looked over at the three dogs sitting side by side drooling. "You've all been fed already." He looked down at the four massive steaks that were almost ready to plate. "These are for us."

Ranger inched forward. Ruby and Boone followed his lead. They all wanted a taste, but none of them seemed to be competing for the first morsel. The Belgian Malinois had changed substantially since Jackson had first met him. He was calmer and far more comfortable with his surroundings. The dog was soaking in Ruby and Boone's combined energy, but he needed to be tested and observed with Willow in a hyper-charged situation. Jackson knew exactly what he wanted to do, but the current case was evolving too quickly. There simply wasn't time to devote to the K9.

"Jax," his mother said from the picnic table. "If you burn my steak, I'm going to tan your hide."

Jackson turned to where his mother was sitting with Willow and Levi. Willow had a strange smile on her face, one that he couldn't quite decipher. Maybe she was enjoying seeing him squirm while his mother teased him. "They're barely medium rare. They need another few minutes."

"You heard me, Jax." Maybelle slapped the palm of her hand on the old pine table. "I don't want a pink center. I want it red. Do you hear me? Red!"

Jackson sucked in a breath through his teeth. Part of him still wanted to caution his mother about her diet, but he couldn't bring himself to deny her this simple pleasure. Her cancer was in remission—a miracle he was still processing—and her renewed zest for life was infectious. He pulled the thickest steak off the grill and placed it on the fancy, flowery platter—the one his mother insisted on using for special occasions. Jackson watched her eyes light up at the sight of the rare steak, feeling both relief at her improving appetite and concern over the strain it might put on her compromised kidneys. The past year had been a rollercoaster since his father's disappearance, and the thought of facing more uncertainty with his mother's health made his chest tighten. But for now, he pushed those worries aside, determined to savor this moment of normalcy. "Does anybody else want theirs still bleeding?" The words caught in the back of Jackson's throat.

"I prefer mine on the rare side as well," Willow said, earning herself a smile from Maybelle. Jackson's mom patted her hand.

"I knew I liked this girl," Maybelle said. "So did Grace. That first day you two met, Grace said this one was full of spit and fire."

Jackson kept his eyes on the meat as he pulled a second steak from the flames. He shot a questioning look at Levi, doing his damnedest to avoid eye contact with either of the two women at the table.

"Pink center, no blood," Levi said with a broad grin. He waggled his eyebrows, forcing Jackson to turn away. It seemed there was a conspiracy afoot.

After refusing to engage for several minutes, Jackson pulled the last two steaks from the grill and placed them next to the others.

With his head still down, he placed the food on the table and made his way to the house. "I'll be back with the sides in a moment. The steaks need to rest."

"Bring that bottle of red wine," Maybelle said. "The one I've been saving. I want to taste it."

Jackson was about to object, but he knew what would happen. They'd argue for two or three minutes, and then he'd give in. His mother was happy and doing better than he'd seen her in the last month. Like the overly rare steak she insisted on, he wasn't going to deny her this little pleasure. It's not like she'd have more than a few sips anyway, and it was a bottle his dad had bought for them to drink on their last anniversary—the same one they never got to share together.

While Jackson was loading up two trays with side dishes, a bottle of wine, and four glasses, the screen door slammed. Some day he would need to fix the spring on that door. "Hey, Levi. Can you carry one of these?"

"It's just me," Willow said as she stepped into the kitchen. "Is this a normal night at the Brooks's? Your mom's amazing."

Jackson's face heated, but he wasn't sure why. "Pretty much. When she was healthy and my dad was still around, the two of them used to tag team me. It seemed like a competition to see who could embarrass me more." He shrugged a shoulder. "I didn't realize how much I missed it until just now."

"How long has your dad been gone?" Willow leaned her elbows on the counter. The intensity of her blue eyes stole Jackson's breath.

"About a year and a half," Jackson said, his voice tinged with pain. Even now, the hurt from his dad's disappearance was still raw. "My dad went on his annual hunting trip in Bankhead National Forest. He was usually gone for a week. When he wasn't home in time for Thanksgiving, we knew something was wrong. A massive search was conducted. After scouring the forests for three weeks, we found no sign of my dad or his hunting party. It was like they had been scooped off the earth. Their camp was pristine and undisturbed. Their truck, long guns, and valuable belongings were all there. When the winter weather turned bad, the Florence PD declared the case closed, saying that they must have *run off*. Nobody believed it, but they shut down the search anyway, citing lack of funding or some other lame excuse. Ruby and I continued searching into late December, but despite our efforts, we never found anything. Every day without him still feels unbearable. I miss him horribly."

Willow rubbed the middle of Jackson's back. "Sorry. I didn't mean to open old wounds."

"Speaking of wounds," Jackson said, eager to change the subject. He pointed to his neck, where Willow had been grazed by the bullet. "How are you feeling? I'll bet that still stings."

"It was a scratch," Willow said. "How's your shoulder? I think you got the worst of it."

"I don't hardly notice it anymore," he said. It did, in fact, still sting like crazy but he wasn't about to let on. He was certain Willow's also hurt, but she wasn't going to say so either. She grabbed the tray laden with food and winced. Her dislocated finger was clearly still bothering her.

"I should have shot her instead of cracking her skull." She was still grimacing, but it didn't slow her down. "But we were in close quarters, and she was standing between us."

"I'm sorry." The words blurted from Jackson's mouth. "It was all my fault. You were nearly killed because of me. We both were. I..." His heart was beating hard. Shame and guilt for his failure to protect himself and his partner burned in his gut. "I won't let it happen again."

Willow slammed the tray onto the counter. "Stop it. It wasn't your fault. It was mine. I... I push too hard sometimes. I... Let's forget about it. Okay? Your mom is in a great mood and she's waiting for us." She picked up the tray, her cheeks reddening slightly. "If we doddle anymore, she's going to start making up more stories about us being a couple. Which we're not."

The last comment was like a punch to the gut, though Jackson couldn't pinpoint why it affected him so deeply. It's not like he had any feelings for the woman. Sure, she was attractive, but he found her overuse of expletives and aggressive approach to everything... off-putting. His eyes lingered as she left the kitchen carrying the tray of food. She was definitely attractive.

***

While Levi and Willow discussed the case, and the likelihood that Savannah was the shooter, Jackson washed and dried the dinner dishes. Though they had both offered to help, he welcomed the solitude that came with the mundane task. As expected, his mother had barely touched her blood-red steak and had only taken a few sips from the wine she had been saving, but it was the happiest he had seen her in months. The lively conversation and bustling activity had worn her out, and now she was sleeping quietly in the den, which had been converted into her bedroom.

Ranger, who had been sleeping under the kitchen table, popped up and ran to the front window. Ruby and Boone followed.

Jackson threw his drying towel onto the counter and strode into the living room to see what had caught their attention. Two large SUVs were parked on the street while two men dressed in dark suits were actively surveying the area. "We've got company. Levi, get upstairs and take Boone with you."

"Who is it?" Willow asked, taking up a position beside Jackson. "They look like government vehicles."

A mix of concern and annoyance coursed through Jackson's veins. Whoever it was could get back in their cars and… "It's Mayor Persie."

"What's he doing here?" Levi asked. He was standing a few feet away, his hands stuffed into his pockets.

"Get out of sight," Willow hissed, pointing towards the staircase. "What are you doing?"

"I'm not hiding anymore." Levi jutted out his jaw. "I didn't do anything wrong. I refuse to cower."

Jackson had no interest in arguing with the man. He pushed his way past the pack of dogs and stepped outside. Ruby and Ranger forced their way through the open door before he closed it. "Sit," he said. He didn't mind they were with him.

The two men in dark suits led the way, while Mayor Persie followed unsteadily in their wake. "I'm sorry to bother you at this late hour but I need to speak with you," he said, his words slightly slurred.

Jackson stepped off the front porch and met the mayor halfway. "What can I do for you, Mr. Mayor?" He had more than a few choice words he would have preferred to say.

The two bodyguards split apart like a pair of sentinels while the mayor moved past them, stumbling slightly. His mouth opened to speak, but no words came out. He appeared to be looking past Jackson, his eyes glassy. "Good evening, Special Agent Banks. Good evening, Levi."

"Mayor," Levi said.

The muscles in Jackson's stomach clenched tight. How stupid could he be?

"I had hoped to have a chance to speak with you. All of you." The mayor stepped forward and paused at the sound of Ranger's growls. The two bodyguards reached for their sidearms.

"Remove those weapons at your own peril," Willow said. Ranger's growls turned to snarls. Ruby and Boone joined in.

The mayor grunted at his men, swaying slightly. They pulled their hands away from their weapons, but neither relaxed their stance. Ruby pressed her shoulder against Jackson's thigh to let him know she was there. Willow and Ranger took up a position on his left, while Levi and Boone stood to his right.

With his palms facing forward, the mayor's expression turned solemn. "Please. I just want to talk to you. I'm not here to cause trouble. I know Levi had nothing to do with my daughter's death. I only..." He closed his eyes for a moment and shook his head, as if trying to clear it. "Go back to the car, gentlemen. I can assure you that I am perfectly safe. Your presence isn't helping." When neither man moved, the mayor's expression turned dark. "Gentlemen. Leave me."

As soon as the bodyguards had closed the car doors, the mayor addressed Levi. "I'm sorry, son. I was given bad information, and I acted brashly. Please forgive a grieving father." The typically stoic politician's façade shattered completely. In that moment, every self-serving, backhanded action he had ever taken melted away, leaving only the raw, devastated man.

"I understand," Levi said. He stepped forward and offered his hand to the man who had wanted to see him arrested. "Despite our differences..." His words fell away as he wrapped his arms around the mayor. The scent of whiskey hung in the air as they embraced, their muffled words lost to all but them.

"Can I come inside?" The mayor asked after the two parted, his voice thick with emotion. "I need your help. Please. I beg of you."

Jackson exchanged a wary glance with Willow. "Come inside," he said. "I'll put on some coffee."

Chapter Forty-Nine

Willow

After the mayor fell into the largest and most comfortable chair in the living room, Willow took a seat on the couch next to Jackson. Being drunk didn't make the man any less of an asshat. Then again, she understood the grief he was suffering. Or did she? She was still devastated at the loss of her friend and partner. This man had lost his daughter. His chin was resting on his chest, and his shoulders were slumped.

"Do you have any bourbon?" the mayor asked. His eyes were red and swollen.

"I've put on some coffee," Levi said. He hadn't sat down. He had chosen to wait by the door and watch from a distance.

"Did I ask for coffee?" the mayor said, slurring his words. He pulled his cell phone out from his pocket. "I have some in my—" The phone slipped from his hand and fell to the floor.

Jackson sprung from his place to pick up the man's phone. "I'm sorry, Mr. Mayor. I don't have hard liquor. My mother won't allow it in the house. You can have coffee or water, or you can leave."

"That's bullshit." The mayor, after several failed attempts, stuffed his phone back into his pocket. "Someone killed my daughter, and I want her body back so I can make arrangements."

And there was the reason for his visit. Despite his political power, the mayor couldn't get what he wanted. The coroner's office wouldn't release the body until they had completed their investigation and performed all the necessary tests. In Willow's experience, even an expedited case could take more than a week to process all the lab reports and forensic analysis. Less than seventy-two hours had passed since the murders.

"Mr. Mayor," Willow said, leaning forward.

"Call me Harlan," the mayor said, waving off the formal title. "I don't want to be mayor right now."

"Harlan," Willow said, starting again. "Do you know why your daughter was meeting with Tanner Montgomery? He drove a long way to have breakfast with her."

"He..." The mayor rubbed his forehead. "She was so excited. He sent her a text message. He had something to discuss with her." He wiped non-existent tears from his cheek. "No. That's not right. It was an email."

"Tanner sent Rachel an email?" Willow glanced at Jackson. Rachel had said during their interaction that Tanner had emailed her, but Willow had been certain she was lying. "Are you sure? It was my understanding that she had emailed him. She said she had something important to share."

Guilt spread across the mayor's face, and he slumped back in his chair. Through hooded eyes he stared up at Jackson. "I am quite certain of my assertion. She... she showed me the email. Jesus Christ. She showed everybody the email. She even posted a picture of it on her social media accounts." He closed his eyes hard. "She went to a beauty salon for hours to get all made up. She wanted to look her best when she posted videos of herself reading his message to her."

"I saw none of that," Levi said, his brow knitted into a tight V. "I've been scouring her social media, looking for any reason someone might have killed her." He shrugged at Jackson, who had shot him a questioning look. "I used your mother's computer. I was feeling useless sitting around the house while you two were hunting down leads.”

Willow understood that. Had she been the one cooped up in a house, she'd have been crawling out of her skin. “I doubt Mitchell would have any trouble spoofing emails or wiping someone's social media.”

“Who's Mitchell, and what do you mean, spoofing?” The mayor clutched the arms of his chair, looking like he was going to puke.

“SSA Alexander Mitchell is the head of cyber crimes in the Birmingham FBI field office,” Willow said. “We think he is responsible for sending out the fake emails that lured Rachel and Tanner into meeting. Do you know him? He works with Savannah.”

“He works with Savannah? You think she's involved in my daughter's death?” The mayor clapped his hand over his mouth. “Where's the bathroom? I'm going to be sick.”

Levi grabbed the mayor by the arm and dragged him from the living room.

“Well, that pretty much confirms Savannah's involvement,” Jackson said, shaking his body like a dog trying to rid himself of water. “She wanted them both in the restaurant. But why? Why was it important to kill them at the same time?”

“I've been thinking about this since Evelina said the killer was a woman,” Willow said. “Savannah needed a diversion. She dressed herself up to look like Levi. She made sure Rachel and Tanner were dosed with mind-altering drugs. Everything she did was measured and calculated. Tanner was onto her. Rachel might have even been giving him inside information. It all fits. She's running for state senate, so she kills off two high-profile individuals and solves the crime in record time.”

“Even if we believe it's Savannah,” Jackson said, his voice tight. “We have no real proof. Everything is conjecture and circumstantial evidence.”

"Maybe," Willow said, lowering her voice. "But she's the most likely suspect. I looked that homeless woman right in the eye and she completely..." The memory of the disheveled woman in the tent flashed in Willow's mind. Long scraggly hair. An N95 mask covering her face. And striking blue eyes. "Savannah has blue eyes. Levi's eyes are brown. The homeless woman... her eyes were bright blue. Her face was hidden behind a surgical mask, and her hair was a mess. Savannah wasn't just planting evidence in Levi's tent. She was getting changed and taking off her disguise. I interrupted her, mid change."

Jackson's expression tightened, his jaw clenching as if trying to hold something back. "All this time... oh, God, save me."

"What?" Willow asked. The man looked like he'd just had his heart ripped from his chest.

"Tanner had been trying to tell me this all along. For the past year, he'd been fixated on corruption in the FBI. He'd been saying how things didn't add up." Jackson held his hands wide. "Tanner was brilliant, but he was also a bit of a conspiracy nut—seeing problems that weren't there. I had laughed at his ideas."

"And now you think he was right?"

Jackson's body slumped, like the weight of the world had suddenly landed on his shoulders. "I do, and I was too caught up in my own self-pity to listen."

"It's understandable," Willow said, moving closer. "It's hard to hear others when we're struggling ourselves."

"Maybe," Jackson said. He recoiled from Willow as she tried to touch his hand.

The mayor interrupted their conversation, pinballing off the walls on his way back to the living room. Levi was walking behind him, making sure the drunk father didn't fall on his face.

"We have someone who might be able to shed some light on this," Willow murmured with an evil grin. She dashed to the mayor, took his arm and draped it over her neck and shoulders.

"Let me help you, Mr. Mayor." The man mumbled something unintelligible in her ear as she led him to his chair. She worried that questioning him in this state of inebriation might have blow black. A good lawyer could easily bring into question whether he had the mental capacity to understand his rights.

"He needs to sleep this off," Jackson said. "We can't question him like this."

"I came here of my own free will," the mayor shot back as he flopped back into his seat. "I want you to catch the motherfucker who blew off my daughter's face. I..." He grabbed hold of the armrests like he was trying to physically stop the chair from spinning.

"We need access to Rachel's email provider," Willow said, ignoring Jackson's protestations. "We've got a suspect, but we can't tie her to Rachel. Not yet anyway. We think there might be something crucial in your daughter's communications."

"Who do you think did it?" He glared at Jackson. "Tell me. Tell me now and I'll have the motherfucker assassinated. I've got friends. Dangerous fucking friends."

"We won't make false claims," Willow said. "Look what happened to Levi. We're not going to do that to someone else."

The mayor grumbled as he dug into his pocket and pulled out his phone. He tapped on it a few times before holding the phone up for everyone to hear.

"Harlan? What's up?" a voice said over the speaker.

"I need you to give the SBI a warrant for Rachel's email provider. They need access to everything. They said that it will tell us who killed my Rachel."

"I've already warned you, Harlan. If you do that, you might give them access to incriminating evidence against you. Against both of us."

Jackson's mouth opened like he was about to speak out, but Willow held her finger to her lips, imploring him to be quiet.

"Then make the warrant narrow enough that anything against me is inadmissible. Do what I goddamn pay you to do and get them what they need. I want them to have access immediately. Get the governor behind it if you have to. I want to know who killed my daughter so that I can get her body back."

"Fine," the judge said. "Marsden will have the warrant within the hour. I hope you know what you're doing, Harlan. Otherwise, we're both going to be royally fucked."

Jesus. Willow didn't know if what he just said could be used against him. The man was completely inebriated and out of his mind, but he had just admitted to paying off a judge, and the judge just admitted to accepting bribes.

"There," the mayor said. He looked pleased with himself. "Now you can catch the motherfucker who killed my daughter, and I can give her a proper burial." He slouched back into the couch and dropped his cell phone to the floor.

"You'd better get his men in here," Levi said. "They'll take him home and he can sleep it off."

"Even if everything he said was inadmissible," Willow said, "we've got the judge by the balls, and I'm thinking that might come in handy at some point."

Chapter Fifty

Jackson

Jackson squinted. The rays of the morning sun were searing into his brain, making every nerve ending in his body feel like it was on fire. Even his pre-dawn run hadn't alleviated the pain. Again, he had left Ruby at home, giving him another chance to see how Ranger did without her support.

"Do you have the extra burner phone to give to Marsden when we get to his office?" Willow's voice pierced Jackson's skull like an icepick, causing him to wince. "What's going on with you?"

"Migraine." Jackson shielded his eyes with his left hand. The hood's reflection was too low for the visor to be effective.

"Jesus. If it's that bad, you should be in bed sleeping. Why don't you let me drive? That way you can close your eyes." At least she kept the last sentences to a whisper.

"It'll pass," Jackson said. "I was too slow taking my medication, but it's already starting to kick in. I can already feel the knot in my head lessening. Which reminds me, we need to stop by the pharmacy. I've only got one dose left."

"I'm really worried about the number of pills you're taking." Willow rolled down the window, filling the cab with cool morning air. "Is it because of your dreams last night?"

The events surrounding this case had triggered old memories, and last night, they had resurfaced with a vengeance. It seemed that no amount of therapy could rid him of his guilt. No matter how many times he heard it wasn't his fault or that he did what had to be done, that poor kid was still dead, and it was by his hand. He could have done something different, something non-lethal. His therapist had said, multiple times, that playing what-if scenarios was unhealthy, but it wasn't like he could tell his brain to stop doing it. When he got into his funk, Jackson went through all the prescribed grounding techniques like counting objects, identifying things he could see, and touching each finger. Those things helped when he was awake, but his subconscious was in control while he slept.

"I had a rough night." Jackson turned a corner, putting the sun to his right. The relief was instantaneous. "Can we focus on the case?"

"You're deflecting," Willow said. "And I'll say you had a rough night. Your dreams kept the entire house up, and your screams really freaked me out. Ranger too. I thought he was going to eat his way through the door to find you."

"I'm sorry about that. I... I have nightmares sometimes."

"Does it have something to do with that kid's death?"

Jackson's head snapped to his right, his breath catching. The memory of that day clawed at the edges of his mind, as he pushed it back. His chest tightened, his mouth went dry, and the words stuck in his throat. He wanted to explain, to say something, but all he could do was gape, unable to escape his never-ending guilt.

Willow's voice softened. "When you left for your run, you woke the entire house, including your mother. She was looking out the living room window when I came downstairs to check on what was happening. She told me about the shooting and how it gave you night terrors. Guilt, even if it's unfounded, is tough to shake."

There was something in Willow's tone and demeanor, a subtle softening of her usually sharp gaze, that suggested she may have understood better than most. He wanted to ask her about it and change the subject, but he feared it would reopen a wound that he desperately wanted to scab over. Jackson's grip tightened on the steering wheel, thankful that the SBI building was directly ahead. "We're here," he rasped. The conversation was more than he could handle.

They made their way to the building's front door with Ranger padding quietly beside them. There were no reporters lining the streets, making for a pleasant surprise.

"You really should be holding Ranger's leash in your left hand," Jackson said. The pain in his head was lessening enough that he could reasonably function. He was about to explain why when Willow showed him how badly swollen her finger was. It had turned purple, and the color had spread into her palm. "Why didn't you say something? We should get you to Emerg."

"Nah. It looks worse than it is, but it hurts badly enough that I can't hold Ranger's leash in that hand."

Jackson was dubious. He was certain she was making light of it, but he didn't want to press her on it.

"Really," she said, making a loose fist to show him it wasn't broken. "If it's not improved by tomorrow, I'll get it checked. Okay?"

"I'm guessing my mother didn't see it," Jackson said as he pulled open the front door to the building. "Otherwise, she'd have forced me to take you to the hospital."

"She did, and I told her I'd go." She tucked her hair behind her ear and offered a coy smile. "I just didn't say when."

The elevator doors closed when Jackson punched seven on the panel. "We're meeting Marsden in his office, away from the war room, in case Mitchell has bugged it."

"What if Mitchell was listening in when you called him?" Willow said. "Wouldn't he find it suspicious?"

"Maybe," Jackson said. The elevator chimed, and the doors opened. "It was a necessary risk."

"What risk was that?" Marsden asked. It seemed that he had been waiting for them in the hallway. He had a number of thick file folders under his arm. "Are you talking about the dogs?"

"Power down your phone," Jackson mouthed. When Marsden's eyebrows drew together in confusion, Willow moved close enough to whisper in his ear. Their closeness got Jackson's blood up.

With a shrug, the SBI agent pulled out his phone and shut it down. "What's that all about?"

"Take us someplace quiet, and I'll explain," Jackson said. "A lot has happened since we last met."

"Tell me about it," Marsden said. "We've been given full access to Ms. Persie's phone records, and we've dug up a shit-ton of evidence from the photos and videos you shared. Maybe what you have to say will help make sense of it." As the trio made their way through the maze of offices, Jackson gave Marsden a burner phone along with a brief explanation of their concerns. They arrived at a tiny meeting room with a table barely large enough to seat the three of them. After unclipping his leash, Ranger immediately settled at Willow's feet, despite the tension in the room. After taking their places, Jackson and Willow told him everything that had happened with SSA Mitchell and the mayor, but neither mentioned Savannah.

"What have you uncovered?" Jackson asked. "Does any of it support what we've told you?"

"Jesus." Marsden scratched at the stubble that covered his chin. "Support it? I'd say so. Before I get into that, we found out why Ms. Shanahan's videos came out clear. Her phone was brand new, and she hadn't yet installed the Yumm app on it. According to her credit card records, she purchased the phone the night before the murders."

"That makes sense," Willow said.

"As for the videos and photos you shared with me," Marsden said, rifling through the loose papers in one of his file folders. "My

IT team worked on them all day yesterday. It felt like I was being hit with a new bombshell every thirty minutes or so." He pushed some of the papers to Jackson. Willow immediately pulled her chair closer, so they could read the information together. "This is a report of the people who were at the raid the PD conducted on your house. Despite them all wearing Florence police department gear, the only two who actually work on the force are detectives James and Spade. The others are all former marines who now work for a paramilitary firm. It's a good thing you took pictures of them because your CCTV cameras had all been disabled."

"How?" Jackson asked. "They're on a closed network, completely cut off from the internet."

"So was the camera at the laundromat," Marsden said. "We were able to find a vulnerability in the server configuration that allowed the cameras to be shut down remotely. We are assuming the same thing happened to yours. Your cameras shut off shortly after Detective Spade arrived at your home. When my team noticed the timing, they checked out the street cams by the laundromat. They spotted the detective just up the road, ten minutes before the laundromat cameras shut off."

The police were definitely corrupt, but during Jackson's investigation into them, these two detectives never came up. In fact, he hadn't even come across their names. The only way that could have happened... "I guess that makes the chief a part of this. During the last six months while I was looking into the captain, there was never any mention of James or Spade. Wheeler was feeding me the intel on only those I needed to investigate, and I can only assume that it was to protect the guilty and implicate the innocent."

"It gets better," Marsden said.

"Of course it does," Willow interjected. She had been leafing through the paperwork Marsden had shared. "From what I can see here, these two detectives were heading up the investigations into the city's drug problems."

"Right," Marsden nodded. "But that's just the tip of the iceberg. Remember that paramilitary company the fake cops work for? It's called Phoenix Security, a wholly owned subsidiary of Belladonna Enterprises."

Jackson scratched his head. "Belladonna keeps coming up. We need to know who owns this company."

Marsden grimaced. "That's where it gets tricky. The company was formed in the Cayman Islands, and the shareholders' names are private. We can't easily compel the government to reveal that information."

"But you found something else," Jackson prompted, sensing his excitement.

"We did manage to get the names of the people sitting on the board of directors," Marsden confirmed. "And let me tell you, it's quite the roster."

Willow leaned in. "We know Rachel Persie was one of them."

"Yes, but she wasn't the most interesting," Marsden said, shuffling through his notes. "We've got Lauderdale County District Attorney Clayton Beauregard—"

"Levi's former boss?" Jackson asked.

Marsden nodded. "And Thomas Neilson, the sitting Alabama State Senator for District 1."

Willow's eyes widened. "Isn't that the same district Savannah would be running for?"

"Exactly," Marsden said. "And here's the kicker: Neilson just announced he's not running this term. Savannah will be running unopposed."

Jackson whistled low. "That can't be a coincidence."

"It gets better," Marsden continued. "The chairman of Belladonna is a man named Juan Chavez. He's the nephew of Emilio Reyes."

Willow tilted her head. "Should that name mean something to us?"

"It should," Marsden said gravely. "Emilio Reyes is the leader of the Los Reyes Cartel out of Mexico. They've been a major player in the synthetic opioid trade since the early 2000s."

Jackson sat back, stunned. "So, we're talking about a drug cartel connection here?"

"Seems like it," Marsden said. "And there's more. The cartel owns the largest casino in Biloxi."

Willow's eyes lit up. "I'm guessing that's important, and not just a random fact about the cartel's holdings?"

Marsden grinned. "You've got good instincts. That casino ties into some other details my team uncovered yesterday."

Ranger shifted restlessly under the table, picking up on the heightened energy in the room.

Jackson leaned forward, matching Willow's position. "Okay, Marsden. You look like you're about to burst if you don't share. What else did you find?"

"Do I?" Marsden's grin widened as he reached for another file. "Well, I guess I'd better tell you what we found out..." He wiggled in his chair as though to ready himself for a long-winded explanation.

Chapter Fifty-One

Willow

Willow's head throbbed as she processed Marsden's revelations. Ranger had settled into a corner of the small room, his eyes alert but body relaxed. "You're telling me that Mitchell flew his plane here the day before the murders even took place. You're certain of it?"

"Absolutely certain," Marsden said. "I thought it a coincidence until you told me about his involvement in this... mess. While my team was digging into everyone involved in the case, I told them to leave no stone unturned, and they turned over some doozies. They discovered Mitchell is a pilot, and that he has his own plane. They tracked his flights over the last year. Using his plane's tail number, they accessed the information via the Automatic Dependent Surveillance–Broadcast. The ADS-B transponders broadcast data openly through services like FlightAware and Flightradar24."

He paused for a moment, seemingly to make sure both Willow and Jackson were following, which they were. Willow was impressed. This man's team was skilled and thorough.

"He made weekly trips to Biloxi," Marsden continued. "Thanks to a friendly judge, we were able to pull his credit card records. It was then that we saw that he always stayed at the El Dorado Casino. While we were digging into the... establishment, I received a call from the DEA. They wanted to know why we were trying to pull corporate records. When I told them, they gave me the details, and they also said to, and I quote, stay away from the Los Reyes Cartel. They've been working their case for over three years, and they were close to making arrests."

"Okay," Jackson said. It seemed his migraine was under control, but he still looked unwell. "That is beyond interesting, but what does it have to do with the case?"

"Apparently, until last year, SSA Mitchell was in deep with the casino... I'm talking nearly a quarter of a million deep. Around the same time that his debt was wiped, Juan Chavez became the chairman of Belladonna enterprises."

"So, even if we don't know who owns Belladonna," Willow said. "We know that the owner or owners are connected to Mitchell. I mean, they wouldn't give up the head of the board for just any-one."

"Do we know who Juan replaced?" Jackson asked.

The question made Marsden grin. "I thought you'd never ask. None other than SAC Savannah Greene."

"You're shitting me!" Willow wanted to smack the SBI agent in the head. "And in doing so, Mitchell is now in debt to Savannah. No wonder he's doing all her dirty work."

"I think there's more to their relationship than just that," Marsden said. "We have some pretty damning evidence that she won't be able to hide from... The crew working the airfield where Mitchell keeps his plane said that a tall, skinny, blonde woman almost always accompanies him when he flies."

The thought of it almost made Willow laugh. "They're a cou-ple? Never in a million years would I have guessed that."

"Maybe not a couple," Jackson said. "At least not in the roman-tic sense. But think about it. If they're working together, Mitchell could be cleaning up behind Savannah. He's got the skills and the access to make sure she leaves no digital trail. If Savannah has the mayor, the chief of police, and the DA in her pocket as well..."

"There's almost nothing she couldn't pull off," Willow said. "Including a double homicide. Especially if the mayor is connected with the governor. If they're all working together... how are we going to take them down? I mean, they've got power and connections and—"

"I think Tanner was going to do it," Jackson said. "I think that's why he was murdered. The man was a genius when digging into financials. I'm willing to bet that he uncovered... something, and Savannah removed him from the equation."

"You think Savannah is the killer?" Marsden's eyes narrowed. "But why kill Rachel? I can't see Mayor Persie sanctioning a hit on his own child."

"Look at the way she was killed," Willow said, turning to Jackson. "Evelina said that Rachel constantly belittled and humiliated Mitchell. If he's with Savannah... maybe she did it for him?"

"Maybe," Jackson said. "I mean, it makes sense if they were in a romantic relationship but..." He scrubbed the back of his neck to try to ease the tension creeping up the base of his skull. "What if Rachel wanted more? What if she... the woman was an egomaniacal..."

"Bitch?" Willow said. "Is that the word you were looking for Agent Brooks?"

"Something like that," Jackson said.

"Why frame Levi?" Marsden added. "Did Savannah or Mitchell have a beef with him?"

"We know Levi had details on the mayor and on Chief Wheeler," Jackson said. "But he's been out of the picture for almost six months. I can't see that being the reason."

"We think it was a part of her campaign for Senator," Willow said. "Two high-profile murders and she delivers the killer in a few days... it put her center stage when she made her announcement. Even if the current Senator isn't running against her, she needed to come out on top." She raised her eyebrows at Jackson, prompting him to respond. When he quietly looked away, she knew he agreed with her.

"How do we prove any of it?" Marsden asked. "We have a pile of conjecture and absolutely no proof to back up any of it. There isn't a jury in the world who'd convict Greene with what we've got."

"We can't," Jackson said. "Savannah's smart and she knows everything about how the FBI conducts its investigations. There is no way she's going to leave any obvious evidence, at least nothing actionable."

"Your admiration of the woman is blinding you," Willow said. "I don't give a shit how good she is. All killers make mistakes, especially when the heat gets turned up, and I plan on boiling the bitch alive. Look, we know she came here with Mitchell the day before the murders. We can prove that, and we can prove Mitchell is involved with the cartel." An idea struck her like a thunderbolt. "Do you remember in Johnnie Walker's video? Tanner scolded Rachel for sending him an email on his FBI account. To me, that implies she had sent others to some *other* email account, likely a secret account. If the emails were spoofed, it means that Mitchell doesn't know about that other account. Otherwise, he'd have used it. I'm almost certain of it."

"It makes sense," Jackson said. "But until we hear back from Marsden's team, it's more conjecture."

"While we're waiting," Willow said, "what do you say we light a fire under Savannah's skinny ass? Maybe we can flush her out, force her into making a mistake." She banged her hands on the table. "And I know exactly how to do it. We're going to use your admiration against her. While Marsden lights a fire under his team to get us email evidence, you're going to go upstairs and tell Savannah something we've learned, something she can't ignore."

"Okay, then," Marsden said. "It sounds like we've got the makings of a plan going forward. If you don't object, maybe I can turn my phone back on? If you need to reach me, you can call me on the burner you gave me."

"I think we're done here," Willow said. She turned to Jackson to see what he thought. He looked ill. She thought it might be another migraine, but it was more likely that he didn't like their plan to force Savannah into revealing herself. Clearly, he still hoped that she was innocent in his friend's death. "Come on, partner. We've got some big game hunting to do."

"And me without my St. Hubert medal," he said in jest. "My dad and I never went hunting without them."

The comment made Willow snort. "What the hell is a St. Hubert medal?"

"He's the patron saint of hunters," Jackson said with a shrug. "Whenever we went hunting, we'd bring our medals with us and hang them in a tree at our camp. It made my mother happy, and my dad swore by it. He said that if he forgot to bring them, his hunting trip would fail." The man's brow furrowed as though lost in thought.

"Crap," Marsden said. "I missed two phone calls and a laundry list of text messages while we were talking. Evelina Rainier's ankle monitor alarm went off last night. They tracked her to Wilson Dam. She was hung off the side, tied to a handrail. Her eyes were gouged out, her lips were sewn shut, and she was stabbed over fifty times. Chief Wheeler says it was a cartel hit."

Jackson pressed his finger to his lips and pointed to Marsden's phone. "I want to go home and get Ruby. Afterwards, we can head to the dam."

Willow scribbled a question on a sheet of paper. "Are you serious?"

Jackson shook his head. "I need to stop at the pharmacy for more meds too. I'm all out and I've got a huge migraine coming on." While he spoke, he wrote his own note. "Check Evelina's house first. Important."

"I'll head to the dam right away," Marsden said. "I hope my phone doesn't cut out on me again. It's been acting up since I dropped it in the sink last night." He powered off his phone. "Look. I'm not going anywhere. I'm going to check if my team has found anything regarding Rachel's emails. I doubt we'll get anything useful from the murder site."

"Savannah did this," Jackson said, his eyes downcast. "We don't need to fake her out—she's unraveling on her own. We need to get to Evelina's house. Her cameras might have caught her killers on video."

"I had the same thought," Willow said, already heading for the door. Ranger rose smoothly to his feet and moved to her side. She clipped on his leash and gave her dog's head a quick scratch. "If we don't move now, those cameras will mysteriously malfunction, just like the ones at the laundromat." She pulled out the burner phone. "I'll call Captain Sawyer on the way. If Savannah's behind this, she'll need local cops to do her dirty work."

Chapter Fifty-Two

Jackson

Jackson stopped in front of a police barricade blocking the way to Evelina's house. Ranger sat alert in the backseat but remained quiet. Two officers were manning the post, including Officer Martin. He grimaced when Jackson stepped out of the truck.

"I'm glad to see you two," Martin said. "The DEA is here, and the captain is behaving very oddly. He won't let anyone else in until the SBI has processed the scene."

"Since when does DEA have jurisdiction on a homicide?" Jackson asked as he and Willow stepped past the barricade.

"They usually don't," Willow said as she pulled out her phone. "But I'm guessing they are aware of Evelina's involvement with drugs. Give me a sec, I got a text from Marsden."

Jackson took in the scene. There were a half-dozen officers milling about in front of the house, including Officers Dawson and Reeves. Jackson was certain Dawson was dirty, but he had no read on his partner.

"Well isn't that fantastic," Willow said, showing her screen to Jackson. "It's a day late, but State's Attorney approved Evelina's immunity deal and WITSEC enrollment. We're not going to be seeing Evelina's secret footage anytime soon. We can't pull it without a valid warrant, otherwise it will all be inadmissible."

"We'll deal with that in a minute," Jackson said. She was right. They needed legitimate access, but right now, he wanted to know what the captain and the DEA were doing.

"Hey, Jax," Dawson said. "Do you think you can talk to the captain? The SBI hasn't shown up yet and we need to process Ms. Rainier's home as quickly as possible."

"If the captain doesn't want you here," Willow said, crossing her arms over her chest, "then why are you wasting your time standing around?"

"Because Chief Wheeler sent us here," Reeves said. "We told the captain, and he said the chief can fuck himself."

"Maybe you should follow Captain Sawyers orders then," Jackson said. "Because if either of you step inside this house, I'll arrest you myself."

Willow stuck her fingers in her mouth and blew an eardrum-piercing whistle. She motioned for Officer Martin to come over. Jackson had no idea what she was up to, but he had no intention of interfering. "Watch these two," she said to Martin when he approached. "They are to stay outside the house, and they are not to leave. If they try to contact anyone, I want to know who it is and what they say. If they try to leave, arrest them under the authority of the FBI."

"You can't do that," Dawson objected. "You have no right."

"Martin?" Jackson said, ignoring Dawson's protests. "Do I need to repeat my partner's instructions to you?"

Wide-eyed, the young officer shook his head. Vigorously.

"Don't screw this up," Willow said. "You've stepped in it enough times already—this is your shot to rectify it."

The captain met Jackson and Willow at the door, his gaze intense. "SSA Marsden called ahead. Don't make me regret trusting you, Agent Jackson."

"Right back at you, Captain," Jackson said with a quick head bob. "Martin said the DEA are here. Do you know any of them?"

"Not a one," he said. "I wish I had eyes on them both. They've split up." He pointed into the living room where one of the agents was flipping couch cushions over. "The other is upstairs."

"Do they have a warrant?" Willow asked. "Otherwise, anything they find will be tossed out."

"We do," the agent in the living room said. "Are you Agents Brooks and Banks?"

"We are," Jackson said. "You seem to have us at a disadvantage. Who are you?"

"Special Agent Tiffany Cadoux, DEA," the woman said, pointing to the small emblem on her golf shirt. Her eyes flicked to Ranger. She pulled off her latex glove and extended her hand in greeting. "SSC Alice Baldwin told us to expect you."

"Alice called you?" Willow asked. "When? Why?"

"Last night," she said. "She said you had a rat in the house, and that you might need our help."

"More like a nest," Jackson said. He looked over at the captain who was quietly observing their interactions. "It's hard to know who to trust."

"Well," Tiffany said with a grim smile, "I'm hoping you can trust us. We've been working with ASAC Baldwin for over three years. We have also been working with your father, Agent Brooks."

Jackson sucked in a breath. His dad had never talked about what he and Alice were doing, and he had certainly never mentioned the DEA. Suddenly, pieces he hadn't known were connected began to snap into place. His dad wasn't missing—he was working undercover with the DEA.

A memory hit him like a lightning bolt: the last time he'd searched his father's camp. At the time, he'd been so focused on looking for signs of a struggle or clues about where his dad might have gone that he hadn't noticed what wasn't there. The St. Hubert medal. His father always hung the medal from a tree in the camp when he went hunting; it was the first thing he did, every single time.

Its absence hadn't registered back then, but now it screamed at him. His father had left him a message, clear as day: *This wasn't a hunting trip.* And Jackson had missed it completely.

The realization turned his stomach. He desperately wanted to ask Agent Cadoux what she knew, but now wasn't the time.

"I never knew he had an association with the DEA," Jackson said. "When my dad was working a case, the only person he ever confided in was my mother."

Tiffany pulled out her phone and turned it to Jackson and Willow. "We've got a warrant from a federal magistrate, and an AUSA on speed dial in case we need more. It seems ASAC Baldwin has some powerful friends."

"Good," Willow said. "Because we've got something to show you, assuming we can find it." She took out her phone. "You don't mind if I call Alice, to confirm you are who you say you are, do you?"

"Alex," Tiffany yelled. "Get your ass down here. We're being vetted by the FBI, and the agents would like to see your face."

"Oh good, they're here," Alex yelled back. "I'll be right there. I found a camera in the victim's bedroom."

"It's fake," Jackson said. "Don't bother with it."

"How'd you know that?" Alex asked, holding what looked like a small video camera in her hand.

"We've got a lot to catch you up on," Willow said while she held her phone to her ear. "Hey Alice, it's Will. I'm standing here with two DEA agents. I'm going to send their photos. Can you confirm their identity?" She pointed the camera at each of the two women and snapped their pictures. With the phone pressed to her ear, she waited for the ASAC's response. "Great! Thanks Alice, for everything. You're a godsend."

Jackson blew out a breath. They needed allies they could trust, and so far, that number was very small. While Captain Sawyer stayed by the front door, the agents made their way to the second floor. It took them no time to locate the four cameras Evelina had talked about. They were extremely high-end, self-contained units with huge storage capacity.

"Did you bring a laptop with you?" Jackson asked. "We'll need one to access the camera's SD cards."

"We also need to talk with Evelina's unattached neighbor," Willow added. "They've got two well-hidden cameras in the ally. You never know…"

"I've got a laptop in my car," Alex said, "but we should talk to the neighbor first. Let's get as complete a picture as we can before we act."

"Do you have agents at the murder site as well?" Willow asked as they descended the stairs.

"Two," Tiffany said. "Hopefully they'll give us an update sooner than later. The Los Reyes Cartel like to leave a calling card when they make a splashy hit like this."

"Hey," Alex said, wordlessly telling her partner to hold her tongue. She turned toward Jackson, her gaze dropping to her shoes. "There are some details we don't share with anyone outside our unit. It's like how you don't tell everything to the media. Where the cartel is concerned, you can't be too careful."

"Keep your secrets," Willow said. "Unless it matters to our murder investigation. If it does, then you'd better spill, and I mean everything."

"Understood," Alex said with a sharp nod. "Likewise. If you've got details about how this case relates to the drug trade, we also want to know everything."

Jackson and Willow shared a silent conversation, each one asking the other how much they should share.

"The SBI are here," Captain Sawyer yelled. "Are you ready for them?"

"This isn't the place to discuss this," Jackson said. "The CSI team are going to want to process the scene. Let's talk to the neighbor and head to my place. I'm thinking it's going to take a while to review the footage, and we've got a lot to tell you about."

"And we have some information to share with you, too," Alex said. "What's your address?"

"Before we go," Willow said. "We split up the SD cards. You take two, and we'll take two. I hope you understand. With all the corruption involved, it's best that we each hold on to a piece of it."

"I'd like to join you," Captain Sawyer said. "If you don't mind. My men are clearly involved, and I want in on taking them down."

"Speaking of that," Jackson said. "I've placed Detectives Dawson and Reeves under arrest. Officer Martin is watching over them."

"I'll have them handed over to the SBI," the captain said. "If the chief catches wind they're in custody, he'll release them pending a sham of an IA investigation."

"I'll call Marsden," Willow said. "On the secure line."

Chapter Fifty-Three

Willow

Willow was lost in thought on the drive to Jackson's house. Like her, he had been quiet while they'd made their way from Muscle Shoals. They were both shaken by the news of Evelina's murder, fearing they, in some way, had played a part in her being targeted.

Jackson's phone rang. He pulled it out of his pocket and handed it to Willow. "Can you answer it?"

"Hello?" she said. There were a limited number of people who had Jackson's burner number, which meant it was likely Levi or Marsden calling him.

"Willow?" Levi said. *"Is Jackson with you?"*

"One sec," she replied. "We're in the truck on our way to you. I'll put you on speaker."

"Good," he said. *"That's why I'm calling. Maybelle was talking with Tanner's mom. Apparently, Tanner had dropped off paperwork the morning of his murder. Paperwork that proved SAC Greene and SSA Mitchell's connection to Belladonna Enterprises and the Los Reyes Cartel. There is a money trail that also connects Mitchell to Beauregard. Apparently, Tanner wrote up a report that summarized all of his findings, including over ten million dollars that was funneled into an offshore bank account belonging to Savannah. We've got them."*

Jackson tromped on the gas pedal as he rounded a turn, sending Willow slamming against the door and Ranger into the wheel well.

"What the hell?" she said, rubbing her shoulder. Ranger had a similar expression on his face as he climbed back onto the back seat.

"Levi," Jackson said, ignoring Willow's outburst. "Did she call mom on the land line? How long ago was this?"

"Yes, and maybe an hour ago," Levi said. *"Why?"*

"Fuck!" Jackson bellowed. It was the first time Willow had ever heard him use foul language.

"Fuck!" she bellowed back. She understood why he was driving like a maniac. "Those lines were likely tapped, and we just told Greene and Mitchell that we're on to them."

"Did the neighborhood watch call?" Jackson said. "Did anyone report any suspicious people or cars in the neighborhood?"

"No. Nothing." Levi said. *"How far away are you? We need to get Tanner's parents here. They're sitting ducks."*

"Too far away," Jackson said. "They live two minutes from my house. Go get them and hide them away." He jammed on the brakes, sending the truck into a four-wheel skid, nearly colliding with the car in front of them.

"Get the address from Maybelle," Willow said, her good hand taking a firm grasp on the *oh shit* handle. "My keys are on the kitchen counter. When you get them back, grab my gear from under the back seat. Get all of it, do you hear me?" She flopped around in the seat as Jackson continued his reckless driving. "Make sure Ruby is inside, too. When you've got that all done, you hide Maybelle and the Montgomerys, and you'd better hide with them too. Are we clear? We can't be worrying about you while we're dealing with this shit."

"I do. I understand completely." There was a brief pause. *"Thank you. Thank you for caring."*

"Why are you still talking?" Willow yelled. "Move it." Another thought dawned on Willow. "Wait! Are you still there?"

"I am," Levi said. It sounded like he was running. *"What else?"*

"Make sure you get Tanner's files. All of them."

"Thank you," Jackson said. "Take care of them. Take care of yourself."

"I will. You, too." The line went dead.

"What's the captain's number?" Willow asked. "We need to give him a heads up."

Jackson drove the truck up onto a sidewalk to get around a car that was going too slow for him. Between radical maneuvers, he called out the digits. After Willow finished filling the captain in, she tossed Jackson's phone out the window. "If the captain's line was bugged," she said. "Mitchell would have your number, and he could trace where we are."

"Good thing I got six of them," Jackson said. "Can you call Marsden? He needs to know what's happening. I wish we got the DEA agents' phone number. It would have come in handy right now."

"Good thing I got Tiffany's business card," Willow said, flashing the flimsy piece of cardboard at Jackson. "I'll call them right after I call Marsden."

"You're the best," Jackson said. "I'm really glad you're here with me."

"Me too," Willow said. "I'm looking forward to seeing Savannah's face when you slap cuffs on her. It's going to be fucking epic."

Jackson took the turn off the highway at breakneck speed, the truck skidding across the loose gravel. They were doing nearly ninety through the winding, hilly street. Willow struggled to drive it at forty. Then again, she had only been down the road once, and Jackson had done it a million times. Even still, she felt like they were a tire's width from dying in a horrible wreck.

"Ease up, will ya," she said. "We won't be of any use if we're dead in a ravine."

Jackson ignored the request, right up until he slammed the brakes to make the turn onto Aqua Vista Drive. "I'm sorry," he said. "I was being stupid. I should have been driving more slowly."

"Don't apologize to me," Willow said, placing her hand on his shoulder. "If it was my family, I'd have likely driven through the fields if I thought it would get me home sooner."

From the lone house at the corner, a rotund woman came bustling out the door. "Jax, is that you? You best hurry home. I've been trying to call May. She's not answering. There are gun-toting men in the forest. Connie called me and said to keep an eye out for them. Do you want me to sic the dogs on 'em? Earl can get his rifle, if you want."

Jackson had opened his door and was standing beside the truck. "Don't do anything," he said. "Tell Earl, and everyone else, that I've got this. The FPD are coming, and I've got some more agents a few minutes behind me. I don't want him shooting a friendly."

The woman waved and hustled back into her house. Before Jackson had gotten back in his truck, she had already drawn her living room curtains.

"Tight neighborhood," Willow said. "You really do look out for each other."

"It's been that way for a hundred years," he said, his expression a mixture of sadness and extreme pride. "These are good people. All of them. There isn't anything they wouldn't give to help each other. Especially my mom and dad."

In less than a minute Jackson pulled into his laneway. Willow's truck was parked right up by the front steps. "Levi got Tanner's folks here. They're safe. You can breathe now."

"I'll breathe when this is finished," Jackson said. "And it won't be finished until Tanner's death is avenged."

Her partner's choice of words wasn't lost on Willow.

Chapter Fifty-Four

Jackson

Jackson threw open the front door, a wave of relief washing over him at the sight of Ruby in the foyer. "I'm going to check on my mother and the others. Draw the curtains and blinds, and make sure every window and door are locked." The third stair groaned as he took the steps three at a time, his heart pounding against his ribs. He burst into the room shared by Willow and Levi and immediately pulled away the wall panel that led to the secret chambers beyond.

"Mom? Levi?" His voice echoed into the darkness. "Is everyone okay?"

A lightbulb flared to life, momentarily blinding him. When his vision cleared, he saw Levi looking up from the bottom of the staircase. "Everyone is here, including Joanna. She showed up while I was fetching the Montgomerys. What do you want us to do?"

"Sit tight, stay quiet, and keep the lights out." The thought of what came next made Jackson's head throb. He'd have to face his demons—there was no choice now. "I'll let you know when it's safe to come out. I'm taking the fight to them."

"Jax," his mother's voice carried up from below as she came into view. "Remember what your father taught you about hunting.

If you're going to carry a gun, shoot to kill and do so without remorse. I love you. Be safe."

His mother knew what this would cost him, what memories it would dredge up. But she also understood what was at stake.

"Everything is locked," Willow said from behind him, giving him a start. "Is everyone okay?"

"I'll be back as quickly as I can," Jackson said, forcing steadiness into his voice. "Levi, I'm counting on you. Mother will show you where the weapons cache is. Use it, if you must."

"I'll protect them with my life," Levi said. "Go. I've got this."

Bile rose in Jackson's throat as he replaced the panel. When he turned, Willow stood ready in her FBI-issued vest, carrying a Colt M4 Carbine rifle. Ruby and Ranger flanked her sides, alert and waiting. "Tell me you're going to carry a gun today."

"I am." The words felt like glass in his mouth, but he forced them out. His hand trembled as he pulled out his medicine container and took the last of his migraine medication. One pill would have to do. "Follow me."

Leading Willow to his bedroom, Jackson yanked open his closet doors. Inside was a heavy metal footlocker he'd sworn to never open again. He pressed his thumb to the biometric sensor, waiting for the green flash and click that seemed unnaturally loud in the quiet room. His FBI-issued body armor lay on top. He pulled it out and dropped it to the floor, followed by Ruby's. Beneath lay his weapons, and there it was—the Glock. The same one that had haunted him day and night. His throat constricted at the sight of it.

"You're going to put those on," Willow said. "Right?"

Unable to face the Glock yet, Jackson reached for Ruby's body armor instead. He'd done this countless times before, but now his hands shook so badly he couldn't manage the quick clips.

"Let me help," Willow said, her hand steadying his. "Put yours on. I'll take care of Ruby's."

Jackson blinked back tears, drawing a deep breath. "I'll be okay." He had to be okay. "Do you have Ranger's gear?"

"He's already wearing it," Willow said. "Are you sure you're up for this?" She grabbed him by the shoulders, forcing him to focus on her. "Get your head in the game, Jax. I need you. Ruby needs you. Your mother needs you."

Her words centered him. This wasn't about overcoming his past—it was about protecting the people who mattered. Jackson sucked a breath through his nose and strapped on his duty holster. His hand still trembled as he lifted the Glock from its foam nest, but he forced himself through the familiar safety check before sliding it home. Three extra clips followed.

Pushing aside another layer of padding revealed his Remington 700 sniper rifle, disassembled but waiting. This felt different—this was about precision, about control. His hands steadied as muscle memory took over: barrel to stock, bolt insertion, scope mounting. Each piece clicking into place felt right, felt purposeful. The dry-test confirmed its smooth operation, and the full ten-round magazine slid home with a satisfying snap.

"Do you need an extra magazine for your rifle?" Willow asked.

Jackson slammed the footlocker shut, a cold certainty settling over him. "If I run out of rounds, it will be time to use my handgun anyway." His lips twisted into a grim smile. "Unless we're going to face an army, I have no intention of running out of rounds."

"Well," Willow said, scratching Ranger's head. "I'm looking forward to seeing your shooting skills. I haven't forgotten your tall tale of shooting a buck at eight hundred yards."

Jackson didn't respond. He hoped he wouldn't have to kill anyone, but for the first time since that terrible day with the boy, he felt ready to do what needed to be done. His family's lives depended on it.

Fully geared up, they headed for the front door. "I figure they'll be here in thirty minutes or so," Jackson said. "Connie lives near

72, which put the gun-toting men about three miles from here. The terrain between here and there is rough, so it's going to slow them down."

"We'll take up positions and wait for them?" Willow asked. "Captain Sawyer and the DEA agents will be here soon."

Jackson blew out a breath. He'd forgotten about the help that was on the way. "I'll call the captain, and you call Tiffany. We'll tell them to come inside and take cover. They'd slow us down if we took them with us."

"Where are we going?" Willow asked.

"We're going to stop the enemy before they get to the gate." He looked around, like he was looking at his childhood home for the last time. "They're here for Tanner's files, and I suspect they'll kill everyone to get them. I'm not letting them shoot this place up, but if they get past us, we've got people here to protect Momma and the others."

Willow held his gaze, like she was taking measure of him. The two stood motionless for several seconds before the corner of her lip pulled into a crooked smile. "I'm assuming you know what direction they'll come from."

"I can't guarantee it, but I expect they'll take the easiest route that also provides reasonable cover." He pulled out his cell phone and dialed Captain Sawyer. "If that's true, we'll likely meet them on Echo Road."

"*Sawyer,*" the captain barked. "*Whoever this is, I'm kind of busy.*"

"It's Agent Brooks," Jackson replied. "I'm at my house. I received a report that there are armed men heading this way. I don't know how many."

"*I'm five minutes out. Stay put.*"

"Willow and I are going to cut them off before they get here," Jackson said. Willow had her phone pressed to her ear as she walked into the living room. She was assumably on the phone with the DEA.

"Wait for backup. I have a good idea who's coming for you, and you can't take them alone."

"I'm hoping it's the mercenaries who ransacked my house. I've got a debt to settle with them."

"They're ex-special forces, Jackson. You'll be outnumbered and outgunned."

"I'm leaving the front door to my house open. My mother is here and she's... hiding. I need you to keep her safe."

"Jackson. Jesus Christ. If you go after these guys, you're as good as dead. Hold your position. I'm nearly there."

Ranger ran into the living room, barking wildly.

"The DEA are here," Willow said. "I told them what's happening."

"I've got to go," Jackson said to the captain. He cut the call and stuffed his phone into his pocket. With his rifle at the ready, he opened the front door.

The two DEA agents were already at the back of their car, donning their body armor. "Agent Banks said you've got evidence that needs protecting," Tiffany said. "Where is it?"

Willow came striding out with Ranger at her hip. The dog's ears were alert, but his body remained relaxed. Despite everything indicating that these agents were allies, she was relieved to see that neither Ranger nor Ruby reacted negatively to them. "The evidence is safely hidden away. After we neutralize the immediate threat, we'll share what we have with you."

The two agents exchanged a skeptical glance. They drew their weapons and spun towards the sound of the captain's car speeding down the street.

"He's with us," Jackson said. "Agent Banks and I are going to do recon. You and the captain will stay here and take a defensive position." He pointed to the home across the street. "Spread the word that a police action is underway. I don't want any of my neighbors catching a stray bullet."

Chapter Fifty-Five

Willow

Willow opened the door to Jackson's truck, inviting Ranger to hop in. Ruby was already inside, and Jackson had started the engine. "Unless they're willing to hump it across the open fields between here and Highway 72, they're going to keep to the edge of the forest." He backed out of the laneway and sped up the street. "We're going to cut them off before they make it to Echo Lane."

"And what are we going to do when we catch up with them?" Willow asked. It was one thing to protect his home, but Jackson was leading her on a hunt. She doubted this qualified as self-defense, and without a clear indication that their lives were in danger, their actions might not go over well in a court of law.

"I don't know," Jackson said as he raced down Aqua Vista Road. "We need to see who we're facing. Once we do…"

"We'll decide how we'll respond?" Willow already knew how she was going to respond, but Jackson's fear of guns made him a wildcard. Between Jackson and Ranger, she didn't know who she was more worried about.

"We're going to pull up here," Jackson said, pointing to a sharp bend in the road. "There's a hill, and we'll be able to get a decent view of them coming… assuming I'm right about their approach."

"They'd have used satellite photos to make their plan," Willow said. She had no doubt in her partner's knowledge of the area, nor of his tactical skills. "They'll know what you know, and they'll use it to their advantage." She flashed an evil grin. "And that will be their downfall."

Jackson drove the truck off the road, nearly putting them in a deep culvert. He slammed the shifter into park and turned to Willow. "If you have any doubt about Ranger, tell me now. We can leave him in the truck. I need you to stay focused on the mission. If he's a distraction—"

"Of course, he's a distraction," Willow said, anxiety burbling up to the surface. "I've never done anything like this with him. Not with me as his handler. I don't want to be the reason you die."

Jackson's head snapped back. "I'm not Kate, and you're not the same dog handler you were when you arrived. I trust you completely. With my aversion to guns, I understand if you don't trust me, but I'm telling you—I won't let you down."

The earnestness in his voice and the resolve in his eyes took Willow's breath away. They had only met a few short days ago, but she had already come to trust him. Completely and without reservation. "I know you won't, and I won't let Ranger down, either." She hopped out of the truck and invited her dog. She moved to the back of the pickup and grabbed her rifle. On the other side, Jackson did the same. "Let's hunt some scumbags." She raised an eyebrow. "I hear they're in season."

"No limit on them either," Jackson said back. "Ruby, heel." He didn't explain where he was going. He simply took off into the woods and up a rather steep incline.

"Ranger, heel," Willow said. "We better hustle if have any hopes of keeping up." The dog barked; his eyes fixed on hers. It seemed Jackson was right, that dogs were far more capable of understanding than she'd have ever guessed. With her rifle held close to her vest, she sprinted into the trees and up the hill. Ranger never left her side, except to move around trees or over logs. By the time they crested the top of the hill, Jackson already had his rifle at the ready, peering through his scope.

"I don't see anyone," he said. "I'm going to send Ruby on recon. Make sure Ranger stays by your side. If he moves to follow her, call him back immediately."

"You can't send her out there," Willow said. It was exactly what she had done to Ranger, and it cost her partner's life. "They'll kill her if they see her."

"We have little choice," Jackson said. "Ruby knows what to do. This is what she's trained for. Every time we take our dogs on a mission, there is a risk to them. If we can't accept that risk, they become a hinderance. I don't want my dog to die, but we have a job to do... she has a job to do."

A huge lump formed in Willow's throat. Why hadn't Kate thought that way? Ranger was doing his job. It was going to cost him his life, and she sacrificed her own to save him. What Jackson said was a contradiction, but now wasn't the time for philosophical debates. "Okay." She took a shuddering breath. "I get it."

Jackson bent down and scrubbed Ruby's head. "Stay low, girl. Be safe." The man's voice was cracking. He was well aware of what he was telling his dog to do, and that the likelihood of her returning safely was low. "Find them!" he said, pointing north.

Ruby bolted into the trees, and Ranger immediately tried to follow. "Ranger, come!" Willow commanded. Her dog skidded to a stop, seemingly unsure which order he should follow. Before Willow could reissue her command, the dog came running back and parked himself at her side. "Good boy." She scrubbed his head and neck. "You'll get your chance."

The minutes dragged on. Ruby was following orders, but Jackson had already raised the whistle to his lips, ready to call her back at the first sign of danger.

"She'll be okay," Willow said. "Ruby's the smartest dog I've ever seen, and you've trained her well. She knows what to do."

Jackson nodded but remained silent. Three rapid-fire gunshots shattered the quiet, and he immediately issued a single blow into his whistle. "They're close," he said as he brought his rifle to his shoulder. The man appeared calm, but the timber in his voice showed the truth. Several more gunshots reported, this time off to the north-west. Jackson's rifle pivoted in that direction; the barrel of his gun was remarkably steady.

Willow blew out a breath at the sight of Ruby bounding through the brush. Her head snapped around when Jackson's rifle sounded off. A split second later, he fired off a second round.

"Come with me," he said, bolting in the direction he'd shot. "Two men are down, but I can't see how many more there are."

"You killed two?" Willow said, racing to keep up. Ranger's uncontrolled barking caused her to stop. "Ranger, heel." The dog was complying, but his eyes were locked on the forest to the north.

Rapid-fire gunshots barely proceeded the explosion of bark from the pine tree she was standing beside. Blindly, Willow spun around and returned fire. She dropped to the ground, and without further instruction, Ranger dropped down beside her. From behind her, Jackson fired off a shot. She had no idea where he was, or what he was shooting at, but she needed to remain focused on her own targets.

Two officers dressed in SWAT gear stepped out from the tree-line. Willow discharged a three-shot burst, sending one of them to the ground. The other had his weapon on auto-fire and unleashed a barrage of bullets, sending branches and leaf litter into the air. When the gunfire ceased, the second officer was out of sight.

"Ranger, attack," Willow said. Her K9 responded immediately, racing to the left of where the SWAT operator was last seen. She swung her barrel in the direction he was heading, fired off another three-round burst, and dashed after her dog. There was a brief scream, followed by another auto-fire burst. Ranger appeared from the brush with his muzzle covered in blood. "Show me," she said. The dog turned and moved back from where he came.

Willow swept a pine bow out of the way, revealing her attacker. It was a female officer. Her eyes were wide, and her throat ripped out. Blood burbled from her lips as she gasped for breath.

Another two shots from Jackson's rifle said they weren't finished yet.

"Ranger, heel," she said, sprinting towards the gunfire. Another gunshot said there was still at least one more. Jackson came into view, his back against a thick tree trunk with Ruby tucked between his legs. Two more shots followed, sending bullets whizzing past Willow's head. Following her partner's lead, she, too, found a tree to back herself against with Ranger on the ground, facing her.

"How many are left?" Willow asked, daring a quick peek from behind her tree.

"I got five." Jackson closed his eyes and sucked in a deep breath. "Detective Spade is still up, but I can't say how many others there are."

"Ranger and I got two," Willow replied, taking a mental count of how many rounds she'd fired. She looked over at her partner. Despite everything he had said about carrying a gun, if it was bothering him, he wasn't showing it. If anything, he appeared to almost be in a calm, Zen-like state.

"Detective Spade," Jackson called out. "Throw down your weapons and give yourself up. This isn't going to end well for you, but it's not worth throwing your life away."

Two more shots followed immediately, cutting through leaves and branches near where Jackson was standing. Her partner motioned for Willow to circle around to her left. Willow nodded, understanding his plan. "Ranger, stay," she murmured. The dog looked up at her, his brown eyes wide and alert. With her M4 held tight to her body, Willow dashed away from Jackson's position, drawing another pair of gunshots. When she reached the next large tree, she turned back to see Ranger right where she'd left him. Jackson and Ruby were no longer in sight.

"Ranger, attack!" she shouted. The dog raced towards his quarry. As he left his position, Willow stepped out and fired multiple bursts from her rifle. She used her K9 as a directional locator, adjusting her aim to where he was heading. Moving forward in a crouch position, she continued to fire until she was out of ammunition. Her K9 disappeared into the underbrush and another shot rang out. She knew the sound of Jackson's rifle.

Willow pressed her fingers to her lips and issued a sharp single whistle. She waited several seconds for her dog to appear. When he didn't, panic gripped her heart. What if it hadn't been Jackson's weapon? What if there were more mercenaries out there?

Ranger bounded over a fallen tree and stopped at Willow's side. She ran her hands over every inch of exposed fur, checking for injuries. Unbidden tears ran down her cheeks. For the first time, she understood why her partner had sacrificed everything to save this incredible animal.

"Ruby's searching for anyone else who might be out here," Jackson said. "But I'm fairly certain that we got everyone." Concern creased his face when he noticed Willow's tear-stained face. "Are you hurt?" He dropped to his knee to check more closely.

"I'm okay," Willow said, wiping away the tears. "I was worried for Ranger. I—"

A barrage of gunfire broke out to the south, in the direction of Jackson's home.

Chapter Fifty-Six

Jackson

Jackson turned and charged down the hill, barely able to keep his feet beneath him. From somewhere behind, Ranger was barking wildly. He had four bullets left in his magazine. He suddenly wished he had packed more ammunition for his rifle. By the time he got to his truck, Jackson's lungs were burning from exhaustion. He opened the door and invited Ruby to hop inside. "Settle," he said, ordering the dog to lie down.

Ranger appeared and leaped into the backseat, landing on top of the other dog. "Settle." Jackson repeated his command. Ruby obeyed, but Ranger was up on the seat looking out the rear window. "Ranger, settle!" The dog refused his order and issued a string of high-pitched barks.

Willow's face was bright red as she approached. "If you left without me..." she wheezed.

"Get in," Jackson said. He wouldn't leave her behind, but he wanted to be ready the moment she arrived. Another series of gun shots sent his already racing heart into his throat.

"I need a moment," Willow said, laying her M4 across her lap. "I need to catch my breath."

"You'll have time," he said, climbing behind the wheel. He passed his rifle over to Willow while he started the engine. "I'm going to stop when we get to the bend in the road. We'll have a good view of my house from there. I don't plan on running in blind."

Willow nodded and sucked in a deep breath. "Good. Once we see what's what, we can work out a plan."

Jackson slid the shifter into gear and pulled out of the ditch, spinning his wheels on the soft ground. In the short time it took to get to their destination, Willow's breathing had eased, and her color had returned to normal. "Give me my rifle and wait here," he said. "I'm going to see what I can see through the scope."

"I'm coming with you." Willow handed him his gun and opened her door. "And don't you dare disagree with me."

Jackson eased his door open and hopped out. He slunk into the ditch and moved forward, keeping his body low. When his house came into view, he raised his rifle and peered through his scope. "Chief Wheeler is there along with... seven uniformed police officers. It looks like there are three down."

"Can you see Sawyer or the DEA agents?" Willow asked. Her head was swiveling as she scanned the trees and nearby homes.

"No," Jackson said, turning back toward the truck. "All I can see is that almost every window in our house has been shot out."

"There may be more around back," Willow said. "I'd be surprised if there weren't."

Anxiety gripped Jackson, sending a throbbing pain up his neck. He had taken the last of his medication, and if he went into a full-on migraine, he'd be powerless to stop it. He rolled his shoulders in a futile attempt to ease the discomfort.

"Take the dogs and follow behind me," Jackson said. "I'm going to take the truck and make as much noise as I can. If I can divert the chief's attention, it will take some of the pressure off the captain."

"No," Willow said. She looked at the dogs over her shoulder. "You've got better control of them than I do. I'll take the truck, and you sit back. You've got four rounds left in your rifle. I'll draw fire and give you time to make them count."

Jackson didn't think she was right, at least, not where Ranger was concerned. Before Willow had arrived, the dog had completely ignored his commands. "Give me his leash," he said. "I don't trust him to leave you behind, not without force." The look of astonishment on Willow's face was almost comical. She snatched up the leather lead from the floor at her feet and handed it over.

With Ruby at his side, and Ranger fully secured, Jackson slipped into a series of bushes that lined the front of Al and Christine's rental property. From there, he moved forward until he had a clear line of sight to his property. "Settle," he said, adding a sharp snap to Ranger's leash. Both dogs immediately dropped to the ground and rested their heads on their front paws. He gave a thumbs-up to Willow to let her know he was in position.

Screeching tires and a blaring horn let everyone know that she was coming down the street. Within seconds, a hail of bullets was unleashed by the Florence Police Department officers. Fighting his desire to ensure Willow's safety, Jackson used the tree he was behind to support the barrel of his rifle. He didn't need it, but he had no intention of leaving anything to chance. He focused his aim on one of the two officers running headlong at his partner. They both had automatic weapons, and they weren't sparing a single shell.

The head of the trailing officer exploded in a pink mist. The lead man hadn't noticed. He slowed slightly while he ejected an empty clip from his weapon. Before he could slap in its replacement, he met his end in a similar fashion. With Willow's immediate threat neutralized, Jackson turned his attention back to his home. The chief was crouched behind a squad car, making him an easy target, but there were two officers standing at either side of the front door. Willow's arrival had seemingly spurred them into action, forcing them to take additional risks to bring their assault to an immediate end.

With the crosshairs squarely over the first officer's left ear, Jackson squeezed off a round. The man's head erupted across the house's cedar siding. Adjusting his barrel to the left, the sights landed on the second officer, who was looking directly at Jackson. His face was pale and his eyes wide. The next bullet entered the man's left eye, and, like the previous shot, left a gory mess on the wall behind him.

It bothered Jackson that he felt no remorse for the lives he had taken. He had spent the last eight months haunted by the destruction he had wrought on the boy in the closet, but the threat to his family had brought his anxieties to an immediate halt. He might have to pay the price for his actions when his blood had cooled, and the threat was neutralized, but right now, he didn't care.

He tossed his empty rifle on the ground and drew his handgun. Willow had vacated the truck, which she had parked sideways on the street. She was standing behind the bed, her legs and feet protected by the rear wheels.

Jackson unclipped Ranger's collar. "Go to Willow," he said. The dog raced down the street, directly for his handler. When he arrived, he immediately moved to her side and waited for her command.

"Heel," Jackson said as he ran from cover to join Willow. Ruby followed at his side, but her head was swiveling about, searching for any nearby threats. When the pair reached Willow, Jackson stole a quick peek at the situation. "We're about one hundred and fifty yards away," he said. "Do you think you can make accurate shots from here?"

"That's pretty insulting, Jax," Willow said. "Of course I can. I've been creating a diversion for you. If you'll do the same, I'll finish them off."

Jackson liked that she had stopped calling him by his full name. "Ruby, stay," he said, flashing his partner a devilish grin. "One diversion coming up."

He dashed from the truck back into the ditch. He popped up and fired off a couple of rounds before ducking low and moving closer. When he reached the next driveway culvert, he paused long enough to take a few breaths. He stood erect and fired off three more rounds, shattering the windows on a squad car. An officer raised his head to return fire. Willow's rifle reported a single shot, and the officer dropped to the ground.

Jackson climbed out from the culvert, his gun at the ready. He couldn't see the chief or the last of the officers he had spotted earlier on. He took aim at another squad car and shot out its windows. "Ruby, come!"

The Golden Retriever burst out from behind the truck and barreled from cover. Together, they moved across the front lawn kitty corner to Jackson's home. When the foot of a police officer came into view, he threw himself to the ground and crawled on his belly. At his side, Ruby followed. From his prone position, Jackson took aim with his pistol and fired off a shot. The target's foot flinched from the impact, but he otherwise hadn't moved. In his heart, Jackson hoped it was the chief.

A squad car's engine roared to life and the vehicle's tires smoked on the pavement as it spun around, turning to leave the scene. Chief Wheeler was hunkered down low in the seat, trying to present as small a target as possible. Before the car had cleared the scene, Jackson emptied the rest of his clip, taking out the vehicle's tires. A handgun appeared out the window and fired blindly.

The windshield exploded as multiple rounds penetrated the front glass. Jackson had already reloaded as he and Ruby moved closer. The interior of the car was painted crimson, and the corrupt cop had three holes in his forehead. Unsure if there were any other enemies around, Jackson ducked beside the squad car and motioned for Willow to come forward. It took all his willpower to not rush the house.

"All's quiet," Willow said as she squatted next to him, "but I doubt this is over. If it was my raid, I'd have sent people around back. Since we're not hearing anymore gunfire, I'm thinking they're working their way inside, or they've already secured the house."

"If they're inside, they're searching the place," Jackson said. "Unless Levi does something stupid, my mother and the others should all be safe."

"And what do you want to do?" Willow poked her head up to take a look. "I vote for going in through the back... or through the kennels. We can get inside without anyone knowing."

"There's no way of knowing if someone is in your bedroom if we do that," Jackson said. "And Ruby can't climb ladders. I don't know about Ranger though."

"My dog could scale the side of a brick house if he was ordered to. A ladder is no harder than stairs for him. I have no doubt we can get in through the kennels." The confidence Willow showed in Ranger warmed Jackson's heart. Every word out of her mouth said that she trusted the Malinois as her partner, and not just as a tool to be used.

"Okay," Jackson said. He didn't like the idea of splitting up, but it was the best approach. Willow could also check in on his mother to make sure she was safe and well. "Head for the lakeshore. There are a series of docks and walkways that will take you all the way to my property. You'll have good cover the whole way. Once you get to the kennels, though, you're going to be exposed until you get into the office. Use Ranger to help identify and neutralize threats. He'll know they're there long before you do. I'll wait here for five minutes. Unless you run into trouble, that should give you enough time to get inside."

"I'll text you when I'm inside," Willow said. "Don't do anything until you hear from me."

Jackson closed his eyes and nodded.

Chapter Fifty-Seven

Willow

Willow grabbed Jackson by the front of his shirt. "Give me your word, Jax. I can see it in your face. You have no intention of waiting for me to get into position. If you're not going to follow the plan, I'm staying here with you."

His indecision was obvious, but she was certain he was thinking the situation through. Willow's own brash actions had cost her partner's life. Jackson might not know the whole story of what happened to Kate, but he knew enough.

"Remember," Willow said, loosening her grip. "I lost my partner because I was an impatient fuckwad. Don't do something that will get Ruby killed. Do you hear me? I've grown quite attached to her, to you both, and I don't want to see either of you hurt because you're a dumbass who can't sit still long enough for his partner to get into position."

"I'll wait," Jackson said. He took Willow's hand in his, his grip warm and gentle. "I swear on my mother's life, I will wait for your message. But if I don't hear from you in five minutes, I'm coming to you."

Willow pulled out her phone and checked the time. "Five minutes," she said, slipping her hand away from his. "Unless I'm in a gun fight, you can assume I'm okay." She checked the number of rounds left in her clip. "Ranger, heel!"

The run from the street to the lake's edge was short, and Willow knew that she and Ranger would be exposed the entire time. She had nearly made it to the far ditch when a bullet struck her chest.

The impact was brutal, like a sledgehammer slamming into her ribs. The force stole her breath, collapsing her world into a moment of shock and searing pain. Her knees buckled, and she staggered, instinctively clutching her chest, feeling the throbbing ache spreading across her ribs and shoulders.

Willow hit the ground, Ranger immediately climbing on top of her. His presence offered some comfort, but his weight only amplified the ache. She slipped her hand beneath her vest, checking for blood. The armor had done its job, absorbing the bullet, but the pain was still sharp and bruising. Dazed and breathless, she fought to stay conscious, her pulse pounding as she reminded herself that she was alive—and had to keep moving.

"Willow!" Jackson yelled from his place. "Willow, are you okay?"

Not wanting to call out, she raised her hand and gave her partner a thumbs-up. She assumed he got the message when he fell silent. After giving Ranger a scratch behind his ears, she pushed him to the side. From her prone position, she couldn't see the front of Jackson's house. She believed that's where the shot had come from, but it was impossible to know for certain. Clenching her jaw tight, Willow belly crawled until she was in the clear. As she stood, she took a moment to check on Jackson. He was still in his position, and visibly relieved.

Docks and paved walkways stretched along the lake's edge. Despite Jackson having said there were no alligators in Wilson Lake, she kept a safe distance from the water's edge. As they neared Jackson's property, a police boat docked behind the kennels came into view. Willow threw herself to the ground, and Ranger followed suit without prompting.

"Jesus, Ranger," she whispered. "I didn't expect that." She waited and watched, looking for any signs of movement at the police boat. With her rifle at the ready, Willow stood and took several tentative steps forward. She had eight rounds left in her gun, and one more clip on her belt. Ammunition was the least of her concerns. The biggest problem right now was that she had no cover if someone was hunkered down in the hull. She glanced down at Ranger whose ears were alert, but he seemed more interested in the kennel than anything else.

"Ranger, search!" she commanded, pointing to where she wanted her dog to go. Without hesitation, the Malinois sprang forward, raced down the dock, and leaped into the craft. After a few seconds, the dog's head appeared, waiting for his next instructions.

Willow raced to the boat, her gaze flicking up towards Jackson's house. From this position, she was completely hidden from view, allowing her to investigate further. The vessel appeared empty, save standard boating equipment. She smiled at the sight of the keys hanging from the ignition. Using the boat to get away wasn't going to be an option for them.

After having tossed the keys into a nearby bush, Willow moved to where she'd have a clear view of the kennel's office. She was going to have to dash across thirty feet of open terrain to get to it, and she feared the building would make for an excellent ambush point.

"Ranger, heel," she ordered. Willow moved toward the building with her gun trained on the lone window. It was the most likely place someone would appear. Her pulse was pounding in her ears by the time she made it to the office's screen door. Unlatching the door with her injured hand wasn't an option, but that would mean not having her gun ready when she opened the door. She glanced down at Ranger. He wasn't reacting like there was anyone inside the room. He was alert, but otherwise calm.

Willow leaned her rifle against the wall and unclipped the safety strap on her Glock, figuring she could get to it quicker than her

M4 if someone was inside. She gripped the door handle, simultaneously telling her dog to search while throwing the door open. As Ranger raced inside, she pulled her handgun and followed him inside.

"I guess they're not expecting anyone coming from this direction," she said. Ranger's head tilted to the side like he was trying to decipher what she was saying. "Why would they? They don't expect anyone to want to get in here." Willow grabbed her M4 and headed for the secret entrance.

Even knowing exactly where it was, finding the seam to open the panel was no easy task. Having only one functional hand didn't make it any easier. The room beyond was pitch black. Beyond groping in the dark, her only option was to use the flashlight on her cell phone, but that meant she couldn't carry her rifle.

"Let's go," Willow said as she stepped inside the secret chamber. Ranger happily followed. Willow leaned her rifle against the wall and closed the panel behind her. Concern crept into her consciousness. She'd never been here before, and she remembered Jackson saying that there was a second secret door that led to the interior. If it was as well hidden as the first panel, there was no way she was going to find it.

Ranger whined while he sniffed at a wall.

"Good boy," she said. "What would I do without you?" The dog unleashed a series of high-pitched barks, as if in response. "Ranger, shut the fuck up!" It was a stupid thing to say, but it was the first thing that came to mind. Surprisingly, the dog obeyed, but he was becoming frantic. He paced back and forth in front of what was likely the secret door. The behavior meant that there was someone in the room beyond. That's what he was barking at. She turned off the flashlight, slipped her phone into her pocket, and drew her Glock.

Sweat blossomed under Willow's armpits. Standing in the dark wasn't helping. Ranger's claws scratching against the wooden floor grated on her nerves. In the pitch blackness, he seemed even more agitated. She needed to act. Jackson wasn't going to wait forever. Shit. Why hadn't she thought of this earlier? He could tell her how to get past the door.

Ranger's shrill barks startled Willow. From the room within, Boone's higher-pitched yip echoed back. "Levi," Willow rasped. "Let me in. I don't know how to open this door."

A whoosh of fresh air struck Willow as the secret panel was pulled away. Ranger bolted forward, enthusiastically greeting the Border Collie. "We've got a lot to fill you in on," Levi said. From the light of his cell phone, the concerned face of Mr. Mongomery was visible. "We can hear most of what Savannah's talking about. We'll tell you everything we know."

"I don't have time for to chat," Willow said. "I need to get to the second-floor entrance. Jax's waiting on me, and I've got a limited amount of time."

"It won't take long," Mr. Montgomery said, motioning Willow forward. "You need to hear this."

Chapter Fifty-Eight

Jackson

Jackson checked his watch for the fifth time in less than a minute. Outside of the wind, everything was eerily quiet. He could see the front of several of his neighbors' homes from where he was. Thankfully, nobody was in sight. Surely, they had hunkered down during the gunfight, but the longer the silence continued, the more likely they'd come out to investigate.

The buzz of his cell phone startled him. His hands shook while he answered the call, desperate for news from Willow.

"I'm in position," she said. *"Savannah's inside. There are at least two others with her, but I can't tell who."*

"You're supposed to wait for me," Jackson growled back. "Not doing recon."

"I'm still in your secret tunnels," Willow said, her voice a harsh whisper. *"I could hear them threatening Captain Sawyer through the walls. Savannah wants to know where the Montgomerys are."*

Hope burbled up in Jackson's chest. "Can you sneak them out the back? I'll draw everyone's attention while you get them out." Tightness gripped his heart when Willow didn't respond.

"Screw that," Willow said. *"If you can keep their attention, I'll come in through the second floor. You're not doing this on your own."*

"Fine," Jackson said. "I'll keep them busy while you get into position. Be careful. Okay?"

"You, too."

The line went dead, and Jackson gripped the muscles at the base of his skull. He closed his eyes and sucked in a deep breath through his nose. It struck him as odd that ending the lives of the people assaulting his house had caused him no grief, and yet, the thought of his partner being in danger triggered a response. He wiped the sweat from his hands on his pant legs. "Let's do this," he said to Ruby, giving her an affectionate scratch behind her ear. "I'm going to need you at your best."

The dog stared back; her brown eyes filled with compassion. There was no doubt in Jackson's mind that she understood the situation, and that she felt every one of his emotions.

With his Glock raised, and his dog at his side, Jackson strode toward his home. If Savannah was there, and if she wanted to know where Tanner's parents were, it was unlikely that she'd shoot him. The hairs on the back of his neck sprung to life when Ruby growled.

"I have what you're looking for," Jackson said. "I'm putting my gun away."

"Throw it away," Agent Crenshaw said, stepping out onto the porch. "You're not coming in here armed."

"I'm not going in unarmed either," Jackson replied. He wanted to shoot his VCAC cohort in the face. "Do you really think I can kill the three of you before you shoot me?" Announcing that Jackson knew how many people were inside had surprised the agent. "If Savannah wants to know where Tanner's files are, send her out."

"Fuck you," Agent Thomlinson said. She moved in beside Crenshaw, leveling her handgun at Jackson. "Give us what we want, or I'll shoot you." She raised a shoulder in a half shrug. "You have no say in any of this."

"Shut it," Crenshaw said, forcibly lowering the female agent's gun. "Jax, listen to me. You don't know the whole story. I'm sorry that Tanner had to die. He wouldn't listen to reason. What Savannah's doing—it's for the good of the country. She's got a deal in place that will make Alabama safe. But she can't make that happen if she's rotting in prison."

"I know you're not the smartest agent in the bureau," Jackson said, "but you're not that dim either. You're a loose end. Just like Rachel and Evelina were. Look what happened to them. It's going to happen to you, too. To both of you."

"They weren't loose ends," Savannah said. She was standing behind the two agents, using them as a shield. "They were obnoxious cunts and thorns in my side."

"You didn't like the way Rachel treated Mitchell," Jackson said. He continued moving forward as he spoke. "And I'm guessing you just found out that Mitchell and Evelina were more than online author buddies."

Savannah's face reddened at the comment. Her upper lip twitched.

"Oh," Jackson said. "You didn't know about it. You killed her because she was going to turn on you. You heard about her deal with the US Attorney."

"You're a fucking liar, Jax." Savannah pushed herself past the two agents. Her momentary loss of poise was gone. "I don't know how you found out about Mitchell... but it doesn't matter. You'll cooperate. You'll get on board or people you love will die. It's as simple as that."

The muscles in Jackson's neck tightened into a knot, sending pain shooting all the way to the top of his head. Did they have Willow? Was Savannah holding her hostage?

"Holster your weapon and come inside," she said. "What I have to say to you isn't for the whole world to hear." Savannah turned and disappeared into the house. Agents Crenshaw and Thomlinson followed her. Their disregard for Jackson being armed was alarming. He refused to put his gun away. He was obviously walking into a trap, but he couldn't see it. Not for the life of him.

Chapter Fifty-Nine

Willow

Willow waited while Levi pulled back the panel that led to their shared bedroom. Ranger was at her side, vibrating with anticipation. She had ordered him to settle, but her whispered words had no effect.

They feel what you feel.

That's what Jackson had said—or something like that. Her dog was picking up on her anxiety, just like when they came through the front door of Trowbridge's Diner. She needed to get her own emotions under control first.

Jax knows what he's doing. Trust your partner. Trust yourself.

"Easy," she whispered into the dog's ear. Willow nodded at Levi, silently thanking him for his help. She stepped through the low opening and breathed out for Ranger to heel. The dog joined her and pressed his body against her leg. He was still agitated, but he seemed more under control.

The bedroom door was wide open, allowing for voices to carry up from the main floor.

"Beverly," Savannah said, with her deep voice. "If Agent Brooks does anything stupid, shoot the captain to help him understand the severity of the situation."

It took Willow a few moments to realize who the SAC was speaking to. It was that fat, blonde bitch who liked to pretend she was tough.

"Why didn't you take his gun?" Beverly said. "Are you fucking stupid?"

"Agent Thomlinson," Savannah replied, her voice clipped. "Don't ever question my orders. Agent Brooks is not a threat to us. With or without a gun, he will comply."

"Fine," she replied. "You're the one he's going to shoot first."

Willow cringed, half expecting to hear a gunshot in response. The stupid girl really had no idea how to keep her opinions to herself.

"I'm here," Jackson said.

The sound of his voice startled and confused Willow. What was he doing, walking in through the front door, acting like it was nothing? She crept forward until she could see him standing at the bottom of the staircase. Ruby was glued to his side, her head turned towards Willow.

"Settle," Jackson said. Ruby complied immediately, dropping to the floor and resting her head on her chin. "If you have any agents upstairs, call them down. I don't want anyone appearing behind me. It will go badly for you if that happens."

Willow's head snapped to her left, fearing that someone had been laying in wait up there. Ranger's attention was focused on Ruby. Had there been a threat upstairs with her, she was certain he'd have picked up on it.

"It's just us," Savannah said. Her voice was airy, like she hadn't a care in the world. "I keep my inner circle small. It's easier to manage that way. I have to say, you did me a favor killing Wheeler. He was getting greedy, and I don't like that in a partner."

"What about the mayor?" Jackson said. "He can't be very happy knowing that you obliterated his daughter's face."

A brief silence followed. Savannah was likely shocked that he had just identified her as the shooter. "I want you to kill Captain Sawyer," she said. "Shoot him in the face three times. If you don't, Thomas will put your dog down."

Shit.

Willow hadn't even thought about the captain or the two DEA agents that were left to guard the house. She needed to get downstairs, and she needed to do it quickly. She looked at the staircase, remembering the squeaky stair. It was no problem for her to avoid it, but there was no way to communicate that to her dog. All she could hope was that he wasn't heavy enough to make a noise.

"Continue to point your weapon at my dog, and I'll kill you right now," Jackson said. He had his gun raised. "Back up until she's out of view. I swear to God Almighty, Crenshaw—do it now or I'm going to empty my gun into your chest." He stepped forward until he was no longer in view.

Attaboy, Jax. He had cleared a path for her to get down without being seen.

"Ranger, heel," she whispered. "Easy." Willow creeped down the stairs and Ranger mimicked her movements. It was a behavior she'd never noticed him exhibit before. Then again, she hadn't paid much attention to how he'd conducted himself in the past. She could have kissed her dog when he followed her action and avoided the third stair. Willow turned right and took the hallway that led to the kitchen. It gave her a clear path without risk of being spotted. Worry gripped her. At no point had she heard Mitchell's voice. What if he was in the kitchen guarding the back door?

Chapter Sixty

Jackson

Jackson recoiled at the sight of the two DEA agents laying dead on the floor. They had both suffered multiple gunshot wounds to their bodies, but it was the holes in the back of their heads that were their cause of death. Captain Sawyer was seated on a dining room chair, his hands tied behind his back, a gag in his mouth. Blood was seeping from what appeared to be knife wounds in his legs. Savannah had likely been torturing him to get him to give up Tanner's parents and the critical information they possessed. Jackson felt bad for having believed the man was corrupt. Levi's assertion that he was a righteous man was an understatement. "I have no intention of harming Captain Sawyer. Do you really think I'm so stupid as to incriminate myself?"

"Where's your partner?" Savannah asked. "We lost sight after Tom shot her."

"She's dead," Jackson snarled. He latched onto the fear that had shattered his soul when he saw his partner take a bullet to the chest. His gun trembled as he pointed it at Savannah's face. "Just like I'll be when you get what you want out of me."

"I don't want you dead, Jax," Savannah said. She strode towards him, completely unconcerned that he held a gun on her. "I want you to work with me. I'll make you wildly rich, and together, we will put an end to the fentanyl epidemic in Alabama."

Jackson lowered his weapon when the reality of her plan became clear to him. "Let me guess. You've made a deal with the Los Reyes cartel."

Savannah raised a shoulder, like working with the cartel was just another Tuesday.

The revelation crushed Jackson. Eight years of mentorship, countless cases solved together, all the late-night discussions about justice and doing what's right—it had been a lie. The weight of that betrayal pressed against his chest, making it difficult to draw a breath. "So, what, you paid them off?"

"Pay them off?" Savannah snorted. "I don't have that kind of money. What I do have is power and connections. I will help them establish themselves as the primary drug supplier in the US. In fact, they're going to pay me, and on top of that, they will stay out of Alabama."

"And in doing so," Jackson said, "you'll come out looking like a superstar. Let me guess, State Senate is a stepping stone for the governorship? Or do your aspirations run even higher?"

"Undecided," she said. Savannah walked over to the captain and tutted. "I'm not sure I care to take such a seat. Sure, it would open more doors for me, but how rich does someone need to be? I don't plan on doing this forever, you know. Just long enough that I can amass a big enough fortune to buy an island and live my life in peace and quiet. You know what it's like, Jax. I know the horrors you've seen. I've seen them too. It changes you. It forces you to look at what's important."

"Family. Friends. The people you love," Jackson said. "That's what's important. Money? It's not even in the top five."

"I knew you'd say that." Savannah rolled her eyes. "I think I'd have been disappointed in you had you said anything different."

"Drop the gun, Jax," Crenshaw said. "I told you, Savannah. He won't help us. The man is too much of a boy scout."

"Easy, Agent," Savannah said. "He'll come around. He's not going to let his father die, not when he understands his life is in my hands."

Jackson swallowed the bile that had risen into his throat. His father's hunting trip had been a ruse, and he was definitely alive. The confirmation overwhelmed him. All those nights his mother had cried herself to sleep, all the times he'd cursed himself for not looking harder, and his father had been alive the whole time. Working undercover? Or a hostage? The uncertainty clawed at his insides. "Where is he? Where did you take him?"

"Me? Take him?" Savannah's feigned innocence grated on Jackson's last nerve. He imagined putting a bullet in the woman's forehead. "I didn't do a thing to him. But the cartel will if I rat him out. Cops don't last long in Mexico when their cover is blown. If I don't leave here, I expect your daddy won't last the day."

"You're leaving here," Jackson said. "But you'll be doing it in handcuffs or a body bag. Those are your options."

Smug satisfaction spread across Savannah's face. "You're in no position to make such threats. You've got two guns on you and if I die, so does your father."

"I hope you're not counting on Agent Mitchell," Jackson said. "Because I'm afraid he's already in custody. The SBI have been at the airport, sitting on his plane since yesterday."

The squeal of the third stair drew everyone's attention. Jackson turned away from Savannah. Agents Crenshaw and Thomlinson had both turned to see who was coming.

"Whoever it is," Savannah said. "Kill them."

Ruby appeared from the hallway, launching at Crenshaw's arm and catching him by the wrist. The man bellowed in agony as his bones were crushed in the dog's powerful jaws. Jackson's heart leaped into this throat as Agent Thomlinson shot twice at Ruby. From the kitchen, Ranger sped past Jackson and slammed into the agent. They went down hard, Ranger rolling across the floor, claws scrabbling on the hardwood as he tried to recover. Thomlinson brought her gun to bear, leveling the barrel at the Malinois. Two shots rang out from Willow's position, striking the agent in the neck and head. Ranger didn't care that she was already dead when he mauled her.

Boone streaked in from the hallway, joining Ruby in her savage attack on Crenshaw who had collapsed to the floor. The two dogs worked in tandem—Ruby locked onto his arm while Boone tore at his leg, pinning him in place.

"Show me your hands," Willow commanded, emerging from behind the kitchen doorframe with her weapon trained on Savannah, who stood isolated in the center of the room. "Greene, lift them up, or I swear to God, I will end you."

"Ruby, off," Jackson said.

"Boone, off," Levi echoed. He was standing in the hallway with Tanner's father, who was holding a shotgun.

"It was you who killed my boy," Mr. Montgomery said, the gun trembling in his hands. "Agent Banks told me so." Tears had gathered in the man's eyes, but they were filled with resolve.

"Mr. Montgomery," Jackson said. "Don't do it. It's over. She will pay for her crimes, and she will never walk free again."

"And what of my boy?" Mr. Montgomery said, his face twisted with hate and rage. "Louise and I will never be free of the grief and torment knowing that she lives on while our boy..." His words fell away, and he raised the shotgun to his shoulder. "I don't care what happens to me, but I will not let her live. My son is dead. An eye for an eye, Jax. It's right in the bible."

"And what of Mrs. Montgomery?" Jackson said. He stepped forward, and the grieving father trained his gun on him. "Don't do this to her. Don't make it worse."

"Make it worse?" Mr. Montgomery said. Tears trailed down his reddening face. His chest was heaving. "We lost our only son, Jax. It can't get worse." The barrel of his gun swung towards Savannah.

As it did, a shot rang out, and Mr. Montgomery buckled over and Levi dove to catch him.

Jackson spun to see Captain Sawyer holding his service weapon, smoke curling up from the barrel. The ropes that supposedly bound his hands lay in a tangle on the floor. His gaze fell on Jackson and a predatory smile pulled at his lips.

"I've been right about you all along," Jackson said. "All the evidence Savannah gave me on you... it was all real."

"The best lies are served with a healthy dose of the truth," Sawyer said. "She's a brilliant woman, an unstoppable force." He turned his gun on Jackson. "And now I finally get to rid the world of your sanctimonious ass."

Two shots reported, and the traitorous officer tumbled from his chair. Willow stepped closer with her weapon poised, ready to shoot him again if necessary.

While everyone's attention was fixed on the fallen captain, Savannah exploded into motion from her position. In two fluid steps, she closed the gap to Willow. Her left hand shot out, fingers wrapping around the barrel of Willow's gun while simultaneously driving an expertly aimed right cross into Willow's face. The strike knocked Willow off balance, and Savannah used the momentum to wrench the weapon free, bringing it to bear in one smooth motion.

Time slowed as the woman Jackson had admired his entire career aimed her gun at him. Her expression wasn't triumph—it was raw, primal fear. And in that moment, as Savannah's finger moved to the trigger, Jackson saw the face of the young boy in the closet again. The abused victim had seen the FBI agent standing in front of him, and he didn't care. He was covered with visible scars, but it was the invisible ones that would forever haunt him, and he had no intention of living with his horror. Instead, the child chose to die.

Jackson pulled the trigger of his Glock.

Savannah stumbled backward, a mix of shock and pain on her face. He fired three more rounds into her chest until her gun clattered from her hand and she crumpled to the floor.

Only when his partner picked up her weapon, did Jackson pause to survey the scene.

"Call an ambulance," Levi said, his hand pressed to Mr. Montgomery's abdomen. "It's bad, Jackson."

Chapter Sixty-One

Willow

Two weeks later.

Willow tugged at the sleeve of her navy blazer, adjusting it to better hide the compression bandage immobilizing her wrist. In the days since the shootout at Jax's s house, the bruises on her face had faded to a yellowish hue that makeup easily concealed, but the sprain from her fall during Savannah's attack still ached. At least her swollen finger was finally healing.

She sat in the front row of the chapel between Ranger and Grace Foster, watching Jackson approach the podium. Ruby sat quietly at his feet as he unfolded his eulogy, her usual exuberance subdued as if sensing the solemnity of the occasion. His hands trembled as he smoothed the paper.

"I've written this speech a dozen times," Jackson said, his voice wavering. "And have torn up every version. How do you sum up a friendship that spanned a lifetime? How do you capture someone's essence in a handful of words?" He paused, swallowing hard. "Tanner Montgomery was more than my best friend. So very much more."

Ranger's head lifted at the catch in Jackson's voice. Willow placed her hand on the dog's neck, steadying him. Just as Jackson had taught her—they feel what you feel. She forced herself to breathe slowly, projecting calm. The Malinois settled against her leg, a far cry from the aggressive animal she'd first brought to Florence. At the podium, Ruby pressed closer to Jackson's leg, offering silent support.

"We went through everything together," Jackson continued. "From grade school to high school, and on to university. We even went through Quantico together. Every step of the way we competed against each other, but the only thing I ever bested Tanner at was growing taller. Each time I lost to him I would say *just wait until next time*. But there won't be a next time."

Jackson's composure cracked. His shoulders shook as he gripped the podium. Ruby whined softly, pressing against him. Before Willow could move, Mr. Montgomery was already rising from his seat, one hand pressed to his healing wound. He climbed the steps slowly but steadily, placing a supportive hand on Jackson's shoulder.

"It's okay, son," Mr. Montgomery said, loud enough for the microphone to catch. "We all loved him, and we'll carry him with us forever."

The sight of the grieving father comforting his son's best friend broke something in the chapel. Willow heard Louise Montgomery's quiet sobs, saw the tears on Grace's cheeks. Even the stone-faced agents from OPR—required to attend given the ongoing investigation—were visibly affected.

The CCTV footage from Jackson's house had cleared them of wrongdoing in Savannah's death within days, but the broader investigation into the corruption she'd enabled would take months. None of that mattered right now. Today was about Tanner.

Jackson straightened, drawing strength from Mr. Montgomery's presence and Ruby's steady companionship. "Tanner died protecting this community from corruption that ran deeper than any of us knew. He discovered evidence that certain people didn't want found. But even knowing the danger, he wouldn't back down. That was Tanner—always doing what was right, no matter the cost."

Willow noticed several people shifting uncomfortably in their seats—people who'd worked with or for the now-arrested Mayor Persie, his cousin Judge Mayfield, and others implicated in Alexander Mitchell's testimony.

Let them squirm.

"But that's not the memory I wish to hold onto," Jackson said. "I want to remember the friend who drove for two hours and showed up at my house at midnight when my mom got sick. The athlete who turned down NFL scouts to answer the call of the FBI. The jerk who never let me forget the time I face-planted during tactical training." A wet laugh rippled through the chapel. "I want to remember my brother."

Mr. Montgomery squeezed Jackson's shoulder as he finished. Together, they walked back to their seats, Ruby padding softly beside them. Louise Montgomery reached for her husband's hand, and Willow saw the older couple exchange a look of deep understanding. They'd lost their only son, but perhaps they'd gained another in their shared grief.

The rest of the service passed in a blur of hymns and remembrances. Willow found herself studying Jackson's profile, noting the shadows under his eyes. Even with Ruby's comforting presence in his bed each night, she knew he wasn't sleeping well. The weight he carried wasn't just about Tanner. It was about Savannah's betrayal, about having to take the life of someone he believed to be his friend. Willow knew he'd started seeing his therapist again. She hoped it would help.

At the graveside, Willow stood back, giving the family space. Ranger sat perfectly at heel, his earlier training issues a distant memory. Like his handler, he'd found his balance. She watched Jackson place his St. Michael's medal on the casket—a gift from Tanner's father, she'd learned, given to both boys when they'd joined the FBI. Ruby sat beside him, her usual golden coat dulled by the overcast day, her head bowed as if she, too, was saying goodbye.

"He would have liked this," Grace said softly beside her. "All these people coming together. Even that ornery dog of yours is behaving."

Willow smiled. "He's not so ornery anymore. He just needed the right guidance." She glanced at Jackson, who was hugging Louise Montgomery, Ruby a steady presence at his side. "Sometimes we all do."

"Speaking of guidance," Grace said, a familiar glint in her eye despite the solemnity of the occasion, "you know about the charity auction next month? For Dr. Simmons's clinic?"

"I might have heard something about it."

"Good." Grace patted her arm. "Because a certain FBI agent has been volunteered as a bachelor. And between you and me, dear, we're not going to let some little hussy outbid you."

Willow felt heat rise in her cheeks. Trust Grace to think about matchmaking even at a funeral. But watching Jackson with the Montgomerys, seeing his strength and his vulnerability, she couldn't help but hope. They'd been through hell together. Maybe it was time to see what they could be in times of peace.

The service ended, and people began to drift away. Jackson caught her eye across the cemetery, and something passed between them—understanding, perhaps. Or possibility. Ranger's tail wagged once, catching the shift in her emotions. Ruby trotted over to join them, pressing against Jackson's leg before offering a gentle greeting to Ranger, the two dogs a symbol of their handlers' growing connection.

"Come on, boy," she said softly. "Let's go home."

They'd all lost something in bringing down Savannah's corrupt empire. But maybe, just maybe, they'd found something too.

Chapter Sixty-Two

Jackson

Four weeks later.

Jackson steered his truck on autopilot, his therapy session playing on repeat in his mind. "You're cleared for duty," Dr. Patterson had said. No qualifiers, no hesitation, just simple confirmation that he'd worked through enough of his trauma to be trusted with a gun again.

No migraines in two weeks. No nightmares in ten days. The guilt that had pressed on his soul since shooting the boy in that closet had finally begun to lift. Adding Savannah's death to his conscience should have broken him, but somehow it had done the opposite. Seeing her face in his dreams, twisted with that raw, animal fear, had helped him understand. Sometimes people choose their own endings, whether they were abused children or corrupt FBI agents.

He turned off Highway 72, toward home. His mother would be waiting. She always seemed to know when he had been to therapy, though he never told her his schedule. His phone buzzed. Marsden's text was brief: "Mitchell rolled on the cartel. Your father's cover is secure but no longer necessary. Extraction team en route."

Jackson's hands tightened on the steering wheel. After all these months of hoping, of hearing his mother cry herself to sleep, his father was coming home. The Los Reyes cartel's influence was crumbling, their pet politicians falling like dominoes. Mayor Persie, Judge Mayfield, DA Beauregard—all in custody. If Alexander Mitchell was willing to testify...

Ruby's head appeared between the seats, her wet nose touching his ear. Like always, she accompanied him to the hospital, though she stayed in the waiting room. When his formal session was completed, she provided her own special brand of puppy therapy.

He pulled into his driveway, noting his mother's freshly planted flowers replacing those trampled during the investigation. The crime scene tape was long gone, the bullet holes patched, but sometimes he still saw it all when he closed his eyes. At least the CCTV footage had cleared them quickly. Savannah and Sawyer's conversation about executing the DEA agents had been caught in crystal clear audio and video.

"Jackson?" His mother called from the porch. "I made cookies."

He smiled despite himself. Some things never changed. He followed Ruby into the house, the familiar scent of chocolate and vanilla wrapping around him like a hug.

"Dr. Patterson cleared me," he said, accepting the cookie his mother pressed into his hand.

"I know." Maybelle's eyes crinkled at the corners. "I could tell by how you're carrying yourself. The weight's lifting, isn't it?"

Jackson sank into his usual chair at the dining room table. "Did you know? About Dad?"

His mother placed the cookie sheet on the table. "Yes," she said quietly. "Not at first. But he found a way to let me know he was alive, that he was working. I couldn't tell you—it would have compromised everything you were doing here."

"He knows about your experimental treatments? Grace's money?"

"Alice had told him all about it. She kept him up to date. It was the only way he'd stay where he was." Maybelle sat across from him. "I'm sorry for letting you think... for letting you see my grief.

But those tears weren't just for loss—they were for worry, knowing he was out there infiltrating the cartel, and not being able to tell you. It was the hardest thing I've ever done."

"Harder than the cancer?"

"The cancer?" She waved a dismissive hand. "Comparatively speaking, that was nothing. Latest tests continue to show complete remission, and no sign of kidney problems. Your father will come home to find me stronger than ever."

The pride in her voice made his chest tight. "Why didn't you tell me after? When you knew I was investigating Savannah?"

"Because you were already carrying so much. The shooting, those horrible migraines, Tanner's death." She reached across the table and squeezed his hand. "A mother knows when her child is at their limit. I couldn't add to your burden."

Jackson thought of all the nights he'd lain in bed and cursed himself for not searching harder for his father. But she'd been protecting him, just as he'd been protecting Florence. Just as his father had been protecting them all.

"SSA Marsden says they're extracting him soon. Getting him out of Mexico."

"I know that too." His mother's eyes twinkled. "Your father called this morning. Said to tell you he's proud of how you handled everything. And that he's sorry he missed all the excitement."

Jackson laughed. It felt good, natural. When was the last time he'd really laughed?

"Now," Maybelle said, sliding the cookie sheet closer to her son, "we need to talk about this bachelor auction. Grace and I have been discussing strategy."

"Strategy?" Jackson groaned. "Mom, no."

"Mom, yes." She drummed her fingers on the table. "That nice Agent Banks needs a little encouragement, and you need to stop pretending you don't light up every time she walks into a room."

"I do not—"

"Ruby," Maybelle said to the dog, "does your daddy light up when Agent Banks comes over?"

Ruby's tail thumped against the floor.

"Traitor," Jackson muttered.

But he was smiling. For the first time in longer than he could remember, the future felt wide open. His father was coming home. His mother was healthy. His mind was clearing. And maybe, just maybe, his mother and Grace were right about Willow.

He took another cookie. Sometimes healing came in unexpected ways.

Chapter Sixty-Three

Willow

Five weeks later.

"That's not how you hold a bidding paddle," Grace hissed, adjusting Willow's grip for the third time. "You need to be ready. Competition will be fierce."

Willow bit back a smile. She sat between Grace and Maybelle in the crowded community center, watching Dr. Jason Simmons work the crowd. The veterinarian had transformed the space into an elegant auction house, with white tablecloths and twinkling lights. He was dressed in a tuxedo, with his hair slicked back. He looked nothing like the day she'd first met him, when he'd helped save Ranger from what could have been his last day on earth.

"Here." Maybelle pressed a glass of wine into her free hand. "Liquid courage."

"I'm not nervous," Willow protested. Jesus. Was it that obvious? She'd thought she'd done a decent job of hiding it.

Both older women snorted in perfect synchronization.

"Of course not, dear," Grace said. "That's why you've checked your makeup six times in the last hour."

"And why you chose that particular dress," Maybelle added with a knowing nod. "Jax's heart is going to stop when he sees it."

Willow smoothed the dark-blue silk self-consciously. She'd bought it yesterday, after Grace had casually mentioned it was

Jackson's favorite color. The two women had appointed themselves as her personal matchmaking committee, and resistance, she'd learned, was futile.

"Speaking of Jax," Grace said, "Levi cleans up rather nicely too."

Willow followed Grace's gaze to where Levi stood chatting with Jackson near the stage. The former "homeless man" looked every inch the Deputy DA in his tailored suit, Boone nowhere in sight for once. His reinstatement ceremony last week had made front page news, right alongside Mitchell's plea deal and the ongoing arrests of corrupt officials.

"Boone misses the kennel," Maybelle said. "But I suppose a prosecutor's dog needs to look more dignified than a street mutt. Though Ruby's been moping about, having lost her playmate."

"Jax says it's good for her to learn that goodbye doesn't always mean forever." Willow watched Jackson laugh at something Levi said, his entire face lighting up in a way she rarely saw. "Some endings are just new beginnings."

Grace and Maybelle exchanged coy smiles that Willow pretended not to see.

"Ladies and gentlemen," Dr. Simmons called from the stage. "Welcome to our annual bachelor auction. As you know, all proceeds go to providing veterinary care for local shelter animals and pets whose owners can't afford treatment."

Willow's hand tightened on her paddle. She'd been saving for this night, picking up extra shifts at the range as a firearms instructor. Her recent commendation for the Florence case had come with a bonus, all of which was earmarked for tonight.

"Our first bachelor," Simmons continued, "is a man you all know. Recently reinstated as Deputy District Attorney, please welcome Levi Benson!"

The bidding was fierce but quick. A pretty paralegal from the courthouse won with an impressive bid, making Levi blush to the roots of his newly trimmed hair.

Three more bachelors came and went. Willow barely noticed them, her attention fixed on Jackson. He'd been watching the proceedings with apparent amusement, but she caught the tension in his shoulders, the way his hand kept reaching for Ruby's ear despite her absence.

"Just remember," Maybelle whispered, "if you get outbid, I'm your backup. Though explaining to my son why his mother bought him at auction might be awkward."

Willow choked on her wine.

"And now," Jason announced, "our final bachelor of the evening. FBI Special Agent Jackson Brooks!"

The room erupted in applause. Jackson stepped onto the stage, and Willow's breath caught. The shadows that had haunted his eyes at Tanner's funeral were gone. He stood straight, confident, at peace with himself in a way she hadn't seen before.

"Opening bid is five hundred dollars," Jason called.

Paddles shot up across the room. Willow waited, letting the initial frenzy die down.

"Two thousand," called a voice from the back. Willow turned to see Sergeant Marcy Jenson, a leggy blonde who'd made no secret of her interest in Jackson since he'd arrived for the auction. The officer had flashed a grin that suggested she had no intention of losing.

"Twenty-five hundred." The words left Willow's mouth before she could second-guess herself.

The blonde's eyes narrowed. "Three thousand."

Grace grabbed Willow's arm. "Show her who's boss, dear. Show her who really knows him."

"Five thousand." Willow's voice carried clear and strong.

A hush fell over the room. The blonde's paddle lowered slowly.

"Five thousand going once," Simmons called. "Going twice..."

Jackson's eyes found hers across the room. Something electric passed between them, something that spoke of shared battles and hard-won trust.

"Sold! To Special Agent Willow Banks!"

Applause and cheers filled the room. Willow barely heard them. Jackson was walking toward her, that crooked smile she loved playing on his lips.

"Ranger's going to be jealous," he said when he reached her. "Spending all that money on another handler."

"Ranger's fine with sharing," she replied. "As long as it's you."

His hand found hers, warm and solid and real.

"Well," Maybelle announced loudly, "I believe that's our cue to leave these two alone. Come along, Grace."

"But—" Grace protested.

"Now." Maybelle's tone brooked no argument. "Our job here is complete. I have things to take care of back home." She practically dragged Grace away, leaving Willow alone with Jackson.

"So," she said softly. "What exactly does five thousand dollars buy these days?" Willow looked up at him, at the man who'd taught her to trust again—herself, her dog, her heart.

"I guess we'll find out." He grinned at her, his tone playful. "I have to say, though, you've put a lot of pressure on me to make it worth your while."

Heat crept up her neck at his tone, but she met his gaze with a challenging smile of her own. "Well, Special Agent Brooks, I've always believed in getting my money's worth."

Chapter Sixty-Four

Jackson

The morning mist clung to the cemetery grass as Jackson approached Tanner's grave. Six months had passed since the funeral, but this was his first visit since that day. Ruby padded quietly beside him, her presence steady and grounding. Behind him, he heard the soft crunch of footsteps—Willow, giving him space but staying close.

The headstone was simple, elegant. Someone, probably Louise, had placed fresh flowers in the stone vase. Jackson crouched down, running his fingers over the engraved letters of his friend's name.

"Got some good news," he said quietly. "They're finally opening that Resident Agency you and I used to talk about." He glanced back at Willow, who stood with Ranger at a respectful distance. "A lot's changed. You'd hardly recognize the place."

And it was true. Mitchell's testimony had triggered a cascade of arrests and resignations that reached all the way to Mississippi. The Los Reyes cartel's influence in Alabama was crumbling. Even the El Dorado Casino in Biloxi had new ownership.

"Also, Dad's settling in well," Jackson continued. "Mom's trying to fatten him up, says Mexico made him too skinny. But he's good. Whole. They offered him Chief of Police, but he turned them down. He said *the Florence PD has lost all credibility with the public, and there is no way on God's green earth that he'll get sucked into that mess.* All told, eleven officers were arrested and charged. I've got to tell you, Savannah and Mitchell had us all twisted up—they fed me evidence that made Sawyer look corrupt and Wheeler seem honest, while telling Levi the exact opposite. It was a masterclass in manipulation, and it nearly worked. But after Wheeler's death and Sawyer's true colors being exposed, the remaining corrupt officers quickly turned on each other. Despite the chaos, the DA's office had a field day. They have described the situation as a 'target rich environment.'"

He paused, his voice softening. "Levi... it'll be a long time before he fully trusts his own judgment again. Thankfully, he's going to get some help from my dad. Levi offered him a role as a special investigator." The thought made Jackson smile. "If he takes the job, they're going to make an interesting pair. My dad's old school and more than a little resistant to change." His smile turned to a chuckle. "Speaking of interesting pairs... I wish you had had a chance to meet Willow. I really think you'd have liked each other. She's been staying with us at Mom and Dad's... in her own separate room. We had planned on getting a place together, but the housing market is really tough. So, for now, we're saving our money until we can afford a place of our own."

Ruby's ears perked up at approaching footsteps. Jackson didn't need to turn to know it was his father—he recognized the deliberate tread and deep, steady breathing.

"Thought I might find you here," Travis Brooks said, stopping beside his son. "Your mother said you needed to have a talk with your best friend."

Jackson stood, feeling both lighter and heavier at once. The new Florence Resident Agency—a small satellite FBI office under the jurisdiction of the Birmingham Field Office, led by SAC Alice Baldwin—was set to open next week, bringing to life a dream he and Tanner had once shared. Willow and Jackson had received commendations in recognition for bringing down Savannah's corruption ring. Willow had also earned her certification as a K9 trainer, turning Florence into a model for rehabilitating problem K9s. Alice—newly reinstated as SAC in Birmingham—had made sure the new office had the resources and autonomy it needed, and the new mayor had pushed hard for local agents he could trust. Jackson and Willow's track record had proven they were the right choice, even if Jackson had surprised everyone by inexplicably turning down the supervisory role.

"He'd be proud of you," Travis said. "Hell, he was proud of you. He'd have never let you know it, but he bragged about being your friend all the time." Travis placed a hand on Jackson's shoulder. "He's the one who warned the DEA about the cartel's plans. Tanner helped get me out before they could take me out."

Jackson absorbed this new piece of information, this final gift from his friend. "He never told me." His voice caught in his throat.

"Couldn't. Would have blown my cover." Travis squeezed his shoulder. "Just like he never told you he'd been pushing Alice for years to open an office here. His last official act was filing a recommendation for you to run it."

The knot in Jackson's chest, one he hadn't realized he was carrying, finally unraveled. He looked back at Willow, watched her quietly working with Ranger, and knew with bone-deep certainty he'd made the right choice. "I turned down being in charge... If I had accepted it, I couldn't have a future with her."

"You going to tell your mother?" Travis asked quietly.

"About turning down the supervisory position?" Jackson smiled. "I told her yesterday. Right before I asked Mom for Grandma's ring."

"About damn time." His father's voice was gruff but pleased. He clapped his son on the back. "By the way, your mother sent me with strict instructions to remind you about Sunday dinner. She's making pot roast. Apparently, it's Willow's favorite."

Jackson laughed. "Where else would we be then? Besides, I think Willow wants to pick Mom's brain. There's a Treasury agent coming into town on Monday. He's got an aggressive German Shepherd, and the man is in desperate need of guidance. He's driving all the way from D.C. just to work with her."

Travis shook his head. "Your girl's building quite a reputation in K9 training circles."

"She's good at fixing broken things," Jackson said softly. "Dogs. People. Even me."

"You were never broken, son. Just bent a little." Travis stepped back. "Take your time here. I'll tell your mother you'll both be staying home on Sunday."

Jackson watched his father walk away, pausing to chat with Willow before heading to his truck. The morning mist was burning off now, sunlight breaking through the trees.

"You'd like how it all turned out," he told Tanner's headstone. "The good guys won. The bad guys are paying. I hope you don't mind that I turned down running the new office." He smiled as Willow started walking over. "Here's your chance to meet her."

Ruby's tail wagged as Willow approached. Ranger fell in beside her, every inch the professional working dog. Not a hint of his former aggression remained.

"Ready?" Willow asked softly.

Jackson ran his hand over his friend's grave in a silent farewell. "Yeah," he said. "I'm ready."

They walked back to the truck together, dogs flanking them in perfect formation. The morning sun caught Willow's hair, turning it to fire. In his pocket, his grandmother's ring seemed to pulse with possibility.

He knew that some wounds never fully healed, but they could become something different. Something stronger. Like his mother's cancer pushing her to help others. Like Ranger's aggression transforming into protective instinct. Like his own trauma teaching him empathy.

Like loss leading to love.

"Let's go home," he said, and took Willow's hand.

Afterword

Thank you so much for reading. I hope you enjoyed the journey as much as I loved writing it.

If you want to be the first to know when the next case drops, join my inner circle for exclusive updates and early alerts on new releases. You can sign up instantly online at:

https://paulmouchet.ca/subscribe

If the story kept you turning the pages, I'd be incredibly grateful if you shared your thoughts in a review. Reviews on **Amazon, Goodreads, and BookBub** help other readers discover my books and allow me to keep writing more stories for you.

Even a few words make a world of difference. Your support means everything.

— Paul/PJ Mouchet

Also By

PJ Mouchet Novels

Brooks & Banks Series (Adult 14+)
Character-driven thrillers filled with high-stakes investigations, intense confrontations, and the human struggles that bind us all.

- Violent Echoes

- Deep Water

- The Crucible

- No Safe Trail

Paul Mouchet Novels

The Last Guardian Series (Adult 14+)
From unwanted outcast to the last Guardian of the Realm. Some paths are easier than others to follow.

- Rosemarked Assassin

- The Olander Legacy

- Realm of Arachnielle

Priest of Titan Series (Young Adult 14+)

Titan called her. The Temple forged her. Gods will fear her.

Life for Kit was difficult, growing up a Nomad human in a Berrat village. At the tender age of eleven, she travelled to a distant kingdom, and joined the Fist of Titan, a temple that worships a foreign god. The Temple priests trained her in the art of war. They taught her to deliver justice. They set her on the path to free their god, Titan. But paths have a way of taking you in unexpected directions and help you to discover things about the world and yourself. They can show you that meddling in the affairs of gods can either save or destroy the world. How can a teenage girl and her eclectic group of friends save the people and still prevent Ragnarök, the end of days?

- Call of Titan

- Hand of Titan

- Hammer of Titan

- Eyes of Titan

- Daemon of Titan

- Wrath of Titan

Fairytale Retellings (Young Adult 12+)

If you enjoy fantasy adventure with a touch of romance, then this is for you.

- Between Land and Sea: A Little Mermaid Retelling